Keep Smiling Through

Keep Smiling Through is Ellie Dean's third novel. She lives in Eastbourne, which has been her home for many years and where she raised her three children.

Also by Ellie Dean

There'll be Blue Skies
Far From Home

Keep Smiling Through

Ellie DEAN

arrow books

Published by Arrow Books 2012

6 8 10 9 7

First published in Great Britain in 2012 by
Arrow Books
Random House, 20 Vauxhall Bridge Road,
London SW1V 2SA

www.randomhouse.co.uk

Addresses for companies within The Random House Group Limited can be found at:
www.randomhouse.co.uk/offices.htm

The Random House Group Limited Reg. No. 954009

A CIP catalogue record for this book
is available from the British Library

ISBN 9780099574620

The Random House Group Limited supports The Forest Stewardship Council (FSC®), the
leading international forest certification organisation. Our books carrying the FSC label are
printed on FSC® certified paper. FSC is the only forest certification scheme endorsed by
the leading environmental organisations, including Greenpeace. Our paper procurement
policy can be found at www.randomhouse.co.uk/environment

MIX
Paper from
responsible sources
FSC® C016897

Typeset in Palatino by Palimpsest Book Production Limited,
Falkirk, Stirlingshire

Printed and bound in Great Britain by Clays Ltd, St Ives plc

Keep Smiling Through

Chapter One

Cliffehaven, June 1940

Rita held back the tears as she sank into her father's tight embrace, her cheek pressed against the rough khaki of his uniform jacket. Jack Smith had completed his enlistment training and was leaving for a Royal Engineers' army camp in the Midlands. It could be months, maybe even years, before she saw him again, and she needed this intimate moment between them to convey how deeply she loved him.

She was only vaguely aware of the rumbling engines of the waiting army trucks that stood in line along the heavily barricaded seafront. The shouts of the Sergeant Major, the cry of fretful babies and sobbing women, and the tramp of heavy boots were barely audible as she pressed her cheek to his chest and concentrated on the steady drum of his heart. She had to be brave, had to keep her smile in place and her tone cheerful, for it was vital she dispelled his misgivings about leaving her.

Jack Smith gently withdrew from the embrace and cupped her head with large, callused hands. His nut-brown eyes were suspiciously bright as he looked down at her. 'This is as hard for me as it is for you,' he said, his voice catching with emotion. 'My brave little girl. There's no need to hide your tears from me. I'll be back as soon as I can. I promise.'

Rita blinked rapidly, determined not to cry. 'I know,' she said, her voice unsteady. 'And you're not to worry about me, Dad. Auntie Peg has promised to look in every week, and of course Papa Tino and Louise will always be next door.'

His smile was shaky as he patted her cheek. 'Thank God for Peggy Reilly and the Minellis,' he sighed. 'I don't know what either of us would have done without them after your mum died. But at least I can leave with an easier heart knowing they'll watch over you.'

'I'm seventeen,' she protested softly. 'I don't need babying.'

'I realise that,' he sighed, as he ruffled her short dark curls. 'But you're all I've got, and I need to know you won't take any unnecessary risks.'

She looked up at him through unshed tears. 'Don't be daft,' she murmured.

'Fall in!' The barked order from a nearby officer made them stiffen. It was time for him to leave.

Rita threw herself back into his embrace, gripping tightly to his jacket. 'Be careful, Dad,' she said urgently. 'And don't play the hero. I want you back in one piece.'

He kissed the top of her head and then firmly but gently broke the embrace. 'Not much chance of heroics where I'm going,' he said with determined cheerfulness as he rammed the beret over his light brown hair and hoisted his kitbag onto his shoulder. 'I'll be spending most of my time repairing machines in some draughty army garage – not dodging bullets.'

Rita's emotions were running too high for words, so she stood on tiptoe and kissed the smooth cheek he'd so carefully shaved before leaving the house.

He gave her a swift hug. 'Watch yourself on that motorbike,' he murmured, glancing at the Norton ES2 which they had rebuilt together. 'Just because I'm not around, doesn't mean you can tear about on it like a hooligan.'

Her smile was tremulous. They both knew she would continue to ride the motorbike with ferocious skill and speed – after all, it had been Jack who'd taught her how, and Jack who'd encouraged her, and her best friend May, to enter the fiercely competitive races that had been held on dirt tracks all over the county before the declaration of war.

'The trucks are leaving,' bellowed the red-faced sergeant major. 'Last man on board will be on jankers for a week. Move it, you 'orrible lot, or you'll feel me boot up yer backsides.'

'Bye, love.' Jack winked, turned swiftly away and ran for the nearest truck.

Rita watched as the flow of scurrying men ebbed. She kept her gaze fixed on her father as he leaned out from beneath the tarpaulin roof and waved, and then the trucks were moving away in a roar of engines and clouds of exhaust fumes. She raised her hand to him, the tears finally rolling hotly down her face. 'Goodbye, Dad,' she whispered. 'Please come home safe.'

She waited until the last truck was out of sight before she turned away and donned the leather motorcycle helmet and goggles. There were other women among the crowd that she knew well, and Peggy Reilly would have been one of them if Rita had not insisted upon coming alone. This was a time for contemplation, not talk – or even offers of comfort – that would have been too hard to bear, and she acknowledged the others' sad, brave smiles with a nod as they slowly and silently left the seafront and headed for homes that would feel so very empty now their menfolk had left.

As she buckled the helmet under her chin and adjusted the goggles, Rita watched the well-wishers disperse, and was suddenly overwhelmed by loss. Her father was gone, and until this war was won, she would have to carry on without his love, guidance and companionship.

The seafront barricades and gun emplacements blurred as the tears fell, and she had to resist the powerful urge to go straight to Beach View Boarding House, fling herself into Peggy Reilly's motherly arms and cry until there were no tears left. She sniffed the tears away. It was time to be brave, to prove she was perfectly capable of standing on her own two feet and getting on with things. She couldn't falter at the first hurdle.

Determined to prove her father's faith in her ability to cope, she swung her leg over the seat, started the engine and headed away from the seafront, the bike's throaty roar drowning out her sobs and the accompanying mournful cries of the gulls.

Barrow Lane was one of a series of narrow cobbled streets that radiated from the high brick wall of the goods yard at the back of the station. A vast gasometer towered over everything, stealing the sunlight for most of the year, and casting its deep shadow across the streets. Life was conducted against the background sounds of steam engines and iron wheels clattering over the rails – noises few of them even heard any more.

Unlike the posh area of Havelock Gardens, there were no trees or pretty flowerbeds and lawns in Barrow Lane, just front doors that opened onto the street, and grim backyards housing the outside lavs. There had been talk of demolishing the whole area, for the terraces were run-down, the red brick darkened by years of soot and smoke from the trains, the paintwork flaking and ingrained with grime. But with the onset of war any plans the council might have had were set aside, and there was a sense of relief within the tight-knit community, for, like Rita, most of them had been born here, and couldn't contemplate living anywhere else.

After leaving the seafront, she had driven the bike hard, taking a roundabout route home in an attempt to recover some semblance of calm before she had to face Papa Tino and Louise. But the pain of parting was still too raw, and it was unsettling to return to an empty house and find none of the familiar bustle surrounding the family garage which was now closed for the duration.

Her slender figure and elfin face belied her strength, and she ably negotiated the cumbersome Norton across the weed-strewn cobbles of the narrow lane and brought it to a halt outside the large wooden doors her father had padlocked that morning. Their terraced house was at the end of the row, with a piece of scrubland beside it that was always overshadowed by the high brick wall of the station shunting yards. The ground floor had been converted into a garage many years ago by her grandfather, the scrubland roughly paved to accommodate a petrol pump and extra service area. She let the engine idle as she eyed the locked and empty pump and deserted side-court, and experienced the new and unusual ache of loneliness which threatened to bring tears again.

Determined not to give in to self-pity, she booted the kickstand down and switched off the engine. She took off the goggles and forced her thoughts elsewhere as she listened to the twilight sounds of

Barrow Lane and its surrounds. She'd played on these streets, gone to the local school and become an intrinsic part of the community where life, although hard at times, had provided many happy moments.

But it was all very different now that her father and the other men had enlisted, and the women had gone to work in the factories. Most of the younger children had been evacuated and the cobbles no longer rang with the sounds of laughter and gossiping from doorsteps, or games of football and hopscotch – or the ring of heavy boots at the end of another shift on the railway or at the nearby tool factory.

Rita hitched the gas mask box over her shoulder and tried hard to control her emotions. June was already promising to be fair despite the darkening clouds of war which had overshadowed everything these past nine months. She could hear soft music from a distant wireless, the cry of a baby and the persistent yapping of a dog. From her next-door neighbours' rooms above their café drifted the delicious aroma of garlic and herbs and fresh bread, and the sound of rapid-fire Italian as Antonino Minelli and his English wife, Louise, discussed what sauce to cook with tonight's home-made pasta.

She felt the warmth of deep affection as she listened, and it brought her some comfort to know they would always be near her. She gave a wry smile. To those not familiar with Italians and their passionate discourses, it must seem Antonino and Louise were always arguing – but Rita, who'd become as fluent as Louise over the years, knew it was just their way. Papa Tino adored his quiet little Louise, and there was rarely a cross word between them.

Their two daughters had already left Cliffehaven for a new life in America when Rita's mother had died of consumption twelve years ago – and although their young son, Roberto, still lived at home, Louise had joyfully taken on the role of mothering five-year-old Rita, who had come to adore her. The Minelli home was as poor as everyone else's in the street, and they'd had to work hard to make their little café a success, but those three upstairs rooms were always warm and welcoming – another home for her and her father.

Rita clambered off the bike and shook out her short dark hair, willing herself to be as adult and independent as she'd pretended to be for her father. She and her best friend May Lynch had been working for two weeks as welders at one of the new factories that had sprung up on the outskirts of town, and were earning a fairly good wage. There was plenty of opportunity for overtime, and the work was demanding, so she would have little time to mope.

But as she turned the key in the padlock and pulled the heavy chain out of the sturdy door handles, she realised it wouldn't be easy to live on her own, even though Louise was only next door. The little things would be the hardest to bear – the evenings would seem longer without him there to talk to over their supper. She would miss the close friendship they'd built over the years as they worked together in the garage – and the smell of his pipe tobacco as he sat by the fire reading the evening paper. It would feel most odd not to be clattering downstairs each morning to find him already at work in the garage, his ready smile greeting her as she handed him his cup of tea.

The garage doors screeched in complaint as she dragged them open, and she made a mental note to oil the metal runners that were set firmly into the cobbles. She hauled the motorbike into the welcoming atmosphere of the dark space, threw the tarpaulin over it, and breathed in the familiar scents of greasy rags, engine oil, metal and petrol. They were reminders of her childhood when she'd sat on a stool and watched her father take engines apart, eager to learn, longing for the moment when she was deemed old enough to help.

She'd learned the trade at weekends and during school holidays, preferring to be here with him instead of out playing with the other children, and after she'd left school, he'd encouraged her to go to technical college and take the exams that would give her proper qualifications as a mechanic. Through their shared fascination for engines and motorcycles they'd forged a deep and abiding closeness which had helped them both to overcome the painful void left by her mother's death.

Rita looked around the dim space, at the tyres stacked in a corner, the tools neatly lined up on the wall, the pulleys and chains hanging from the ceiling rafters, and the deep pit where she'd spent many hours craning her neck to inspect and repair the customers' cars. They had been good times, happy times, but until the war was won there would be no classes at the college, and no cars to repair. She had to accept that it could be some while before she was fully qualified and life could return to normal.

'*Ciao*, Rita. I hear you come home, and want to make sure you are all right.'

She turned to find Antonino Minelli standing in the doorway. The short, rotund little Italian had a mop of black, unruly hair and a bushy moustache of which he was very proud. His ever-cheerful smile and enthusiastic approach to life belied his years, and no one would have guessed he was almost sixty – but today his eyes were troubled, his smile soft with sympathy and love as he opened his arms to her.

Tears welled on seeing him and all the emotions she'd been holding back poured out as she fell into his embrace. 'Oh, Papa Tino,' she sobbed, 'I'm going to miss him so very much.'

'*Cara mia*,' he soothed, his hand gently stroking her short curls. 'Of course you are sad, but Mamma Louise and I will take care of you, I promise.'

Rita found comfort in the soft Italian endearments and the fierce embrace, and she clung to him until the storm of tears and jagged emotions were soothed. 'You must think I'm being a terrible baby,' she said as she finally drew away and blew her nose.

His brown eyes were wet with his own tears – Tino had never been one to hide his emotions. 'You must always cry when the need is great,' he soothed. 'And yes, you are still very young, but you are strong, Rita. You will get through this.'

She gave him a watery smile. 'I know,' she admitted, 'but . . .'

He tried to look stern but his warm smile shone through. 'We will make sure you do, and for now, you will come home with me and eat pasta. Louise has cooked it just the way you like.'

The thought of Louise's delicious pasta made Rita's mouth water despite her sadness. 'I'd love to come, but I need to get out of these clothes and have a wash first.'

He shook his head as his gaze drifted over her heavy boots, leather trousers and the old flying jacket that had survived the first war. His moustache twitched in disapproval. 'You are pretty girl,' he said in his heavily accented English. 'Why you dress like boy all the time?'

This was a familiar grumble, and Rita replied as she always did, but with a rather shaky smile. 'Because I can't ride the Norton in a skirt.'

His dark eyes flickered with disdain over the motorbike before regarding her solemnly. 'Perhaps it is not fitting to ride bike at all,' he said. 'In Italy the girls ride side-saddle – these bikes are for boys.'

Rita had had this argument with him before, and they both knew it would never be resolved. But it was good to be having a normal conversation after the trauma of her day, and she loved him all the more for it. She kissed his cheek and gently steered him out of the garage. 'Give me half an hour, Papa. And I promise not to wear trousers.'

'Roberto, he is home tonight,' said Antonino, his eyes twinkling now. 'You dress pretty, eh? Maybe take *la passeggiata* after dinner with Roberto and his *famiglia* before he have to leave for guarding the factories?'

To give Papa Tino his due, he never tired of match-making, for he seemed convinced – against all their protests – that she and Roberto were meant for one another. *La passeggiata* was a slow amble through the streets in the company of your betrothed and his family or, if unpromised, with a *mamma* who had a sharp eye open for a suitable husband. In Antonino's Naples it was an age-old custom carried out during the soft, warm and scented evenings, but in Cliffehaven where the wind tore in from the Channel and the gulls squabbled overhead, it would lose any of the romance of the moment and simply get tongues wagging amongst the small Italian community.

Rita chuckled and shook her head. 'No *passeggiata* tonight, or any other, Papa. I'll see you in half an hour.'

'You are sure?' He looked crestfallen, the very embodiment of a man devastated by crushed hope.

Rita had seen this act before and wasn't fooled. She grinned. 'Positive. Now, let me close these doors and get on, or Louise's pasta will be ruined.' She watched him shrug before he turned away and knew he was already plotting something else so she and Roberto could be alone.

She was still chuckling as she drew the heavy doors to, snapped the padlock over the thick chain and headed to the back of the garage and the door that led to a flight of stairs. Running up the bare boards, she entered the main room at the front. Even her own father seemed anxious to see her and Roberto together, and although she adored Roberto, he was more like a brother than someone to fall in love with, and she refused to play along with their scheming. The war had meant life was opening up to her with endless exciting possibilities and new challenges. She wasn't about to do something so radical just to please the people she loved. If she and Roberto were meant for one another, then it would happen. Meanwhile, she had a war to get through.

The front room served as kitchen and living space,

with a small range in the chimney breast, a narrow table, two chairs and a sagging couch. A photograph of her mother had pride of place on the mantel next to the new one of her father in his uniform, and a wireless stood in one corner, the mahogany casing gleaming dully through the layer of dust that had settled since this morning. It wasn't a big room, but it was the heart of their home, and as Rita eyed her father's empty chair, she felt his absence even more keenly.

The sadness threatened to overwhelm her again, so she drew the blackout curtains and lit the gas lamps – the electricity supply had recently come to this end of town, but not every house had been fully adapted. She eased off her sturdy boots, then stripped off the heavy leather trousers and moth-eaten flying jacket and slung them over the back of the couch where she'd left the dungarees she wore to work. Wriggling her toes, she pulled off the thick socks and, dressed only in her camiknickers and vest, padded across the faded linoleum into her bedroom.

It was a small, rather untidy room – there never seemed to be enough time for housework these days, which suited her just fine – with a single iron bedstead, chest of drawers, wardrobe, and a view out of the window over the tiny backyards of the houses in the next terrace to the shunting yards beyond the high brick wall. There was no bathroom, and it would take too long to fill the big metal tub which hung on a hook in the outside lav, so she would have to make do with a quick wash in the kitchen sink.

Now the sun had gone down it was chilly, so she pulled a warm knitted dress and cardigan from the wardrobe and returned to the front room. Standing well back to avoid getting her eyebrows and lashes singed, she lit the ancient boiler and washed as well as she could in the tepid water.

Her stomach rumbled as she finished dressing, reminding her she hadn't eaten since the paste sandwiches she'd shared with her father at lunchtime. She hadn't had any appetite then, but now her mouth watered at the thought of Louise's pasta. But her main concerns were far from the family dinner awaiting her as she rubbed her hair dry and tried to restore some order to its dark, wayward curls. They were still centred on her father, and the memories and passions they shared.

The airfield to the north of Cliffehaven had fascinated her from the moment her father had taken her there as a small child. She'd stood holding his large warm hand, not at all afraid or overwhelmed by the noise of the place, and over the years she had become a familiar figure about the hangars and runways, asking endless questions of the mechanics and pilots as her father tinkered with the engines on his one day off.

She had never had a yen to actually go up in a plane – she preferred to have her feet firmly on the ground – but the yearning to be a part of that exciting world and to work in the hangars had remained with her, growing stronger with every passing year.

Rita gave a deep sigh as she ran a comb through her damp hair. The airfield had been enlarged over the past year, with more runways, a new control tower, Nissan huts and extra hangers to house the steady influx of planes and pilots. It was now an important RAF airbase and therefore off limits for the duration.

She had been to the RAF recruiting office and asked about joining the WAAFs as a mechanic, but she was still too young, and her qualifications incomplete. The woman there had suggested she wait until her eighteenth birthday to apply for an administration post, but that didn't appeal at all. The thought of being stuck in an office all day made her shudder.

Her dad had understood, but even he couldn't get round the ever-stringent rules and regulations that were now in force. He'd suggested the job in the factory as a stopgap until she found something else, and she supposed she should be satisfied she was doing her bit by welding parts of planes together. But she couldn't quite dismiss the thought of how much more satisfying it would be to become a useful member of the engineering team that ensured the planes' engines were running smoothly so the courageous pilots could be brought home safely.

Dragging her thoughts into order, she glanced at the clock and gasped at how quickly time had passed. Louisa's pasta would be ruined if she didn't hurry up.

Chapter Two

Peggy Reilly was in her early forties and had lived in Cliffehaven all her life. She and her husband, Jim, had taken over the running of Beach View Boarding House when her parents retired, and it was there that she'd raised her four children. Jim had recently returned home unscathed after taking part in the rescue of the troops from Dunkirk's beaches with his older brother Frank, and she gave nightly thanks they'd been spared.

Her father-in-law, Ron, and his large Bedlington-cross, Harvey, lived in the basement of Beach View, sharing the two small rooms and scullery with her young sons, Bob and Charlie. Her much older girls, Anne, who was a teacher, and Cissy, who was theatrical, shared a room at the top of the house. Anne's future husband was an RAF pilot who had to live on the base nearby, and Peggy fretted as much as her daughter over his safety now they were flying so many missions across enemy territory.

The elderly Mrs Finch lived on the first floor. She'd become a permanent boarder once she'd admitted she could no longer live alone. She was as deaf as a post and refused to replace her ailing hearing aid – not that it mattered a jot, for the family had come to love her as their own, and her confused, but cheerful twittering always made them smile – and in these dark times a smile was worth a great deal.

The holiday trade had dried up once war had been declared, but with the evacuation process in place and more service personnel arriving all the time, Peggy's home was once again full to the rafters – which was the way she liked it.

Cliffehaven was changing and growing rapidly as the war progressed, but despite the influx of foreign servicemen, and the barbed wire and gun emplacements on the seafront, it still felt like home to Peggy. There were numerous new factories being built on what had once been wasteland to the north-east of the town, the airfield to the north had become a strategically important centre for the RAF, and the grand hotels on the seafront had become billets to allied servicemen from all over the world. A vast Canadian camp had been built in a distant valley to the west, close to the permanent American airbase which had been there since the last war. Although the Americans had yet to join in the hostilities, they could often be seen about the town helping to fix things, and using their jeeps and heavy machinery to good advantage when called to do so.

Peggy rather liked the Americans; they were so terribly polite, calling her 'ma'am' all the time and offering to carry her shopping. But she wasn't daft enough to be taken in, for she knew only too well that their real interest was in her youngest daughter Cissy and the girl from London who was billeted with her.

She smiled as she packed away the last of the blankets and locked them in a cupboard. She'd been in the boarding house business long enough to have a sharp eye for shenanigans, and she kept to the strict rule of no men in the house – unless they were lodgers, or too old to cause trouble.

Peggy eased her back and yawned. She had just finished her afternoon stint at the WVS centre which was now based at the Town Hall, and although she was tired and there was a great deal still to do at home before she could put a meal on the table, she was determined to visit Rita. This would be her second visit in the ten days since Jack had left, and she wanted to make sure the girl was still coping.

The old bike had seen better days, but her father-in-law, Ron, had fitted new tyres and chain, given it a lick of black paint, and managed to find a lovely new basket which he'd tied to the handlebars with thick leather straps. Peggy dumped her handbag, gas mask and parcels in the basket and wheeled the bike out of the Town Hall, down the steps between the great wall of sandbags and out into the road.

It was a steep climb to the station, taking her up the High Street, away from the shops, the cinema and the seafront, and over the hump-backed bridge to the north of the town. She decided it might be better to push the bike most of the way, for gone were the days when she could have cycled up this hill with ease – gone too were the days when she used to drive up here to get her dear old car serviced.

Her journey was made longer by friends stopping her for a chat, and although she liked a good gossip, and was desperate to share the news of Anne's impending wedding, she didn't really have time to stand about. Beach View Boarding House was full of people waiting to be fed, not least of all her husband, Jim, who would no doubt be filching anything he could find in her woefully understocked larder to ward off his imaginary starvation.

With that thought in mind, she pushed harder and crossed the railway bridge. It was much flatter on this side of the line, and the wheels hummed nicely as she rode through the narrow back streets of crowded terraces and headed for Barrow Lane. It was still early June, and the day had been pleasant, but now the sun was dipping behind the hills she felt chilled by the light breeze she stirred as she raced along.

Barrow Lane looked more forlorn than ever now most of the children had been evacuated, and Peggy despaired for the families who had to live in those damp, dark little houses. The council should have done something about this whole area years ago, and the mayor – who was the landlord – should be ashamed of himself for letting things deteriorate so badly.

The brakes screeched as she came to a halt outside the wooden doors which stood open. She propped the bike against the wall and peered into the gloom. 'Hello? Rita?'

'Aunt Peg!' Rita was grinning with pleasure as she appeared from the deep shadows clutching a spanner. 'What a lovely surprise.'

Dressed in her dungarees and heavy boots, she'd covered her hair in a knotted scarf and looked so young it made Peggy's heart hurt. 'Just thought I'd pop in with a few bits,' she said, her voice catching as she gave the girl a hug. 'How are you coping, dear?'

Rita smiled as she put down the spanner and dug her hands into her pockets. 'I'm all right,' she replied. 'Work at the factory keeps me out of mischief, May and I have our bikes to tinker with, and I go next door most nights. Mamma Louise is feeding me so well I've probably put on pounds,' she added wryly.

'I'd like to know where,' muttered Peggy, who was just as slender and slight. 'You still look as if a breeze would knock you over.' She plucked one of the parcels out of the basket. 'It's only a bit of brisket and a couple of kidneys, but I'm sure Louise could do something tasty with them.'

Rita beamed with pleasure. 'Thanks, Auntie Peg. I'm sure she will. Her herb garden is coming on a treat and Papa Tino still goes to the allotment every day, so there's always plenty of veg.'

Peggy breathed in the heavenly aroma of cooking that wafted from the next-door top window, and was reminded rather sharply that she had to get home to her own kitchen. 'Cissy sends her love, by the way, and wants you to know she can get you tickets for one of her shows should you feel like going.'

Rita giggled. 'So she finally made it into a proper theatre, has she? Good for her. I know how much she wanted to go on the stage.'

Peggy nodded. Her youngest daughter had always been theatrical, and she couldn't for the life of her understand where she'd got it from. No one in her family had ever been that way inclined, and she didn't know if she should approve or not. 'She's been badgering me and her father to let her join ENSA, but thankfully she's too young and they won't take her without our permission.' She cocked her head. 'What about you, Rita? Still hankering to join the WAAFs?'

The girl's large brown eyes became sad. 'I'd love to, but I'm too young and they won't take me on as a mechanic until I've passed my final exams – and of course the college is closed now.' She chewed her lip. 'It looks like I'm stuck at the factory until something more challenging comes up.'

Peggy nodded, but her thoughts were racing as she eyed the motorbike in the corner. Anne's fiancé had mentioned something about the need for motor-cycle dispatch riders with the RAF – but whether that included girls as young as Rita she had no idea. She made a mental note to ask next time she saw him – and then dismissed it. Racing about on motorcycles was dangerous at the best of times, and with the war on and the airbase bound to be a prime target, Rita's father would have her guts for garters if she encouraged the girl in such a foolhardy enterprise.

'Never mind, dear,' she said. 'I'm sure something will come along, and at least you're doing your bit at the factory, and that's got to count for something.'

Rita sighed. 'I know, but it's not very exciting.'

Peggy thought about the all-too-recent 'excitement' over the Dunkirk rescues. Jim had suffered from nightmares ever since he'd been back, for not all those little fishing boats had returned home, and thousands of men had died in the most terrible way. 'Excitement isn't everything,' she muttered, 'and your father wouldn't want you taking any unnecessary risks. How is he, by the way?'

'He's settling in and enjoying the work, though the sergeant major's an absolute beast who does nothing but shout all the time.' Rita grinned. 'I don't think Dad takes too kindly to being ordered about.'

Peggy chuckled as she pulled on her gloves. 'It certainly can't be easy after running your own business for years. I must go, Rita, or no one will get fed tonight.' She gave the girl a hug and a kiss and headed for her bicycle. 'If you need me, you know where I am – and don't leave it too long before you come and visit us. Cissy and you used to be close as children and it would be a shame to let your friendship dwindle away.'

'We don't really have that much in common any more,' said Rita, eyeing her dirty hands and chipped nails. 'But it would be nice to catch up with her again, and hear all about life on the stage.'

'Come to lunch one day soon,' said Peggy as she wheeled the bike into the street. 'Once this wedding's over, we'll have more time to chat.'

'How's everything going with the wedding plans?'

Peggy heaved a sigh. 'It's not been easy, but I think everything is about done. Anne got extra rations for the cake, my evacuee, Sally, is making the dress, and the neighbours have been very generous with their donations for the wedding breakfast.' She gave a wry smile. 'My sister Doris has bought a new hat, which no doubt will outshine anything I can put together.'

'You'll look lovely, regardless of what you wear,' replied Rita. 'You shouldn't let her wind you up, Aunt Peg.'

'She manages that by simply walking into the same room as me,' said Peggy with some asperity. 'I don't know where she gets those airs and graces. My younger sister Doreen and I are chalk to her cheese.'

'How's Doreen getting on in London?'

'She's finally seen sense and sent her two girls to

the country, but she insists upon staying up there.' Peggy tugged at her gloves. 'Doreen has a very good job as personal assistant to a businessman and she seems to think he can't manage without her,' she said rather sharply. 'Which is why she's not coming down for the wedding. Anne's quite disappointed, actually. She and Doreen get on very well.'

'That's a shame,' murmured Rita. 'Please give Anne my very best wishes for a happy day.'

Peggy smiled and nodded, realising she'd said more than she'd meant to. Rita had enough to think about without her blathering on. 'Are you sure you don't want to come?'

Rita shook her head. 'I can't, Auntie Peg. I'm working, and Major Patricia only gives us days off if we're at death's door.'

Peggy grinned. 'She sounds a fright.'

'She's not that bad really,' Rita conceded. 'Not when you think of what pressure she must be under to fulfil all those contracts.'

Peggy nodded. 'Well, let me know when you can come for lunch then, and I'll make sure Cissy's at home.'

Rita kissed her cheek and gave her a swift hug. 'Thanks, Auntie Peg.'

'TTFN, as they say on the wireless. Take care of yourself, dear, and I'll see you soon.'

Peggy stood on the pedals as the bike jolted over the cobbles, and before she turned the corner she looked back at Rita and waved. The girl might be small and seemingly fragile, but there was a tough core to her that was lacking in Cissy. There had been too many tears and tantrums these past few weeks, and it was time Cissy was made to realise that life was not all about dancing and make-up and frothy, sparkling frocks. It would do no harm to get the two girls together again, for Cissy needed a good dose of reality, and by the look of it, Rita needed as many friends as she could find. Feeling much more positive about things, Peggy headed for home.

The great bowl of steaming spaghetti was a delicious concoction of garlic, onions, tomatoes and shredded chicken, accompanied by the crusty yellow bread that Louise made each morning. The crust was hard enough to break teeth, and had to be chewed thoroughly, but when used to mop up the fragrant sauce, or to dip in the precious dish of olive oil, it tasted wonderful. To add to this feast was the rough red wine Antonino had hoarded in the cellar beneath the café.

Roberto knew there were enough bottles down there to see the family through at least a year, and he hoped it would be enough. His father had bought a substantial consignment from an Italian friend who'd imported it secretly from Naples before the hostilities in Europe had begun. Antonino Minelli might have embraced the English way of life for over forty years, but he was still very Italian when it came to his food, and regarded a meal without wine as an intolerable privation.

Roberto surreptitiously watched Rita as the meal progressed. She looked so fresh and bright-eyed, and he wondered if she even knew just how beautiful she was – wondered if she'd guessed at how much his feelings for her were changing.

He ate the delicious pasta, content just to listen as she chattered away to his parents in fluent Italian. Small and dark-haired, with a raucous laugh and fearsome Irish temper – he guessed a legacy from her mother – Rita Smith had been a part of his life as far back as he could remember. He'd pulled her pigtails at school and teased her with dead frogs, earning himself many a deserved clip round the ear. They'd played in the street together, made secret camps out near the airfield, and sat next to one another in church. Rita was two years younger, but she could give as good as she got, and it had sometimes galled him to discover she could climb trees and race along the cobbles much faster than he – and that she could fight like a boy when necessary and knew more about engines than he'd ever learn.

He bit down on the grin as he finished the pasta and wiped the bowl clean with a bit of bread. Rita was a tomboy, racing about on that infernal motorbike in her leather trousers and ridiculous goggles, and there were times when he wished she'd just be a girl – but, he admitted, he loved her the way she was, and hoped that one day she might think of him as more than a brother, and love him back.

Roberto pushed his plate aside and sipped his wine. He held few illusions about his chances with Rita, for he was no handsome hero, nothing special – just a nineteen-year-old youth who would one day inherit the family café – if it survived the war and the strict rationing which had begun in January. He was of average height with the dark hair of his father and the creamy skin and blue eyes of his mother which, but for fate, might have made him handsome.

He fingered the scar that puckered his brow and eyelid. The childhood accident with a gas boiler had left him blind in his right eye, the scar a permanent reminder of that day. But not all the scars were visible. He was all too aware of the curious looks he still got, of the almost imperceptible shudder of the girls he tried to impress, and the fact that even now it set him apart. For, when he'd gone to enlist, they'd turned him down for active service, and he'd had to watch his friends excitedly leave for war while he had to settle for working in the canteen at the local hospital, and a position with the local Defence Volunteers along with his father and all the other old men.

The bitterness of his situation caught him unawares and he lit a cigarette to mask his emotions. There were others far worse off than he; he should be grateful he hadn't been blinded in both eyes and had half his face blown off. At least he got to wear a uniform of sorts and was doing his bit to protect the vast sprawl of important factories on the other side of town from enemy raids, which were expected at any moment.

The meal continued in the usual leisurely fashion, even though there was no soft mozzarella cheese, no fruit or dark, rich olives to eat with salty biscuits and slivers of hard, strong-tasting parmesan cheese. The quiet chatter continued around him in the homely, loving atmosphere of the candlelit room and Roberto was reminded of all the other nights he'd sat at this table, and prayed that the war wouldn't change things too much, and that it would soon be over.

With the blackout curtains closed, the room was like a cave, his mother's brightly coloured home-made tablecloth, napkins and cushion covers adding a touch of further warmth to the ambient glow of the range and the candles on the table. The room where he'd once played as a toddler on the worn rug before the range was sparsely furnished. Apart from the table and chairs, there were two comfortable armchairs placed before the range, pictures of Naples on the walls, and a treasured statuette of the Madonna and Child taking pride of place on the mantelpiece. To Roberto, who had never been to Naples, it was a tiny corner of Italy, and he knew Rita felt the same, for it had become her second home.

His father finally pushed back from the table and

lit a cigarette as Rita and Louise gathered up the dishes and put the kettle on to boil. There was no rich, dark coffee to finish the meal, no little almond *biscotti* to dip in it, but they'd become inured to the English habit of drinking tea – even though it was often as weak as the dishwater in his mother's kitchen sink.

Antonino was off duty tonight, but Roberto was already dressed in his Defence Volunteer's uniform, ready to leave the house in an hour's time for his late-night stint of fire-watch duty on the new factory estate. The nine o'clock news would be on the wireless soon and his father was, as usual, twiddling with the knobs to try and get a better reception. He caught Rita's eye as she stacked the clean plates in the rack above the wooden draining board, and they shared a knowing grin. Papa was forever messing about with the wireless, and it was a miracle the damn thing still worked at all.

The sound of concert music drifted into the homely room as his mother made a pot of tea and finally sat down. Rita hung the cloth above the range to dry just as the tranquillity was shattered by the sound of heavy bombers taking off from the nearby airfield. They were heading south again for another raid on enemy ports.

They all looked up, not voicing their fears for the young men who flew so bravely towards conflict, but silently praying they would all return safely. There had been no serious enemy attacks on England so far, but with the Nazis now in Denmark, Norway, France, Belgium, Luxembourg and the Netherlands, it could only be a matter of time.

The music came to an end and the pips sounded, heralding the news. They sat facing the wireless which was perched on a cupboard next to the range, hoping beyond hope that for once there would be good tidings.

The solemn announcement stunned them. Italy had declared war on Britain and France.

'Oh, dear God,' breathed Louise through trembling fingers. Her blue eyes were bright with tears as she looked at her husband. 'What does this mean, Tino?'

He took her hands and gently held them to his heart. 'I don't know,' he murmured, 'but I think it will not be good for us.'

'But *we* are not at war with this country,' she protested, snatching her hands away. 'We have no allegiance with Germany's Nazis. You and Roberto are with the Defence Volunteers. We will be all right, yes, Tino? Promise me, we'll be all right.'

Roberto was as shocked as his parents, but he couldn't bear to see his mother so distraught. He swiftly moved to her side and put his hand on her shoulder. 'Papa has lived here for over forty years,' he said calmly in Italian. 'He married you, an English girl, and together you have run a good, honest business in this town. We have broken no law. We are not fascists, and have never got involved with politics. We will be fine.'

His soothing words and quiet manner had little effect on his mother, whose fear was palpable as she clung to him and his father. He glanced swiftly at Rita, who was ashen-faced and clearly as upset as his mother – though she was able to keep her emotions in some kind of check for once.

Louise wrung her hands, her face twisted in anguish. 'I want to believe you, Roberto, but I remember what happened to the German families in the first war,' she sobbed. 'The mobs came and smashed their houses and shops, calling them terrible names, dragging them out into the streets and setting fire to their homes.'

'It won't happen here,' said Rita firmly. 'You've been a part of this community all your life, just as I have. They know and respect you, and . . .'

The sound of smashing glass interrupted her and all eyes turned towards the front of the house.

Before Roberto could stop her, Rita had rushed to the window to peek between the blackout curtains, and he had to drag her back out of sight of the mob that was gathering in the street below. 'Get on the floor,' he barked, 'and stay away from the window.'

'What is it?' shrieked Louise as Antonino bundled her into a corner. 'What's happening?'

A brick came crashing through the window and Louise screamed as it landed with a thud in the middle of the kitchen table, scattering glasses, the red wine spilling across the tablecloth like blood, candles toppling, flames spluttering and dying in the deluge.

Roberto and his father shielded the cowering women as a cobblestone exploded through the glass and bounced across the carpet. He felt Rita wince, and in the flickering light of the range fire, saw blood on her face and realised a tiny shard of glass was embedded in her cheek. With infinite care he plucked it out and made a pad of his handkerchief which he ordered her to hold against the wound.

'We have to get them out of the house,' he said urgently to his father.

'They'll be safer staying up here,' Antonino replied grimly. 'Come on, Louise, let's get you and Rita into the bedroom and away from that window.'

'I'm not hiding away up here while that mob chucks bricks through your windows,' stormed Rita as she wrestled from Roberto's embrace. 'I recognise at least two of them, and if it's a fight they want, then I'm quite willing to give them one.' She reached for the poker and curled her fist around the handle.

'You will stay in the bedroom,' ordered Antonino as he snatched the poker from her and pushed them both out of the room. 'This is for the men to settle.'

Roberto could see Rita was ready to argue the point. 'He's right,' he said, grabbing his mother's heavy wooden rolling pin which was the only weapon to hand. 'Mamma must not be left alone, and we need you to look after her.'

'But . . .'

The sound of hammering and the splintering of wood silenced her. They were breaking down the café door. Roberto and his father headed for the landing. '*Silencio!*' roared Antonino over his shoulder. 'You will stay with Mamma.'

'No,' pleaded Louise. 'They will kill you. Come back, come back.'

Her cries were ignored as the two men thundered down the stairs ready to do battle.

The mob was smaller than it sounded, but they were a rough lot, intent upon venting their spleen as the café door finally yielded to their heavy boots and the window was divested of its glass. They poured into the small café wielding spades and clubs and yelling obscenities.

Roberto stood beside his father, ready to protect their property. 'Get out of my café,' yelled Antonino, 'or I will call the police.'

'The rozzers ain't interested in protecting Nazi sympathisers,' growled their spokesman – a large, swarthy individual who was well known in the neighbourhood for drunken brawling.

'We're not Nazis,' snapped Roberto.

A club smashed through the glass of the counter. Another swept through the shelves of cordial bottles and jars of sweets, and from the streets came more men, drunk on ale, and the promise of a bit of excitement.

The ringleader grinned as he towered over

Antonino. 'You ain't gunna stop 'em,' he said with a snarl. 'And when they've done with down 'ere, they'll be setting fire to this place. It's the best way to get rid of vermin.'

Roberto shoved the man back, making him stumble, but he was surprisingly nimble and the right hook seemed to come from nowhere. Within seconds he and his father were embroiled in a vicious fight for survival, with fists and boots flying. But, inch by inch they were being forced into a corner of the café, and with rising panic, Roberto realised there could be no escape – there were just too many of them.

Rita could hear the terrible noise downstairs as she grimly held a sobbing, terrified Louise. She was furious at what was happening to the Minelli family business, and had been quite prepared to help defend it – but was wise enough to realise she wouldn't have stood a chance. From her brief glance through the window, the mob seemed to consist mainly of known troublemakers, rough types who drank hard and fought hard – men who had few allegiances to anything but beer and fist fights.

As she and Louise huddled in the corner of the bedroom, the sounds worsened from below. The yelling had grown and was more menacing as it was accompanied by smashing glass and splintering wood which drowned out the Minellis' attempts to shout for calm.

Rita knew she couldn't just sit here and wait for the mob to burn the place down. 'I need to see what's happening.'

'No, no, Rita. We must stay here.' Louise's clutching fingers bit into her arm.

Rita firmly prised her fingers away and gathered the older woman into her arms, rocking her like a child until her sobbing had subsided. But at every thud and every crash she could feel Louise wince as she moaned, and Rita's own fear escalated. It sounded like a fearsome battle and she was as terrified as Louise, but she simply couldn't sit here any longer.

Moving away from Louise, and deaf to her pleas to return immediately, she left the bedroom. Carefully stepping over the shattered glass on the carpet, she risked another peek through the blackout curtains.

'Get away from there, Rita Smith,' came a voice out of the darkness. 'You don't want to get involved with those greasy eyetie Nazis.'

'Yeah, get out, Rita, if you know what's good for you. We're going to burn this place down.'

Rita was shaking with anger as well as fear as she recognised some of the hate-filled faces that looked up at her from the street. They were men she'd known since childhood – men who'd used the garage and café and had passed the time of day with Antonino and his son quite happily before the war. And yet they were now part of a mob, seemingly intent upon carnage.

'Go home, and leave us alone!' she yelled. 'I've called the police.' She hadn't, of course, Antonino didn't possess a telephone, but she hoped it would be enough to make them stop.

They took no notice of her and continued to smash up the café. There was a roar of jubilation from below as something heavy crashed to the ground amid the splinter of broken glass. And Rita could clearly hear the scuff of heavy boots and the thud of what she suspected were wrestling bodies being thrust against the walls and the door that led to the stairs.

'You're a bunch of cowards,' she yelled through the shattered window. 'You should be ashamed of yourselves.'

One of the men separated from the others and stood looking up at her. 'You should watch what yer say, Rita Smith. Talk like that could get you into trouble – and we all know where you live.'

Her heart was hammering and her mouth was dry. The threat had been all too real, and she knew the man was perfectly capable of carrying it out – his wife often turned up at the factory with a black eye. She melted behind the curtain, her legs threatening to give way as she stumbled back to the bedroom.

'You shouldn't have said such things,' sobbed Louise. 'It only stirs them up.'

Rita admitted to herself that Louise was probably right, but she stayed silent and held the other woman close, the fear growing with each crash and blow, her gaze fixed to the far door in dread. Men drunk on power and ale were capable of terrible things; she'd seen fights in the streets after closing time – had heard some awful stories from the women she worked with in the factory. But these were their neighbours – surely they wouldn't set fire to the house knowing she and Louise were up here?

'There's a fight outside the ice-cream shop,' came an excited yell from the street. 'Gino and a bunch of dagos have got together and our blokes need some help. Come quick before you miss out.'

Rita felt Louise stiffen. Gino and his six burly brothers ran several successful businesses in the town including a butcher's and market garden – they were distant cousins of Antonino, with wives and young families to protect.

'Oh, Rita,' Louise moaned. 'What is to happen to us all?'

'I'm sure the police will deal with it,' said Rita with more certainty than she felt. 'Gino and his brothers are big men and perfectly capable of handling themselves in a fight.' She didn't like to voice her concern that there had been no sign of the local policeman – or even some offer of help from those who lived nearby. It had also gone far too quiet downstairs now the mob had raced off.

She tiptoed across the main room to the door that opened onto the landing and, with Louise cowering behind her, hesitated at the top of the stairs. There were no yells or scuffles, no sound of thudding boots and breaking glass.

But then the door opened at the bottom of the stairs and a shadowy figure appeared.

Rita stifled a cry of alarm and stepped back into the shadows, keeping Louise behind her. There was nothing up here to use in defence. They were trapped.

'It's all right, *cara*,' said Antonino with great weariness. 'They are gone. It is safe now.'

Rita and Louise raced down the stairs and Louise flung herself into Antonino's arms, the relief so great they could barely speak.

'Come,' said Antonino softly. 'We will go upstairs and rest. I am very tired and Roberto needs some attention to his face.'

Rita couldn't see much in the dim light of the stairwell, and it wasn't until they reached the main room and collapsed into the chairs that she realised how battered they were.

'Oh, my God,' breathed Louise. 'Antonino, Roberto. What have they done to you?' She stroked their battered faces as if her touch could heal them, and then rushed for clean cloths and a bowl of water.

Rita placed a cool damp cloth over the swelling on Roberto's cheekbone and tried not to wince at the amount of blood coming from his nose and the cuts on his chin.

'It looks worse than it is,' he said with forced

cheerfulness as he took the cloth from her. 'See to Papa, Rita. Mamma is too shaken by everything and needs to sit down.'

Rita nodded and, having pressed a distressed Louise into a chair, hurried to help clean the older man's wounds and put ointment on the swellings that were already darkening into bruises. Louise was weeping and wringing her hands as she muttered to herself, and Rita was shocked at how badly she'd been affected. This was not the calm, stoic Louise she'd known all her life and she feared that the events of this evening had sent her over the edge.

'How much damage has been done?' she murmured to Antonino.

'Too much,' he muttered. 'A life's work ruined in minutes.' He shook his head in confusion. 'I don't understand these people. Why do they do these things? Since when are we their enemy?'

Rita had no answer to this, and she was about to wring out a fresh cloth to wipe away the last of the blood on Antonino's face when the door opened and the local copper, Sergeant Williams, stepped into the room. 'You're too late,' she snapped. 'The mob has gone to Gino's. No doubt to do the same sort of damage they inflicted here.'

'I've sent some men to put a stop to it,' he said.

'Then I hope there will be some arrests,' said Rita crossly. 'They've not only beaten both Roberto and Antonino, but ruined the café and sent Louise to the edge of reason. I recognised at least three of them, and would be quite happy to give a statement and go to court.'

Sergeant Williams cleared his throat, his expression doleful. 'Well now, miss, that might prove a bit of a problem. You see, things get heated at times like these, and what with Mr Minelli being Italian and all, and that Mussolini bloke declaring war on us – well . . .' He tailed off into silence as he avoided eye contact.

'You're supposed to protect everyone in the town,' Rita retorted. 'And that includes the Italians. It's not their fault Mussolini declared war.'

'I know, luv.' His expression grew even more lugubrious. 'And I can assure you it won't happen again.'

'Let's hope not.' Rita stood with her arms folded against her chest in an attempt to disguise how badly shaken she was. 'But I was threatened tonight as well, and if those men aren't punished, it will be your fault if anything happens to me or the garage.'

'Shhh, *cara*. Be still.' Antonino stood and, with his arm about his wife's trembling shoulders, faced the sergeant. 'I thank you for coming, but the trouble has passed,' he said quietly. 'Will you perhaps have a glass of wine with us?'

Sergeant Williams flushed a deep scarlet. 'I'm sorry, Mr Minelli, but I'm not here to drink wine.'

'Then why are you here?' Rita knew she was being belligerent, but she couldn't help it.

The burly policeman took a deep breath and finally looked Antonino in the eye. 'I'm sorry, Mr Minelli, but I have to arrest you and your son under regulation 18b of the Defence of the Realm Act.'

'*What?*' Rita stared at him, unable to believe what she was hearing.

The sergeant glanced swiftly at the dumbstruck Minelli family before replying. 'They are of hostile origin, Miss Smith. I have no choice,' he said unhappily. 'But at least they'll be safe from attack in prison.'

'But Roberto is British,' she stormed. 'He was born here – and Antonino has been living here for most of his life. They've done nothing wrong.'

Louise broke into heart-rending sobs, clinging to her husband and son as she let forth a stream of anguished Italian. 'I won't let you take them,' she babbled. 'You cannot take them. We must repair our business. This is our home, Antonino is my husband, Roberto my son. You will not take them from me.'

Sergeant Williams looked flummoxed. 'Look, missus, this is hard enough as it is, but it ain't no use spouting all that Italian at me. I don't understand a flaming word.'

'My son is a British citizen,' said Antonino calmly. 'Take me if you must, but leave him with his mother who needs him.'

Sergeant Williams was clearly out of his depth.

He gave a great sigh, his expression making it clear he wished he was anywhere else but in this room. 'Look, Antonino, I know you and your boy ain't no fascists, but the law is the law. I have to take you both in. Once it's proved you're no danger to security, you'll be released. Probably be home for breakfast tomorrow,' he finished lamely.

'I don't believe you,' wailed Louise.

Sergeant Williams looked helplessly to Antonino, who gently took his sobbing wife in his arms and tried to soothe her. 'I must go with him,' he murmured against her hair. 'Please do not make it harder than it already is. They will see that Roberto and I are innocent victims of this, and will soon let us go. Now, please, *cara mia*, stop crying. I want to see your smile before I leave.'

Rita was furious at the unfairness of it all. She saw Louise make a tremendous effort to calm herself, but noticed how she trembled, how she had to hold onto Antonino to stay on her feet. 'Where are you taking them?' she asked, her voice rough with pent-up emotion.

'To the local nick,' he said. 'It'll be up to the powers-that-be what happens next. But I'll see to it you're kept informed.' He attempted a smile that failed miserably. 'Don't fret, girlie. You'll soon have them home again.'

Rita didn't appreciate his patronising air but realised the situation was tense enough without her causing further trouble. She stood back and battled with her tears of frustration and bewilderment as she watched the little family say their goodbyes.

Roberto kissed his mother and turned to Rita as his father tried to placate Louise. His lips brushed her forehead. 'Mamma isn't strong,' he murmured as he embraced Rita. 'Please, look after her until we get back.'

Rita could only nod, for her tears made it impossible to speak. What had begun as a warm family gathering had turned into a night of violence and unpleasantness, and it seemed there was little she could do to change it.

'Rita.' Antonino enfolded her in his embrace. 'Look after your mamma – and take care of yourself. I love you as my own, and want no harm to come to either of you.'

Rita hugged him fiercely. 'I'll take care, Papa. I promise.'

Sergeant Williams stood awkwardly by as the men fetched hats, coats, scarves and gloves, the two pairs of handcuffs dangling from his meaty fingers as he waited to escort them downstairs.

'There is no need for those,' said Antonino with dignified calm. 'My son and I are not dangerous criminals to be handcuffed. It is shame enough to be arrested.'

Louise clung to Antonino and he had tears in his eyes as he had to wrest himself from her grip. 'You will stay with Rita,' he said firmly. 'Do not come downstairs.'

Rita gathered her into her arms and they were both sobbing as the three men slowly made their way to the ground floor. Within moments they heard the police car drive away and were left with only silence and the terrible fear of not knowing what the future held for any of them.

Chapter Three

There was a long silence after the sound of the police car faded into the distance, and Rita had to steady Louise as she sank like a rag doll into a nearby chair. It was clear she was in shock, and although Rita was still reeling from the night's events, she swiftly made fresh tea, adding two spoons of precious sugar to give her a boost.

'Drink that,' she murmured, 'then we'll tidy up. It's probably best we keep busy.'

Louise nodded, but she made no move to drink the tea. Staring in bewilderment at the toppled candlesticks and wine glasses which lay next to the brick on her table, it seemed she was in a trance.

Rita was shocked at how swiftly she'd seemed to age. Louise's once upright, bustling little figure had shrunk, her fair, silver-streaked hair had come undone from its pins, and the round blue eyes that had always shone with love and contentment were now dull, the lines on her face etched deeper than ever.

Rita held the cup to those pale lips. 'Drink, Mamma,' she coaxed. 'It will make you feel better.'

Louise took a sip as she stared at the horribly

stained tablecloth and the ugly brick which sat in the middle of it. She was too lost in her misery and bewilderment to really know what she was doing.

Rita cupped Louise's cold fingers around the warm china and gently encouraged her to drink some more. 'Please, Mamma. Papa Tino would want you to drink this,' she said in soft Italian. 'You must keep up your strength.'

The big blue eyes were reddened as they regarded her over the lip of the cup. 'Antonino and Roberto will be back soon,' she murmured.

Rita wasn't so sure about that, but it wasn't the moment to voice her doubts. Louise needed to be distracted – and so did she. 'Finish drinking that while I make a start with the clearing up.'

She picked up the brick and the cobblestone. Avoiding the glass strewn across the floor, she placed them on the windowsill, resisting the urge to hurl them into the darkness. The window was in ruins, and the night air was cold, so she fastened the heavy blackout curtains over the yawning hole with some of Louise's wooden clothes pegs.

Glancing over her shoulder, she saw Louise finishing her tea, the colour slowly returning to her face. 'Why don't you clear the table and put that cloth in to soak while I sweep up the glass and see if I can find something to nail over the window for tonight?'

Louise nodded and plucked at the tablecloth with trembling fingers, but the very action seemed to stir her from her stupor and she soon began to clear the table with determination. 'They'll be home soon,' she muttered as she plunged the cloth into a bowl of soapy water to let it soak. 'Antonino and Roberto will be hungry and tired. I must clean my house and make more pasta.'

Rita stilled her as she reached for the large cooking pot that hung above the range. 'They won't be back before morning,' she said softly, 'so why don't we just clear up here, and then you can come back to my place and stay the night?'

Louise's eyes filled with tears again, her face gaunt as she stared back at Rita. 'I can't sleep – not without Antonino beside me. We have not been apart since the day we married – not one night. I will stay here and wait for him.'

Rita knew there was little point in arguing. Once Louise got a thought in her head it was impossible to shift. She kissed her soft cheek and went to fetch the broom, the dustpan and carpet sweeper. There were still shards of glass glinting in the rug, and Louise was often barefooted about the house.

As Louise scrubbed at the tablecloth and wept silent tears, Rita finished clearing the glass and tried to think where she might find something to nail over the window. Despite her best efforts, the blackout curtains couldn't shut out the night air which was winning the battle over the fire in the range and chilling the room.

'I'm just going home to see if there's some

plywood to put over this window,' she said, reaching for her gas mask box.

'No.' Louise spun away from the sink and grabbed Rita's hand. 'I don't want to be alone here. They might come back.'

'I'll only be a matter of minutes,' she soothed. 'You'll be quite safe, I promise.'

'No.' The soapy fingers tightened on her wrist. 'We'll find something here. I don't want you going outside. It's too dangerous.'

Rita gave in. Louise had been a mother to her for years; had dried her tears, fed her pasta and tidbits of bread and sweet cake, told her stories and given her cuddles when she was feeling sad or unwell. How could she go against her wishes now? 'All right, Mamma. I'll go downstairs and see if there's anything in the café.'

'I'll come with you.' Louise dried her hands on her apron, hesitated on the landing, and then made a tremendous effort to be brave and cautiously followed Rita down the stairs.

The moon provided the only light in the strict blackout, but the sight that greeted them broke their hearts. The large display cabinet that had once held a variety of delicious pastries, cakes and pies had been smashed and kicked into a buckled, broken mess. The Italian coffee machine Antonino had been so proud of was a mangled wreck, and the shelves behind the counter had been swept clean, the sweet jars and cordial bottles shattered on the floor, their contents trampled underfoot into a sticky mess.

The linoleum that Louise scrubbed every night was also spattered with blood and smears of dirt, and the imprint of a heavy boot could clearly be seen marking the once pristine wall. Tables and chairs had been systematically broken, the little hand-sewn tablecloths Louise had so lovingly made left trampled among the debris, and all that remained of the front window was a few daggers of glass clinging to the frame. The door had been kicked in so hard the brass knob had become embedded in the wall and both hinges were buckled.

'*Mamma mia*,' breathed Louise through her fingers. Her shocked gaze trawled the devastation and she had to lean against Rita as her legs threatened to give way.

Rita felt sick. Antonino and Louise had been so proud of their little café – had worked long hours to make it a success, had treated each customer as a welcome friend, and each neighbour as warmly as one of their own. Louise was always lending a hand in times of trouble, helping to look after children when they were sick, doing an extra batch of bread when times were hard, slipping a handful of sweets or a sticky bun to the little ones who so rarely got a treat. But where were those friends and neighbours now?

She stood in front of the shattered window and looked out at the deserted cobbled street. There were no lights, no anxious neighbours coming to help, not even the flicker of a twitching curtain or a curious face at a window. She felt like yelling for them to come out – wanted to bang on those doors and shame them into admitting how deeply they had betrayed one of their own by ignoring them in their time of need.

But reason took over and she had to concede that she and Louise were alone in this and must do the best they could. 'There's nothing we can do in here without any lights,' she said, the bitterness sour in her throat.

She yanked on the door, using all her strength to loosen the knob from the crumbling plaster and push it into place. Miraculously, the key still turned in the heavy lock, but she knew it wouldn't take much to cave it in again.

Jamming the back of a surviving chair against the knob for added security, she looked round for something to use to cover the shattered windows. But there was nothing left that was big enough, so she turned to Louise who was still eyeing the scene with stunned disbelief. 'Come on,' she said softly. 'Let's go back upstairs.'

With the door locked at the bottom of the stairs, Rita checked the back gate and door were secure before they trudged back to the living quarters. The mob hadn't had time to do any damage there.

'You'll stay with me tonight?' Louise grasped Rita's hand, her eyes pleading.

'Of course,' she replied swiftly. 'I'll sleep here by the fire.' She kissed Louise's cheek. 'But I have to leave early in the morning,' she warned. 'My shift starts at seven, and I'll get it in the neck if I'm late.'

Louisa nodded reluctantly and went to find spare blankets and a nightdress. When she returned, she looked slightly more in control of her emotions, but it seemed she took comfort in speaking Italian, even though it was just the two of them.

'I will cook a big breakfast and make some more bread in the morning. I have one last bag of flour, and you will need something to fill you up for your day's work.' She nodded, as if satisfied with her plans. 'Antonino and Roberto will be glad of my home cooking when they get back. It can't be very nice down at the police cells.'

Rita thought it was probably far from nice down there but kept those thoughts to herself. The other thing that struck her was that, in the light of the night's events, it would probably be wiser if Louise spoke English from now on. With such animosity infecting the neighbourhood, it might not take much to stoke more trouble. But she would leave it for now. Louise had had enough for tonight – and so had she.

Rita weighted the heavily pegged curtains down with the brick and cobblestone and finally settled into the armchair by the range, glad of its warmth and the two cosy blankets.

She was exhausted and downhearted from the

night's events, but sleep eluded her as the clock on the wall slowly ticked away the minutes. Tormented by visions of Tino and Roberto being locked in a prison cell, she guessed Louise was having the same problem in the other room and, after an hour of restlessness, she went to check on her.

The room was not quite in darkness, for a votive candle burned in a saucer on the bedside table where Louise had placed photographs of her husband and son. She was sitting up in bed, her hair trailing over one shoulder in a ragged plait as she slipped the tiny pearl rosary beads through her fingers.

On seeing Rita, she turned back the blankets. 'Come, *cara mia*,' she murmured, 'come into the warm with me like when you were a *bambina*. Together we will make it through the night.'

Rita climbed in beside her, nestled into her warm, familiar embrace and was a child again – comforted and protected, safe in her mother's arms.

As the candle flickered and Louise finally succumbed to her exhaustion, Rita watched the shadows dance on the wall, her thoughts in turmoil. She had to hope and pray that Papa and Roberto would come home in the morning, for she didn't dare contemplate what the consequences might be if they were kept in custody.

Rita had left a far more cheerful and optimistic Louise the next morning with a promise to come home straight after work to welcome the men. But as she approached the series of large sheds on the industrial estate, she was surprised to see her best friend, May Lynch, parking her BSA motorbike before she rushed towards her.

'Hello, not like you to get here so early,' she said. Her smile faded as she saw the grim expression on May's pretty little face. 'What's the matter?'

'I heard about what happened last night,' May replied, sweeping off her leather helmet and goggles before brushing back the over-long fringe of fair hair from her eyes. 'Are you all right?'

'I'm fine,' Rita reassured her, 'but Louise is in a terrible state and we're both worried sick about Papa and Roberto.'

'I'm not surprised.' May grabbed her arm to stop her from going into the factory. 'I should warn you,' she said urgently, 'there's some in there wanting to cause trouble over what happened last night.' She shot a glance at a small knot of women who were standing just inside the doorway. 'And Aggie's appointed herself as ringleader. Don't let her wind you up, Rita. You know what you're like when you lose your temper.'

Rita frowned. 'What's it got to do with Aggie?'

'She doesn't need an excuse to cause trouble, we both know that.' May's big blue eyes regarded her solemnly. 'Don't worry,' she muttered. 'You've got me on your side.'

'Come on, then. Let's get it over with.' Rita smiled as they linked arms and headed for the factory. They were the same age and height, May's fair hair a perfect foil to Rita's dark curls. May's father had long since done a runner, leaving her mother to wallow in bitterness and resentment, and May had realised very quickly that if she was ever to achieve anything in life she had to do it on her own. Like Rita, she was a little battler who stood no nonsense when it came to defending herself. Their friendship was firm, their shared passion for motorbikes welding them even tighter.

Rita didn't want to believe such nastiness could exist in Cliffehaven, but as they marched into the enormous shed arm in arm, she was made all too aware of the huddles of women who fell silent as they passed, their suspicious eyes following them as they approached their lockers to hang up their coats and gas mask boxes.

'Just ignore them,' muttered May as she shed the leather jacket and adjusted the straps on her overalls. 'They're mostly full of hot air anyway.'

Glad of her friend's support, Rita tried to follow May's advice – but it was difficult. The talk was all about Mussolini's declaration of war and the ensuing battles that had been fought in the town. She heard the snide comments and the sniggers and stoically tamped down on the urge to answer back, but as she and May approached their work stations in the welding bay Aggie Rawlings deliberately blocked their way.

'We need to know what side yer on,' Aggie said

belligerently, her meaty arms folded beneath her large bosom.

Rita noticed how several of Aggie's cohort of grim-faced women had sidled over, and were now surrounding her and May. Refusing to be daunted, she lifted her chin. 'I'm here to do a job and help win the war against Hitler,' she said clearly into the deathly hush that had fallen over the vast echoing shed.

'Yeah, that's right,' said May, 'so bugger off and leave us alone.'

'Lie with dogs and you'll get fleas, May Lynch,' snapped Aggie. 'This ain't your business.'

'It ain't yours neither,' retorted May.

'Keep out of this, May, if you know what's good fer yer,' snarled Aggie.

'She's my friend, and all the while you've got something to say to her, then you'll say it in front of me.'

Aggie glared at her. 'You ain't right, the pair of yer,' she snapped. 'What with yer motorbikes and men's clothes. It ain't normal.'

'If normal means having a fat arse and hairs on your chin, then I'm glad we're different,' said Rita tightly. 'What's your real beef, Aggie?'

'What about them Eyeties yer so friendly with? I 'ear you practically live with them, and that you was there last night.'

'So?' Rita eyed each woman in turn as she balled her fists deep in her overall pockets. 'Every one of you has been in that café at some time. And I bet most of you go to the market garden, the ice-cream parlour and the butcher's as well. The Italian families aren't a threat – just decent, hard-working people who have earned the right to feel safe in their beds at night.'

'That don't make no difference when there's a war on,' Aggie retorted. 'They're our enemies now, and if you ask me, prison's the best place for 'em.'

'With a husband like yours, you'd know all about that, wouldn't you?' Rita fired back. 'How many years has he done so far? Or have you lost count?'

Aggie's expression hardened and the light of battle gleamed in her eyes as she took a step towards Rita. 'I'll 'ave you fer that,' she snarled. 'My old man ain't no saint, but at least he ain't a greasy Eyetie collaborator.'

Rita eyed her with loathing. 'Tino is no collaborator,' she retorted. 'Take that back, Aggie.'

'I ain't taking nothing back.' Aggie swiftly glanced at the other women who'd edged forward. 'And we all reckon you ain't all you make out to be and all. You look Italian, you speak their lingo and spend all your time with 'em. Perhaps you should have been arrested as well.'

'My mum was Irish, as you very well know,' Rita said with dangerous calm.

Aggie sniffed. 'If you say so.' She looked for approval among the others. 'But we don't like you working here, so sling yer hook, Eyetie lover.'

'I'm not going anywhere.' Rita and May took a pace forward, both ready to stand their ground as the other women formed a tighter circle round them.

'Right, that's enough.' The knot of women reluctantly parted as the sturdy, no-nonsense figure of Major Patricia Marshall marched through to stand between Rita, May and Aggie.

Dressed in the uniform of the Royal Engineers, Major Marshall was a formidable presence and not someone to argue with. Her steely blue gaze raked over them. 'I will not have that kind of talk in my factory,' she said coldly. 'Rawlings, go to your workbench and stop causing trouble. Lynch, your loyalty is to be commended, but I will not have fisticuffs in the workplace. The rest of you, get on with your work.' The flinty gaze settled on Rita. 'Smith. In my office.'

Rita shot May a look of gratitude, but she could taste the bitterness of that short, nasty spat, and could hear the sniggering and whispering as she followed the broad beam of the woman in charge, and braced herself for what she suspected might be a stern dressing-down.

According to the gossip, and verified by Rita's father who knew about such things, Major Marshall was an Oxford graduate who, before the war, had designed and built aircraft for the RAF, as well as for the burgeoning number of private flying enthusiasts. She and her husband, who was a hugely respected Wing Commander at the local airfield, had run this successful business together. Now Patricia was in sole charge of the government contracts to build aeroplane parts in this area, and took her duties very seriously indeed.

Closing the door behind her, Rita stood in the small, cramped office and waited nervously for the other woman to tear her off a strip – or worse, to question her loyalties.

Major Marshall sat down in the battered chair and eyed Rita across a desk strewn with paperwork and technical drawings. 'You have an important job here, Smith, and I don't want it compromised by your relationship with your Italian neighbours.'

Rita was about to protest when she was silenced by an impatient wave of Major Marshall's hand. 'The events of last night were unfortunate. I do not agree with mob rule – never have. But the fact is we are at war with Italy and, as with all enemy foreign nationals living in this country, it is the law to take them into custody.'

'But Antonino has lived here since he was a boy, and Roberto's a British citizen. They had no right to arrest him.'

The Major took a deep breath and eyed Rita down her long, patrician nose. 'I suggest you make sure you are familiar with the salient facts before you make such wild statements.'

Rita frowned. 'What do you mean?'

The older woman stood, clasped her hands behind her back and stared out through the heavily taped window to the yard in front of the shed and the enormous barrage balloons that swayed above it. 'Because of their connection with you, I have made enquiries,' she said, 'and it appears the Minelli son was actually born in Naples.'

Rita stared at her in shock. 'That's not right,' she protested. 'Louise has always . . .'

The Major turned from the window, her impatience clear. 'It is of no matter to you, Smith, and we are wasting valuable time discussing things that don't concern either of us. Go back to your work and don't rise to the baiting of the other women. Not everyone feels the same as Aggie Rawlings, and last night's shocking events will soon become of less interest as this war progresses.'

She relented somewhat with a stiff little smile. 'You are a valuable member of my team despite your youth, Smith. It would be a shame to blot your copybook now.'

Rita knew better than to speak and, at the other woman's nod of dismissal, she hurried out of the office and headed to the welding bay which was at the far end of the enormous shed.

May was already busy welding, but on Rita's approach, she switched off the blow torch and raised the heavy leather visor. 'What did she say?'

'Nothing much,' Rita replied, reaching for the sturdy gloves. 'But Major Patricia has her beady eyes on us, so we'd better get to work. I'll tell you more during our lunch break.'

'All right, but don't let them upset you, Rita. Their opinions don't matter a jot.'

Rita shot her a grin and, ignoring the sly glances of the others, she fastened the heavy leather hooded visor over her head, pulled on the thick gloves and sturdy apron and adjusted the oxyacetylene supply. Having tested the strength of the flame coming from the blowtorch, she focused her attention on welding the two pieces of metal together that would form an intrinsic part of an aircraft wing.

As the blindingly bright sparks flew and the sweat began to sting her eyes beneath the stifling visor, her thoughts kept returning to Louise and the lie she and Papa Tino had maintained for almost twenty years. It made no sense, and she was impatient for her shift to be over so she could get the truth from Louise.

Beach View Boarding House was in one of the many terraces of Victorian villas that climbed the hill from the seafront on the eastern side of Cliffehaven. It was not aptly named, for the view of the sea could only be glimpsed from the corner of one of the top-floor bedroom windows.

Tall and narrow above the two basement rooms and scullery, its depth provided six other bedrooms, a bathroom, dining room and kitchen. The garden at the back housed the outside lav, a coal bunker and shed, and the ugly, rather menacing hump of the Anderson shelter. The washing line was stretched between poles to hang over the neat rows of vegetables that had replaced the lawn, and every inch of fence was covered with sprouting beans, peas and tomato plants.

The boarding house was conveniently close to Camden Road, where there was a small row of shops, the school where Anne taught, a pub, the fire station, clothing factory and the hospital. Cliffehaven's High Street and main shopping centre could be accessed at the far end of Camden Road, but it was a steep climb to get to the top of it, and most of Peggy's neighbours preferred the easier option of shopping locally where they were registered for their rations.

It was almost lunchtime and Peggy was peeling potatoes. The elderly Mrs Finch was reading the newspaper at the kitchen table, and Ron was outside weeding his vegetable plot, his every move closely watched by Harvey, his shaggy lurcher. Charlie and Bob were at school, Cissy was rehearsing for her show and everyone else was at work. Jim was not on duty in the projection room of the Odeon cinema until this evening, but he'd left the house several hours ago – no doubt up to something he shouldn't be.

She cut the potato into chunks and dropped them in the saucepan of salted water, then stood gazing out of the window at nothing in particular as she let her thoughts ramble. She had known Jim was a rogue when she'd married him, and despite his roving eye and penchant for a dodgy deal, Peggy still adored the Irish charmer But she did wish he wouldn't sail so close to the wind. Black market-eering was illegal, and if he was caught, then it would be prison or enforced enlistment. At over forty, with experience of war the first time round and used to his home comforts, she doubted he'd appreciate either.

Pulling her thoughts together, she reached for the kettle that always stood filled and ready on the side of the Kitchener range that she'd spent half the morning blacking and polishing. 'Would you like a cup of tea, Mrs Finch?'

There was no reply. Mrs Finch had turned off her hearing aid – not that it made much difference, the damned thing was useless most of the time. Peggy gave a wry smile, wiped her hands on her wrap-round apron and reached for the cups and saucers.

'I think I'll make a cup of tea,' said Mrs Finch as she set the paper aside. 'Reading all that news has made me thirsty.'

'The kettle's already on the boil. Do you want a biscuit?'

Mrs Finch frowned as she twiddled with her hearing aid. 'I didn't know tea could spoil,' she muttered, 'but if you're prepared to risk it, then so am I.'

Peggy chuckled. Conversations with Mrs Finch were always confusing, but at least they brought a smile. She poured the water over the leaves, dragged the knitted cosy over the brown china pot and sat down.

Mrs Finch was aptly named, for she was birdlike and twittered a great deal, especially when Jim and Ron were around. But Peggy felt a deep affection for the old lady and was glad she could make her last years more comfortable by bringing her into her home and making her part of the family. She had been worried the war would unsettle her, but it appeared she'd discovered a new lease of life with the house so full of young people, and Peggy could only hope that would last.

As they waited for the tea to mash, Peggy dug her packet of Park Drive out of her apron pocket, lit one and tried to relax. But there were so many things to think about, what with the wedding only three days away, that she found it impossible. She gazed around her kitchen, noted the worn lino, the faded oilcloth on the table, the flaking paint on the window frames and the dust lining the shelves next to the range. This was the heart of her home and although it was shabby, and a world away from her sister Doris's pristine kitchen in Havelock Gardens, she drew comfort from it, and the lovely memories it recalled.

Ron tramped into the kitchen, closely followed by an equally dishevelled Harvey. 'Can I smell tea brewing?'

Peggy eyed them in horror. 'Take your boots off,

Ron. You've got half a garden of mud on them and I've just scrubbed the lino.'

'To be sure, you're a hard woman, Peggy Reilly,' he said with a deep sigh, his brogue as strong as ever despite having left Ireland many years before.

Peggy eyed him with a mixture of exasperation and affection. Ron was a widower of many years and, at sixty-three, was as fit as a butcher's dog, with strong shoulders and arms and a rather disconcerting habit of wearing the first thing he picked up from the floor each morning. His favourite clothes were baggy corduroy trousers, threadbare sweaters and the large poacher's coat he wore when he took Harvey up into the hills hunting for game and anything else that might just happen to fall into the many hidden pockets.

The only times he looked passably smart were when he was in his Defence Volunteers' uniform, or on his way to court Rosie Braithwaite, who was the middle-aged but very glamorous landlady of the nearby Anchor pub. He'd lusted after her for years, and despite the fact that Rosie was at least ten years younger than him, he remained determined to snare her.

Peggy wrinkled her nose as Harvey investigated the biscuit tin. 'You can take him out of here as well,' she said in disgust. 'He's been rolling in something and absolutely stinks.'

Ron grabbed the dog's collar and grimaced as the aroma finally hit him. 'He got in the compost before

I could stop him,' he grumbled. 'Go on, ye heathen animal – downstairs.'

Harvey put his tail between his legs and, with a look of utter dejection that was meant to change Peggy's mind, reluctantly made his way down the steps to the basement scullery where he slumped on the bottom step with a defeated sigh.

Ron pulled off his boots to reveal unsavoury socks and reached for the cup of tea Peggy had placed in front of him. 'To be sure, and that hits the spot, so it does,' he murmured.

Peggy was about to ask him how the tomato plants were coming on when she heard the front door slam. Jim was back. She looked up as he strode into the room and her pulse gave a little jump as it always did every time she saw him. He was still so handsome with his dark hair and twinkling eyes – how could she ever be cross with him?

'You'll not believe what happened last night,' he said without preamble as he flung his cap on the table. 'And in Cliffehaven of all places.'

'My goodness,' chirped Mrs Finch as she patted her hair, adjusted her hearing aid, and gazed at him in admiration. 'Whatever have you been up to, you young rogue?'

'We'll no doubt find out soon enough,' said Peggy dryly as she fetched another cup and saucer, happy to let him have his moment of drama.

Jim winked at Mrs Finch. 'To be sure, 'tis not me causing the trouble this time.'

Mrs Finch frowned, clearly not understanding a word he'd said, and rather than repeat himself, he turned back to Peggy. 'I was chatting to Alf the butcher,' he said as she put his tea in front of him. 'He said the police had to be called and the amount of damage done would probably amount to hundreds of pounds.'

He blew on his tea, took a sip and grimaced. Reaching for the almost empty bowl of sugar, he tipped most of it into his cup and stirred it vigorously.

'Jim,' protested Peggy. 'You've got to take it easy on the sugar. It *is* rationed, you know.'

'War or no war, I'll not be drinking tea without sugar,' he declared. 'And besides, there's plenty more where that came from.'

Peggy didn't want to know about illicit sugar. 'Never mind all that,' she replied. 'I want to hear what sort of trouble had the police out.'

He looked at her over the lip of his cup, his expression solemn. 'The local Italian families had their businesses and homes wrecked last night. Alf said Gino and his brothers put up a hell of a fight, but they were outnumbered and the police got there too late to stop the mob from burning down two of their shops.'

Peggy stiffened. 'Dear God,' she breathed. 'Was anyone hurt?'

'They got the women and children out in time, but two of Gino's brothers had to be taken to hospital with broken bones.'

'I can't believe it,' she gasped. 'Not here. Not Cliffehaven.'

Jim slurped his tea. 'There's always been a rough element over on the other side of the rail tracks, and they need little excuse to start trouble.'

'What about the Minellis?' Peggy's voice was sharp with concern.

'Their café was wrecked, but the mob moved on without setting fire to the place.' He eyed Peggy over the cup. 'Rita and Louise are all right, Peg, but that's not the half of it.'

'What?' Peggy's fear for Rita made her tone sharper than she'd meant.

'The police let the hooligans go free and promptly arrested all the Italians, including the women, children and old folk.'

'But why?'

'Defence of the Realm Act, according to Alf,' he muttered darkly. 'The same thing happened to the German families in the last war, if you remember.'

Peggy could remember it all too well. She stood and reached for her coat and scarf which were hanging on the back of the door. 'I must go to Rita and make sure she and Louise are all right.'

'You'll not be going anywhere near that side of town until things calm down,' he replied firmly. 'Feelings are still running high and it's not safe.'

'Safe or not, I'm going.' She kicked off her slippers,

pulled on her coat, grabbed her handbag and gas mask and slid her feet into her outdoor shoes. 'Louise isn't strong at the best of times, and relies on Antonino for everything. I dread to think what all this must have done to her.'

'Sit down, Peg,' he growled. 'It's not our business and it won't do any good to meddle.'

'Of course it's our business,' snapped Peggy, who was now thoroughly overwrought. 'Rita's been coming here since she was a little girl, and she relies on the Minellis – they've been a second family to her. I need to make sure Louise hasn't been arrested along with the others.'

'For God's sake, woman, would you listen to yourself?' Jim rose from his chair and towered over her, his eyes glinting with what looked suspiciously like amusement. 'Louise won't have been arrested. She's one of us.'

'My point entirely,' she retorted, 'and because she's one of our own she'll need all the support she can get until her husband and son are released. Now, are you coming with me, or do I have to go alone?'

He heaved a great sigh, finished his tea and reached reluctantly for his cap. 'God preserve me from interfering women,' he muttered, tipping a wink at his father who was grinning like a Cheshire cat. 'If I'd known you'd make such a fuss, I wouldn't have told you anything.'

Peggy wasn't even listening to him as she hurried

into the hall. 'Hurry up,' she said over her shoulder, 'or we'll miss the trolleybus to the station.'

'Thanks for standing by me today.' Rita gave her friend a hug. 'I'll see you tomorrow.'

May hugged her back and climbed onto her BSA motorbike. 'I'll be here waiting for you, so don't be late.' She kicked the bike into life and shot out of the estate, the powerful bike barely missing the broad, wobbling beam of Aggie Rawlings – earning a shaken fist and some ripe language.

It was after four, and Rita walked quickly past the furious Aggie, the gas mask box bumping on her hip, her heavy, steel-capped boots ringing out on the pavement as she hurried home. The day had not been a pleasant one, for a lot of the other women had refused to speak to her at all. At least she'd had May at her side, and two or three of the other younger girls had come forward to offer their sympathy and make it clear they wanted no part of her being sent to Coventry.

Rita had never been a victim of bullying before, had never experienced such suspicion and spite, and it had unsettled her more than she liked to admit. Still, she thought with some relief, now she knew where she stood and who her real friends were – and May had proved to be a stalwart.

As she entered Barrow Lane she felt her spirits rise as she saw the café had been boarded up with heavy sheets of plywood, the door replaced, and the ruined furniture piled neatly outside awaiting the rubbish collection. Perhaps their darkest dread had been in vain, and Roberto and Tino had come home.

But hope faltered as she stood there. It was hard to tell if anyone was at home, for the upstairs window had been boarded up, too, and it was rather worrying that she couldn't smell cooking or hear voices.

With rising panic, Rita hurried to the narrow alley that ran between two of the houses and headed for the Minellis' back gate. As she unlocked the gate and stepped into the neat concreted yard with its array of potted herbs and seedlings, she looked up at the rear window. The curtains were drawn and the sash window was tightly shut, which was most unusual at this time of day.

Her mouth dry, she let herself in through the back door. This was where Antonino and Roberto baked their pies, cakes and pastries, but since plentiful supplies of cream, sugar, flour and eggs had become almost impossible to maintain, they'd had to cut down on production, and Roberto had gone to work in the hospital kitchens. The fire in the range in the corner had gone out, the mixing bowls and baking tins were neatly stacked on shelves, and the cool slab of marble where Papa Tino rolled his pastry and made his bread had been polished clean. The paraphernalia of rolling pins, knives, spatulas and spoons were neatly stacked in jars, waiting for him to return. The only sound came from the quiet hum of the gas fridge.

Fearful for Louise, Rita ran into the shop, noted it had been cleaned of all trace of the brawl, and raced up the stairs. 'Louise,' she called, hurtling into the main room.

There was no reply, and she quickly checked the two bedrooms before finding the note Louise had left on the mantelpiece.

'Have gone to police station. Please come.'

'Oh, no,' she groaned, and fled back downstairs again. She didn't have enough petrol in the tank to use the motorbike, and although she had a couple of cans stowed in the garage for emergencies, it would take too long to top it up, so she locked the back door, grabbed Roberto's bicycle and pedalled furiously into town.

Louise was waiting for her beside the great stacks of sandbags that guarded the door to the police station. Her face was drawn, her eyelids swollen as she gratefully clasped Rita's hands with her cold fingers. 'I waited,' she murmured in Italian, 'knowing you would come as soon as you could.'

'Have you had any news?'

Louise shook her head as the tears welled again. 'They haven't come home and I'm frightened, Rita.'

Rita noted the straggle of untidy hair drifting from beneath the headscarf, the deep lines of worry etched into the sweet face that was usually wreathed in smiles. Louise was slowly falling apart, and Rita

73

realised she had to be strong for both of them. 'Come on,' she said, taking her hand. 'I'll see if we can get any sense out of anyone.'

They climbed the concrete steps and pushed through the heavy door into a vast hall with a desk at one end. Sergeant Williams stood behind it, and when he caught sight of them he ducked his head and continued to write something in a large ledger.

Rita hurried forward, Louise alongside her. 'We want to know what's happened to Roberto and Antonino,' she said. 'You told us you would keep us informed, but they still haven't come home, and you said . . .'

'They won't be coming home, miss,' he interrupted. 'Not for a long while yet.'

'Why not?' Rita snapped. 'They aren't criminals.'

'Where are my husband and son?' pleaded Louise as she twisted the strap of her gas mask box in her fingers. 'I must talk to them; make sure they are all right.'

Sergeant Williams stood tall, his expression implacable. 'They've been taken to Wormwood Scrubs for questioning.' He glared down at Louise. 'It's no good you looking like that, missus. You want to thank your lucky stars you're English and didn't go with them. All the other Italian families have been rounded up and sent to camps where they'll stay for the duration.'

'All of them?' breathed Louise. 'Even Gino's *nonna*

Frizzelli?' At his nod she burst into tears. 'But she's eighty years old. What possible risk could she be?'

'It's not my place to question the law, madam, just to see it obeyed.'

'But Wormwood Scrubs is miles away. How am I supposed to get to them?' wailed Louise.

Rita could feel her temper rising and had to struggle to remain calm in the face of his inflexibility. 'Can we visit them at the Scrubs? Or perhaps write to them?'

'There's no visiting or correspondence allowed. Not for internees. Besides, you won't be allowed travel warrants.'

'Murderers are allowed visitors,' Rita retorted. 'I don't see why . . .'

'It's out of my hands, miss. But the way things are going, I doubt they'll be there for much longer. The German and Italian nationals are being processed pretty swiftly to get them away from strategic areas before the invasion comes. You'll just have to wait until they can write to you.'

Rita stared at him as Louise sobbed. 'But this is England,' she said, her own voice trembling with emotion. 'We don't treat people like this.'

The sergeant slammed the large logbook shut. 'There's a war on,' he said grimly. 'Things happen whether we like it or not.' With that, he pushed through the nearby door and was gone.

Rita put her arm round Louise's shoulder. 'Come, Mamma,' she murmured. 'Let's get you home.'

She gently steered the weeping woman out of the police station, past the sandbags and into the almost deserted High Street. There was no sign of a bus and neither of them could afford a taxi even if, by some miracle, one happened along. Rita retrieved the bicycle from where it leaned against a nearby lamp post. It was going to be a long, slow walk home.

The air-raid siren went off before they could reach Barrow Lane, and they hurried down the concrete steps of the public shelter that had been dug beneath the recreation ground. It was dimly lit and reeked of damp and too many bodies crammed into a tight space. Babies were crying, women were chattering and complaining at the inconvenience of it all as they puffed cigarettes and shared flasks of tea, and Rita had to push her way through to find somewhere to sit.

She recognised many faces but, as she held Louise's hand and tried to comfort her, she noticed how their gazes shifted away, how they shrank from making contact with them, and whispered to each other behind their hands.

'It's all right,' she consoled Louise. 'Let them turn their noses up. Roberto and Papa are worth ten of them.'

Despite her brave words, they suffered an uncomfortable half-hour down there until the all-clear rang out. It was yet another false alarm, and everyone trudged back up the steps, more concerned with getting home than continuing their gossip.

Louise tied her headscarf under her chin, gripped her handbag and gas mask box to her chest and, head held high, walked alongside Rita who was pushing the bicycle. They went into the house through the back door and, after making sure everything was locked, wearily climbed the stairs to the main room.

'You've worked hard today,' said Rita as she pulled the blackout curtains over the fresh plywood, lit the gas lamps and put the kettle on to boil. 'It must have taken ages to clean up the mess downstairs.'

Louise sank into her favourite armchair with a deep sigh and pulled off her gloves and headscarf. 'I had plenty of help. Peggy and Jim Reilly came over and she got him to board up the windows and carry the heavier stuff out to the pavement while we scrubbed the floor and cleaned the mess. Jim even managed to find a replacement door. They were both so very kind.'

'They're lovely people,' agreed Rita. She prodded the poker amongst the few coals in the range fire and coaxed it to burn more brightly as her thoughts whirled. It was a great pity their neighbours hadn't rallied round, and she hoped they'd felt at least a twinge of shame as they watched the Reillys help clean up.

'Peggy was all for going to the police station and

giving the superintendent a piece of her mind, but I managed to persuade her not to make a fuss. It would have only made things worse for Tino and Roberto.'

'It might not have done,' said Rita as she let the tea steep in the pot and reached for cups. 'Peggy knows a lot of influential people in this town, and she might have been able to pull some strings.'

'There are no strings left to pull,' said Louise, who was close to tears again. 'You see, it's my fault Roberto is in prison, and I didn't want the shame of having to tell Peggy how stupid I've been.'

Rita perched on the arm of Louise's chair and took her hand. 'What is it, Mamma?' she asked softly.

Louise sniffed back the tears and tried her best to remain composed. 'Antonino and I had taken the girls to Naples for his brother's wedding. We thought we'd have plenty of time to get back before Roberto was born – but he came early. I left Italy only a few days after he was born and planned to deal with the paperwork when I got home. But Roberto was a demanding baby, Tino needed help in the café and I had the two girls to look after. It slipped my mind.'

'I'm not surprised,' murmured Rita. 'You had enough to worry about by the sound of it.'

Louise nodded and dabbed her eyes with her handkerchief. 'When I finally remembered, there were so many forms to read, so many places that had to be signed and witnessed and stamped – and I couldn't understand half of them.' She dipped her chin, her voice softer now. 'I was never much good at reading and writing, and I got more and more confused and upset about it all. I finally decided it wouldn't really matter if I didn't fill them in. Tino had made his home here since he was fourteen, the girls were born in this house and I was already British anyway. Roberto was less than a week old when I brought him home, and I didn't think there was any harm in pretending he was English too.'

'But surely Papa Tino must have known?'

Louise burst into tears. 'I was ashamed to admit I couldn't understand all those forms. So I lied to him. He didn't question it because he trusted me.'

Rita held her as she sobbed into a handkerchief. The whole thing was a terrible mess. If only Louise had had more courage, Rita was certain Tino would have understood and perhaps paid for advice on how to fill in those damned forms. But it was too late now, and all they could do was wait and see what happened next.

Louise eventually blew her nose and then scrabbled in her handbag for a rare cigarette. She lit it, coughed on the smoke and determinedly carried on puffing. 'He will know now that I lied to him, but it was the only time, Rita, I swear. And look what it has done.'

Rita didn't know what to do or say. Events had whirled out of her control to the point where she was as confused and upset as Louise. But one thing was certain. Louise could not cope alone. It was now up to her to make sure they both got through this – no matter how long it took, or how hard it became.

Chapter Four

As the weeks passed and there was still no news of her husband and son, Louise slowly lost hope and became a shadow of her previous self. The allotment where Antonino had once worked so diligently was all but abandoned. The three rooms above the boarded-up café began to look shabby as she couldn't dredge up the energy to cook and clean, and she'd lost any interest in her appearance, rarely leaving the sanctuary of her home for fear of the real and imagined slights of the neighbours who mostly still kept their distance.

Louise had become a lost soul – a prisoner in her own home, and Rita despaired at ever seeing her smile again. Peggy was a frequent visitor, and she and Rita did their best to clean the house and try to bring some order to Louise's life. Ron turned up to weed the allotment now and again, but there were too few hours in the day for any of them to do much. Peggy had a houseful, Ron had his own garden to keep as well as helping in the pub and attending to his Defence Volunteer duties. Production at the factory had been stepped up, and everyone was encouraged to work longer hours to complete the quota, which meant Louise was often left alone to mope.

Rita had all but abandoned her own home, sitting night after night with Louise, encouraging her to eat the dismal little meals she'd cooked as she attempted to persuade her to take up some sort of work – or at least to spend time in the allotment. Peggy would often arrive with a tin of something to eat, but with no income from the café, and few savings, Louise had effectively come to rely on Rita's slender pay packet. Although their needs were few, it was getting harder to cope each week.

But all these worries faded into insignificance at the beginning of July when they heard that the *Arandora Star* had been sunk by a German U-boat. She'd been on her way to Canada with 1,562 internees on board. Over eight hundred lives were lost, the majority of them Italian, and although there was a public outcry, it didn't stop the government from sending another, larger ship, the *Dunera*, to Australia with even more internees on board, including German Jews who had escaped the terrors of Europe only to find themselves imprisoned alongside Nazi POWs.

It took Rita and Peggy many days to reach the right people and confirm that the Minelli men had not been on board, or sent to Australia on the *Dunera* along with the survivors from the *Arandora Star*. But their whereabouts was still being kept secret, and all communication banned. This lack of knowledge was almost the undoing of poor Louise and she retreated further into her shell of despair.

As the summer waned, the war news became ever more alarming. The Channel Islands had fallen to German occupation. Italy had invaded Southern France and bombed Abyssinia and Eritrea, capturing the British outposts of Kassala and Gallabat on the Sudanese border, and the Italians had bombed the British protectorate of Palestine. Cardiff and Liverpool had come under attack by the Luftwaffe and August saw the first enemy bombing raid over London. Hitler's blockade of the British Isles was swiftly followed by massive enemy raids on London, Southampton, Bristol, Cardiff, Liverpool and Manchester.

The activity at the airfield increased tenfold as the RAF began night raids on Kiel, Wilhelmshaven and Berlin. Prime Minister Winston Churchill declared that 'The Battle of Britain' had begun, and now there were daily air-raid warnings as seaports, airfields, radar stations and factories came under attack. Shipping was under fire in the Channel as Hitler's blockade of Britain tightened, and everyone was on high alert as the activity in the skies increased and the danger of invasion became ever more likely.

Cliffehaven was in the direct flight path of the enemy bombers which came across the Channel to attack London, and was being called 'Fire Alley' in the newspapers. Because of the military camps, the factories and the airfield in the hills behind it, the sprawling seaside town had suffered numerous heavy bombing raids during August and September, which had caused several deaths and a great deal of damage.

Beach View Boarding House had escaped a particularly fearsome explosion nearby, and no one had been hurt, but the front door and most of the windows had been blown in, leaving it looking rather forlorn.

Barrow Lane's proximity to the railway added to Rita's concern for Louise's safety, and she'd made her promise she'd run for the public shelter the moment she heard the sirens. But she had a sneaking suspicion Louise hid beneath Tino's marble-topped table at the back of the café rather than face the other women from the street. So far, they'd been lucky, and the only real damage had been further up the railway line in open country, which was inconvenient, but at least no one had been hurt.

It was now late October, and everyone was too occupied with their own problems to get involved in Aggie's troublemaking, or to be concerned over the Italian families who'd been forcibly removed from Cliffehaven. Rita's dark hair and olive skin caused a lingering suspicion among some of the women that she was closer to the Minelli family than she let on, but with the constant raids and the need to increase their output, they were kept busy at the factory and they left Rita in peace. However, she had learned a sharp lesson in how quickly this could change, and she kept her thoughts and her personal business to herself as she went about her work.

It had been another long, fraught day and she was exhausted, but Rita's mind was working busily as she buried her chin in her coat collar and ran through the rain out of the factory gates. She'd come to the conclusion it was time to talk seriously to Louise about finding some kind of work, and she'd spent the day mulling over what she should say, and the best way to say it without upsetting her. Yet, as she hurried down Barrow Lane in the darkness, she knew that no matter how she dressed it up, Louise would not take kindly to her suggestions – or to Rita's latest news.

The night was black and wet, the wind tearing down the narrow streets and whistling round the corners and rooftops. Rita slipped into the alleyway between the houses and quietly let herself in through her own back door. She was glad to be out of the appalling weather, and needed a few moments to wash and change and catch her breath before she went next door. The day had been interrupted by numerous air raids and what felt like hours huddled in the shelter beneath the factories, and she wanted to sit quietly for a moment over a cup of tea and read her father's latest letter.

With the blackout curtains pulled and candles lit, she kicked off her boots, stripped and washed at the sink. Her last sixpence had been used in Louise's meter this morning, so she had to make do with candlelight and cold water.

The chill dowsing made her shiver, and she swiftly pulled on a thick sweater and slacks, knitted socks and sturdy shoes. Giving her wet hair a vigorous rub with a towel, she eyed the dust on the furniture, the hastily discarded clothes on the back of the couch, and wrinkled her nose at the pervasive smell of damp walls and musty rugs. The house was neglected and shabby, and she made a mental note to do something about it as soon as she could – but it wouldn't be tonight.

She poured the last of the tea from the flask she'd taken to work, but with only a dash of milk and no sugar, the weak concoction was barely drinkable. She curled up on the sagging couch, pulling the blanket round her to ward off the chill as the candles threw flickering shadows across the walls. Her only consolation was the thought that there probably wouldn't be any raids tonight if this weather carried on, and that, for once, she and Louise could get a good night's sleep.

She had revealed none of her struggles to her father, who had enough to worry about, and had kept her letters cheerful and hopeful, telling him only about her trip to the theatre to see Cissy in her show, her afternoon teas at Peggy's when time allowed, the matinees she'd gone to with May to watch the latest films, and how Louise had struck on the idea of trying to make pasta out of potato. The result was a disaster, but even Louise had seen the funny side of it and for the first time in months, Rita had seen her laugh.

Rita grinned at the memory as she opened the envelope. The postal service was erratic, and some of his letters took weeks to get to her. This one was almost a month old. Jack Smith wasn't a natural letter writer, and his offerings were usually short, but they were so heavily censored it was difficult to make much sense of them.

He was kept very busy, with only a few hours off a week to go to the nearest town, where there seemed to be a pub on every corner. He was enjoying the camaraderie of the other men, and Rita suspected he was finding this sudden independence rather liberating after having had the responsibility of raising her on his own for so many years. The army was a man's world, and her father was clearly revelling in it.

Rita had had to tell him about Tino and Roberto's arrest, and he was so concerned that he'd also written to Peggy to ask her to keep an eye out for them – which of course she had done. He suggested that it might be better if they moved away from the coast and the constant threat of attack or invasion, but Rita doubted she could persuade Louise to do so until they'd had word from Tino.

His letter wasn't long and he finished with the

usual warnings to stay safe and leave the motorbike at home. His scrawled *'Love, Dad'* was followed by a row of kisses.

Rita carefully folded it back into the envelope and tucked it away with the others in the shoebox she kept on the mantelpiece. She touched his photograph and blinked back the ready tears that always came after reading his letters. He'd only been gone a matter of months, but to Rita it felt like a lifetime and she longed to see him again – longed to hear his voice, and to feel his steadying, reassuring presence in these troubling times. Losing Tino and Roberto so swiftly after his departure had given her the weighty responsibility of caring for Louise, and without her father's guidance, she often felt alone, vulnerable and far too young.

She sniffed back the tears and grabbed her coat and gas mask. There was no point in feeling sorry for herself; there were far more important things to deal with tonight than her childish needs. Running down the stairs, she locked the back door and gate and hurried along the twitten that ran between the terraces to Louise's backyard.

'Where have you been?' Louise was at the stove, stirring something in the big pot she'd once used to cook pasta. 'You were due back half an hour ago.'

'I went home to wash and change.' Rita kissed Louise's cheek and slipped off her coat. 'There was a letter from Dad, and I lost track of time while I read it.'

Louise sighed as she continued to move the wooden spoon through what looked like a very thin vegetable stew. 'He is well?'

Rita held her hands out to the warmth of the fire in the range. 'He's the same as always, and being kept very busy. He sends his regards, by the way.'

'There was no letter from Tino or Roberto,' Louise murmured in Italian. 'You're lucky.'

'I know,' Rita said softly. 'But they'll write once they're given permission, and I'm sure it won't be too long to wait now.'

The spoon stirred a little more raggedly. 'It's been four months, Rita. How do I know if they are even still alive?'

Rita stilled Louise's hand, took away the spoon and pulled the pot from the heat. 'Of course they are,' she said firmly. 'They'll have been sent somewhere far from harm, and I'm sure we'll hear from them any day now.'

'You've been saying that since June,' Louise replied, her voice breaking. 'But we've heard nothing, nothing.'

Realising Louise was on the brink of another storm of tears, Rita took her hands. Noting how cold they were, she gave them a rub. 'Mamma, we have to have a serious talk about what we're going to do until they come home. We can't go on like this.'

Louise snatched her hands away. 'We're fine,' she said stubbornly. 'I have made a start on the allotment again, and as you see, there are plenty of vegetables to eat. And Peggy brought over some tomato chutney and sugar this morning.'

'We mustn't rely on Auntie Peggy too much. She has a house full of people to feed, and the rationing is as tough for her as it is for us. We have to fend for ourselves, Mamma, and my wages just won't stretch that far.'

'I'm sorry, *cara*.' Louise's shoulders sagged as she dipped her chin. 'I've let you down, haven't I?'

'Not at all,' she said hastily, 'but there's plenty of work, well-paid work, and it would do you good to have something else to think about.'

'But what can I do?' Louise twisted her apron in nervous fingers. 'I'm not clever like you, *cara mia*. I can't read and write very well and I've only ever helped Tino in the café and raised my *bambini*. I wouldn't know where to start.'

'But you must have had a job before you married Tino?'

Louise shook her head. 'I did a bit of cleaning and mending at one of those posh hotels down on the seafront until Tino and me got married on my sixteenth birthday. I've never had a proper sort of job really.'

As Rita's gaze fell on Louise's Singer sewing machine, she was struck with a bright idea. 'There's a uniform factory in Camden Road, and they're recruiting machinists. You know how to use a sewing machine, and they're offering really good pay, especially for the night shifts.'

Louise's blue eyes widened in horror. 'I couldn't leave you on your own all night, Rita. It wouldn't be safe.'

Rita couldn't quite meet her gaze. 'That was the other thing I wanted to tell you, Mamma . . .'

'What is it?' The blue eyes widened further with alarm.

'May and I have signed up to do fire-watch. I'll be sitting on some roof somewhere three nights a week with at least two others and a radio, so you won't have to worry about me being on my own.'

'But that's a man's job, and you're only a little girl. I forbid it.'

'I'll be eighteen soon,' Rita reminded her gently. 'And lots of other girls my age are signing up to do the jobs men used to do. We have to keep the country running while they're away fighting, Mamma. And I want to do my bit.'

'You already work in that factory,' she retorted. 'It's enough.'

'No, Mamma, it isn't.' Rita relented at the sight of Louise's unshed tears, and reached for her hands across the table. 'We must both learn to adapt to what's happening, Mamma. It won't be easy, but think how proud you'll be when Tino and Roberto come home to find we haven't given in to the bombings and the rationing. This is our chance to make a difference – however tiny it might be – and I know you'll find the courage to face your fears, roll up your sleeves and get on with it.'

Louise's smile was uncertain. 'You seem to think I'm far stronger and braver than I really am,' she said, her voice catching. 'But I will do my best not to let you down.'

Rita rounded the table and gave her a hug. 'You've never let me down, Mamma,' she murmured, 'and I love you very much.'

'This factory. Camden Road, you say?' At Rita's nod, she stood and returned to stirring the stew. 'I will go there tomorrow morning,' she said.

Rita chewed her bottom lip, hesitant to say what she needed to now. 'Can I offer just one piece of advice, Mamma?'

Louise stiffened. 'What advice is that, *cara mia*?'

'Mamma, you will have to speak English all the time from now on. Even when we're alone.'

Louise turned from the stove, the ready tears rolling down her lined cheeks. 'It is all I have of Tino,' she murmured. 'How can I not speak Italian – especially if it is only us to hear it?'

'Because it wouldn't be wise,' Rita replied gently. 'There are still people who enjoy nothing better than to stir up trouble, and now Italy has invaded Greece they need little excuse. You'll find it much easier to get on with things if you speak English all the time.'

Louise thought about this and finally nodded. 'Peggy has said the same thing,' she replied softly in Italian. 'I will do my best, but you must be patient with me, *cara*.'

'Then let's start tonight,' Rita cajoled. 'The sooner you get used to it, the easier it will get.'

Louise gave a deep sigh, and Rita was about to offer to go with her to the factory in the morning when the wailing siren heralded yet another air raid. She reached for their gas mask boxes, handbags and overcoats as Louise took the stew off the heat, damped down the fire in the range and stuffed the Madonna and Child into her shopping bag alongside the family photos she always kept in there now.

They hurried down the stairs, locked the back door and gate and raced down the alleyway to join the tide of running people who were all heading away from the station towards the nearest public shelter, which was four streets away.

It was pitch-black outside and still raining, the searchlights cleaving the sky as the Spitfires raced to intercept the enemy before they reached the English coast. The noise was deafening, the wailing siren sending chills up their spines as the roar of the numerous fighter planes made the very air tremble.

Louise stumbled on the cobbles outside the burnt-out shell of Gino's ice-cream parlour and Rita grabbed her arm before she fell. They were jostled on all sides as the crowd began to funnel towards the steep steps and narrow entrance of the vast shelter that had been made in the cellars of a block of tenements.

It was a gloomy, claustrophobic place deep below

ground and sparingly lit. Rita and Louise had always tried to avoid it in the past, for the shelter on the other side of the railway lines was much more pleasant, built as it was beneath the playing fields, and with proper ventilation. But beggars couldn't be choosers, and they didn't have time to get there tonight.

The warden shouted for them to hurry up as they negotiated the steps and tried to find somewhere to sit. Wooden benches lined the dank walls of crumbling mortar and worn bricks, and a few more were set out in the middle of the vast space. The floor was unevenly laid with concrete that had been painted dark green, but the paint was already blistering from the damp and the tramp of many feet.

Rita found them a place on one of the side benches and took Louise's hand. She wasn't afraid of the dark, had never really suffered from being enclosed, but she knew Louise was terrified, and some of that fear was transmitted to her as the warden slammed the door shut and they were plunged into further gloom.

The three ceiling lights flickered and buzzed inside their metal cages, and then mercifully settled, but Rita was suddenly all too aware of how deep beneath the building they were, and of how ramshackle that old tenement was. One blast from a nearby bomb could bring it down, and they would be buried alive.

Determined to keep these thoughts at bay, she

rummaged in her coat pocket, found the bag of broken biscuits she'd put in there this morning and offered it to Louise, who shook her head and pressed it back into Rita's lap.

The siren no longer wailed, but the sound of many aircraft rumbled through the walls and made the earth vibrate beneath their feet. The lights flickered again as the deeper, heavy-bellied drone of the enemy bombers approached. Their fearful power filled the gloomy basement, making the earth tremor and the walls shudder. The answering rat-a-tat-tat of the anti-aircraft guns on the surrounding hills was joined by the heavy boom of the Bofors guns on the seafront and the sharp machine-gun fire of the duelling fighter planes. There was the heavy crump of a distant explosion, swiftly followed by another – and then another.

Rita put her arm round a trembling Louise, finding comfort in their closeness, even though she too was terrified that the enemy bombs seemed to be getting nearer by the minute. Dust and debris rained down on them as the tenement miraculously withstood the blasts, and they both flinched as yet another explosion threatened to rock it from its foundations.

Whimpers of fear and muttered prayers mixed with the sound of crying babies, further explosions and the roar of enemy bombers. It was clear to everyone that the nearby railway station was the enemy's target.

The deadly whine of a stricken plane screamed overhead, followed by an earthshattering explosion that made them all gasp. No one said anything, but everyone was wondering whether it was an enemy plane, or one of their own.

Rita thought of Martin Black, whom she'd met once at Peggy's, and understood how deeply Anne and Peggy must worry about his safety up there in his Spitfire night after night. Their fear must be even greater now Anne was expecting their first baby, and she gave thanks that her father was safe in the Midlands. She refused to admit that nowhere was really safe any more, for Liverpool and Manchester had been hit by massive raids, and the whole country was in the midst of an enemy blitz.

The barrage ceased as swiftly as it had begun, and all eyes turned towards the warden, waiting for the all-clear so they could escape this awful place. But he resolutely ignored them as he sat firmly by the door, and they had to accept that the enemy would come back as they always did after they'd finished their attack on poor old London, which was suffering more than anyone.

The enemy bombers returned half an hour later, harried by the Spitfires and Hurricanes, and defended by their own fighter planes. To gain speed and height, several bombs were dropped before they escaped across the Channel – this was known as 'tip and run' – and everyone flinched as two explosions once again rocked the very foundations of the old building.

It was another twenty minutes before the all-clear sounded, and as the warden opened the door they shuffled impatiently towards it, hungry for fresh air and open space despite the fear of what they might find.

Rita and Louise were cold and stiff after their long incarceration. They emerged to the urgent clamour of fire-engine and ambulance bells, and the stench of acrid smoke which stung their eyes and hit the back of their throats. It was still dark, but there was a fiery orange glow above the High Street which illuminated the changed landscape of those once familiar streets.

A vast crater was all that was left of the little church where Rita and the Minellis had gone to mass every Sunday morning. The nearby houses had been blasted into scattered remains of bricks and tiles and slabs of concrete, leaving the rest of the terrace adrift. Telegraph poles and street lights were bent and buckled, electricity cables writhed across the uprooted cobbles, hissing like giant snakes amongst the debris of glass shards and the remnants of people's lives, and a huge fountain of water shot skyward from a broken main. Two houses on the edge of the blast had been opened as neatly as a can of sardines, their pathetic interiors exposed as fire hungrily devoured what was left of the furniture and the precious last pieces of family treasures.

A woman screamed and tried to scramble over the debris to get to her ruined home but was forcibly held back by the men who were trying to put the fire out, mend the water main and repair the electricity cables. Other women began to move as though in a trance towards what remained of their own homes, faces set, the fear and anguish clear in their eyes.

Rita and Louise glanced at one another and moved as one, running as fast as they could towards Barrow Lane. The damage was everywhere, and the stench of smoke, the hiss and spit of electricity cables and the shouts of the rescue workers followed them. They stumbled and tripped, helping each other over the piles of rubble, dodging the twisting cables, wary of the glass and the thick wire that stuck out of the shattered concrete and threatened to rip their legs.

They slowed as they reached the end of Barrow Lane and just stood there, arm in arm, staring in disbelief at the damage.

The wall that had once run along the far end was all but gone. The coils of barbed wire that had topped it now swung malevolently back and forth in the cold wind, making a grinding, scratching noise that set their teeth on edge. Bricks and mortar were strewn across the narrow street, or piled in a great mound on the piece of waste ground that had once been her father's service area. There was no sign of the petrol pump, and the chimney was leaning precariously, ready to collapse at any minute. Almost every window in the street had been blown out, doors hung on buckled hinges, chimneys had toppled and slates had been shattered.

'At least the houses are still standing,' murmured Louise.

'I suspect the wall took the brunt of the explosion and absorbed the blast enough to protect them,' Rita replied, her gaze trawling the narrow lane before searching for the gasometer. It still stood a street away, ugly as always, and seemingly untouched. 'It's a miracle that didn't get hit,' she said, 'otherwise there'd be nothing left of these streets.'

Louise nodded, gripped her handbag and gas mask box and began to pick her way through the rubble to the yawning hole in the wall. As Rita joined her, they both stared down the exposed siding to the buckled rails, the mangled goods train and the shattered platforms and sheds. It would take a long time to get the trains moving again, and they were a lifeline for Cliffehaven, for they brought in precious supplies.

'Come, Mamma,' Rita murmured. 'Let's go and inspect the damage, even though there's nothing much we can do in the dark. At least we still have beds to sleep in – not like some.'

Chapter Five

Following the close shave they'd had in Barrow
Lane, Rita and Louise now kept their most precious
things with them every time they left the house.
Rita's treasures were kept in a holdall in the motorbike pannier.

Over the next three weeks there were other raids
but Barrow Lane was spared further damage, for
most of the bombs had fallen harmlessly into the
sea. The Americans, although still neutral, came in
their trucks and diggers and helped to clear the
rubble, board doors and windows, and secure Rita's
chimney before it went through the roof.

Their arrival caused a stir among the women, who
suddenly found an inordinate amount of time to
stand on their doorsteps handing out tea in exchange
for packs of Lucky Strikes and some earnest flirt-
ation. It was noted that some of the younger women
had started wearing make-up again and having their
hair set – and this was fuel for gossip, stoked by
the fact that these young women seemed to go out
at night much more than they had when their
husbands and children were at home.

The tittle-tattle went back and forth as meaty arms

were crossed beneath self-righteous bosoms, chins quivered in delicious disgust and gimlet eyes peered through twitching net curtains at every footstep and door slam. It was common knowledge that Vi Charlton at number four was entertaining a Yank most nights, and could be seen brazenly stepping out with him, nose in the air, silk stockings flashing as they headed for a night in the town. The general consensus amongst those who felt it was their duty to keep an eye on such things was that she was no better than she was meant to be – and that when Cyril Charlton came home on leave, it would serve her right if he blacked her eye.

Rita had always liked Vi. She was young and pretty and one of only a handful of neighbours who'd actually offered help and understanding over the past months. Of course the sour old biddies just loved it when she proved them right about her being flighty. But Rita could understand how tempting it must have been for Vi to make the most of her brutal husband's absence now her three children had been evacuated to Wales, and rather admired the way she ignored the gossips and carried on regardless.

The nightly news at nine o'clock did little to lift the gloom of rationing and air raids. The Axis pact which had been signed by Germany and Italy now included Japan, Hungary and Romania. The city of Coventry had been almost annihilated and the RAF had bombed Berlin and Turin. Enemy planes once again ravaged London and the days and nights were shattered by wave upon wave of Messerchmidts, Dorniers and Fokkers heading for the Midlands.

There had still been no news of Papa and Roberto, and Louise despaired of ever discovering what had happened to them. There had been rumours of a huge internee camp being set up on the Isle of Man, but no one seemed to really know what was going on, and the authorities weren't telling.

Rita was as anxious as Louise for news, but she also fretted over her father's safety. The hardest part was the not knowing, for his letters couldn't even tell her where exactly he was based. One thing was clear from the news broadcasts: the Midlands were suffering as much as they were down here in the south.

It was only two weeks to Christmas, and Rita had a rare day off which she was determined to enjoy. Her eighteenth birthday was only two days away, and although it wouldn't be the same without her dad and the others at home, she was looking forward to at last being considered old enough to join one of the services and really get stuck in. She still hankered after the WAAFs, but if that meant being confined to a stuffy office all day, then she'd see what the others could offer.

Louise had settled down to work at Goldman's after a shaky start and seemed much more cheerful now she had other things to think about and new friends to talk to. She still spoke Italian occasionally, but only when they were alone, and now there was a bit more money coming in things were getting easier. Their evenings were less solemn and there had been fewer tears of late, and Rita at last felt more confident about leaving her to pursue her own adventure.

Rita was enjoying her job at the aircraft factory now the sniping had ended, and felt she was really doing some good on her night shifts of fire watching, but she wanted more – an indefinable more that she hoped would soon offer itself.

She ran down the stairs to the garage and wrestled to open the doors, forgetting that one of the Yanks had kindly greased the runners. They shot apart with a clatter and she giggled as at least three sets of curtains twitched opposite. It seemed her neighbours had little better to do than spy on everyone.

Giving them a cheeky wave, she dragged the tarpaulin off the motorbike, carefully filled the tank with the last of the petrol she'd stored and wheeled it outside. With the doors closed and padlocked again she adjusted the goggles and old flying helmet, zipped up the moth-eaten jacket and swung her leg over the broad leather saddle.

The engine roared into life and she tweaked the accelerator, filling the narrow lane with its deep rumble so the nosy neighbours could fully appreciate its power before she drove it over the cobbles and round the corner.

Vi Charlton was waiting to cross the road and Rita returned her wave as she roared past, noting the new winter coat and smart hat that had replaced the worn, sagging cardigans and headscarf of last winter – more fuel for gossip, no doubt, but at least Vi was keeping warm.

The railway tracks had been swiftly repaired but the humpbacked bridge was still missing, so it was a circuitous route into town, but that didn't matter a jot. Rita could have happily ridden the bike all day if only she'd had enough petrol.

The backstreet terraces were soon behind her as she headed west and then south, down to the bottom of the High Street. The Woolworth's building, the bank and Plummers, the large department store, had taken a direct hit some weeks before, and the debris had been shifted from the road and the pavement into a vast heap that filled the crater. The trolleybus was in service again after the rails and electricity cables had been repaired, and there were the usual long queues outside the bakery, grocery and butcher's.

Rita headed down to the seafront and let the engine idle as she took off the goggles and helmet and let the crisp salty wind ruffle her hair and sting her face. The gulls were wheeling and calling as they rode the wind, the sea crashed against the shingle beyond the coils of barbed wire, splashed against the great concrete blocks that had been set across the bay, and swirled round the iron pillars of the abandoned pier which had been cut adrift from the promenade to discourage enemy landings. A closer look revealed viscous clumps of tar and oil which swept in with every wave and clung to the wire, the pier and the pebbles. This offering from the sea was the horrifying reminder that too many ships had been sunk in the Channel.

Rita breathed in the tang of salt and tar, glad to be out of the factory and away from Barrow Lane. It was a beautiful cold, bright day, the white cliffs at the far end of the bay gleaming in the sun, the dark sails of the fishing fleet flapping in the brisk wind as they negotiated their way through the barricade and onto the steeply shelving shingle which had been fenced off from the rest of the heavily mined beach.

There were gun emplacements all along what was left of the promenade, and she could see more up on the cliffs where she and May had often been posted to watch for fires. The big hotels along the front were still acting as billets for allied servicemen, but the smaller guest houses had closed for the duration and were looking a little shabby now.

This had been her childhood playground, and the sight of it invoked memories of how she and May and Roberto used to sneak off to play in the sand at low tide – memories of how they'd hunted for crabs in the rock pools and used special nets to scoop shrimps from the sandy shallows. There had always been music coming from the pier, which had been wreathed in pretty lights, and lines of deckchairs along the prom, stalls selling ice cream and fizzy pop, and Louise's jam sandwiches which always became gritty from the sand on their fingers, but tasted delicious anyway. She felt a twist of longing for those precious days and gave a deep, regretful sigh. It felt like a lifetime ago.

Closing her eyes, she clung to those memories, praying that Papa and Roberto were safe, and that they would know in their hearts that they hadn't been forgotten.

On opening her eyes again, she blinked back the ready tears, looked at her watch and quickly donned her helmet and goggles. Peggy and Cissy would be waiting, and she was in danger of being late.

She set off down the seafront, towards the fishing fleet which was now anchored beneath the white cliffs, and then turned left and headed up the hill towards the terrace of Victorian houses three streets up on the far eastern side of Cliffehaven. There was another vast crater where there had once been a row of houses and she negotiated carefully around it before turning into Beach View Terrace.

As she drew up outside the Beach View Boarding House, the front door opened and Peggy came down the steps, covering her ears until Rita had turned off the engine. 'I could hear you coming half a mile away,' she said, and gave her a warm smile. 'My goodness, your face is cold,' she added as she kissed her cheek. 'Come into the warm. I've got the kettle on.'

Rita clambered off the bike, propped it on its stand

and ran up the short flight of stone steps, past the shattered lamps that once stood at the bottom, to the elegant, but slightly damaged portico. The front door had been replaced, she noted, and the lovely coloured glass panes on either side had gone, their place now covered in ugly hardboard. She stepped into the square hall and breathed in the familiar scents of furniture polish and good cooking.

'Cissy has only just got in,' Peggy said on her way to the kitchen. 'She's having a bath, and you know Cissy, she could be ages yet.'

'That's all right,' Rita replied cheerfully as she dumped the gas mask box on a nearby chair. 'I've got all day.'

'You might need it,' said Peggy with a wry smile. 'I've never known anyone sit in three inches of bath water for so long.'

Rita grinned, took off her helmet and goggles and shook out her hair. It was lovely and warm as usual in Peggy's homely kitchen. She did envy Cissy the luxury of a proper bath where hot water gushed at the turn of a tap. It was like a military manoeuvre to bath in the tin tub at home.

'Hello, dear,' said Mrs Finch, who was sitting by the range with a bag of knitting on her lap. She peered over her half-moon glasses. 'That is Rita, isn't it? My goodness, you look like a boy in that get-up. I don't know what things are coming to, I really don't.'

Rita could barely remember what her own

grandmother looked like, for she lived in Ireland, and had only visited once – but Mrs Finch was the epitome of everything Rita regarded as important in a granny, and she loved her to bits. She kissed the peachy cheek that smelled of lavender. 'It's lovely and warm and practical,' she said loudly. 'It gets cold on the bike.'

Mrs Finch gave her a wry look. 'I have no doubt of it,' she muttered, 'but it's not very feminine, is it?' She plucked at her knitting with a frown. 'It's all very different to my day,' she rambled as if to herself. 'Young women dash about, paint their legs with cold tea and do the butter-jig and googy-woogy with gay abandon, and seem to forget they're supposed to be ladies. I don't know what my dear husband would have made of it all, I really don't.'

Rita caught Peggy's eye and they shared an affectionate smile. Mrs Finch was always muttering to herself, but they wouldn't have it any other way.

'Sit down, and thaw out, dear,' said Peggy, bringing the teapot to the table. She settled comfortably on a nearby chair, poured the tea and passed round the cups. 'It's a bit weak, I'm afraid. These leaves have been used at least three times.' She lit a cigarette. 'There are rumours that we'll get extra rations of tea and sugar for Christmas, but I doubt it.'

Rita sipped the hot tea gratefully and began to warm up enough to strip off the old flying jacket and hang it on the back of her chair. 'The papers also say we won't get any more bananas – though I can't remember the last time I saw one.'

Peggy grimaced. 'Neither can I,' she agreed, 'but I suppose the supply ships have to have room for more important things than bananas – though I have the feeling that a bit of fruit would buck people up no end.' She puffed on her cigarette. 'How's Louise getting on at Goldman's?'

'She's doing very well, and she's started to make friends with some of the other women.' Rita smiled with warm affection. 'She's much happier now she has other things to keep her occupied, and often comes home with a funny story to tell. It's lovely to see her smile again.'

'I'm glad,' murmured Peggy as she watched Mrs Finch make a complete hash of her knitting. 'Would you like me to sort that out for you, dear?' she bellowed.

'There's no need to shout. I'm not deaf.' Mrs Finch sniffed. 'You know very well I dislike beer, so I can't quite see the point of asking me if I'd like one.' She gave up on the knitting with a cluck of frustration. 'Can you make sense of this, Peggy? I seem to have lost my way.'

Peggy began to unpick several rows so she could get to the problem. 'This is supposed to be a matinee jacket for Anne's baby,' she said quietly to Rita. 'Though if it ever gets finished it'll be a miracle.'

'How's Anne doing? It can't be easy for her with Martin flying so many missions now.'

'She's doing very well, considering. They've bought that sweet little cottage in Wick Cross, which is too close to the airfield for my liking, but at least she gets to see Martin a bit more often. But I do worry about her when he's away, and I've made her promise she'll come back home for her last few weeks.' She gave a sigh. 'I know she has a telephone, the RAF insisted upon that, but the thought of her being alone and in labour doesn't bear thinking about.'

'I'm sure Anne's sensible enough not to take any risks,' murmured Rita. She studied Peggy and saw the weariness in her. 'But what about you, Auntie Peg? How are you holding up now the boys have been evacuated?'

Peggy rested the knitting in her lap and gave a beaming smile. 'I've arranged to go and visit Bob and Charlie in Somerset,' she said, 'and I can hardly wait. Jim managed to get me a travel warrant, and I leave tomorrow. I'll be gone for three weeks, which is why it was so important you came today. I couldn't leave without making sure you and Louise were all right.'

'That's wonderful news,' Rita breathed. 'They'll be so happy to see you.'

Peggy's expression was soft with love. 'Yes, I know they're not babies any more, Bob's almost thirteen, but I couldn't bear to think of them being so far away over Christmas, and Jim's been very understanding. It's just a shame he can't come with me, but there's his job at the cinema, and his Home Guard duties.' She looked at Rita and smiled. 'I just hope I don't come home to chaos. You know what men are like when left to their own devices.'

They shared a knowing grin. 'I'm sure he and Ron will manage just fine, and of course you've got Cissy and the other girls to keep an eye on things.'

Peggy picked up the knitting again, the smile still playing on her lips. 'Cissy has some news of her own, which I won't spoil by telling you. But my two evacuees have left for pastures new, and the three nurses are either at the hospital or out on the tiles dancing the night away. I doubt they'll be of much use to anybody.'

Rita was intrigued as to what Cissy had been up to, but no doubt she would soon hear all about it. Cissy was not one to keep a secret for long. 'I'm sure your sister would be only too pleased to lend a hand,' she teased, knowing full well that Peggy and the extremely snooty Doris could barely be in the same room together for more than five minutes without falling out.

Peggy grunted. 'Doris would be about as useful as a chocolate teapot,' she said, 'and she's the last person either Ron or Jim would want in the house.' She looked up, caught the glint in Rita's eye and laughed. 'You are naughty,' she scolded softly. 'Poor Doris, she's far too grand to roll up her sleeves and get stuck in here – and I doubt it would even cross her mind to do so. I just hope she never gets bombed out, because the thought of her moving in with us makes me shudder.'

They were both startled by the loud snore coming from the fireside chair. Mrs Finch had gone to sleep.

Peggy giggled and shook her head. 'Poor old duck. She can go to sleep at the drop of a hat these days. But at least it means she sleeps through all the air raids. We've had to rig up her deckchair in the Anderson shelter with pillows so she doesn't fall out of it.'

'Will Jim and Ron be able to cope with her while you're away?'

'They adore her as much as she does them, and will look after her like cut crystal.' Peggy grinned. 'Actually, Mrs Finch has been helping with the cooking lately, and she's doing a sterling job. I suspect the men will mostly leave her to her own devices as long as their stomachs are attended to.'

'Hello, Rita.' Cissy breezed into the kitchen looking refreshed and lovely, her blonde hair swept back from her perfectly made-up face in an elegant chignon, the fetching little cap placed just so over one finely plucked eyebrow. 'What do you think?' She gave a twirl to show off the neat WAAF's uniform which enhanced her narrow waist and hips.

Rita gasped in admiration. 'Since when . . .?'

Cissy giggled and gave her a swift hug. 'I'm glad you're suitably impressed.' She carefully settled her pert bottom on the edge of a kitchen chair and crossed her long, shapely legs. 'After the dancing troupe folded, Amy and I decided it was time we did something sensible for a change, so we enlisted a few weeks ago.' She gave a delighted grin. 'It's ever so exciting, Rita. You should give it a go.'

Rita was infused with the other girl's excitement. 'What sort of work are you doing, Cissy?'

She shrugged and stirred her tea vigorously. 'It's only shorthand and typing, but there's lots of other girls to chat to and have a giggle with, and of course we're surrounded by all those lovely, lovely pilots.' Her expression grew dreamy as she sipped her tea. 'There's the Poles and the Free French, the Canadians, the Aussies – and of course our own lovely boys. Amy and I are having the time of our lives.'

Rita regarded her friend with admiration. Cissy had always been a pretty girl, but now she was positively glowing. 'You certainly look well on it,' she murmured, feeling the teeniest bit jealous of the uniform. 'But I'd be hopeless in an office, and they've already turned me down as a mechanic.'

'But there's other things you could do,' said Cissy excitedly.

'I think Rita's got enough on her plate with the factory and fire-watching,' interrupted Peggy sharply.

Cissy frowned. 'But she's been wanting to join up ever since the war started.'

'Rita has other responsibilities,' said Peggy, giving Cissy a warning glare. 'Louise couldn't cope without her for a start.'

Now it was Rita's turn to frown, for she couldn't understand why Peggy was putting a dampener on her and Cissy's enthusiasm.

But Cissy was made of sterner stuff and obviously decided to ignore her mother's warning. She turned back to Rita with sparkling eyes. 'You won't have to be stuck in an office, Rita,' she began. 'There's a posting that would suit you down to the ground.'

'Cissy.' Peggy's voice was low and warning.

Cissy hesitated before ploughing on. 'I just thought Rita might be interested in becoming a motorbike dispatch rider,' she said defiantly.

Rita felt a thrill of hope. 'Really? They have them in the WAAFs? Do you think they'd take me on?'

Peggy butted in again. 'I don't know that your father would want you haring about on that bike – not up at the airfield. It all sounds very dangerous, if you ask me – and I doubt very much if they'd take on a slip of a girl like you.'

Rita's hopes plummeted.

'Actually, Mum,' said Cissy fearlessly, 'they are recruiting women of all ages. Rita would be perfect.'

Rita looked at Peggy, waiting for her approval – longing for her to give her blessing for this miraculous chance to do something extraordinary.

'It will probably mean having to leave Cliffehaven for several weeks to be trained,' Peggy said with rare asperity. 'Would Louise be able to cope without you?'

Rita tamped down on the sliver of doubt. 'She's

working now, and much happier. I'm sure I wouldn't be away for long – after all, I could handle a bike by the time I was ten, so I wouldn't need *that* much training.'

Peggy gave a deep sigh, her face still etched with worry. 'It's obvious you'll go ahead and apply no matter what I say,' she murmured. 'So I suppose I'll have to give this madness my blessing. But I don't like it, Rita – I really don't.'

'Then that's settled,' said Cissy. She clapped her hands in delight. 'What fun. You, me and Amy, all in the WAAFs. Who'd have believed it?'

'It strikes me that the RAF have enough problems without scatterbrained girls cluttering up the place,' muttered Peggy, her lips twitching with a reluctant smile.

Rita's eyes were shining and her cheeks were flushed with hope and excitement. She'd never even considered such a thing as becoming a motorbike dispatch rider – but now she could, she realised it was a job she was born to do. 'Do you think they'll let me take my own bike?'

'I expect so. You'll have to ask at the recruitment office.' Cissy glanced at the sleeping woman in the chair and stood, smoothing the neat blue serge over her slender hips. 'Come on, let's go upstairs and I'll tell you all about life in the WAAFs and the brilliant time you'll have. I'll even let you try on my spare uniform if you promise not to get it creased.'

'You've got a letter from Joe Buchanan,' said

Peggy, still out of sorts at having been defeated by her garrulous daughter. She retrieved it from amongst the litter of ration books and lists on the mantelpiece above the range and held it out.

Cissy studiously ignored her mother's disapproving expression as she took it. 'Thanks, Mum. I'll read it later.'

Rita followed her friend upstairs to the top floor and made herself comfortable against the pillows on one of the single beds as Cissy perched on the dressing stool. The room was decorated with dainty sprigged wallpaper, the pale pink bedspreads and quilts matching the heart of each little flower perfectly. The same material covered the padded stool and fell in pleats around the kidney-shaped dressing table, which was smothered in make-up, cheap jewellery and perfume bottles. It was an intensely feminine room and a world away from the rather austere, damp and untidy surroundings Rita slept in back at home.

Cissy noticed her surveying the room. 'It's heaven not having to share with Anne any more,' she said, carelessly dropping the letter in amongst the debris on her dressing table then turning her attention to her smudged, lipstick. 'I have plenty of room for all my things, and it doesn't matter if I come in late when I'm on leave, or keep the light on half the night while I catch up on my magazines.'

'You don't seem terribly keen on reading your

letter,' said Rita. 'I thought you and Joe Buchanan were sweethearts?'

'We are – or at least, I thought we might be.' Cissy opened the window, offered a cigarette to Rita, who refused it, and lit one for herself. 'You'll have to learn to smoke if you don't want to stick out like a sore thumb in the WAAFs,' she said, watching herself blow smoke in the mirror. 'Everyone smokes – it's quite the thing, you know.'

'I won't be able to smoke and ride a motorbike at the same time,' said Rita reasonably, 'so I'll pass on it for now.' She eyed Cissy, who was puffing smoke out of the window as if she was in a Hollywood film. Peggy had always banned smoking in the bedrooms, and for all Cissy's sophistication and devil-may-care attitude, she was still in awe of her mother's rules. 'You were telling me about Joe Buchanan,' she prompted.

'He's lovely and I adore him, I really do, but I wonder now if we weren't just caught up in the moment – he was leaving, you see, and we only had that last day together. But it's terribly difficult to keep up any romance with someone who isn't even in the same country, and there's an awful lot of distraction at the base. It's hard for a girl to make up her mind about what she wants.'

Rita had heard all about the quietly spoken, handsome Australian soldier who'd turned up at Peggy's with two of his mates, and a coat full of chickens. He'd sounded really nice. 'I can see it must be a bit of a dilemma,' she murmured, 'but if you're having doubts, you really should write and tell him.'

Cissy forgot she was supposed to be emulating Bette Davis and puffed furiously on the cigarette before grinding it out in a glass dish on her dressing table. 'I know. But he's right in the middle of things, and I don't have the heart to let him down.' Her smile was uncertain as she looked at Rita. 'Those "Dear John" letters are ghastly, Rita. I've seen what they can do to a chap.'

'Then I suggest you just keep the letters light and friendly and promise nothing,' said Rita, who knew nothing about romance other than what she'd read in books and magazines or been told by May, who was inclined to exaggerate. She fidgeted on the bed. 'Now, come on, Cissy. I want to hear all about the WAAFs, and I especially want to hear about these motorbike dispatch riders. What do they do exactly?'

'I don't know a lot about it, to be honest,' Cissy confessed. 'I see them rushing about, of course, but what they actually *do* is a mystery.' Her face brightened, 'But I can tell you all about the fun we have. Those fly boys are always up for a party, you know, and . . .'

As Cissy happily prattled away, Rita's thoughts drifted. Louise was settled at the factory and they only spent the occasional night together when they were not doing night shift or fire-watch. The recruitment office was in the High Street, so surely it wouldn't hurt to go and ask for a form? She could get one for May, as well, and they could have them filled in and returned before tomorrow.

She tuned back into Cissy, who was in full flow about the car one of the Poles had borrowed, so they could get into town for one of the many dances. 'Of course it was all highly irregular,' she said happily, 'and we all got a terrible ticking off. But that's half the fun, isn't it?'

Rita nodded, but she had no real idea, and would probably never have the chance to find out. Not many boys would be interested in a girl with dirty nails and smears of engine oil on her face. Roberto wouldn't have minded, of course, but then he was just like an older brother and didn't really count. 'Do you really think they'll take me on?' she persisted. 'I mean, they are recruiting girls – you're sure about that?'

Cissy's eyes widened. 'I said so, didn't I?' She gave a sigh of exasperation. 'Honestly, Rita. Don't you ever think about anything but machines?'

'Not often,' she admitted, and grinned. 'You said I could try on your spare uniform.' She waggled her hands. 'My nails are clean – I won't get muck on it. I promise.'

Cissy giggled and gave her a hug. 'You are a caution, Rita Smith, but it's lovely to be friends again – quite like old times.' She opened the wardrobe to reveal acres of dresses, skirts and suits. The floor of the cupboard was littered with shoes and handbags, and the shelf above the hanging rail was stuffed with hat boxes.

Rita stared at this bounty in amazement. Cissy could have opened a shop, and it made her own paltry collection of worn clothes fade into further insignificance. But then Cissy had always loved clothes – it was probably why she'd gone on the stage. Rita smiled fondly at her friend, glad that they were so different – glad that they'd found each other again, for life had become far too serious of late, and Cissy was injecting fun back into it.

Cissy finally found what she was looking for and held it out. She puckered her lips as she eyed Rita thoughtfully. 'It'll probably be far too long in the skirt, and the jacket will swamp you. I'd forgotten how tiny you are.'

'All the best things come in small packages,' Rita retorted as she pulled off her jumper and trousers and almost reverently stepped into the lovely blue serge skirt.

It swam at her waist and fell almost to her ankles, and she and Cissy burst out laughing. 'Here, put on the jacket and I'll hold it at the back so you can get a good idea of what you'll look like when you have your own.'

The sleeves covered her hands, sagged at the shoulders and poked at the front. Cissy did a great deal of judicious pulling and tugging and then they looked in the dressing-table mirror to see the effect.

Rita's eyes widened. 'Gosh,' she breathed. 'Don't I look different? All sort of grown-up and posh.' She shot Cissy a grin and put on her plummiest voice.

'A bit like you, Corporal Cecily Reilly – all glam-orous and *terribly, terribly* sophisticated.'

They burst into gales of laughter and it was a few minutes before order was restored and the uniform was put carefully back into the wardrobe.

'Come on, Rita. It's time to make you look gorgeous.' Cissy pushed her down on the dressing stool. 'You're far too serious about everything. You simply can't go about without make-up and a decent haircut. Sit still and I'll show you just how lovely you can look.'

'But I don't like wearing make-up,' Rita protested.

'All girls like make-up,' retorted Cissy as she flung a towel round Rita's shoulders and picked up her scissors.

'What are you doing?' Rita gasped.

'Taming this mop,' she replied, and without further ado, began to snip at Rita's curls.

Rita closed her eyes. With a mixture of dread and excited anticipation, she listened to the snip of the scissors and felt the scrape of the comb. 'Just don't cut it too short,' she pleaded, 'or I'll look like a half-witted pixie.'

'Keep your eyes closed while I do your make-up,' murmured Cissy as the scissors clattered onto the glass top of the dressing table.

Rita tried to relax and sit still as Cissy smoothed cream on her face, dusted it with powder, and began to brush something on her eyelids and lashes. She could smell Cissy's perfume and feel her warm breath on her face as she carefully applied lipstick and gave her hair a final tweak. It was an intimate moment, reminding her of their childhood when Cissy had insisted upon dressing her and May in frothy frocks and bejewelled tiaras so they could be princesses to Cissy's queen in her little plays.

'There,' sighed Cissy. 'You can look now.'

Rita opened her eyes and stared at her reflection. Her unruly curls had been tamed into a side parting, the thick sweep of hair carefully brushed back from her face to enhance the cheekbones she never knew she had. Her eyes looked enormous and very dark brown against the dusting of blue eyeshadow and black pencil, the lashes were long and curled with mascara, her lips a deep scarlet. 'I can't believe how different I look,' she breathed.

'But do you like it?' Cissy's face was anxious.

Rita nodded. 'I look just like the photograph of my mother,' she murmured. 'I never realised . . .'

Cissy seemed satisfied, and she whipped off the towel, shaking the hair out of the window. 'That's no bad thing,' she said. 'From what I can remember, your mother was a beauty.' She rummaged about in the mess on her dressing table, picked out powder, eyeshadow, rouge, eyebrow pencil and lipstick and pressed them into Rita's hand. 'Keep practising,' she said. 'You'll soon get the hang of it.'

'I can't take these,' Rita gasped. 'They're far too expensive.'

Cissy pressed her beautifully manicured hands

on Rita's shoulder. 'Of course you can,' she replied. 'Think of them as an early birthday and Christmas present.'

Rita slipped the gifts into her trouser pocket and had to blink back the tears as she gave her friend a hug. 'Thanks, Cissy. Thanks ever so.'

Cissy waved away her thanks and tried to look stern. 'Don't you dare cry, Rita Smith. You'll spoil the effect.'

Rita took another long look at her reflection and smiled ruefully. 'I'll spoil it the minute I put on my helmet and goggles.' She glanced at her watch and gasped. 'I'd better go if I'm to get to the recruitment office before lunch.'

Cissy laughed and gave her a hug. 'It's been so lovely, Rita, and I wish you the very best of luck with enlisting.' She too glanced at her watch. 'Goodness, I didn't realise how late it was. I'd better spend some time with Mum before I have to be back at base.' She blushed prettily. 'Someone's coming to give me a lift in a couple of hours, and I won't see Mum again until the New Year.'

Rita noted the blush. 'Think about what I said about Joe,' she said softly, 'and take care of yourself. I'll need a friendly face when I come to the airbase.'

'I'll make sure to look out for you – and don't worry, Rita. You'll sail through the interview and training. I just know you will.'

Rita followed her down the stairs and went into

the kitchen to fetch her coat and say goodbye to Peggy and Mrs Finch, who was still snoring fit to bust.

Peggy eyed the make-up and haircut. 'Well,' she said, 'I can see Cissy has been hard at work.'

'What do you think?'

Peggy smiled. 'You look just like your mother,' she said softly, 'and very lovely.' She picked up three neatly wrapped parcels from the kitchen table. 'This is for your birthday,' she said, handing one over, 'and these are for you and Louise on Christmas Day.'

'Aunt Peg,' Rita gasped. 'You shouldn't have – and I didn't bring anything . . .'

'It's what aunts are for,' said Peggy as she gave her a hug. 'Now, we won't disturb Mrs Finch, but you have a lovely Christmas and I'll see you when I get back.'

Waving goodbye to Cissy and Peggy on the doorstep, Rita placed the packages alongside the gas mask box in the motorcycle pannier before carefully donning helmet and goggles and buttoning the jacket. She kicked the Norton into life and roared down Camden Road. The warmth of Peggy's love and Cissy's friendship and kindness stayed with her all the way to the recruitment office in the High Street.

It was an austere-looking place, wedged between two shops and almost hidden by the vast wall of sandbags in front of it. The only clue to its purpose was a large poster in the window exhorting all and sundry to do their bit by joining up.

Rita's heart was pounding, the blood rushing in her ears as she took off the goggles and helmet, ran her fingers through her hair and pushed the door open.

The room was empty and stiflingly hot and smelly from the kerosene heater that stood in one corner. Rita could already feel the perspiration rolling down her back as she tried not to make too much noise with her heavy boots on the bare floor-boards.

'I hope you wiped those boots before you came in here.' A stern-faced woman suddenly appeared from the doorway behind the scarred desk. Middle-aged and sturdy, she was dressed in blue serge and sensible laced-up shoes.

Rita hadn't, but she wasn't about to admit it. She gripped the helmet and goggles more firmly. 'I've come to apply for the motorbike dispatch riders' unit in the WAAFs,' she said before her courage failed her.

The woman's grey eyes trawled over her leather trousers, elderly flying jacket and sturdy boots. 'You certainly look the part,' she said grudgingly. 'How old are you?'

'I shall be eighteen in two days' time.'

The woman puckered her lips thoughtfully, her gaze fixed on Rita's face as she settled ponderously behind the desk. 'Despite all the make-up, you don't look much older than fourteen or fifteen. Do you have proof?'

Rita felt a rising tide of panic. She couldn't fail now – not when she was so close to achieving her goal. 'Not with me,' she said. 'But if I could just have a couple of forms for me and my friend May, we'll fill them in and bring our birth certificates with us next time.'

The woman eyed her for another long, heart-stopping moment and then reached for something in her desk drawer. 'These forms are highly confidential and must not leave this office. You will fill the form in here, and then return with proof of your age within twenty-four hours or your application will be scrapped.' She pointed to the single metal chair in front of her desk. 'Sit,' she ordered.

Rita sat.

A pen was pushed towards her. 'I assume you can read and write?' At Rita's dumbfounded nod, the woman slid the application form across the desk. 'At least that's a start, I suppose,' she said on a sigh.

Rita's hand was shaking as she picked up the pen. The words blurred as she quickly read through the form. This was worse than sitting any exam, and her nerves were threatening to let her down. Taking a deep, steadying breath, she filled in her name, address, date of birth, father's name, mother's name and all her qualifications. She'd been an able student and had sailed through her School Certificate with ease.

They seemed to want to know a great many things, including her height and weight, and her reasons for applying – but she supposed that was necessary security. The WAAFs wouldn't want just anybody, and she could only hope and pray she was good enough for them.

She filled in every section and then signed the bottom of the last page with a flourish and pushed everything back across the desk. 'How long before I know whether they'll take me?' she asked.

'Once we have proof of your age the application takes only a matter of days.' The pale grey eyes raced over the paperwork, widened when they reached the long list of qualifications and examination passes and moved swiftly on to the end. 'Thank you, Miss Smith. That all seems in order.'

Rita realised she was being dismissed, but she still had questions to ask. 'How long is the training?'

'About three weeks.'

'And will I have to leave Cliffehaven to do this training – and if so, where will I be sent?'

The grey eyes narrowed. 'You certainly will, but that is classified information.'

Rita was about to ask something else when the woman stood and made it clear the interview was at an end. 'Goodbye, Miss Smith. This office will be open tomorrow morning at ten. I look forward to seeing you then.'

Rita nodded, glanced up at the enormous clock on the wall, and backed away from the desk. Once outside, she rammed on her helmet and goggles, fired up the Norton and within minutes was racing for home. Her birth certificate was in a tin box under her father's bed. There was still plenty of time to get back to the office before it closed this afternoon – and then she would go and see May and tell her all about it.

May lived in a narrow backstreet of terraced houses some distance from Rita. It was even more down-trodden than Barrow Lane, and May lived with her mother on the ground floor of a house which was shared with another family. The outside lav was also used by the two houses next door, and water had to be collected from a communal tap further down the street. The only good to come out of the heavy bombing was the disappearance of the rat popula-tion, which had fled after the first raid for easier pickings amongst the debris.

Rita could see May sitting on her front step, the BSA parked at the kerb as she sipped from a mug of tea. There was a smear of grease on her cheek and her hands were filthy, the oily rag poking from the pocket of her dungarees.

Rita steered the Norton along the rough cobbles and drew to a halt in front of the BSA. 'Hello,' she said once the engine had died. 'Doing repairs?'

May grinned and stood to greet her. 'Just been oiling and adjusting. Nothing too serious.' She lifted the mug of tea. 'Fancy a cuppa?'

Rita took off her helmet and goggles. 'I certainly could,' she said.

May's blue eyes regarded her suspiciously. 'You're looking very pleased with yourself,' she said. 'And what's with all that make-up? You got a bloke on the go?'

'Don't be daft,' said Rita. 'I've got something far more exciting than that to tell you.'

May grinned. 'So have I, but let me make your tea first.'

Rita was intrigued as she followed her friend into the house, which was dark regardless of the time of day, and headed into the main room. It was shabby and cluttered with old newspapers and magazines and far too many cheap ornaments. Thankfully, there was no sign of May's mother, although the smell of her cheap perfume permeated the room.

Rita perched on the arm of a sagging chair as May poured the tea. 'I obviously have no idea what your news is – but it's clearly exciting, 'cos you're positively bursting with it. But I've found the perfect job for both of us, and if you're quick, you can get down there today and sign on.'

May frowned as she handed over the mug of very weak tea. 'You'd better start at the beginning, Rita, 'cos I've got no idea what you're on about.'

Rita quickly told May about her visit to the recruitment office. 'If you apply today, then we'll be able to join together,' she said breathlessly. 'Just think, May. It's the perfect job for both of us.'

'Um, yes . . .'

Now it was Rita's turn to frown. 'You don't sound very keen,' she murmured. 'I thought . . .'

'I'm sorry, Rita, I should have told you.' May leaned against the rickety kitchen table, gazing at the mug in her hands. 'But I didn't want to say anything until I knew for sure.'

Rita's own excitement ebbed. 'What is it, May? What have you done?'

May took a deep breath and finally looked Rita in the eye. Her face was alight with excitement, and her words tumbled over each other in her eagerness. 'I've been accepted into the Women's Air Transport Auxiliary. They're going to teach me to fly planes, Rita, and soon I'll be ferrying supplies and troops all over the country.'

Rita stared at her, stunned into silence.

May perched beside her and took her hand. 'I know I should have said something,' she murmured. 'But I didn't have the nerve to tell you until I was sure I'd be taken on.'

'But when did all this happen?'

'About a week ago,' May admitted. She squeezed Rita's hand as if to emphasise her regret for not sharing her secret. 'It's something I never thought I could ever do,' she said breathlessly. 'When I saw all them posh women enlist, I thought I wouldn't fit in, but it doesn't seem to matter where I come from, or how I speak – and the woman at the base was ever so nice and encouraging. She even took me out to have a look at the planes and to meet some of the other women pilots.'

'I never knew you wanted to fly planes,' said Rita, still struggling to absorb her friend's news – and the fact that she'd kept it to herself for a whole week.

May grinned. 'Neither did I until I saw that poster outside the Town Hall. Then I got to thinking, why not? Other women are doing it, and it has to be about the most exciting thing any girl could do, don't you think?'

Rita laughed. 'I think you're mad,' she replied, giving her a hug. 'But well done you. Who would have thought it? May Lynch flying planes.'

May's enthusiasm was brimming over. 'Why don't you apply as well? They're crying out for more crew and the pay is terrific. We'd be on the same wage as the RAF pilots, and that's not to be sniffed at.'

Rita chuckled. 'It's two feet on the ground for me, May, so I'll stick to motorbikes.'

May's little face became solemn. 'I'm sorry I didn't tell you, Rita, but I only got the confirmation this morning.'

'Don't be daft,' Rita replied. 'We'll probably see one another on the airfield – you in your plane and me on my bike. Cissy's joined the WAAFs with her friend Amy, so it'll be quite like old times.'

May giggled. 'I hope not,' she managed. 'Cissy was always trying to dress us up in frocks and tiaras, and plastering us in powder and rouge.' She eyed Rita's make-up. 'She's still at it I see,' she said dryly.

'I quite like it,' said Rita, not wanting to be disloyal to Cissy. 'But when I'll get the chance to wear it again, I don't know.' She eyed her friend with affection and sadness. This war was providing opportunities that none of them could have dreamed of, but those opportunities would change them, make them drift apart. 'When will you start your training?'

'In four days,' May replied softly.

'But that's so soon,' Rita gasped.

May took her hand. 'At least we can celebrate your birthday together and have a bit of fun before I leave.' Her expression was tearful. 'I'm sorry,' she said again, 'but there's nothing here for me – Mum couldn't care less, and if I'm to make anything of my life then I have to get out. This is my chance to really do something, Rita – to make a difference.'

'I know, but I'm going to miss you, May.'

'Me too, but we must promise to keep in touch, no matter where we're sent or what we do.'

Rita gave her friend a swift hug to reassure her, but the thought of another goodbye broke her heart. Plastering on a smile, she tried to dispel the gloom. 'Let's take the bikes out for a run and to hell with the petrol rationing.'

May grinned and reached for her jacket and helmet. 'Race you to the old water tower up in the hills. Last one there pays for tickets to the flicks tonight.'

They raced out of the room and onto the pavement. Within moments the two motorbikes roared down the street and headed for the hills, leaving the echoes of the powerful engines ringing in the silence.

Chapter Six

Peggy had finished packing the day before, but there was still plenty to do before she left. It had been lovely to have Cissy home for a few hours, but having kissed her goodbye and waved her off as the young pilot officer drove her away, she felt the full impact of what she was about to do.

With Mrs Finch busy at the sink peeling the potatoes Ron had dug from the garden, she determinedly ignored the cavalier way the old lady was wielding that paring knife, and checked on the provisions in her larder.

There were still Christmas puddings, made long before the war, and an absolute godsend now the rationing was so severe. There would be no cake this year, and certainly no mince pies, but Ron had a couple of pheasants hanging downstairs, and Mrs Finch had assured her she knew how to cook them. Vegetables would be no problem, Ron's garden was bountiful, and she knew for a fact there was enough whisky and rum to keep Jim and his father in a stupor for most of the Christmas holiday. But her larder was woefully understocked for this time of year, with only a few tins, half a bag of flour, and a few jars of preserves she'd made during the summer.

She closed the larder door and stood for a moment deep in thought. Was she doing the right thing? Could Jim and Ron really cope? Was she being selfish by leaving them for so long?'

'It's no good you standing there worrying,' said Mrs Finch. She wiped her hands on the wrap-round apron she'd borrowed from Peggy and which swamped her. 'You need to see your children, and I'm perfectly capable of keeping this house in order while you're away. So stop fretting.'

Peggy gave her a warm smile. 'I know you are,' she said, 'but it doesn't feel right, leaving you all . . .'

'Stuff and nonsense,' the old lady retorted, dropping the potatoes into the saucepan. 'You're a mother and it *is* Christmas.'

Peggy was about to reply when she heard two sets of footsteps crossing the hall.

The kitchen door creaked and a happy face peeked round it before it was flung open. 'Hello, Mum. We thought we'd surprise you.'

'Anne! Martin! Oh, my darlings, how wonderful.' Peggy flew across the room and gathered her eldest daughter into her arms as she grinned a tearful hello to Martin over her shoulder.

'Careful, Mum,' laughed Anne. 'You're squashing the heir to the family dynasty.'

Peggy stepped back and admired the enormous bulge between them. 'Goodness,' she laughed shakily, 'you have got big, haven't you? Are you sure it's not twins?'

Anne tossed back her lovely dark hair and giggled. 'It feels like it at times, but the doctor says there's only one in there.'

She grabbed their hands. 'Come in, both of you, and sit down. This is such a lovely, lovely surprise, I feel quite giddy.'

She slammed the kettle on the hob as Anne and Martin kissed Mrs Finch and shed their heavy coats. Martin was in his RAF uniform, and Anne was wearing something that resembled a smocked tent beneath a thick cardigan Peggy remembered knitting some time ago. How lovely it was to see them, and how radiant Anne was.

'You're both looking very well,' said Mrs Finch, twinkling up at Martin. 'I do so like to see a handsome man in uniform.'

Martin twirled his magnificent moustache like a pantomime villain and twinkled back. 'There's nothing like a pretty girl to cheer a chap up,' he said gallantly.

Mrs Finch collapsed into giggles and had to sit down.

Peggy made the tea and they settled by the fire to catch up on their news.

Half an hour later they were still talking and Mrs Finch had gone to sleep. 'I brought presents for the boys,' said Anne, her elegant hands folded on the top of her bump. 'I hope you've got room for them in your case.'

Peggy pointed to the bulging string bag sitting on the dresser. 'Their presents are all in there, and I'm sure I can find room for more.' She took the gifts and, with a bit of judicious prodding and poking, managed to get them in. 'By the way,' she said, returning to her seat at the kitchen table, 'have you given any thoughts to a name for this baby?'

Anne and Martin exchanged soft, loving smiles. 'We thought Peter James Ronan Black if it's a boy, and Rose Margaret if it's a girl.'

'Just like our sweet Princess Margaret Rose,' Peggy sighed. 'How lovely.'

'Actually, Mum, the Margaret bit is after you.'

She hugged her happiness. 'How darling of you, but only your Aunt Doris calls me Margaret, and she does that to wind me up.' She saw the startled concern in their expressions and hurried to reassure them. 'But Rose Margaret is a pretty name, so much nicer than plain old Peggy, and I'll be very proud to know my name will live on in my granddaughter.'

She eyed the pair of them, looking so content and happy. 'Have you told your parents yet, Martin?'

'I went to visit them a few weeks ago. Thought it better face to face, don't you know? They said all the right things, of course, but we've heard nothing from them since.'

Peggy thought grimly of Martin's snooty family, and the way they had virtually cut their son off once he'd married her Anne. Well, they would live to regret it, she was sure of that, and she could only wish she had the chance to give them a good piece of her mind about their disgraceful behaviour. It was all very well being rich and well connected, but without your children and grandchildren about you, what good was any of it?

'It's all right, Mrs Reilly,' said Martin. 'Really it is. Anne and I are perfectly happy, and we know we'll always have you – and that's far more than any of us could hope for.' His handsome face lit with a smile, making him seem so terribly young that it made Peggy's heart ache.

'Martin Black, you're a flirt,' she chided softly. 'But don't think you can get round me as easily as you do Mrs Finch.' She cocked her head and eyed him thoughtfully. 'I get the feeling you're after something, so you'd better get on and tell me what it is.'

'I knew it wouldn't take long for her to cotton on,' Anne said to Martin before turning back to Peggy. 'Mum, I hope you don't mind, but Martin and I have come to a decision.'

Peggy was immediately alarmed. 'What?'

Anne laughed. 'Don't panic, it's nothing too serious.' She licked her lips, her hands fidgeting with her voluminous dress. 'It's just that Martin is on duty all over Christmas, and with you away in Somerset, we thought it would be a good idea for me to move in here until you get back.'

'But, darling, that would be perfect.' Peggy took her hand and held it between her own. 'Are you sure, though? You know what your father and granddad are like – and of course there's Mrs Finch and the three nurses to think about as well – and you mustn't do too much, not in your condition.'

'I'm as fit as I ever was, and I don't intend to scrub floors or redecorate the dining room,' Anne said wryly. 'But it will be nice to have company, and a bit of cooking and cleaning will keep me out of mischief.'

'Oh, dear,' sighed Peggy, torn between wanting her home, and not wanting to thrust the responsibility of her household on her young shoulders. 'Are you really sure?'

Martin rested his hand on Peggy's shoulder, his gaze level. 'Mrs Reilly, you really must stop worrying about everyone and think about yourself for a change. Anne needs company over Christmas, and with the baby due in less than two months, it's the perfect solution. I would be so much happier knowing she was here, safe with her family and close to doctors and the hospital.'

Peggy caved in willingly. 'I'll push the two beds together in the spare room, and hunt out some fresh sheets.'

'I won't be staying tonight, Mrs Reilly,' he replied sadly. 'I have to be back on base before midnight.'

'Oh.' She gazed at him, noting for the first time how weary he looked and how deeply etched the lines on his face had become. 'Will you be able to visit Anne at all?'

'When I can,' he assured her. He took Anne's

hands and kissed the knuckles as he gazed adoringly into her eyes. 'It's hard for both of us, but this war has to be won. Anne understands that and has been an absolute brick, and as long as I know she's with her family I can get on with my job in an easier frame of mind.'

'Bless you,' murmured Peggy, once again close to tears.

Peggy hadn't expected to be able to sleep, what with all the excitement of having Anne home again, the worry over leaving the family to fend for themselves, fear for the long, possibly dangerous journey ahead of her, and the excited anticipation of seeing her sons again. But when she opened her eyes and looked at the bedside clock, she realised it was almost six and time to get up.

The wind was howling outside and a chill draught whistled under the door. Peggy steeled herself to throw off the blankets.

'Stay another minute,' murmured Jim, his arm heavy across her midriff. 'To be sure, I'm going to miss you, Peg.'

She snuggled down happily into his embrace. 'I'm going to miss you, too,' she said against the reassuring, steady beat of his heart. 'But you have to promise not to get up to any mischief while I'm away.'

He eased his head back on the pillow, his eyes widening in feigned shock. 'Mischief? Me?'

She giggled and poked his chest. 'Yes, you, Jim Reilly. I know all about those cigarettes and bottles of rum and whisky you've hidden in the shed, and I don't want to see them still there when I get back.' She looked him in the eye, trying desperately hard not to laugh. 'And that doesn't mean you can replace them with anything else illicit. I won't have this house become a den of iniquity.'

His chuckle was low and rumbled in his chest. 'A den of iniquity, is it now?' He grabbed her and held her tightly. 'If it's iniquity you're after, then I'm your man,' he growled into her neck, his hand slipping possessively over her hip.

'Jim,' she softly protested, pushing feebly against his chest.

'Shhh,' he whispered in her ear as his hand softly caressed the warm skin of her thigh beneath the winceyette nightdress. 'Be still, me darlin' girl, and let me love you.'

Peggy gave in to the glorious sensations he'd aroused. The rest of the world could wait a few minutes more.

Breakfast was a bit late, but it didn't seem to matter, for everyone was reluctant to leave the warmth of the kitchen for the blustery, cold dark day outside. Peggy knew she still glowed from their lovemaking, and wondered if it was at all obvious to anyone – and rather wished that Jim wouldn't keep winking at her from across the table. Mrs Finch was eyeing them both suspiciously, and it was disconcerting to say the least.

Anne went back upstairs to wash and dress as Suzy, Fran and June helped to clear the dishes before they wished her luck and sped off for their shift at the hospital. Peggy had warned them to behave while she was away, and although they'd promised faithfully, she couldn't quite dismiss the feeling that they were only humouring her. June was a bit of a man-eater, Fran was always up to some kind of mischief, and Suzy – well, Suzy was just too pretty to be safe anywhere.

'I hope you'll be as strict with them as you are with Cissy,' she said to Jim as Anne came to join them for a cup of tea before she and Jim had to leave for the bus. 'And watch out for June. She and Cissy aren't the best of friends since their falling out over Joe Buchanan, and I don't want any unpleasantness – especially now that Anne's here.'

'Mum,' protested Anne. 'I'm perfectly capable of dealing with June and Cissy.'

'Will you listen to yourself, woman?' muttered Jim. 'Stop fretting, will you? Everything will be fine.' He winked at Ron, who was slurping his tea on the other side of the kitchen table. 'Me and Da will keep the home fires burning, won't we, Da?'

Ron finished his tea and nodded. 'That we will, Peggy.' He reached for his poacher's coat and clicked his tongue. Harvey leaped from his favourite place by the range and barked excitedly at the promise of a day's hunting.

Peggy kissed Ron's stubbly cheek and wrinkled her nose at the pungent aroma drifting from the weatherproof coat. 'What on earth have you got in there?'

He grinned. 'Nothing for you to worry about.' With that, he headed for the steps that led down to the basement. 'I'll feed the chickens, and then see if I can find something for the pot. Anne's promised a stew for tonight.'

Harvey raced back and licked Peggy's hand as if he understood she was leaving, then almost bowled Ron over as he shoved his way through the door and down the steps.

Ron grasped the doorjamb to steady himself before he turned and rammed his cap over his silvery mop of unruly hair. 'Take care, Peg, and make sure those young rapscallions have a good Christmas.' His thick, bristly eyebrows lowered. 'You did remember to pack those presents, didn't you?'

Peggy's eyes swam with unshed tears as she nodded and listened to him clump down the concrete steps and slam through the back door. She turned back to the others. 'Oh, dear,' she sniffed. 'Are you sure you can all cope without me?'

Mrs Finch's grey head bobbed as she smiled at Peggy and placed her soft, warm hand on her cheek. 'Go and see your boys,' she said, 'and be thankful they aren't on the other side of the world like my family. Anne and I will keep an eye on things here, don't you fret.'

Peggy carefully gave her a hug, wary of brittle bones and unsteady feet. 'Don't let them wear you out – and ask for help when you need it,' she ordered, mouthing the words clearly so the old lady understood.

'We'll be fine,' said Anne as she stood and eased her back in the way of all pregnant women. 'Go, Mum, and give those boys a big kiss and hug for me.'

Peggy kissed her and gently patted the bump. 'You take care of my grandchild, and don't do anything silly,' she murmured.

Jim held out her coat, gas mask box and handbag. 'You'll miss the bus,' he warned. 'Come on. Time we left.'

Peggy slipped on her coat and gloves, her gaze settling on the beloved faces that looked back at her. Then she followed him into the hall and out of the front door without looking back. It was better that way, for then they wouldn't see her tears.

She hastily blew her nose and tucked her hand in the crook of Jim's arm. He was carrying her suitcase as well as the large string bag stuffed with presents, and was looking very smart in his best overcoat and soft trilby. But as she trotted along beside him down the steep hill to the trolleybus stop on the seafront, her emotions were in turmoil.

They had rarely been apart during their marriage, and three weeks was a long time. Jim had a habit of flirting with anything in a skirt, and there had been many a time she'd threatened to either murder him or leave, but she'd carried on loving him. Now she was putting that love to the test, and she wasn't at all sure she was ready.

It was bitterly cold on the seafront, the wind threatening to tear off her hat as the foamy heads of the thundering waves tossed spume in the air, crashing against the shingle. Peggy stood and watched the sea, never tiring of its majesty. She would miss it in the heart of Somerset.

'You've gone very quiet,' said Jim, as they found a seat and the trolleybus jerked away from the stop. He took her gloved hand and held it between his own. 'We'll be fine,' he soothed.

She looked into his eyes and knew he understood her fears. 'Are you sure?'

He nodded. 'There's only one woman for me, Peggy Reilly, and she's sitting right beside me.'

Peggy would have liked to kiss him, but they were surrounded by strangers and it wouldn't be seemly. She squeezed his fingers instead. 'That's all right then,' she murmured as she looked into his handsome face and prayed that it would be.

The trolleybus whined and juddered up the High Street then came to a halt outside the bus station.

Jim collected the case from the luggage rack, grabbed the string bag and helped Peggy alight. She was wearing her high heels, her best coat and dress, and one of Doris's cast-off hats, and knew she looked very smart, but probably not at all practically turned out for the long journey ahead. Clutching his arm again, she walked slowly towards the green and yellow charabanc which was already waiting at the kerb with its engine running.

In a sudden moment of panic, Peggy tightened her grip on his arm. 'What if something happens and I can't get back?' she said, her mouth dry, the fear coursing through her. 'What if Beach View is bombed? What if—?'

'What if you get on the damned bus and stop fretting yourself into a standstill?' Jim said softly. He put down the case and in front of an interested and amused audience of bus passengers and passers-by, swept her into his arms and kissed her so ravishingly that she almost lost her hat.

'Jim,' she hissed, red in the face and unable to think straight as she rescued her hat and tried to tidy herself.

'Get on the bus,' he ordered softly, 'and give those boys of ours a big hug for me and Da.'

Peggy stood on tiptoe, held onto her hat and kissed him softly on the lips. 'I love you, Jim Reilly,' she murmured. Before he could say anything, and before she showed herself up by bursting into tears, she took the string bag from him, turned away, clambered onto the bus and showed the driver her ticket.

She heard Jim talking to the driver as he stowed her case in the luggage rack, but continued her way along the narrow aisle between the seats, resolutely ignoring everyone until she found an empty place near the back.

Sitting down, she kept her face turned towards the window, her handbag, gas mask box and the string bag tightly gripped in her hands as if they were the anchors that kept her tied to Cliffehaven and her precious family.

The driver closed the door, clambered back into his seat and revved the engine. With a deep rumble, the charabanc slowly moved away from the kerb. But where was Jim? She couldn't see him.

And there he was, tall and handsome, the trilby pulled raffishly over one eye as he kept pace with the bus. Peggy put her hand on the glass, her expression saying so much more than any words could – and he seemed to understand, for his eyes held her until the last moment.

She twisted in her seat as she was carried away from him, and the last she saw of him was the hat being waved in the air as he stood like a rock in the middle of the busy High Street and defied the oncoming traffic.

Peggy sagged against the back of the seat and closed her eyes. All she could do now was pray that this war would spare her family and that she would see all of them again.

Ron was where he loved to be: high above Cliffehaven, the wind tearing at his hair and plastering his long coat around his legs as Harvey raced back and forth, nose to the ground, tail windmilling in the pursuit of rabbit and hare.

It was bitterly cold, making his eyes water and his cheeks sting, but Ron felt more at home here than sitting in front of the fire in Peggy's kitchen. He knew these hills so well, and they gave him the time and space to breathe and think, provided the family with good food according to the seasons, and offered a chance for Harvey to be carefree again.

He hitched the rifle's broken stock over his shoulder and smiled as he watched the lurcher chase after something through the long, windswept grass. Harvey had proved to be an excellent rescue dog, his finely tuned nose sniffing out people who had been buried beneath their bombed out homes and businesses. He'd become quite a hero during these past months, and he deserved these few hours of freedom to be just Harvey.

Ron was hardly out of breath as he tramped up the steep incline and paused for a moment to take in the view from the highest peak of the chalk cliffs. There were numerous gun emplacements all along the cliff-tops which marred the beauty of his surroundings, but he could look back on Cliffehaven from here and see how it stretched beneath him, the bay curving from these tall white cliffs to the western hills that softly undulated towards the sea. The landscape had changed over the past months, and several gaps denoted where a church spire, a tenement block or a row of shops had once been – but for all that, it was still home and Ron felt at peace.

He made himself comfortable on a convenient tuft of sturdy grass and lit his pipe, content to while away the time and leave Harvey to chase and forage and roll about in fox droppings. It would mean having to scrub him down when they got home, but with Peggy away, it probably didn't matter too much.

Then he remembered that his granddaughter Anne had moved in – which meant he would definitely have to clean Harvey up. The girl was as fussy as her mother, and he didn't want to start off on the wrong foot – not while she was carrying his first great-grandchild.

The thought rather shocked him. He didn't feel old enough for such things, and it was sobering to realise how many years had flown by without him even noticing. Where had they gone – and what had he to show for them but a few old clothes, a couple of guns, fishing rods and rabbit nets?

He gave a deep sigh as he thought about the years he'd run his small fleet of fishing boats down on that shore – of the two sons he and Emily had raised in the tiny cottage that had once stood nearby – and of the loving family Peggy had warmly allowed him to join when Emily died and he was left all alone. They had been good years, and he was a lucky man. His only wish now was to see his sons, Jim and Frank, reconciled, and he had hoped their rescue mission to Dunkirk would be a beginning – but it seemed that whatever it was they'd fallen out about still kept them apart.

Preferring not to dwell on such things, he leaned back on his elbows, puffed on his pipe and let his gaze drift towards the elegant lines of Victorian terraces that climbed the hill to the east of Cliffehaven, and on to Camden Road and the Anchor pub. Rosie would be getting ready to open for the lunchtime crowd, and he could just picture her behind the bar, her voluptuous curves drawing every red-blooded man's eye as she sashayed back and forth, opened bottles, and pulled pints.

'Rosie,' he murmured around the stem of his pipe, 'you're a wonder to be sure. And 'tis a wonder you give an old reprobate like me the time of day.' He puffed contentedly as he thought of the afternoon ritual they'd fallen into, with him sitting in her little upstairs parlour drinking tea after the pub was closed for the afternoon.

The view was forgotten as he pictured Rosie in her chintz-covered chair, her high-heeled shoes kicked off, her long, finely shaped legs curled beneath her, the blouse undone just enough to give a tantalising glimpse of warm, peachy flesh. Rosie Braithwaite was perfect in every way, and Ron became lost in erotic fantasy.

Harvey spoiled the moment by flopping down beside him, reeking of fox. 'Ach,' he said in disgust. 'Ye're a heathen animal, so you are.'

Harvey panted and wriggled his eyebrows before rolling with vigorous relish in the grass.

Ron ruffled his shaggy fur and was rewarded with an enthusiastic lick across his face. 'Get away with ye,' he growled, giving him a gentle push. 'Go on. Find something for the pot and leave an old man to his dreams.'

Harvey raced off and Ron got to his feet. Dreams and reality were not easy bedfellows, and he doubted he'd ever get further with Rosie than helping her in the bar and drinking tea in her parlour. But an old man could dream, couldn't he? And there was still plenty of life in him, even if he was over sixty and had nothing much to offer.

Feeling much more cheerful, he whistled to Harvey, hitched the rifle over his shoulder and tramped towards the distant copse of trees where there would be plenty of burrows, and perhaps even a pheasant or two that had escaped from the big estate further north. With the gamekeeper and estate workers busy soldiering, there was always a good chance of something to be had – and he was certain Rosie would appreciate a nice fat bird for her Christmas dinner. He grinned at the thought that she might even invite him to help her eat it – and with a few tots of whisky to follow, who knew what might happen?

Rita had been on tenterhooks ever since she'd returned to the recruitment office with her birth certificate. The woman had clearly been surprised at her eagerness, and had softened enough to tell her more about the kind of work she might be doing.

It was a bit of a worry that she'd have to be billeted in one of the large accommodation blocks on the airbase and therefore would have little chance to keep an eye on Louise. But it all sounded terribly exciting, and she was bursting to tell someone other than May – yet, like May, she knew it wouldn't be wise to say anything until she had confirmation.

The hardest part was keeping it from Louise, who was already suspicious about what she was up to, and not at all pleased at the amount of make-up she'd been wearing. Rita had so wanted to tell her last night, but didn't dare in case she caused her any unnecessary anguish only to discover that her application had been turned down.

It was a dilemma, and it played on her mind so much that she'd made several mistakes this morning, and Major Patricia was not best pleased with her.

'Concentrate, Smith. You've made a complete hash of that.'

She lifted the visor, looked at the welded joint and reddened with shame. It was indeed a shoddy piece of work. 'I'll do it again,' she mumbled.

'Yes, you will. But I suggest you take a break and concentrate your mind first. It's clearly not on your work.'

Rita dumped the heavy leather visor and apron on the workbench, glad of the respite. Despite the cold wind that rattled the corrugated roof and sang in the wires supporting the barrage balloons, she was drenched in sweat, her hair sticking to her head, her shirt and dungarees clinging to her back and chest. She gave a wry grin as she ran her fingers through her lank hair. Cissy would be horrified, but there was little point in putting on make-up and making her hair look neat when she spent most of the time covered from head to foot in sweltering leather.

Reaching for the flask of tea and the Spam sandwich she'd made that morning, she perched on the bench and mulled over her plans for her birthday. She would have to work, of course, and tomorrow night was her turn to fire-watch, but she knew Louise had planned a special dinner, and she was really looking forward to seeing what she could possibly have conjured up from the bit of scrag end she'd so victoriously carried home last night.

As she munched her sandwich and washed it down with the weak tea, she watched May and the other women. The enormous hangar was a gloomy place, and every sound was magnified, echoing to the rafters as the women bent to their various tasks and shouted to each other to be heard. They were all dressed in dungarees and shirts, their hair covered with knotted hankies, their hands swathed in thick gloves. Some were welding, others were hammering, or working the vast rollers and lathes, while others painted the sheets of metal a uniform grey.

It was strange to think she might not be coming here for very much longer, and in a way she felt a bit uneasy. This was what she knew, and now the others had set aside their prejudices and offered friendship again, she was quite surprised to realise how much she would miss them.

Her reverie was rudely interrupted by the wailing sirens, and she swiftly reached for her gas mask and jacket. Racing for the door, she and May were almost carried out into the windswept concrete yard by the tide of women, and jostled towards the enormous shelter that had been built beneath it.

Men and women from all over the industrial compound raced to join them, and in the moment before she plunged into the darkness of the shelter, she heard the steady, ominous rumble in the distance. The enemy was fast approaching.

Ron had eaten the strong-smelling cheese Rosie had given him with a pickled onion and a hunk of bread for his lunch. It had been a successful trip, for they had bagged a couple of pheasants which were nestled nicely in his coat's deep pockets alongside the duck Harvey had managed to catch close to the big pond that was on the very edge of Lord Cliffe's estate.

It had been a close-run thing, for they'd been spotted by the elderly Lord Charles, and had had to make a quick escape. The old boy had proved to be quite nifty on his feet as he'd given chase, his shouts of fury following them right into the woods. But the old fellow's age had finally caught up with him and he'd run out of steam – leaving Ron and Harvey to saunter victoriously back towards the cliffs with their booty.

'It's your fault, Harvey,' he muttered to the dog that bounded along beside him. 'You know better than to go for the ducks. Now the old fool will probably have the law on us for poaching.'

Harvey waggled his eyebrows, tongue lolling, tail wagging like a metronome as he looked up at Ron. It wouldn't be the first time, he seemed to say. And we've got away with it before.

'Very pleased with yourself, aren't ye, y'old scoundrel?' Ron growled. 'But now I have to be hiding these birds and make sure the cops don't find 'em.' He stomped across the rough tussocks of grass, his cap firmly jammed low over his bushy brows. 'Still,' he muttered more to himself than the dog, 'I suppose Rosie might like a nice duck for a treat.'

He ruffled the dog's ears to show he was forgiven, and then tensed, eyes searching the horizon, alert to the ominous sound of distant thunder. But this was no storm coming across the Channel, he realised. It was the Luftwaffe.

'Come,' he ordered the dog, and broke into a run towards the thicket of trees that grew in a nearby dell.

Ron dived into the shadows, making for the heart of the thicket in the certain knowledge that Harvey was right behind him. He came to a halt beside a particularly tall oak and waited for the lurcher to join him. 'Harvey,' he snapped. 'Where the divil are you, you heathen animal?'

Harvey trotted up to him, a rabbit hanging from his mouth, thorns spiking his muzzle.

'Eejit beast,' he murmured affectionately. He stuffed the dead rabbit in one of his pockets, encouraged Harvey to lie next to him in the deep shadows and began to carefully divest the soft nose of its thorns.

The thunder was coming closer, drowning out the many sirens that had gone off round the town, and soon the air and the earth vibrated with it.

Ron looked up through the leafy canopy and shook his fists as the first wave of bombers ponderously rumbled over them. Their shadows stole the sun in that clear blue sky, stained the windswept grass and chilled the man and his dog who watched them.

The answering boom of the guns on the headlands shook the earth and resonated through them, and Harvey whimpered as he rested his sore nose on his paws, his eyebrows jiggling, his ears flat to his shaggy head.

Ron laid a reassuring hand on his head and fondled the silky ears. The noise was so loud there was little point in trying to talk to him, so Ron lay beside him and held him close as he heard wave after terrible wave of enemy bombers and fighter planes head inland.

And then, within that awful noise, came the lighter, quicker sound of the brave little Spitfires and Hurricanes, racing from the nearby airbase to cause as much disruption as they could before the bombers reached their targets.

As Ron and Harvey moved to the outer edge of the copse they watched them peel off from their tight formation, swooping, diving, climbing, picking out their separate targets, harrying them while they dodged the enemy bullets and fired off their own.

'Come on, me boys,' yelled Ron. 'Show the bastards what you can do.'

His heart was pounding, swelling with pride as two of the enemy fighters were hit, and the Spitfires continued to attack. He could hear the sharp rat-a-tat-tat of the bullets – had a front-row view of the deadly dogfights that were being carried out high above him, and could hear the deep, rapid booms of the Bofors guns further along the cliff and the rattle of the anti-aircraft guns on the seafront.

He held his breath as one of the Spitfires streamed black smoke from its wingtip. It began a slow, deathly spin, the engine screaming as one of the enemy fighters closed in for the kill. 'Come on, boy,' he muttered fiercely. 'Pull out, get 'er straight again.'

The brave little plane was hit again and again – the German pilot making sure of a kill before he banked away and hunted for another target.

Ron searched the skies as the Spitfire spun out of control, its fate already clear. But where was the pilot? Had he managed to eject? He screwed up his eyes, straining to see the billow of white silk that would mean the pilot had escaped.

And there it was, drifting down, spinning in the strong wind coming off the sea and the down-draught of the enemy planes. He could even see the pilot struggling to control its flight as it came ever faster towards land. 'Yes,' he breathed. 'Yes, my lad, you keep a steady bearing and you'll be all right.'

Forgetting how exposed he was to stray bullets or trigger-happy Huns, Ron left the shelter of the trees and followed the parachute's path. He had no need to whistle to the dog, for Harvey was already at his heels, and they set off at a quick pace towards the spot where Ron suspected the pilot might come down.

It was soon clear that the lad was injured and struggling to control the parachute, and Ron feared that if he didn't watch out, he'd have a heavy landing in the trees that edged Lord Cliffe's estate and cause himself further damage.

Disregarding the enemy planes that still thundered overhead, Ron picked up his pace as the pilot disappeared behind the nearby hill and the parachute deflated like a pricked balloon. 'Seek 'im, Harvey,' he ordered.

Harvey shot off and Ron tramped steadily after him until he'd reached the summit and could see what had happened. The lad had missed the trees by some way, but he was lying very still – too still.

With fear making his heart thud, Ron raced down the hill. He'd seen too many young men killed in the first war – and somehow it had become imperative that this one should live.

The parachute had been unhitched and gathered up by the pilot, who'd also had the time to peel off his flying helmet and goggles. But this great effort must have drained him, for he now lay on his side, head cushioned by the parachute, unaware of Harvey's rasping tongue on his face and the prodding, inquisitive paw nudging his shoulder.

'Leave him be,' muttered Ron as he pushed the dog away and got on his knees beside the pilot. Tears blinded him. He was just a boy – a boy who was white with pain and terror – a boy with a child's soft face and a lick of fair hair which fell across his closed eyes.

Ron's heart ached as he gently brushed back that lick of hair. 'It's all right, son,' he murmured. 'You're home now. You're safe.'

The boy stirred and the long lashes fluttered against the downy cheek. 'Dad?' he rasped. 'Dad, I tried to save her, but she was hit too badly.'

'Shh now, son. Be still,' muttered Ron as he examined the bloody mess above the heavy flying boots and checked there were no other injuries. The boy had lost a lot of blood and was obviously delirious. What did it matter if he thought Ron was his dad?

He sniffed loudly and scrubbed away his tears impatiently. Stripping down to his shirt, he pulled it off and tied it tightly above the leg wound in the hope it would stem the bleeding. The cold made him shiver and he swiftly put his jumper and coat back on then reached into the many pockets, found the flask of tea and carefully poured some into the plastic cup.

Gently easing his hand beneath the boy's head, he tried to get him to drink. It was sweet enough to counter the shock, for he'd sneaked four teaspoons of sugar into it when Peg wasn't looking, so it should do a bit of good. But the heavily sugared, milky tea dribbled from the slack lips and darkened the pale sheepskin at the neck of the flying jacket.

Ron sat back on his heels, the boy's head cradled against his legs. He eyed his remote surroundings, realised the enemy bombers were no longer flying over Cliffehaven and came to a decision. 'Well, Harvey,' he said, 'it looks as if you and me are going to have to get him home by ourselves.'

He gently lowered the boy's head back onto the parachute silk. 'Stay,' he ordered the dog, and hurried off to find enough sturdy branches to make into a travois.

He kept a close eye on the time as he used the deadly sharp hunting knife to hack down several branches and strip them clean. The bombers would be back soon, and he had to hurry. Returning to the valley, he saw the boy was awake, and that Harvey was happily trying to wash his face again.

'Leave him,' he growled. 'How do you feel, son?'

The blue eyes that looked up at him were cloudy with pain. 'I'm fine, sir. Is this your dog?'

'His name's Harvey,' muttered Ron. 'And he and I are going to get you home so that leg can get seen to.'

'I'll be all right, sir, really.' He made a tremendous effort to sit up. The blood drained from his face and he fell back in a dead faint.

'Just as well,' Ron muttered. 'At least he won't feel any pain.' He hurried to lash the two longest poles together at the top with the thick string he always kept in his pocket, then took off his coat, emptied the pockets, and threaded the poles through the sleeves. He then slashed the parachute free of its strings and used them to lash the two shorter poles crosswise so the travois formed a rough triangle, and used the last of the string and the parachute lines to thread around the buttons and through the button-holes to anchor the coat firmly.

'Let's just hope it holds,' he muttered, giving it an experimental prod. He eyed the parachute and the sturdy canvas bag that had carried it. The rabbits and birds fitted in the bag very nicely. Now for the tricky bit.

It didn't take long to lift the boy onto the make-shift stretcher – he didn't weigh much. Ron worked quickly, tying the parachute across the boy's body and lashing it firmly to the poles. They couldn't stay out here in the open much longer – he could already hear the distant droning of the returning bombers.

His fears were confirmed by the cacophony of wailing sirens that had Harvey howling – he hated them – and Ron told him to shut up and get into the trees. Picking up the canvas bag, he slung it over his shoulder, placed his rifle on the boy's chest, and took the weight of the travois. Aware of the rough terrain, he tried to make his hasty dash into the trees as steady as possible so as not to cause the boy any unnecessary pain.

Ron and Harvey waited with the boy until the last of the enemy had been chased back over the Channel, then set off on the long journey home to Beach View.

The winter's day was closing in, darkness coming early as it always did in December, and Ron shivered as the cold penetrated the ragged jumper and settled into his old bones. But he trudged purposefully on, pulling the travois behind him. There would be no afternoon tea with Rosie today, he thought sorrowfully, for there was at least another half-hour to go before he reached Beach View, and the pub would be opening soon. But none of that mattered. The boy had to be got back to safety and into the care of a doctor.

Harvey loped beside him, turning now and again to check on the airman who was falling in and out of consciousness. He whined when the lad was awake, and Ron would stop and try to encourage him to drink a bit of tea, but these short stops were exhausting, and it became harder and harder to get going again.

Ron plodded on in the darkness, the scrape of the travois and the moans of the boy accompanying him across the rough terrain he knew so well. They were almost there now, he could make out the shapes of the houses against the sky, the alley behind Beach View – the bomb-damaged wall – the gate.

He was almost spent. The travois was too wide to go through the gate, and he simply didn't have the strength to haul it through the hole in the wall. He put the travois down and rested, hands on knees as his chest heaved. 'Jim,' he rasped. 'Jim, I need some help.'

Harvey gave three sharp barks and Jim finally appeared at the back door. 'What the divil are you doing, old man?'

'Stir yourself and help me get him inside,' Ron panted. He saw Anne and Mrs Finch appear in the doorway. 'Telephone for an ambulance,' he ordered, 'and be quick about it, I've got an injured man here.'

Jim helped him hoist the travois over the hole in the wall, but then discovered it wouldn't fit through the back door. 'We'll have to get him off this thing,' said Jim. 'Give me your knife.'

Ron was drained but still had his wits about him. 'Don't cut the parachute. It's valuable.'

'To be sure, I know that much,' retorted Jim. 'And I suppose you'll be claiming the silk for yourself?'

'I think I've earned it,' Ron replied wearily. He

watched his son cut the strings holding the coat to the travois and carefully untie the parachute, then used the last of his strength to help carry the boy inside and settle him in the chair by the fire.

The room seemed to spin round him, the familiar faces blurring, the concerned voices muffled as wave upon wave of darkness filled his head. He stumbled towards the other chair, desperate to sit and dispel the giddiness.

But he never reached it and didn't feel the thud as his head caught the corner of the table and he sank into oblivion.

Chapter Seven

'It's no use you coming in here every five minutes,' said the woman sternly. 'I don't have the authority to tell you anything.'

Rita felt she was being a bit unfair, this was only the third time she'd been in since yesterday. She shuffled from one foot to the other. The reek of the oil heater was exacerbating the queasy feeling in her stomach that had been troubling her all day. 'I just thought you might know if my application got through all right?'

'It has been less than twenty-four hours,' the woman said, her expression softening. 'I admire your enthusiasm, Miss Smith, but please go home. You will be notified soon enough, I assure you.'

Rita was forced to accept that the agony of waiting was to continue. She left the enlistment office carrying her helmet and goggles and swung her leg over the motorcycle's saddle, sitting for a moment to quell the squirms of doubts that were plaguing her.

This was probably the most daring thing she'd ever done outside racing the motorbike on the pre-war circuits, and although she was desperate for her application to be accepted, that yearning was tempered by her responsibility for Louise. Her acceptance into the dispatch riders' unit would mean leaving home to live in the barracks at the airfield, and giving all her attention to the needs of the WAAFs. Would Louise be able to manage without her? She gave a deep sigh and told herself she must stop worrying.

It was late afternoon and the town was already in darkness, with only a few hardy souls finishing their shopping before they hurried home. Heavy waves of enemy planes had been coming over most of the afternoon, and although it was quiet now, the blackout meant there was no tree with fairy lights twinkling in the centre of town – no gaily decorated shop windows, or glimpses of tinsel, streamers and silver balls in the upstairs apartments. Christmas would be very different this year, and without her dad, Papa Tino or Roberto to celebrate with, it was all a bit depressing.

'Hey, great bike.'

She snapped out of her reverie, looked up at the brash young American, and couldn't help returning his broad smile. If this was his idea of a pick-up line then he'd chosen well, for any praise of her bike was certain to be appreciated. 'Thanks,' she replied.

He eyed the Norton with delight before he looked back at her. 'I guess you're waiting for your boyfriend, huh? This his bike?'

Why did men always assume a girl couldn't own

a motorbike? 'It's mine,' she told him, with rather more than a hint of pride and annoyance.

He gave a low whistle as his gaze swept her from head to toe. 'Boy, oh boy, but you're just an itty-bitty little thing. You sure you can handle that monster?'

Now he'd spoilt it. She had long grown weary of this question, which had been asked repeatedly since she started riding the bike. 'I've handled bigger.' She rammed the helmet over her lank hair and prepared to kick-start the engine.

It seemed he was impervious to her hurt feelings and cool response. 'You don't say,' he breathed in admiration. 'My brother had one of these back home in Oregon.' His hand ran over the front mudguard. 'It's a powerful piece of machinery.'

Rita heard the longing in his voice and decided she was being a little harsh with him. He was probably homesick, and the bike had become a sort of symbol of all he was missing. 'Me and Dad rebuilt it,' she said. 'It was in a bit of a state when we found it.'

His brown eyes widened. 'You found it? But they're worth a heap of money.'

Rita grinned. 'This one wasn't at the time. It had been left to fall apart behind an abandoned house. It took me and Dad two years to sort it out.'

'You helped your dad rebuild it?' The disbelief was clear in his expression.

Rita laughed. 'Just because I'm a girl doesn't mean I can't mess about with bikes. My dad has his own garage, and I was training as a mechanic before the war.'

She reddened as she caught his glance at her heavy trousers and boots, the moth-eaten flying jacket and old leather helmet. 'I'm a welder now – hence the get-up,' she quickly explained. It was suddenly rather important that he knew she didn't always look quite so scruffy.

He gazed at her in silence, and then seemed to remember his manners. 'The name's Chuck Howard, by the way,' he said, snatching the American Air Force issue cap from his head.

'Rita Smith.' She tried not to wince as her hand was smothered in a vice-like grip. 'Been over here long?'

'A few months,' he replied, his gaze still trawling the Norton. 'I'm based up at the camp yonder.' He pointed vaguely in the direction of the hills. 'We feel kinda useless not being allowed to join your RAF boys. But I guess President Roosevelt will get us involved soon enough now the conscription bill has gone through.'

Rita nodded. 'Still,' she said, 'you Americans are doing a sterling job clearing up after the bombing. Our street was in a terrible mess.'

'We do what we can.' He grinned down at her.

As silence fell between them Rita felt a rush of awkwardness and began to fiddle with the strap on her goggles. 'I should be getting home,' she murmured.

He looked crestfallen. 'Aw, shucks, I was hoping you might like to come for a drink. We could talk about bikes,' he added hastily. 'My brother used to race them, you see.'

'So did me and Dad before the war,' she replied. 'Is your brother here too?'

He shook his head. 'Nah, he joined the navy and is based somewhere in Hawaii.' He reddened. 'I guess I shouldn't have said that, what with all the warnings about spies and such.'

She smiled back at him. 'I won't tell anyone.'

'So,' he prompted. 'About that drink? There's one of your great little pubs on that corner.'

She was tempted, for he was young and handsome and seemed like a really nice chap. It might be fun – and it was her birthday the next day. Then she saw a group of young women hurrying down the street in their high heels and best coats and remembered how much of a fright she must look. It would just be embarrassing.

'I'm sorry,' she said with genuine regret, 'but as you can see I've only just finished work and I need to get home.'

'I have a night pass,' he said quickly. 'Maybe you could meet me later?' He looked at her hopefully.

His open, honest face and friendly smile made Rita hesitate. She chewed her lip and gave it some serious thought. It wouldn't take long to wash and change into something more respectable. But Louise was expecting her home for the evening, and as it was the first time they'd both had a night off for some time, she couldn't let her down.

'I don't think I can,' she replied softly. 'You see, I have someone waiting for me back home.'

He stiffened and took a step back. 'Oh, gee. I'm sorry, ma'am. I didn't realise you were married.'

There seemed little point in putting him right when they probably wouldn't see each other again – but she felt a twinge of regret, for their short interlude had been flattering and pleasant. 'It was nice to meet you, Chuck,' she said, and smiled. 'Now, I really must be off.'

'Well, so long, ma'am. You take care on that bike now.' He snapped off a salute and stepped back onto the pavement.

Rita shoved the goggles over her eyes and kick-started the bike, revving it just a little more than necessary before she shot down the road and reluctantly headed for home.

The kitchen at Beach View Boarding House was in chaos as Anne returned from telephoning for the ambulance. Harvey was barking and whining and trying to lick Ron awake. The young airman was groaning with pain, Mrs Finch was muttering and wringing her hands, and Anne was torn between the needs of the boy and her grandfather.

'Da!' shouted Jim, as he fell to his knees beside the inert form on the floor and shoved the dog out of the way. 'Da? Can you hear me?'

'It's no good yelling at him,' said Anne. 'He's out cold.' She struggled to her knees, the bulk of the baby making it awkward, as she wrestled to grab Harvey's collar. 'Get Harvey out of here, Dad, he's making it impossible to get to Granddad.'

Jim made a grab for the dog, which skittered out of reach and continued to bark and paw at Ron.

Anne was shocked by the prodigious amount of blood coming from Ron's head wound. 'How did this happen?'

'He fainted and hit the corner of the table with a terrible thud,' said Jim.

Anne could see that her grandfather was the colour of old porridge, his skin cold and clammy to the touch. She'd done a first-aid course as part of her teacher training, so understood how vital it was to keep him warm and his airway free. 'Help me get him on his side,' she ordered her father. 'And then get a couple of blankets and some pillows. We must keep them both warm until the ambulance arrives.'

'It's not his heart, is it?' Jim's eyes were wild with fear as he wrestled to keep Harvey out of the way while they saw to the old man.

'I really don't know,' she said softly. 'Just get the blankets, Dad. The ambulance should be here soon.'

Jim dashed off and Anne looked across at the young flier who was slumped in the armchair, his injured leg stuck at an awkward angle in front of him. He was a ghastly colour too, and although he was moaning, he was clearly out of it – which could only be a good thing. That leg looked nasty. 'I wouldn't undo the tourniquet, Mrs Finch,' she warned sharply as the elderly woman began plucking at it. 'He'll start to bleed again.'

'Oh, dear,' flustered Mrs Finch. 'He's so young. Poor boy,' she muttered, stroking back his hair and patting his pale, soft cheek. 'I feel so helpless. What can I do to help him, Anne?'

'See if you can get a drop of brandy down him,' said Anne, feeling for Ron's pulse as she shoved the dog away. 'I hid the bottle at the back of the dresser drawer.' She counted the thready beats beneath her fingers. Ron's heart was definitely struggling. 'What the hell have you been up to, Grandpa?' she muttered.

Harvey barked and whined and pawed at Ron's inert body. 'Be quiet,' shouted Anne as she batted him away. 'You're really not helping.'

But the animal was too upset to obey her and continued to whine and paw at Ron as he licked his face.

Anne gave up the struggle and made herself as comfortable as possible on the hard floor, nestled Ron's head against her thighs and kept an eye on Mrs Finch, who had scrabbled in the drawer, found the bottle Anne had hidden from her father and grandfather, and was now dribbling a thimbleful into the bottom of a glass.

Gently lifting the boy's head, she tried to get some of it in his mouth without choking him. 'Come on, young man,' she crooned softly. 'Try and swallow some of this. It'll do you good. I promise.'

'Here you are,' panted Jim, racing into the kitchen loaded with blankets and pillows. 'What do you want me to do with them?'

Anne took two blankets and a pillow. 'Take the rest and wrap up the boy while I see to Granddad.' As Jim hovered, she spoke more sharply. 'See to the boy, Dad – and then get this damned dog out of here.'

Jim stumbled away to do as he was told, but Mrs Finch soon became impatient with his ineptitude and shooed him away. 'Isn't there something else you should be doing before the ambulance and police arrive?'

'Police?' His eyes widened. 'What would the police want here?'

Mrs Finch finished cocooning the boy in the blankets and looked back at Jim as if he was half-witted. 'They always turn up when something like this happens,' she said calmly. 'Hadn't you better see to that?' She nodded towards the canvas bag that lay forgotten on the kitchen floor, its contents strewn across the lino.

'Oh, bejesus, what's the auld fool been up to now?' He hastily gathered up the rabbits and birds and stood in the middle of the kitchen in a panic. 'Where shall I put them – and what about the two birds he's got hanging in the cellar?'

Anne looked up at him. 'The rabbits are nothing to worry about,' she told him calmly. 'Wrap the birds in newspaper and bury them under the compost heap. It won't do them any harm, and as long as you keep Harvey away, they won't be found.'

'To be sure, you're a clever wee girl.' He grabbed the newspapers that were piled on the floor next to the range and began to parcel the birds. 'How's Da? Any change?'

'He's still out cold,' said Anne. 'But he's a better colour and his breathing is less ragged. He'd do better without Harvey climbing all over him,' she added crossly. 'Please, Dad. Get him out of here.'

'In a minute,' he rasped, still fumbling with paper and string.

Anne realised her father was more interested in getting rid of the evidence of Ron's poaching than seeing to the dog. She gave up trying to still the animal and turned instead to Mrs Finch. 'Could you get me a bowl of warm water and a cloth? I need to clean Granddad up and see how deep this head wound is.'

Jim was still making a hash of his parcels when he heard the loud clanging bell of the fast approaching ambulance. He froze as a terrible thought struck him. 'The stuff in the shed,' he shouted. 'I forgot about the stuff in the shed.'

'You mean the cigarettes, rum and whisky?' Mrs Finch looked at him sternly. 'There's no time to move them now. You'd better shut Harvey in there. He'll be frantic enough to bark non-stop, and that should keep the police away.'

'To be sure, you've a mind like a first-class criminal,' Jim said admiringly.

'Takes one to know one,' retorted Mrs Finch, 'and I've lived in this house long enough to learn lots of new tricks. Now get on with you.'

Jim grabbed a protesting, struggling Harvey by the collar and raced down the cellar steps, grabbing the two hanging birds on his way to the compost heap.

Anne struggled to her feet as she heard the ambulance come along Camden Road. She grabbed the canvas parachute bag and quickly stuffed it under the wool and needles in Mrs Finch's enormous knitting bag before peeking through the blackout curtains of the kitchen window.

She saw her father slam the shed door on a ferociously barking Harvey before he began to dig furiously in the compost. Her gaze caught the gleam of parachute silk lying across the vegetable patch, and she quickly unlatched the window.

'The parachute, Dad!' she hissed, as the ambulance drew up into the road. 'Don't forget the parachute.'

She heard him curse before she slammed the window and saw him hastily gathering up the parachute and stuffing it down the hole he'd just dug. She let the blackout curtain fall back over the window, took a deep breath to calm herself, and went to let the ambulance crew in. As was expected, they were accompanied by a policeman.

Rita locked the motorbike in the garage and went upstairs to wash and change before she went next door. She was smiling as she ran a brush through her hair and thought about the young American. He was a bit brash, but it had been lovely to be asked out for a drink – even if he was more interested in the Norton than her.

'Ah, well,' she sighed, reaching for her coat and gas mask box. 'At least I had the offer, and they don't come too often.' She hurried downstairs, locked up behind her and made her way in the darkness to the house next door.

Louise was busy at the stove and there was a delicious aroma lingering in the air. 'You're looking pleased with yourself,' she said as she turned and smiled at Rita. 'Had a good day?'

Rita grinned as she pulled off her coat and hung it on the back of the door. 'I got propositioned this evening,' she said gaily, 'by a Yank.'

Louise turned sharply from the pot on the stove. 'You don't want to be starting all that,' she said in rapid Italian. 'You know how much trouble Vi is causing in the street, and you have your reputation to think of.'

She might have known Louise wouldn't approve. 'He only asked me out for a drink,' she replied deliberately in English. 'And as I turned him down, there's no need to get so hot under the collar.'

'I'm sorry,' Louise murmured, still in Italian. 'But with Papa and Roberto away, it's a big responsibility for me to make sure you're kept safe. You're a pretty young girl, and there are too many men on the prowl who would take advantage.'

'I might be young, but I'm not daft,' Rita retorted.

Louise put her hands on her hips, her face scarlet with emotion. 'You have no experience of life,' she said, her voice wavering. 'What do you know of men, eh? This war brings trouble to girls like you. It's important you are careful.'

Rita was taken aback by her vehemence. If she was like this over a passing chat with an American airman, how would she react when she told her about the dispatch rider's application? She decided to change the subject before things got even more fraught. 'What's that heavenly smell?' she asked instead.

'Tomorrow's dinner, and you're not to look in the larder,' Louise replied with unusual sharpness. 'It's a surprise.'

'I'm sorry if you're upset, Mamma,' Rita said softly. 'But you really shouldn't worry about me. I'm quite sensible, you know, and wouldn't do anything silly.'

Louise gave a great sigh, left her cooking pots and sat at the table. 'I'm sorry too,' she said, remembering to keep to English, 'It's just that I'm afraid for you with so many servicemen about.' She gave Rita a watery smile. 'So,' she said, clearly making an effort to remain calm. 'Tell me about this American.'

Rita decided it would do no harm – after all, nothing much had happened. 'He was young and pleasant, and of course his manners were impeccable. He came from Oregon, wherever that is, and I think he's a bit fed up with not being allowed to work with our airmen.' She giggled. 'He was more interested in the motórbike, really,' she confessed, 'and I think he just wanted to talk about his brother, who has the same model Norton.'

'That's what he wanted you to think,' said Louise, her eyes narrowing.

'Oh, Mamma, don't be so . . . so cynical. Of course he was genuine.' Rita giggled again. 'Honestly, Mamma, what man could possibly want to be seen in a pub with a girl dressed in ratty old clothes with grease on her face and sweaty hair?'

'Roberto wouldn't mind,' Louise said softly.

'Roberto doesn't count,' said Rita firmly. 'He's known me since I had droopy drawers and a face smothered in jam.'

There was a long silence and Rita suddenly had an awful feeling she knew where this was about to go.

Louise looked at her and frowned. 'You don't love my Roberto?'

This was dangerous ground, and Rita knew she had to tread carefully. 'I love him as a brother, Mamma,' she said softly in Italian. 'And I miss him as a brother.'

The tears sprang to Louise's eyes and she hastily wiped them away with her apron. 'You know Papa and I have always wished for you and Roberto to be married? Can you not love him just a little?'

Rita took her hand across the table. 'I'm sorry, Mamma. Perhaps when he comes home and we're both a bit older things might change. But for now . . . Well, for now it's best to keep things simple.'

Louise considered this and then nodded. 'You are right,' she said. 'Both of you are too young to make such decisions now. After the war it will be different. Roberto will come home and you will know then that you are right for each other.' She nodded as if to confirm this. 'Then everything will be just as it should be – you'll see.'

Rita kept her thoughts to herself as Louise returned to her cooking.

'We have cabbage, parsnip and potato cakes tonight. I'm saving everything else for tomorrow.' She fell silent and dipped her chin. 'Tino loved my potato cakes,' she said unsteadily. '*Mamma mia*, how I miss him.'

Rita hurried to her side, saw the tears spilling down her face and took her in her arms. 'I miss him too,' she said softly. 'Come, Mamma, don't upset yourself.'

Louise gave her a hug and kissed her cheek. 'You are such a good girl, Rita,' she murmured through her tears. 'I thank God every day that you are with me in these terrible times, for I don't know what I'd do without you.'

Ron was swimming against the tide of darkness which seemed determined to ensnare him and pull him into its clutches. He could hear the murmur of voices, the soft squeak of shoes on a polished floor and the rustle of clothing. As he struggled to emerge from this sea of black he caught the tang of disinfectant and the unmistakable smell of hospital.

He shot out of the clinging darkness and opened his eyes. He hated hospitals. He had to get out of here.

'Granddad, lie still.'

He paused in the act of trying to throw off the restricting sheet and blankets. 'Anne?' he asked, bewildered by his surroundings and the fact that he couldn't see her properly.

'It's all right,' she said softly. 'You've had a nasty bump on the head and the doctors want you to stay in overnight.'

His senses cleared a little and he became aware of the tightness in his chest and the awful pounding in his head. 'I'm fine,' he rumbled. 'Help me get out of here.'

'You are not going anywhere until I give you permission.'

Ron looked up at the stern face of the middle-aged woman who loomed over him in pristine blue and starched white. 'I'll be going whether you like it or not,' he retorted, struggling to breathe and deal with the pain in his head at the same time.

The heavily starched wings on her cap seemed to stiffen further at his impudence. 'I'm in charge of this hospital, Mr Reilly. You will do as I say.' She forcibly tucked in the sheet and blankets, making it impossible for him to move.

'Sour-faced old baggage,' he muttered with a glower.

'Sticks and stones, Mr Reilly. Sticks and stones.' With that, she rammed a mask over his face, checked the dials on the oxygen tank and then marched purposefully back to the other end of the ward.

He ripped the mask away. 'Who the divil was that old battleaxe?' he rasped.

'Matron Billings,' said Anne, fighting back a giggle. 'She's a bit of a tartar, isn't she?' She reached for the mask and gently put it over his mouth and nose. 'I know you hate this, but it will help you breathe more easily.'

Ron's chest felt heavy, and his head was hurting so badly it was difficult to think. But Anne was right, blast her, his breathing did feel easier with this blessed thing on his face. 'What happened?' he asked, his voice muffled by the hated mask. 'Why am I in this godforsaken place?'

Anne told him about how he'd come home carrying the injured pilot and then hit his head as he dropped in a dead faint on the kitchen floor. 'You're quite the hero, Grandpa,' she said fondly as she took his hand. 'That young pilot has you to thank for saving his life.'

'The boy's here too?'

She nodded. 'In another ward. He's broken his leg in three places and lost a lot of blood, but he's young and strong and will pull through.' Her expression grew solemn. 'Grandpa, the doctor thinks you may have pneumonia. It could be a while before you can come home again. Please be good and do as they ask.'

Ron looked at her over the mask, and was about to tell her not to treat him like a child when he had an awful thought. He ripped the mask from his face and grabbed her hand. 'The pheasants and duck,' he rasped, 'and the stuff in the shed.'

'I was wondering when you were going to remember,' she replied with a soft smile as she rescued the mask and put it back over his face. 'It was a close-run thing. Dad shut Harvey in the shed so his barking would keep everyone out of there, and he'd only just finished hiding everything else when the ambulance and police arrived.'

Ron's heart was thudding. 'Police?' he managed.

Anne nodded and patted his hand. 'It's all right. It was Sergeant Williams, and he was only there because of the downed pilot.' She eyed him sternly. 'But he did take Dad aside and asked him if he knew anything about ducks. It seems Lord Cliffe has made a complaint about someone poaching from his pond.'

Ron feigned ignorance. 'Harvey caught that duck on his own. I have no idea where he got it.'

'Of course you don't.' She grinned. 'I don't know, Grandpa. Mum's only been gone a matter of hours and look where we are. Let's hope there won't be any more dramatics before she gets back.'

Ron closed his eyes. It was a good thing Jim had

been quick off the mark, but those cigarettes and bottles of drink would have to be moved – and soon. He squirmed against the tight bindings of sheet and blanket and wrestled to free himself of the mask. 'Tell your father I need to see him,' he said urgently. 'And it has to be tonight.'

'Visiting hour is almost over. It will have to wait until tomorrow.'

He grabbed her hand. 'Tell him to move the stuff from the shed. Rosie will put it in her cellar for me. She's done it before.'

'He's already started on that,' she said. 'Honestly, Grandpa, is it worth it for all the trouble it causes?'

Ron was too weary and in too much pain to reply, but he would have told her that it was – for the excitement of putting one over on Sergeant Williams and Lord Cliffe and, more to the point, for the money that contraband would bring in.

Chapter Eight

Rita had stayed at Louise's as she usually did when their nights off coincided, and she had spent it restlessly in Roberto's bedroom, fretting over her application and Louise's reaction to it.

She lay in the comfortable bed in almost total darkness – it was still very early and the sun had yet to rise and penetrate the thick blackout curtains – and tried not to think where Roberto and Tino might be at this moment. There had been so many rumours, but no one seemed to really know or care where they had been sent. And that made her very sad.

She could just make out the bulk of the wardrobe and the heavy chest of drawers where Louise had carefully tidied all of Roberto's clothes away, and knew, without being able to see, that his shaving kit and hairbrush still stood on the top of the chest, and his dressing gown hung from the back of the door. They were stark reminders that he'd been snatched away without even these most basic personal possessions, and it made her angry to think of how badly he and Papa had been treated.

The door creaked open and light flooded in from

the gas lamps in the main room as Louise stepped over the threshold. 'Happy birthday, Rita. Time to get up and open your presents.'

She swung out of bed and returned Louise's hug. 'Gosh, I don't feel another year older,' she said, doing her best to dispel the weariness with a bright smile.

'You don't look it either,' replied Louise, running her fingers through the tangled mop of Rita's hair. 'Come on, hurry and get washed and dressed. I've made a special breakfast, and there's a pile of presents waiting in the other room.'

Rita sniffed the air. 'Can I smell bacon?'

Louise smiled. 'You can – and that's not all. Hurry up.'

Rita cleaned her teeth and washed in the kitchen sink then hurriedly got dressed in a clean shirt, sweater and dungarees. The delicious aroma of frying bacon made her mouth water as she tugged on thick socks and ran a brush through her hair. The weariness had fled, and she felt ready for her special day as she excitedly began to open her presents.

There was a lovely warm sweater in the softest moss green from Louise, a pretty winceyette night-dress from Peggy, and a pair of beautiful leather gloves from her father accompanied by a letter and a silky scarf. 'My goodness,' she breathed. 'I will look smart.'

'Only if you don't wear the sweater and gloves

on that bike of yours,' said Louise. 'I spent too long knitting that to have it ruined with oil.'

Rita gave her a huge hug. 'Thanks, Mamma. It's beautiful and I shall take enormous care of everything, I promise.'

'There is one more gift,' said Louise, taking a neat package out of the table drawer. 'Papa Tino saw them months ago and he and Roberto agreed they would be perfect for this very special birthday.'

Rita carefully undid the lovely red ribbon and opened the box. 'Oh,' she breathed. 'How lovely. How simply . . .' She could feel the onset of tears as she took the pearl earrings out of the box. 'They're perfect, Mamma,' she sighed, holding them to her ears to get the effect in the mirror on the wall, 'but Papa Tino shouldn't have spent so much.'

'It was no matter to Tino,' said Louise. 'You are his little girl, and he wanted you to have something to mark your journey into womanhood.'

'I'll have to get my ears pierced,' Rita replied, looking this way and that and admiring her reflection in the spotted glass.

'I can do that tonight,' said Louise. 'I have some simple gold rings you can wear until the holes heal. My daughters used them when I did theirs.'

Rita wasn't at all sure if she wanted Louise sticking a hot needle through her earlobes, but she would just have to grin and bear it if she wanted to wear those gorgeous earrings. She carefully put them back in their nest of cotton and closed the box.

'All the excitement has made me ravenous, Mamma. Where's that breakfast you promised?'

Louise carefully took the two plates out of the warming section of the range, and proudly placed them on the table.

Rita gasped at the sight of half a sausage, a rasher of bacon, fried bread and – wonders of wonders – a beautiful golden egg. 'Where on earth did you manage to get this lot?' she breathed. 'It must have taken all your coupons and cost half a week's wage.'

Louise sat down and picked up her knife and fork. 'That's for me to know,' she said smiling back. 'It's worth it just to see you smile, and we both deserve a treat now and then.'

'Thank you, Mamma,' Rita said softly.

'Eat,' she ordered, waving her fork at her and sniffing back her tears. 'It's getting cold.'

Several minutes later their plates were empty and Rita was mopping up the last of her delicious breakfast with a hunk of bread. She couldn't remember the last time she'd had such a meal, and was feeling pleasantly full and rather sleepy.

'You must go,' said Louise, as she cleared the plates. 'It's getting late. I'll see you and May back here at five sharp.'

Rita struggled into her heavy boots and tied the laces before slipping on her coat. 'I'll take the bike so I can get there and back quicker. I've got enough petrol.'

'You be careful. Now go, and leave me to prepare our special supper before I leave for work.'

Rita kissed her goodbye, ran down the back stairs and quickly got the motorbike out of the garage. There were no letters in the box below the slit in the door, but then it was hours before the postman was due to deliver. Aware of how early it was, and that most sensible people would still be tucked up in bed, she pushed the bike to the end of the road before starting it.

As she rode through the twilight of the quiet streets she experienced a rush of hope and excitement. She was eighteen at last, and the only thing that would make this day even more perfect than it already was, was a letter from the WAAFs telling her they wanted her to join them.

Setting aside all the doubts that had plagued her ever since she'd filled in that form, she breathed in the cold December air and concentrated on the deep, satisfying rumble of the Norton's engine, and the sense of power it always gave her to be in command of such a machine.

The factory was a hive of industry despite the hour, with the night shift leaving and the early shift drifting in. May was already busy welding and gave her a wave in greeting. 'Happy birthday,' she shouted above the noise. 'We'll catch up during the break.'

Rita grinned back and nodded. She hung her gas mask box and coat on her hook and placed her packet of sandwiches and flask of tea on her bench. Reaching for the protective leather apron, she slipped it over her head and began to tie it round her waist.

'Good morning, Rita.' Vi Charlton emerged from the small canteen where she worked as a cook, and was pulling on her coat and scarf. She gave a vast yawn. 'I'm ready for me bed, and that's a fact. I hate working nights.'

Rita stifled her own yawn. 'I'm not too fond of these early starts either, but someone's got to do it.'

Vi placed a beret neatly over her glossy hair. 'I saw you talking to Chuck Howard yesterday,' she said, her eyes glinting with curiosity. 'Are you stepping out with him?'

Rita laughed. 'He was only asking about the bike, Vi.'

Vi regarded her evenly. 'You're a pretty girl, Rita. There's no harm in having a bit of fun.' She came closer so those nearby couldn't overhear. 'Did he ask you out?'

'Just for a drink, but I turned him down.'

'But why?'

Rita shrugged. 'I'd come straight from work and looked a fright.' She grinned back at Vi. 'It was a good thing I did turn him down,' she confided. 'You should have heard Louise hit the roof when I told her.'

Vi pulled on knitted gloves and wound the scarf more tightly about her throat. 'You're young and free and should make your own choices,' she said flatly. 'Louise should realise that and not keep you tied to her apron strings.'

Rita felt a jolt of defensiveness. 'She's only looking out for me, Vi.'

'Is she?' Vi arched a finely plucked brow. 'Or is she looking out for herself now she's only got you to rely on?'

Rita bristled. 'That's unfair, Vi. She's been like a mother to me and we rely on each other.'

Vi gave a deep sigh. 'I know, and I didn't mean to cause offence, but you have a life to live, Rita – and it seems to me you're wasting it by hiding away with Louise.'

'I think you've said enough,' warned Rita.

Vi's pretty eyes clouded. 'Yes, I probably have. But think about what I've said, Rita. You'll thank me for it in the end.' With that, she hitched her gas mask box and handbag over her shoulder and stepped out into the dawn.

Rita was seething as she snatched up the visor and put it over her head until it settled firmly, and then donned the heavy gloves. Vi had a cheek, she thought. It was all very well for her – she had nobody to worry about but herself since her children had been evacuated. And as for suggesting Louise was holding her back – well, that was just ridiculous.

She picked up the blowtorch, examined the job in hand and set to work.

It was breaktime and Rita and May had found a relatively quiet corner to eat their sandwiches. 'Happy birthday, Rita,' muttered May through a mouthful of bread and Spam. 'I've got you a present, but I'm saving it until tonight.'

'You didn't have to get me anything,' Rita protested.

May shrugged. 'I wanted to, and anyway, this could be the last birthday we'll share until this war's over, so why not make it special?' She regarded Rita from beneath her heavy blonde fringe. 'What's Louise doing for tea tonight? I love her cooking.'

'I don't know.' Rita chuckled. 'She's keeping it a secret.' She went on to tell her friend about her lovely presents. 'Louise promised to pierce my ears for me, but I'm not sure I'm brave enough.' She eyed May's earlobes where tiny gold studs glistened. 'Does it hurt very much?'

'Yeah, a bit at first, but you soon get over it.'

'Smith. In my office, please.'

Rita looked up at Major Patricia and quailed. What on earth had she done wrong now? She set aside her sandwich and, with a grimace at May, hastened to follow the striding figure into the office.

'Shut the door.'

Rita shut the door and waited nervously as the

older woman reached for some papers on her desk.

'I have had a letter from the Air Force Administrators,' she said without preamble. 'They have asked for a reference.'

Rita swallowed as excitement fluttered in her midriff. 'For me?' she managed.

'I'd hardly be discussing this with you if it wasn't,' the Major replied dryly. She eyed Rita sternly. 'Are you unhappy here, Smith?'

'Not at all,' she stammered, 'it's just that I . . . I . . .'

'Want something more exciting than welding,' the other woman finished for her. She clasped her hands behind her back and stuck out her chest. She looked formidable. 'You have an important posting here, Smith. Not many young women are as efficient and skilled as you, and the RAF relies absolutely on their aircraft being fitted out to the highest standard.'

Rita really didn't know what to say.

'I see from your records that you are eighteen today and therefore entitled to sign up to any of the forces. But before I send this reference off, I want you to be absolutely sure you wish to join the WAAFs and not continue your sterling efforts here.'

Rita was quaking, but she realised that in a backhanded sort of way she'd been given enormous praise by this hard-to-please woman. 'Thank you, Major,' she managed, not daring to meet those gimlet eyes. 'I have enjoyed working here, but I'm quite sure about joining the WAAFs. It's something I've wanted to do ever since war was declared.'

'I see.' The Major's expression softened as she eyed her. 'You will be missed,' she said. 'It's rare to find a girl with such a feel for working in this environment, and you can be assured that your reference from me will be positive.'

'Thank you, Major.'

'Off you go, Smith, and remember to give me as much warning as possible before you leave. I'll need to fill your placement.'

'How long do you think I'll have to wait to hear from them?'

'I have no idea, but I doubt it will be long.' She dismissed her with a wave of her hand and Rita fled the office.

'What did she want?' May was preparing to get back to work, but her curiosity had been too great to ignore.

Rita told her. 'They're obviously processing my application, May,' she breathed, 'and she's promised to give me a good reference.' She hesitated.

'But?' May coaxed.

'But now the waiting will be even harder – and how do I tell Louise?'

'I'd cross that bridge when you come to it,' said May. She pulled the visor over her head and gave her friend a wink. 'You'll think of something.'

Rita slowly donned her protective garments, her thoughts in a whirl, the excitement making it hard to concentrate on the job in hand. This was turning out to be quite a birthday, and she just prayed that nothing would spoil it.

Ron was not enjoying hospital, and even though he was wise enough to realise it was the best place for him, he couldn't wait to escape. His chest felt tight and his breath rattled, but at least the pills had put a stop to his headache, and the fears about pneumonia had turned out to be a false alarm. The doctor had assured him he wasn't suffering from anything more than a nasty chill and a couple of pulled muscles in his chest.

As for Matron Billings, she was a battleaxe who seemed determined to truss him as tightly as she could in this damned bed, her beady eye settling on him every time she came into the ward.

He lay there tugging at the sheet and blankets in a desperate attempt to free himself, when he caught the welcome sight of his granddaughter coming through the doors with the other visitors. 'Help me loosen these,' he mumbled through the oxygen mask.

Anne obliged, kissed his cheek and sat down. 'You're obviously feeling better.' She shot him a smile. 'These will probably cheer you up further.' She placed the evening paper on the bed, along with the latest copy of the *Field* – a specialist magazine for the hunting, shooting and fishing brigade, to which Ron had always subscribed.

'To be sure, and you're a good girl, so you are,' he muttered. 'They'll help to pass the time away. How's Harvey?'

'Feeling sorry for himself,' Anne replied dryly. 'We couldn't leave him downstairs all night because he just howled and kept everyone awake. Now he's lying on the front doormat and refuses to move.'

'Bring him in to visit. That'll settle him down.'

'Don't be daft, Grandpa. They won't let dogs in here.'

He thought about it for a moment and then reluctantly nodded. 'Matron Billings doesn't like her patients much – I dread to think what she'd make of Harvey.'

Anne giggled. 'We had a telephone call from Mum, by the way. She's arrived safely in Somerset, and the boys are well and growing like weeds. She sounded very happy, so we didn't tell her about your adventures.'

'Probably best. Peggy worries too much as it is.' He eyed his lovely granddaughter and noticed how well she looked. 'I don't need to ask how you are, me darlin,' he muttered. 'You're positively blooming.'

'It's the walk to the hospital,' she said lightly. 'The wind is coming off the sea today and it's bitterly cold.' She looked up as the ward door opened. 'I'll be getting home if you don't mind, Grandpa,' she said, gathering her things together. 'Mrs Finch is in charge of tea and will probably need a hand.'

'But you've only just got here,' he protested. 'The

days are long enough, and visiting time is the only chance to have a decent conversation.'

She kissed his cheek. 'You have another visitor,' she said softly.

He followed her gaze. 'Rosie,' he muttered, desperately plucking at the oxygen mask and checking that his pyjama jacket was buttoned properly. 'Bejesus, Anne. Don't let her see me like this.'

'She's already seen you, Grandpa. Be still, enjoy the visit and I'll come in tomorrow.'

Ron lay helplessly in the bed as Anne greeted Rosie and rushed off. He watched the light of his life sashay down the ward, noted how every man's eyes followed her and felt a swell of pride that he was the one she was visiting. But he felt old and decrepit, thoroughly useless, and wished suddenly that she hadn't come.

'Hello, Ron,' she said with a beaming smile. 'You're quite the hero by all accounts. Thought I'd better come in and see how you're doing.'

Ron took off the hated mask. 'I'm fine,' he said.

As if unaware of the admiring glances of every man in the ward, Rosie slipped out of her glamorous fox fur coat to reveal a pencil-slim skirt and frilly white blouse which set off her admirable figure. Taking off her headscarf, she shook out her platinum blonde curls and perched on the chair beside the bed. With her long, shapely legs crossed at the ankle, she looked the picture of elegance.

'To be sure, Rosie, ye're a sight for sore eyes,' he wheezed.

'Put the mask back on,' she said softly, reaching for it and gently placing it back over his face. 'There, that's better. Now you can breathe properly.'

'I feel such an auld fool,' he muttered.

'You're a very brave man,' she replied firmly. 'That boy owes you his life, and I want you to promise me you'll behave yourself and get well quickly.' She leaned her elbows on the bed, resting her chin on her hands. 'I've missed not having you about the place helping with the barrels and bottles – and afternoon tea isn't the same without you.'

Ron caught her perfume and a glimpse of soft, rounded flesh amid the ruffles of her blouse and had to tear his gaze away. Her words had warmed him enough and he was in danger of making a complete fool of himself.

'I'll be back before you know it,' he replied. Then he caught sight of the big clock above the door. 'It's after six. Shouldn't you be opening the pub?'

Rosie took off her gloves and kept her gaze lowered as she smoothed them onto her lap. 'Tommy Findlay came round, so I left him in charge for an hour.'

Tommy Findlay was the sort of man Ron disliked intensely. He was in his fifties, wore sharp suits, oiled his hair and considered himself to be a lady's man – and the worst part of it was that the stupid women fell for his smooth talk. 'I didn't realise

Findlay was back in Cliffehaven – or that you knew him well enough to trust him behind your bar,' he said gruffly.

'We go back a long way,' she said dismissively. 'And it's only for an hour.'

Ron saw how she avoided looking at him, and he experienced a sinking feeling in his stomach. 'Well, Rosie,' he said, trying to shift himself up the pillows, 'you know your business better than me – but I wouldn't trust him.'

'He has his faults,' she admitted. 'But an hour behind the bar won't do much harm.' She must have seen the sudden panic in Ron's eyes, for she leaned forward and patted his hand. 'I've locked the cellar door,' she said quietly. 'I don't trust him that much.'

Ron gave a deep sigh of relief and decided he'd better say no more – it would only antagonise her and spoil her visit.

'Don't fret,' she murmured. 'It's all quite safe, and Jim promised to shift it on as soon as he can.' She shot him a cheeky grin. 'Old habits die hard, eh? I remember when you used to come back from your fishing trips with bottles of whisky and French brandy.'

Ron glanced swiftly round. 'Shhh!' he hissed. 'There's no need to let the whole of Cliffehaven into our business.'

Rosie giggled and began to delve into her handbag. 'I brought a drop of something to keep out the cold,' she said. Using her body as a shield, she showed him the small bottle of brandy. 'I'll put it in here, shall I?' She reached to open the locker beside his bed.

'Give it here,' he whispered urgently. 'Matron searches the lockers.' He took a crafty nip and swiftly buried it down his pyjama trousers.

'It'll get a bit warm down there,' she murmured, laughter tugging at her mouth and sparkling in her eyes. 'Do you want me to bring some ice with me on the next visit?'

Ron actually blushed and was, for once, glad the mask hid his face. 'To be sure, Rosie girl, you're a tonic, and if I wasn't stuck in this bed, I'd dance you all over the ward, so I would.'

'I think you'd better leave the dancing a while yet,' she giggled. 'I don't think Matron would approve at all.'

He gazed into her lovely face and wished that he had the gift of the gab like Tommy Findlay. 'How long have you known Tommy?' he asked hesitantly.

'A long time,' she said evasively. 'Look, Ron, I didn't come here to talk about Tommy. I want to hear all about what happened the other night. The local paper are calling you a hero.'

Ron shrugged as if such praise was an everyday occurrence – but he was astute enough to realise that Tommy Findlay would never be a hero, and this was the moment to prove to Rosie that there was far more to Ronan Reilly than what she could see confined in this damned bed. 'Well now,' he began. 'Me and Harvey were up in the hills and . . .'

Rita's ears still felt sore where Louise had plunged the hot needle through the lobes, but the little gold hoops glittered in the lamplight and showed off May's pretty jewelled haircombs to a treat. She thought they made her look very sophisticated, and was rather disappointed that she wasn't going out on the town tonight to show them off. It was also a bit of a shame about the stench of Dettol which Louise had used rather too liberally to clean the punctures, but she supposed that would soon fade.

Louise had excelled herself tonight. The home-made ravioli had been stuffed with minced meat, onions and garlic and was as light as a feather, and the rich tomato sauce was heavenly. Accompanying this treat was a bottle of Papa Tino's rough red wine, home-made bread, and a dish of pickled artichoke hearts. May and Rita ate in awed silence, savouring each wondrous, melting mouthful until their plates were clean.

'Thank you, Mamma,' Rita sighed as she sat back and rubbed her full stomach. 'That has to be the best meal we've had for months.'

May swiped bread over the last of the sauce on her plate and chewed happily. 'I wish my mum could cook like you,' she said. 'Rita doesn't know how lucky she is.'

Louise flushed with pleasure as she cleared the

plates. 'We don't eat like this every day,' she said, 'but I'm glad you enjoyed it.' She carefully poured a little more wine into the glasses. 'I would like to make a toast,' she said quietly. 'To Rita on her birthday, and to Tino, Roberto and Jack, who are not here to celebrate with us.'

They raised their glasses and sipped in silence, each with their own thoughts.

'It's a shame you have to be on fire-watch tonight,' murmured Louise. 'We might have gone to the pictures or something.'

'We'll do that another night,' said Rita, glancing at the clock. 'I'm sorry, Mamma, but we've got to go. The fire officer is a stickler for timekeeping.' She took out the precious jewelled combs and tucked them safely into Louise's capacious handbag.

'I've made sandwiches and a flask of tea,' said Louise, rising to fetch them, 'and found a couple of scarves in Roberto's cupboard to give you a bit of added warmth.'

Rita and May reluctantly reached for the heavy-duty overcoats the fire service had provided along with a tin hat, sturdy trousers and jacket. It wasn't the most flattering of uniforms and threatened to swamp them, but at least she and May were kept nice and warm during the long, cold nights.

'You both look like little girls playing dress-up in your father's clothes,' said Louise, a ghost of a smile touching her lips as she wound the knitted scarves tightly round their necks. 'Please be careful, girls.'

'We will, Mamma.' Rita gave her a hug and a kiss. 'And if the siren goes, you're to promise to go to the shelter.'

Louise kissed them both. 'Of course I will, and I'll put your special earrings in my handbag to keep them safe. Now run along.'

Rita and May left the warm, cosy room for the dark stairs and the freezing wind that blew down the alleyway. They opened the garage door, which no longer screeched, thanks to the American's judicious oiling of the runners, and wheeled their motorbikes into the lane.

Having padlocked the doors, Rita pulled on her helmet, wincing as it caught the earrings and tugged at her earlobes. 'I don't know that I'll ever get used to these,' she muttered.

'You will,' said May, swinging her leg over the BSA's saddle. 'They won't be tender for long, and you'll soon not even notice them.'

Rita climbed onto the Norton, pulled on her gloves and adjusted her goggles. She shot May a beaming grin as they kicked their bikes into life and headed towards the fire station. The great bonus of working for the fire service was the extra ration of fuel they were allotted for their bikes so they could get to their posts easily – and that more than made up for the often tedious, cold and lonely watches they kept during the long nights.

The chief fire officer, John Hicks, was already waiting for them as they drew up outside the fire station. He was a handsome, well-built young man who had only recently returned from his honeymoon. Rita had learned that he'd been badly injured during the Dunkirk rescue mission, and although he still walked with a limp, he showed no sign of letting his injuries hamper his responsibilities. He was a tough, no-nonsense man, used to being obeyed – but he was also good-humoured and fair, and that made him popular amongst the men and women who worked under him.

'Happy birthday, Rita,' he said, glancing at his watch. 'Glad to see you and May are on time for once.' He shot them a grin. 'Right, you two little hooligans, I need you up on the cliffs with Gladys. Word is we're in for a noisy night, so keep your radio on and your eyes peeled.'

'How come we always get to be up there?' asked Rita.

'Because you've got transport, and I can't spare a truck to take anyone else that far.' He dug his hand in his pocket and pulled out a small paper bag. 'Here you go, Rita. These should help keep you all warm. Now be off with you.'

Rita's eyes widened as she saw the large white peppermints – they were the really strong sort, and would certainly warm their mouths and throats if nothing else. 'Thanks, ever so,' she murmured as she stuffed the paper bag into her pocket and climbed back onto the Norton.

'You take care up there,' he replied.

Rita and May grinned at one another as they kicked their bikes into life. It was a fairly lengthy ride up to their watching post, and although the headlights had been heavily masked, they knew the way so well it didn't much matter how fast they went.

'See you there,' Rita shouted above the roar of the engines, and sent the bike hurtling along the street. Looking over her shoulder, she could see May only feet behind her. Perhaps, tonight, they would break the ten-minute record they'd set the previous week.

The rough terrain of the hills slowed them both down as they passed the heavily sandbagged gun emplacements along the cliffs. The soldiers manning them were sneaking crafty fags which would get them into trouble if their commanding officer caught them. A fag end could be seen glowing for miles. The girls waved back at the men's cheerful shouts of encouragement and headed for the promontory of white cliffs which would give them the best view over the town.

A circle of sandbags was their only protection against the bitter wind that was coming off the sea, and they hurried through the narrow gap into the relative warmth and comfort of hard benches, kerosene lantern, and a battered oil heater.

'Thank goodness you've arrived,' said Gladys Albright, who was trying to knit in the dubious light of the lantern. 'I was getting a bit fed up with my own company.'

Rita and May liked Gladys. She was a widow in her late forties and plump, with an endless supply of biscuits, gossip and humorous, rather risqué stories, and was the perfect companion on a night like this.

'How did you get up here?' asked May. 'I didn't see your bicycle.'

'Getting a bit too old and well padded for cycling up these hills, dear,' replied Gladys, setting her tin helmet at a less raffish angle. 'I got a lift from one of the army boys manning the guns further along.' She smiled and abandoned her knitting. 'Lovely young chap. Might do for one of you young things. He's not married and has his own little flat, you know, and he's just about the right age to be thinking of settling down.'

'How on earth do you find all these things out, Gladys?' asked Rita.

'I ask,' she replied happily. 'There's nothing like a friendly chat to get all sorts of things out of people. My poor Bert was never one for gossip, and I realised pretty quick that if I wanted to know anything I'd have to find out for myself.'

Rita and May set their gas mask boxes aside, took off their goggles and helmets and replaced them with tin hats. 'I shouldn't think any man would fancy either of us looking like this,' said May. 'These tin hats are hardly flattering.'

Gladys laughed. 'It's not the hats they're interested in,' she replied. 'Bert took one look at my legs and that was that.'

Their conversation was cut short by the roar of several squadrons of RAF planes heading across the Channel. 'It looks like Jerry's on the move,' muttered Gladys. 'I've checked the stirrup pump is working, but we've only two buckets of water and I doubt it will be much use if this place goes up in flames.'

Rita and May settled down within the lee of the sandbags, and Rita passed the mints round. There was silence as they dealt with the strength of the peppermint, which seemed to burn through their tongues. She felt pleasantly sated after that lovely tea and the thought of snuggling down for a bit of a sleep was enticing – but it was cold and blustery despite the sandbags and the old heater, which wasn't making a jot of difference.

She looked up at the sky and the numberless twinkling stars. There was a bomber's moon tonight, and it cast a golden glow over the town, gilding rooftops and chimneys, the shadows beneath the trees and in the hollows of the hills made deeper still where it couldn't reach.

May was excitedly telling Gladys about the training she would be starting in two days' time, and Rita felt a pang of sadness. Her best friend was already prepared for leaving her behind, her mind set on the excitement of starting a new life, her gaze settled on a very different future to the one they'd thought they'd share.

'What about you, dear?' said Gladys. 'Have you had confirmation about the Dispatch Riders' Unit?'

Rita shook her head. 'It's probably a bit soon yet,' she replied, 'and there's no guarantee they'll take me on.'

'Never you mind, dear,' Gladys said comfortably. 'If they turn you down, you could always apply for a full-time paid post with the fire service. John Hicks was only talking about it the other day, and with so many raids over the town, he's desperately short of good drivers.' She cocked her head. 'I assume you can drive?'

'I used to drive cars in and out of the garage, but I've never really learned properly.' Rita shifted on the uncomfortable bench and tucked her hands under her armpits to try and garner a bit more warmth.

'I don't suppose it would matter much,' said Gladys. 'You could learn on the job, as they say and . . .'

The wailing siren had them on their feet even before it reached its highest pitch. Gladys killed the lights from the lantern and heater, and wound the radio into life, settling the earphones over her head and twiddling the knobs so she could get the best reception. Rita grabbed the night-sight binoculars and leaned on the sandbags next to May to begin a trawl of the skies as yet more RAF planes hurried to fend off the attack.

The searchlights were going on all over town, along the seafront and the crests of the surrounding hills. They were pale at first, growing stronger into blinding blue-white, reaching into the sky, converging on the watery horizon like giant illuminated fingers.

The radio crackled into life. 'Incoming at six o'clock,' came a distorted voice from the Observer Corps bunker, which was situated some distance away on another cliff. 'Enemy approaching. Enemy approaching.'

They didn't need the warning; they could see and hear for themselves. The black swarm on the horizon was still out of range of the big guns, but it thundered ominously nearer, the heavy-bellied drone of the bombers accompanied by the lighter buzz of the fighter planes echoing across the water, filling the air with their menace.

Then, high up and coming in fast, was a single enemy plane – the leader of the pack, the bellwether leading his demonic flock towards their target. The night sky was suddenly rent with blinding blue stars that illuminated the huddled town beneath. Swaying, drifting, dancing across one another, these tiny chandeliers were marking the path for those that followed.

The earth shook as the big guns boomed, and within seconds there were bursts of bright white stars punching holes in the night sky, their explosions rolling over the water in waves, the echoes repeated in every cliff and bay until distance faded them.

The searchlights converged on the lone enemy plane, catching it like a moth in their beams as it twisted and writhed to escape. The guns boomed and rattled, making the very skies tremble as tracer bullets stitched through the blackness.

And then the searchlight beams lost their target.

As Rita and May searched the skies, a bright red flame blossomed beneath the searchlights, growing into a spiralling comet that plunged into the sea and was extinguished forever.

Rita shivered as the vibration of those guns and the rumble of the fast-approaching enemy planes trembled in the sandbags and the ground beneath her feet. Her ears rang with it as the ominous black swarm came towards the headland, the guns boomed and the Spitfires became embroiled in desperate dogfights. The sheer number of planes was daunting, and now they seemed to stretch right across the town, blacking out the moon and the stars, casting their evil shadow over everything.

Rita felt quite helpless as she watched the blizzard of white explosions follow the enemy planes, the arcs of red tracer bullets climbing towards their targets, the blossom of pom-poms lighting up the sky above the town as shrapnel from the guns whistled through the air.

She ducked her head, plastering herself tightly against the wall of sandbags as shrapnel thudded all around them. She was sweating despite the cold, her ears were still ringing, her hands shaking as she put the special binoculars to her eyes and scanned the town below her. This was no time for fear, no time to forget the important job she was here to do, for the people of Cliffehaven depended upon her staying alert.

She breathed a sigh of relief. There were no fires – not yet. It seemed Cliffehaven was not to be their main target tonight. But they would return from their raid and dump the last of their deadly arsenal over the town so they could outrun the RAF boys. It was going to be a long night.

Chapter Nine

'I'll not be pushed about in that t'ing,' protested Ron. 'I'm no cripple.'

'You will do as I say, Mr Reilly.' Matron Billings shoved the wheelchair against the back of Ron's legs, forcing him into the seat. Before he could complain or catch his breath, he found himself being wheeled out of the air-raid shelter and into the dawn at determined speed, up the ramps and along the endless hospital corridors.

Ron had to admit it was quite fun – he hadn't moved this fast in years – but it was a bit daunting to be crashed through the swing doors of the ward in such a way. 'Bejesus, woman,' he snarled. 'Is it me legs you'll be wanting to damage now?'

'Be quiet, Mr Reilly, and get into bed.' A strong hand grabbed his arm and virtually lifted him out of the chair. She quickly divested him of the hospital dressing gown and was about to hang it on the hook by the bed when something in the pocket clanked against the corner of the bedside locker. 'What have you hidden in here?' Her tone was ominous.

'Nothing to do with you,' said Ron, making a grab for it.

She held it out of his reach, her hand slipping into the pocket. She pulled out the almost empty bottle of brandy, her narrowed grey eyes regarding it with distaste. 'Any more of that sort of thing and I'll have you put on the isolation ward where visitors are barred,' she said coldly.

'Anyone would think this was a prison,' muttered Ron.

Matron ignored him as she handed the bottle to one of the nurses. 'Pour it down the sink,' she ordered.

'That's good expensive brandy,' Ron protested.

'Get into bed, Mr Reilly.' Her tone brooked no argument.

Ron slumped on the bed and glared up at her. She was worse than any of the hard-faced nuns who'd taught him at the convent school back in Ireland. 'I thought nurses were supposed to be angels of mercy,' he muttered. 'To be sure, ye're the devil's handmaiden.'

'And you're the worst patient I've ever had to deal with.' Matron Billings' expression was stony as she finished searching his locker and then deftly imprisoned him with tightly tucked blankets and sheet and placed the oxygen mask over his face. 'Go to sleep,' she ordered.

Ron grimaced at her retreating figure and shook his fist.

'Go to sleep, Mr Reilly, and stop behaving like a five-year-old.'

Matron hadn't even looked at him on her way out of the ward, and Ron gaped in amazement at the swinging doors. 'The auld witch has eyes in the back of her head, so she does,' he muttered, ripping off the hated mask.

'You're not wrong there, mate,' said the man in the next bed. 'Proper tartar and no mistake.' He leaned on one elbow, ready for a bit of a chat. 'You should have heard what she said to me when I had the audacity to ask for another pillow. Blimey, I thought, it wasn't as if I were asking for a gold-plated chamber pot.'

Ron grunted in reply and tried to find a way of loosening the damn sheet and blankets. 'Where's a nurse when you need one?' he grumbled.

'They're on shift changeover,' the man replied. 'But you can guarantee that the minute you doze off one of them will wake you up to give you a sleeping pill.' He flopped back onto his pillows. 'I'll be glad to be going back to the tool factory next week, and that's a fact,' he said on a sigh. 'Anything's better than being stuck in here.'

Ron agreed wholeheartedly as he gave up trying to free himself and sank back into the pillows. He wished he had the strength to get out of this blasted bed and walk out of here, but just the effort of trying to free himself of the bedclothes had been enough to exhaust him.

Closing his eyes, he turned his thoughts to the cluttered basement at Beach View Boarding House where Harvey and all his precious possessions would be waiting for him. It would be wonderful to smell damp dog and gun-oil again; to put on his old poaching coat and boots and tramp about in the hills, free of Matron, the stench of disinfectant, and the cloying heat of this blessed hospital.

Ron realised he must have fallen asleep, for as he opened his eyes and caught sight of the clock above the doors, he was disconcerted to find he'd missed breakfast and elevenses. It was another hour until lunch and his throat felt parched.

He wriggled up the bed, hoping to catch a nurse's eye and charm her into getting him a cup of tea. But they seemed to be occupied with their charts and their gossip at the far end of the ward, so he had to make do with a glass of water from the jug on the bedside locker.

Ron lay there feeling sorry for himself as he idly watched the nurses tend to one of the more seriously injured patients. He could smell boiled cabbage and fish – not the most appetising offering for lunch, but at least the meal would fill in a bit of time.

He heaved a great sigh which only made him cough. The boredom was getting to him, and that was a fact. He'd read the newspaper and magazine Anne had brought in, had borrowed a book from the WVS lady who did her rounds of the wards once a day, found it not to his liking, and abandoned it. Visiting wasn't for ages yet, and the long day stretched before him without a glimmer of hope.

He was about to reach for the newspaper he'd read twice before when the doors opened to reveal an extremely elegant and attractive woman swathed in an ankle-length mink coat. Her fair hair curled away from her lovely face in what the women called 'victory rolls' to reveal pearl studs in her ears, and a pheasant feather wafted gaily from her nifty little hat as she spoke to one of the nurses.

'Blimey,' breathed the man in the next bed. 'She's a sight for sore eyes and no mistake. I wonder who she is.'

Ron still had an eye for a pretty woman, even though he was incarcerated in this bed with a mask over his face. He gazed at her appreciatively, taking in her slender legs, shapely ankles, and the way she seemed to glide down the ward in her high-heeled brown leather pumps. He watched in fascination as she stopped at each bed, exchanged a few smiling words and moved on. If Ron hadn't known better, he'd have thought she was visiting royalty.

'How do you do, Mr Cooper? I understand you are to be discharged tomorrow. Well done.'

She had reached the man in the next bed, and Ron could hear her well-modulated tone as she asked about his work and his family. It was the voice of a real lady, and her smile was warm and genuine – perhaps she was indeed royalty.

As she began to move away from the next bed, he quickly straightened his pyjama jacket and ditched the oxygen mask before smoothing his hands over his hair.

'Good morning, Mr Reilly,' she said, taking off her leather gloves to reveal sparkling diamonds as she offered him her hand and gave him a beaming smile. 'Sylvia Anstruther-Norton, but you must call me Sylvia.'

Ron wouldn't dream of doing such a thing. He cautiously took the elegant, soft hand in his great rough paw, and wondered if he was supposed to kiss it like the toffs did in the films.

But she rescued him from the dilemma by withdrawing her hand so she could unfasten her coat.

'Good morning,' he managed. She smelled lovely – like a garden of freesias, and her eyes were the colour of wild violets.

'I expect you're wondering what I'm doing here,' she began. She slipped the mink from her shoulders and let it pool round her as she sat on the edge of his bed. She was dressed in a beautifully cut heather-coloured tweed jacket and skirt, the collar of a crisp white blouse revealing three strings of pearls at her neck.

Ron's eyes widened. Women like her didn't perch on the bed of an old ruffian like him, but he was too dumbstruck to answer her.

She gave a little chuckle. 'I'm sorry, Mr Reilly. You obviously haven't a clue as to who I am. I'd better explain before that ghastly matron catches me here.'

'Aye, it would be wise,' he said, stifling his own

chuckle as his gaze shot down the ward to the door. Every man in the place was watching them and he felt horribly uncomfortable.

'You saved my son's life, Mr Reilly,' she said, her beautiful violet eyes misting with tears, 'and there are not words enough to express how very, very grateful I am.'

'You're the boy's mother? But you don't look old enough.'

Her laughter was soft and musical. 'Bless you, Mr Reilly. They told me you had the Irish gift of a silver tongue.'

He reddened. 'There's no need to thank me, Mrs Anstruther-Norton,' he said gruffly. 'I just happened to be in the right place at the right time.'

She pressed her warm, soft hand over his as it lay on the blanket. 'You carried my Christopher to safety, disregarding your own health and the dangers during that bombing raid.' She blinked rapidly to clear the onset of tears. 'My thanks seem meagre compared to what you did for me and my husband that night.'

He regarded her uneasily. He hated it when women cried – he never knew what to do or say. And this woman was like no other he'd ever met. He cleared his throat and awkwardly patted her hand. 'How's the boy doing? They won't let me visit him yet.'

She opened her handbag and pulled out a pristine handkerchief with the initial S embroidered in one corner, and delicately dabbed her nose and eyes. 'He's making a very good recovery, thanks to you,' she replied. 'The surgeon expects him to be up and about within a few weeks, and after some physio-therapy, he'll be as good as new.'

'That's good,' he murmured. 'I'm glad he's pulling through, and once I'm allowed out of this bed, I'll be going to see him.'

'He'll be delighted,' she replied softly. 'He asked me to find a nice juicy treat for your dog as soon as I settle in. Harvey, isn't it?' At his nod, she continued. 'We have dogs at home, and I think Christopher found Harvey such a comfort.'

'Aye, he's a good old dog, so he is, and he'll be glad of a bit of a treat, so he will.'

The swing doors crashed open, they both turned, and the atmosphere on the ward was suddenly elec-tric with alarmed anticipation.

'Oh, dear, she muttered. 'It looks as if we've been discovered.' She swiftly gripped his hand. 'Leave me to do the talking,' she said urgently. 'I know how to handle women like Matron Billings.'

Ron lay back on the pillows as Sylvia Anstruther-Norton stood to meet the woman who was determinedly marching towards them. This could be interesting.

'Lady Anstruther-Norton,' boomed Matron. 'You should have told me you wanted to visit the wards, and I would have escorted you.'

'My dear Matron,' replied Sylvia with a beaming

smile. 'I wouldn't dream of taking you away from your important schedule when I am quite capable of finding my way round your hospital.'

So, she *was* royalty, thought Ron – or as near as damn it – and Matron was clearly flustered. He settled back comfortably to enjoy the show.

'Of course you are,' said Matron, her hands tightly clasped at her waist, 'but these general wards are hardly suitable for . . .'

'For people like me?' The pheasant feather waved as she laughed. 'You're too kind to think of any discomfort I may encounter, Matron. But I assure you I am quite safe in Mr Reilly's delightful company.'

Matron threw Ron a glance of sheer venom. 'Mr Reilly and the others on this ward are not permitted visitors outside the appropriate times, Lady Anstruther-Norton.'

'Oh, dear,' Sylvia chuckled. 'How naughty of me to break the rules.' She placed her hand on Matron's arm. 'But I'm sure you understand that it was imperative I see Mr Reilly as soon as I could. After all,' she went on, 'he did save my son's life, and Lord James is frightfully grateful to you and your staff for looking after them both so well.'

Matron was clearly struggling to make up her mind what stance she should take in the face of this charming, titled lady who seemed to be getting the better of her. 'Of course,' she said with as much grace as she could muster. 'But Mr Reilly needs to rest, and I understand you have yet to arrange accommodation for your stay in Cliffehaven. May I suggest we retire to my office so we can discuss the most appropriate accommodation over coffee?'

Sylvia turned to Ron and winked. 'Are you tired, Mr Reilly?'

'To be sure, I've never felt more awake,' he replied and gave her a wink back – which elicited a furious glare from Matron. He decided to play the devil's advocate. 'If it's accommodation you'll be wanting, then my family has a boarding house and we've a spare room at the moment.'

'I don't think Lady Anstruther-Norton—'

'I'm sure it will be just perfect,' interrupted Sylvia. 'Thank you so much, Matron, for taking the time to come and see me. But you must be terribly busy, and Mr Reilly and I have several more things to discuss before I have to go and see Christopher again. Perhaps you could arrange for Mr Reilly and me to have coffee here?'

Matron went quite white. 'I'll see what can be arranged,' she stammered. 'But it's most irregular.'

'How very kind,' Sylvia murmured. 'Thank you so much.' She turned her back on the other woman and perched once more on Ron's bed as Matron snapped an order at one of the passing nurses for two cups of coffee.

'Tell me, Mr Reilly,' said Sylvia. 'What is the name of your family boarding house, and where can I find it?'

Ron looked into her eyes, saw the laughter there and tried not to crack up as he caught a glimpse of Matron hovering uncertainly nearby. 'Beach View is away along Camden Road to the left as you leave the hospital,' he said, his voice breaking. 'To be sure, 'tis not a palace, but it is a home. Me daughter-in-law's away at the moment, but me granddaughter and son will look after you, so they will.'

Matron was within earshot as she brought the coffee cups to the bed. 'I really don't think such an establishment . . .' she blustered.

Sylvia turned a beaming smile on her as she took the cups. 'Ah, coffee. How simply lovely. You will thank the nurse for me, won't you?'

Matron dithered, clearly anxious to get Sylvia out of her ward and away from Ron and all the other gawping men.

'Please don't let us hold you up, Matron,' said Sylvia pleasantly. 'I'm sure you have far more important things to do than chaperone me.'

Matron Billings went the colour of beetroot, turned on her heel and marched out of the ward. The swing doors slammed behind her in condemnation.

Sylvia giggled. 'Good heavens,' she breathed. 'What a simply *ghastly* woman. Where on *earth* did they dig her up?'

Ron roared with laughter. 'You're a caution, so y'are, Lady Anstruther-Norton.'

'I insist you call me Sylvia,' she said sternly,

although her eyes still sparkled with fun, 'otherwise I shall refuse to speak to you at all.'

'Let's compromise. You call me Ron, and I'll call you Lady Sylvia.'

'It's a deal.'

They regarded one another like conspirators as they drank the almost tasteless drink which bore little relation to proper coffee. Sylvia finally gave up on it with a shudder, but Ron was grateful for anything that had been wrung out of Matron and finished the last drop.

Sylvia took his empty cup and then leaned forward and patted his hand. 'I've driven all the way from Wiltshire almost non-stop and am desperate for sleep,' she confided. 'Do you think your family would mind very much if I went there tonight and simply climbed into bed without going through the rigmarole of social chit-chat?'

Ron was rather regretting his hasty and ill-thought-out invitation. 'The offer was genuinely made,' he said, 'but I won't be at all upset if you'd rather stay at one of the big hotels.'

She shot him a beaming smile. 'I realised you were tugging the tiger's tail, Ron, but large hotels are rather impersonal, aren't they? Beach View sounds absolutely perfect.'

Ron reached into the locker, found the stub of a pencil and tore a bit off the end of the newspaper. 'This is our telephone number. Give them a ring and explain who you are and that I sent you. They'll have the room ready for you by the time you've visited Christopher and found your way there.'

She took the slip of paper and tucked it into her handbag. Her smile was soft. 'Bless you, Ron. I don't know how I can ever repay you.'

He decided to push his luck. 'To be sure, a drop of brandy and a cheese and pickle sandwich wouldn't come amiss,' he said. 'The food's like the coffee. But you've got to be careful. Matron searches us for contraband.'

She patted his hand and gathered her things. 'Leave it with me,' she said and smiled. 'See you tomorrow, Ron – and don't cause too much trouble until then, otherwise we'll both be for the high jump.'

Ron watched her leave the ward, smiling at each man as she passed and wishing them luck. 'Now that,' he murmured appreciatively, 'is a real lady.'

Sylvia Anstruther-Norton softly brushed the lick of fair hair from her youngest son's forehead and blinked back the tears of weariness and anxiety. He was sleeping peacefully, and his wounds would soon heal, but the fear that had overwhelmed her on hearing he'd been shot down still remained, and she knew that all the time her three sons were involved in this terrible war, she would never sleep easily.

Closing the door to the private room, she slowly made her way down the endless hospital corridors to the front entrance. The night was cold, the wind coming off the sea in gusts as the clouds scudded over the moon, and she drew the mink coat tighter to her neck as she hurried through the darkness to the Rolls-Royce she'd parked rather haphazardly outside the main gate.

The car was splattered with mud after the long, exhausting journey, but the interior smelled reassuringly of soft leather and the heater soon blasted out welcoming warmth as she checked Anne's instructions on how to reach Beach View Boarding House.

As the delightful Anne closed the bedroom door behind her and plodded back down the stairs, Sylvia took in her surroundings. Beach View was a little shabby, but nevertheless far more homely and welcoming than she could have wished for. Ron hadn't warned her that his granddaughter was heavily pregnant, and she hoped very much that the girl hadn't gone to too much trouble on her behalf.

The room was as neat as a pin, with fresh linen and towels, the pretty bedspread and downy quilt making the narrow single bed look enticing. Sturdy furniture gleamed with polish, the floor had been swept, and every drawer in the dresser had been lined with crisp white paper. She walked into the bay and peeked between the blackout curtains, but it was too dark, and all she could see was the huddled mass of nearby roofs.

She shivered in the chill and kept her mink coat on as she slotted several sixpences into the meter then lit the gas fire. With a wry smile, she took off her hat and began to unpack. It had been a long time since she'd stayed in a lodging house, and this one far outshone those stinking, flea-infested East End hovels of her youth. But perhaps it was a good thing to be reminded of those years of hardship and struggle – of the times when she'd not known where her next meal was coming from – for she'd had things far too easy of late and had taken for granted the privileged lifestyle and happy family life that her marriage to James had provided. Christopher's close shave with death had shaken her to the core, woken her to the harsh realities of this war and the fact that no one, however well cocooned, was safe.

Once the room had warmed, Sylvia prepared for bed and finally slipped in between the freshly ironed sheets and soft blankets with a sigh of pleasure. As she lay in the darkness listening to the whispers and creaks of the old house, she thought of James and wondered if he too was lying wakeful in their London flat, or if he was working through the night in the Cabinet room of Downing Street. They had spoken briefly on the telephone during a short visit to Matron's office, so he knew their boy was on the mend, but that wouldn't make sleep any easier – not when their two other sons were in battleships somewhere out in the Atlantic.

Closing her eyes, she remembered that night twenty-five years ago when they'd met. It was 1915 and London had been smothered in thick, choking fog. She'd been seventeen, and hurrying out of the hotel where she worked as a chambermaid. James had been in uniform, dashing up the steps, already late for a meeting with friends when they had collided.

He'd caught her before she fell, but her handbag hit the pavement, spilling the contents everywhere. Apologising profusely, he'd helped her retrieve her belongings, and then insisted upon taking her out for supper at a nearby café. The hours flew as they ate and talked and strolled along the Embankment, and when dawn lightened the sky they had both known that despite their wildly different backgrounds, this was the start of something very special indeed.

Sylvia sighed as sleep softly claimed her. There had been ructions, of course, and his family had been horrified to learn they'd married at the town hall before he went back to his regiment in France. She had been shunned by them, spending the remainder of the war in his flat in London. But on his return, his love and gentle encouragement had sustained her through those early years of marriage, and little by little she'd learned to fit in and become accepted. Now it seemed she could play the part with ease, but never again must she forget her humble origins, or take anything for granted, for she had been blessed with far more than any one person deserved.

It was May's last day at the aircraft factory and the other women gathered to wish her luck. Rita rode pillion as May stuffed a change of clothing in the pannier, fired up the BSA and hurtled out of the factory compound, heading for Barrow Lane. She clasped her hands round May's waist as they took the sharp bends at speed and rattled over the cobbles. It was a precarious ride, and Rita preferred to be in charge of the bike rather than being a passenger, but as this was May's final evening in Cliffehaven, she had readily agreed to the lift home.

May brought the bike to a skidding halt outside the garage doors and switched off the engine. Rita clambered down and took off her helmet and goggles. 'Whew,' she breathed. 'That was a bit hair-raising.'

May grinned as she wheeled the motorbike into the garage. 'It's good to get the wind in your hair now and again,' she said, 'but I suspect flying a plane will be even windier.'

'You're not having second thoughts, are you?'

May shook her head as she took her bag out of the pannier. 'I'm nervous, that's all, and just wanted to have fun on my last ride.' She patted the BSA and slowly pulled the tarpaulin over it. 'You will look after her for me, won't you?'

'Of course I will, though I can't guarantee the Luftwaffe won't drop a bomb on it.'

'Rather that than Mum selling it, which she'd do the minute I leave. Thanks, Rita.' Her gaze dipped to the floor beneath the slit in the door that served as a letter box. 'Hey, it looks as if the postman's been.'

Rita picked up the envelope with a shaking hand. It was franked with the insignia of the RAF. 'I'm almost afraid to open it,' she breathed. 'What if they've turned me down?'

May grew impatient as Rita turned it over and over in her hand. 'Just open it, Rita. The suspense is killing me.'

Rita's heart was pounding as she carefully slit the envelope and drew out the two sheets of closely typed paper. Her gaze flew across the words, her breath caught in her throat, and she could hardly believe what she was reading, for they were offering her far more than she could ever have wished.

'I'm in,' she breathed. 'They want me. Oh, May, they really do want me, and they say that if a position arises in the engineering department for an apprentice mechanic, they will arrange for me to finish my course so I can get my final qualifications and work for them.'

May grabbed the letter and read it swiftly. 'There, see, I told you they wouldn't turn you down. You have so much to offer, Rita – and this proves it.'

May's eyes were shining with laughter as she handed it back. 'And they've even let you stay at home for Christmas before you start your training. Lucky old you – I'll be eating my Christmas lunch in some draughty air-force canteen in the middle of nowhere.'

Rita grabbed May and they danced an awkward jig among the piles of tyres and abandoned boxes of spare parts, their happy laughter ringing into the rafters. Once they had sobered a little, they stood hand in hand in silence, finally letting the full import of what they were about to do sink in.

'Things are going to be very different from now on, aren't they?' murmured May. 'I wonder where we'll be this time next year?'

'You'll be flying planes, and I'll be rushing about on the Norton at some airfield, or better still, helping to mend aeroplanes.'

'You'll have to tell Louise soon, because you're due to take your medical and initial interview in less than a week,' said May. 'Want to do it tonight while I'm here?'

Rita thought about it then shook her head. 'I'll tell her after you've gone.'

'You can't leave it too late, Rita,' May warned. 'Christmas is going to be hard enough for her as it is, and you leave for your training on the twenty-ninth.'

'I know,' Rita sighed, the euphoria seeping away. 'Let's just hope she hears from Papa or Roberto before Christmas. I'll feel so much easier about leaving her once she knows where they are.'

May squeezed her arm. 'Come on, she'll have heard us coming home and will be wondering why we haven't gone up.' She gave Rita an encouraging smile. 'I expect she'll read me the riot act as well once she hears I'm off to fly planes. Perhaps it would be better if you did tell her tonight – get it all over in one fell swoop.'

'Maybe. I'll let you tell her first and then play it by ear.'

May grinned. 'Coward,' she chided softly.

Rita silently acknowledged that she was being cowardly, but it was important she found the right moment, and the right words, to break her news. This letter was promising everything she'd ever wanted and now it was even more vital to have Louise's blessing. She carefully folded the letter into her trouser pocket and prayed fervently that nothing would happen to stop her from following her dream.

Louise's kitchen was warm, the firelight glinting in the ragged bits of tinsel she'd hung from the mantelshelf and over the mirror. Sprigs of holly and mistletoe had been tied together with scarlet ribbons and suspended from the picture rail, and some rather tatty paper chains which Rita and Roberto had made many years before were stretched from one side of the ceiling to the other. There was no Christmas tree, no fairy lights, and only four little gaily wrapped presents sitting on the sideboard. It would be a very different Christmas this year.

'Hello, May,' said Louise, drying her hands on a tea towel. 'I can offer you a cup of tea, but I'm afraid there isn't much in the way of food tonight.'

'I'm not stopping long, Mrs Minelli. I've just popped in to say goodbye before me and Rita go off for our last night in town.'

Louise paused in the act of putting the kettle on the hob. 'Goodbye? But where are you going?'

Rita watched Louise's expression as May told her about the training she was about to do. She noted how her face paled, how her eyes clouded with tears and how she wrung her hands in her apron, and with a sinking heart, was made to realise how very difficult it would be to tell Louise her own wonderful news.

'But you're just a child,' Louise finally managed. 'You can't possibly fly planes.'

'I'm the same age as Rita,' May replied, 'and there're plenty of other girls flying planes, driving fire engines and ambulances – even working for the gas board and sewerage works.'

'But it's dangerous.' Louise sank into the kitchen chair. 'And girls like you and Rita weren't meant for such things. I've seen some of those posh women up at the airfield, May. You won't fit in at all.'

'Things are different now,' May said firmly as she sat next to her. 'Girls like me and Rita are doing things we never thought possible before the war.

You see, it's offered us a way of getting out of these streets and trying other things. You know how it is at home with Mum. I don't want to end up like her, Mrs Minelli, and this is my chance to make something of myself.' She looked across at Rita for support. 'Rita understands, don't you, Rita?'

She nodded, all too aware of Louise's close scrutiny.

'Rita has a good life here,' said Louise comfortably. 'She has no need to do such a foolish thing when she has me to look after her and give her a proper home.'

Rita knew May was willing her to say something, but realised that if she did it would spoil their last evening together. 'I'll make us all a cup of tea,' she said instead, 'and then me and May are going to get changed and go out for a drink. As we're both eighteen, we can now legally go into a pub.'

'I don't like you going into those places,' muttered Louise, rising from her chair to fetch cups and saucers. 'You'll get a bad reputation, and then how will I face Papa Tino?'

'We're just going for a drink, Mamma,' Rita replied. 'It's all quite respectable.'

'I just don't understand it. In my day no respectable woman would be seen anywhere near a public house.' Louise shuddered. 'Nasty rough places full of drunken men with only one thought on their minds. My father would have taken the strap to me if I so much as went near one.'

The moment was over for now, but as Rita made the tea, she could hear the rustle of the letter jammed in her trouser pocket and feel the awful churning of excitement and dread that knotted her stomach. Louise had to be told, and soon – but not tonight.

It was almost dawn by the time they returned. There had been two air raids during the night and several hours had been spent huddled in the shelters, but it had been a good, happy evening, and they were both pleasantly tired.

'I'll leave my stuff at your place so I don't disturb Louise,' said May as they halted at the crossroads which would take them on their separate ways. 'I won't need most of it, and it's only fit for the bin anyway.'

'I'm going to miss you, May,' said Rita, her voice wobbling dangerously.

They embraced, their tears mingling. 'You'll soon be far too busy to miss me,' managed May as she drew back. 'We'll both be up to our eyeballs in learning new stuff, but I'll never forget you, I promise.'

'What time are you catching the train?'

May looked at her watch. 'In just over two hours.'

'Want me to see you off?'

May shook her head. 'Better not. It's hard enough saying goodbye as it is, and the WAAFs won't appreciate me blubbering like a baby on the platform.' She gave a shaky smile. 'Bye, Rita. Best of luck.'

'Bye, May.' Rita stood at the crossroads and watched as her friend walked into the gloom of a foggy dawn. Her footsteps rang in the silence and then faded as she was lost from sight. The tears blinded Rita as she turned away and headed for home.

Not wanting to disturb Louise, she quietly let herself in through her own back door and slowly climbed the stairs. It had been a hectic evening, with riotous singing round the old piano in the smoky, overcrowded pub, followed by dancing at one of the hotels. Now she was tired and ready for bed.

'What time do you call this?'

Rita's heart jumped as Louise emerged from the gloom at the top of the stairs. 'What are you doing here?'

'Waiting for you to come home.' Louise's expression was thunderous. 'Where have you been?'

'Only to the pub, and then on to a dance. We've spent half the night in an air-raid shelter,' Rita gabbled. 'I'm sorry you were worried.'

'Worried?' Louise shrieked. 'Of course I've been worried, you careless, thoughtless girl. How *dare* you stay out all night?'

'I'm sorry, really, but you knew it was May's last evening at home, and I didn't think you'd—'

'That's the point, Rita. You didn't think. You don't think of me at all.'

'That's not true,' she protested, following Louise into the main room. 'I'm always thinking of you.'

'Then perhaps you'd like to explain this.' Louise held out the letter.

Rita stared at it in horror. 'Where did you . . .?'

'I was tidying up and it fell out of your trouser pocket.' Louise threw it onto the scarred and battered table and folded her arms. 'Were you thinking of me when you applied for this posting? Did you think of me tonight when May was talking about her flying?'

'I was going to tell you,' Rita stuttered.

'When? Tomorrow? The day after? Perhaps a couple of hours before you leave Cliffehaven?'

'No.' Tears sprang in her eyes as she reached out to Louise. 'I was going to tell you today, Mamma. I promise.'

'How am I to believe your promises when you keep such a thing from me?' yelled Louise in a rush of rapid Italian. 'How am I to tell Papa you wish to abandon me to the enemy bombers? How can you love me so little that you plot and plan to leave this home we have given you?'

'Please, Mamma, it's not like that. It really isn't.'

Louise shrugged off her hand, sank into a chair and burst into tears. 'You are my *bambina*, my heart, my little one, but you betray me,' she sobbed, her words tripping one over the other, the Italian flowing as rapidly as her tears. 'You leave me just as my other daughters have. I have no one, no one.'

Rita stood there helpless against the storm. 'I just wanted to do something different, something more exciting than welding bits of planes together. Please, Mamma, try and understand how important this chance is to really make something of myself. It may never come again.'

'No. I do not understand – I will never understand. Why do you wish to leave me all alone without Papa and Roberto when this is your home?'

'I can't stay here forever,' Rita reasoned softly. 'I'm eighteen. It's time I made my own way. It doesn't mean I don't love you, or appreciate everything you've done for me, Mamma.'

Louise grabbed her arm. 'Then don't go,' she said urgently through her tears. 'I have lost too many people I love. I can't bear losing you too.'

'You won't lose me, Mamma. I'll only be away a short while for training, and then I'll be based at the local airfield.'

'It does not say that here.' Louise grabbed the letter and waved it in Rita's face. 'It says only you will go away to be trained and then it is up to the WAAFs as to where you will be posted. They could send you anywhere.'

Rita sank into the other chair, Vi Charlton's words ringing in her ears. 'Mamma,' she began, 'please try to understand how much I want to do this. Let me go and do the initial training at least.'

'No. I will not give my permission. You will stay here with me.'

Rita swallowed the angry retort, aware that losing her temper would simply make things worse. But she had to fight for what she knew was right. 'Mamma,' she said as calmly as she could, 'I do not need your permission. I'm eighteen and have every right to enlist in whatever service I wish.'

'You will defy me?' Louise raised her tear-streaked face and glared at her with reddened eyes.

'I don't want to defy you. I want your blessing, but if you refuse, then I'm sorry, Mamma, I will do it anyway.'

Louise broke into noisy, hysterical tears. 'How can I give you my blessing when you wish to wound me with this defiance – this cruelty?' she gabbled in Italian. 'You wish to leave me here, all alone with the enemy bombing me, our house in danger every night, the streets unsafe. How can you do this to me when I am alone – when there is no Papa Tino to protect me?'

Rita realised she would get no sense out of Louise tonight, for she wasn't listening, couldn't comprehend how much this posting meant to her, or understand that Rita wasn't abandoning her, merely growing up and moving on to make her own way in life. 'We'll talk more after we've both had a good sleep,' she murmured, gathering her into her embrace.

Louise sank into her arms. 'You will change your mind,' she murmured. 'Come the morning you will forget all this silly talk of motorbikes and see that you have a duty to your Mamma to stay with her. For this is what Papa and Roberto asked of you on that terrible day they were taken away – and I know you will not break the promise you made to them.'

Rita fought her tears as she held Louise and tried desperately to think of a way round this terrible emotional blackmail. Vi Charlton had been right – she'd seen how it was with Louise because she could view their relationship from a distance. If only Peggy was not in Somerset she could have gone to her for advice. As it was, she had little choice but to weather Louise's tears and try to make her understand how important it was for her to make her own choices in life, and not to be forever tied to Louise's apron strings.

Chapter Ten

Rita had given in to Louise's pleas not to be left alone for the next few hours, and returned with her to her house. But as Louise slept fitfully in the other room, Rita paced the floor, unable to settle to anything more than making endless cups of tea.

She had a thudding headache and her emotions and thoughts were in turmoil as she tried to work out the best way of appeasing Louise without giving in to her demands. Yet, at every juncture, she came up against that great wall of Louise's neediness, and her own profound reluctance to cause her further anguish.

If only she had someone to talk to, to advise her, but May would have left by now, Peggy was in Somerset, Anne had enough to worry about with running Beach View, and she didn't really know Jim Reilly well enough to talk to him about it. Even her own father was out of reach – how she yearned to be able to talk to him, to hear his soothing voice and feel the comfort of his embrace.

She drank the last dregs of the cooling tea and glanced at the clock on the mantelpiece. It was time to go to work, but she had no idea how she would get through the next eight hours. Her concentration was all over the place, her head pounded and she felt sick – not the best way to begin a new day in the heat and noise of an engineering factory.

Rita left a note for Louise and hurried next door to get changed back into her working clothes, make a flask of tea and stuff down a Spam sandwich. She hesitated as she saw the discarded letter on the table and then folded it carefully and tucked it in the inside pocket of her old flying jacket. There was one person she could trust to give her good advice, but it could prove a bit tricky to get to him.

With this thought, she hurried downstairs, opened the garage doors and fired up the Norton. It was too early yet, the doctors would be on their rounds and Matron would be prowling the wards, but she could try and see Ron during the lunch hour.

The hours dragged as she tried not to make too many mistakes. Luckily, Major Patricia was busy for most of the morning showing the bigwigs from the RAF around the factory and entertaining them in her office, so she managed to avoid a dressing-down for the shoddy work she was producing today.

Discarding yet another attempt to get the welding correct, she gave up and stripped off the protective apron, helmet and gloves. Reaching for her jacket and gas mask box, she ran out of the factory, fired up the bike and was gone before anyone noticed. She would get it in the neck, that was for sure, but this was urgent, and surely Major Patricia would prefer her to be fully concentrated rather than careless and worried sick about her predicament?

Rita decided she didn't really care what others thought of her as she raced on the bike towards Camden Road and the hospital. She'd been given the chance to do something very special and was determined not to be thwarted.

The hospital was busy as usual, with doctors, nurses and porters all going about their varying jobs with a bustling sense of importance and urgency. Rita parked the Norton round the side of the vast grey building that sprawled across an entire block, and swiftly took off her helmet and goggles, tucking them away in the pannier.

Her work clothes and heavy boots would make it difficult to blend in with the neat uniforms and long white coats, but there was not much she could do about that. She just had to hope Matron was occupied elsewhere, and that the sister on the ward would let her sneak in.

Rita ran up the steps and into the echoing reception hall. She knew where Ron's ward was, she'd been to visit him only two days ago, but it meant going up the marble staircase and along a great many corridors before she reached him, and she just had to pray that no one stopped her.

Hurrying along, she was aware of the curious looks of those she passed, but she kept going until she reached the double doors of Men's Medical. The corridor outside was empty, but she could hear the nurses chattering in the sluice as they made cups of tea and put their feet up for a few minutes.

She took a peek through one of the round windows set in the doors. Ron was sitting up, and looked a great deal better as he chatted to the man in the bed next to him and ate his lunch. There seemed to be no nurses on the ward, so she pushed the door open and slipped inside.

'Hello, darling,' said the man cheerfully from the bed close to the door. ' Come to give us a bed-bath then?'

'Not today,' she muttered, hurrying towards Ron.

'Hey, Ron,' yelled the man. 'How come you get to have all the pretty visitors when all I get is the mother-in-law?'

'Keep your voice down, you eejit,' growled Ron. 'Do you want Matron to hear?' He grinned up at Rita. 'This is a nice surprise, so it is,' he said, pushing away the tray of food. 'Come to rescue me?'

'It's me who needs rescuing, Ron.' She perched on the edge of the chair beside his bed and shot an anxious look at the doors.

'Tell me quick,' he muttered.

Rita let it all pour out as he scanned the letter. 'I don't know what to do for the best, Ron,' she finished, close to tears.

'There, there, girlie, don't fret yourself.' Ron patted her hand. ''Tis a tricky business, trying to please everyone, and I can see how much you're wanting to do this thing. But you have to understand Louise better if you're to be persuading her to let you go.'

Rita frowned. 'I don't see . . .'

'Louise has always had someone to look after her, so she has no real confidence when it comes to making decisions and standing on her own two feet. I remember her as a wee girl. Pretty little t'ing she was, but shy, terrible shy.'

'She still finds it a bit of a trial to make friends,' Rita agreed. 'But she seems to be doing all right at the factory, and I thought . . .'

Ron eyed the abandoned plate of unappetising food with a sigh. 'She'll not change now,' he murmured. 'It's the fault of her parents, of course, but they thought they were doing the right thing by protecting her from the real world.'

He became thoughtful as the memories returned. 'Louise was the baby they'd longed for and never thought they would have. Her mother was over forty when she was born, and from that moment they smothered her in love.'

'But surely they realised she'd have to learn to stand on her own eventually? With much older parents there was always the possibility that . . .'

'Aye, you're right there, Rita. But, you see, they were blinded by their love for her, unable to see that tying her so closely to them meant she would never really have a normal life. They couldn't see that it was in the nature of things to let their young fly and make the mistakes and the decisions that would ensure a happy, fulfilled life.'

'That's terribly sad,' said Rita. 'Poor Louise.'

He grimaced. 'They didn't even really want her to go out to work, afraid she might be influenced by the wrong sort of people and led astray, but of course they barely had two pennies to scrape together, so they had to let her earn something. Even then, they found her a bit of a job working for a close friend of theirs so they could keep an eye on her.'

'Louise did tell me she worked at a hotel for a while before she married Tino.'

'Ah, Tino. Yes. That was the only time she rebelled.'

'She was only sixteen when they married,' murmured Rita. 'I'm surprised her parents gave their consent with her being so young and precious.'

'Her father was in his late sixties by then, and not in good health. I think they realised suddenly that if anything happened to either of them, Louise would be left on her own. Tino was a hard-working, honest man with good prospects, who clearly adored their Louise, and as she seemed so determined to marry him, they gave them their blessing.'

'So Louise went straight from being an adored daughter to become an adored wife. I know she relied on Tino for everything, and is totally lost without him.'

'Which is why she's clinging to you, Rita.'

'A friend said much the same thing only the other week,' murmured Rita. 'I didn't want to believe her, but it seems she was right.' She regarded him through her unshed tears. 'What can I do, Ron?'

He took her hand. 'Perhaps if I spoke to her it would help – I don't know. I wish to God Peggy was here. She'd know how to sort this out.'

'I wish I did,' sighed Rita. 'But Louise has lost everyone she's ever held dear. Even her own daughters fled the nest early to start new lives in America – how can I possibly persuade her to let me go too while Tino and Roberto are as good as missing?'

'What are you doing in here?'

They both looked up guiltily at the ward sister.

'I needed to see Mr Reilly urgently,' said Rita.

'We have set visiting hours,' the sister replied, darting a glance at the doors. 'And if Matron catches you it'll be me in trouble. Please leave – now.'

'I'll be off too,' said Ron, throwing back the bedclothes.

'The doctor said you were not to be discharged until this evening,' said the ward sister. 'It is only one o'clock. Please get back into bed, Mr Reilly.'

'Sure, and it won't matter a jot if I leave a little earlier.' Ron grabbed the hospital dressing gown and began to rummage in the bedside locker.

The nurse wrung her hands in distress. 'Please, Mr Reilly. You can't just discharge yourself. There are rules and forms and—'

'Give me the forms and I'll sign 'em,' he muttered. 'I'll even beard Matron in her den and tell her my decision to leave has nothing to do with you.'

'That won't be necessary, Mr Reilly, but I do think you should wait until we can arrange some kind of transport for you. You really aren't well enough to walk home.'

Ron gathered up his clothes, balancing his boots on top of them. 'How did you get here, Rita?'

'On the Norton, but—'

'Well, that's good enough for me. I'll meet you outside once I've filled in Sister's forms and put me clothes back on. Sure a ride on a motorbike will blow the cobwebs of this place away.'

'Mr Reilly,' the sister gasped in horror. 'You can't possibly—'

'Nothing's impossible, Sister – not when I set me mind to it.' He jerked his head in the direction of the ward doors. 'Go and start 'er up, girlie. I'll be with you in a jiffy.'

Rita shot an apologetic look at the flabbergasted nurse and hurried out of the ward. She heard the swing doors clatter behind her and Ron's cheerful voice as he said goodbye to the other patients, but she didn't hang about – Matron could already be on her way, and she didn't fancy the ructions Ron's escape would incur.

She raced down the stairs, dodged trolleys and porters and hurried outside to the motorbike. She doubted the wisdom of letting Ron ride pillion, but the darling old man knew his own mind, and it wasn't up to her to question him.

Rita was grinning as she kicked the starter,

tweaked the accelerator, and let the engine rumble. Life was always an adventure with Ron, and although he hadn't really solved her problem, she was profoundly grateful that she'd thought to ask for his help, for now she didn't feel quite so alone. Between them, they would find a way of persuading Louise to change her mind, she was certain of that.

Rita checked her watch, gauged how long it would take Ron to dress, sign the forms and get down all those stairs. She then slowly drove the bike to the bottom of the front steps. The engine rumbled idly as she waited, and her pulse began to race. She wondered if this was how it felt to break out of prison. She'd seen a film once where the getaway car was waiting outside, the escaped man clambering over the wall, running to the car and shouting at the driver to put his foot down as the alarms began to ring inside the prison and police cars raced to stop them.

Ron appeared at the top of the steps, dressed for once in a decent pair of trousers, shirt, jumper and thick tweed overcoat which no doubt Anne had brought in. His boots had been polished and a cap was pulled low over his eyes to hide the bandage that covered the wound on his head. He carried his pyjamas and washbag rolled up under one arm.

'Quick, girlie,' he rasped, stuffing everything into his coat pockets and making them bulge. 'Matron's been seen upstairs. It won't take a moment for the old witch to find I'm gone.'

Rita felt the suspension dip under his weight as she waited for him to settle behind her. 'Hold on tight, Ron. I don't want you falling off the back.'

'To be sure, I was riding bikes before you were a glint in your daddy's eye. Now get me out of here.'

Rita chuckled as she carefully drove the Norton through the hospital gates and headed along Camden Road. She kept the throttle low and the bike steady, making sure she didn't swerve too sharply round the potholes in the road, or have to brake too suddenly.

'I'd kill for a pint of beer, so I would,' he yelled above the roar of the engine. 'Would you be after dropping me off at the Anchor for a wee chat with Rosie?'

'I've already broken too many rules today,' she shouted back. 'You're going home, Ron, and that's an end to it.' She grinned as she heard him muttering something about the young having no sense of adventure any more and kept on driving past the Anchor to the T-junction at the end of Camden Road.

She rode into Beach View Terrace and parked behind a very swanky Rolls-Royce, which looked as if someone had spent an age washing and polishing it. Switching off the engine, she admired the Rolls as she waited for Ron to clamber off. 'Doris bought a new car?'

'Not even in her wildest dream could Doris afford that,' said Ron. 'It belongs to Lady Anstruther-Norton – our latest lodger.'

Rita stared at him in amazement. 'You have a titled lady staying here? How did that happen?'

'It's a long story. I'll tell you sometime,' he muttered, fiddling with his bulging pockets and trying to retrieve his pyjamas.

The front door opened and Anne came carefully down the steps. 'What on earth do you two think you're doing?' she demanded. 'Granddad, why are you on the back of Rita's bike when you should be in your hospital bed?'

''Tis a long story, so it is,' said Ron cheerfully. 'Get the kettle on, lass. Rita and I could do with a decent cup of tea. 'Tis thirsty work, all this escaping.'

'I should be going back to the factory,' said Rita.

'Not until you've explained to me why my grandfather has absconded – and why you thought it appropriate for him to ride on the back of that thing.' Anne was clearly furious as she stood aside, pointed towards the hall and ordered them both indoors.

Rita followed Ron meekly into the hall. Anne was every inch the stern schoolmistress, and Rita felt as if she was about five years old. 'It wasn't my idea,' she began.

'I don't doubt it,' said Anne, closing the door firmly behind them and heading for the kitchen. 'But I have enough to worry about without you and Granddad causing trouble. Matron has already been on the telephone, and I do *not* appreciate being harangued in such a way over something which I had no part in.'

'I'm sorry, Anne,' Rita said quickly, 'but it was a spur-of-the-minute thing.'

Anne turned and regarded her evenly. 'You haven't explained why you were at the hospital in the first place.'

'Rita needed to talk to me,' said Ron, shrugging off his coat. 'That's all you need to know, Anne, me darling. Now get that kettle on.'

'Well, well, if it's not Bonnie Parker and Clyde Barrow.' Jim was grinning widely from his seat at the kitchen table. 'How does it feel to be on Matron Billings' "most wanted" list?'

'Ron,' twittered Mrs Finch, turning from the washing-up in the sink. 'You are a naughty man, but it's lovely to have you home, it really is.'

Her words were drowned by the furious sound of barking and scrabbling as Harvey desperately tried to break down the cellar door to get to Ron.

Ron acknowledged his son's and Mrs Finch's welcome and hurried to release his dog.

Harvey flew into the kitchen, leaping and bouncing in ecstatic delight as his tail thrashed dangerously close to a pile of china on the table, and his tongue tried to wash every inch of Ron's hands and face. It was several minutes before order was restored, but the noise had brought everyone into the kitchen, and now it was almost impossible to move about.

'You'll be getting us all into trouble, so you will, you bad man,' said Fran, the Irish nurse with fiery hair. 'But to be sure it's good to have you home.'

'It's glad I am to be back,' he replied, slumping into the armchair next to the range and trying to ward off Harvey, who had clambered into his lap and was enthusiastically trying to continue his ablutions. 'Where's that tea, Anne? To be sure, and I could be doing with something decent for me lunch. Got any pickles and cheese?'

'I'll give you pickles and cheese,' muttered Anne, trying to maintain a stern expression as she collected cups and saucers. 'There's a war on, Granddad, or hadn't you noticed?'

'To be sure, it's a war I've been waging in that blasted hospital,' he grumbled. 'Me shrapnel's playing up again with all that sitting about, and 'tis certain a cheese and pickle sandwich would improve me altogether.'

'I doubt anything would improve you, you auld divil,' said Jim fondly. 'To be sure, you're a sight for sore eyes, Da. We've missed your moaning about your shrapnel.'

'Moaning, is it?' Ron's eyes narrowed beneath the bushy brows, but they glittered with amusement. 'You see how you like it with shrapnel up yer ar . . . nether regions. It'd not be me moaning then, I can tell you that for sure.'

Rita loved this kitchen, loved this house and the people within it. There was a warmth here, a gentle understanding and love in each and every word spoken and gesture made. She could have stayed all day.

But time was rapidly moving on and she had to get back to work. She was about to turn down the offer of tea and reluctantly leave when a very attractive woman came into the kitchen, took one look at Ron and hurried to kiss his cheek. She stared in amazement as the old man went scarlet.

'You've not met our new lodger, Rita,' he said, catching her astonished expression and clearing his throat. 'This is Lady Sylvia. She's the mother of the young pilot.'

'How do you do?' The woman's voice was soft, her smile warm and friendly as they shook hands. 'I understand you and Ron have colluded to escape Matron. I don't blame you. Ghastly woman.'

Rita smiled back at her, uncertain of how one should speak to such a well-bred, titled lady. 'I just hope no one gets into trouble because of it,' she said.

'I'll have a quiet word with Matron and ensure no one gets punished, don't you fret, Rita,' she said with a warm smile before turning back to Ron. 'Now, Ron,' she said purposefully. 'I promised you cheese and pickle, and cheese and pickle you shall have.'

There was a hush as Lady Sylvia quickly left the kitchen and returned moments later with a cardboard box filled with jars of pickles, a slab of cheese, a packet of crackers, a pat of butter, and a loaf of bread. 'I was going to bring it in this evening, but you seem to have ruined all my best-laid plans.' Her eyes sparkled with fun as she set about making him a doorstep sandwich.

'To be sure, I've a terrible hunger for one of them, Lady Sylvia,' said Jim, eyeing the cheese before turning on one of his most appealing smiles. 'How the divil did you manage to get hold of such a feast?'

She cocked an eyebrow at him. 'One has one's contacts, as I'm sure you do, Jim Reilly.' A smile tweaked the corners of her mouth. 'The real test was hiding it well enough so you wouldn't get to it first and eat it all.' She looked round the room. 'Would anyone else like a sandwich?'

There was a chorus of acceptance, and soon everyone was happily munching – even Harvey – which would soon have dire repercussions, for pickled onions made Harvey fart.

Anne looked skyward, sighed deeply and poured the tea. 'I'll be glad when Mum gets back, and that's a fact,' she muttered to Rita. 'How she keeps everyone in order, I'll never know. They don't do anything I tell them and simply go headlong into one scrape after another – and with the house full to the rafters, it's a wonder I get anything done.'

'Where on earth does everyone sleep?' asked Rita. 'I thought you and Martin had taken over the front bedroom?'

'I've put Lady Sylvia in there. Martin and I will share Cissy's room, and if she manages to get home for Christmas, she'll either have to sleep on the couch in the dining room, or use the bunk bed down in the cellar room next to Grandpa.'

Rita chuckled. 'I can't see her being too pleased about that.'

Anne shrugged. 'There's nothing much I can do about it, so she'll just have to muck in like everyone else.' She leaned closer, her voice barely above a murmur. 'Lady Sylvia has insisted upon paying full rent on top of the grant we get from the government for those who billet with us. I could hardly put her down in the basement with Grandpa and Harvey, who both snore and blow off all night – she'd think we were complete plebs.'

Rita giggled at the thought. 'How long will she be staying?'

Anne shifted on the hard chair and caressed her swollen belly. 'I don't know,' she sighed. 'Until her son's able to be discharged, I suppose. But she'll certainly be here for Christmas; she said she wanted to stay at least until Mum gets home.'

The kitchen cleared a little as the three nurses went upstairs to prepare for their afternoon shift at the hospital, and Jim accompanied Ron and Harvey out into the back garden to inspect the winter vegetables and argue over the best way to sell the parachute silk.

Rita finished her cup of tea and the delicious sandwich, washed the china and prepared to leave. 'I'd better go. Major Patricia will be furious, and I'll end up having to work through the night to make up for the time I lost this morning.'

Lady Sylvia looked up from the knitting she was

trying to unravel for Mrs Finch. 'Ron's told me all about you, and I'm sorry to hear about Roberto and Antonino. It must be a difficult time for all concerned when one doesn't know where one's family is.'

Rita felt a bit embarrassed at being the focus of such earnest attention from one so smart and posh. 'It's harder for Louise,' she managed, 'but we rub along. I'm sure we'll hear from them soon.' She picked up her jacket, leather helmet and goggles. 'It's been nice meeting you,' she said with unusual shyness.

'Why don't you join us for Christmas?' said Anne. 'There won't be too much in the way of turkey and all the trimmings, but at least it will be cheerful with so many people in the house.'

'We'd love to come,' breathed Rita. 'And I'm sure we can share our rationing stamps to eke out whatever there is.'

'You may find you'll have rather more to eat than you expect,' said Lady Sylvia, giving up on the knitting. 'I do hope you don't mind, Anne, but I've asked my husband to order a Fortnum and Mason's hamper, and he's assured me it will arrive in plenty of time.'

Rita and Anne stared at her in disbelief. 'A hamper from Fortnum and Mason's?' breathed Anne. 'Do they do such a thing in the middle of a war?'

'Oh, yes,' said Lady Sylvia, with a delicate sniff of what could have been interpreted as disdain. 'The rich don't expect to go without their little treats just because there's a war on. Mind you, it helps to be in the know, and my husband's office is only round the corner from Piccadilly.'

'Goodness,' sighed Anne.

Lady Sylvia grinned. 'As I said to your father earlier, one has useful contacts to be exploited at will when necessary. And this Christmas is one of those important occasions.' She stood and smoothed back her silky blonde hair. 'Now, if you'll excuse me, I must go and unruffle Matron's feathers and visit Christopher.'

Silence fell in the kitchen as Lady Sylvia fetched her coat from the rack in the hall and softly closed the front door behind her.

Rita and Anne looked at one another in amazement. 'Blimey,' muttered Rita, 'how the other half live, eh?'

Anne giggled. 'Don't they just? I wonder what you get in a hamper from Fortnum's.'

'I've no idea, but I'm looking forward to finding out,' Rita replied.

Chapter Eleven

The atmosphere in Barrow Lane didn't improve over the following three days, and although Rita had done her best to persuade Louise to change her mind, it seemed she was determined to make Rita feel so guilty that it was impossible to talk to her about even everyday things.

It had been a noisy day with planes taking off from the local airfield and several air-raid warnings, which luckily had come to very little. Darkness had fallen early as it always did at this time of year, and by five o'clock, they'd closed the blackout curtains and lit the gas lamps. They had become adept at preparing for the inevitable wail of the sirens, with small bags packed with their few precious possessions, the flask of tea and packet of sandwiches waiting on the table beside the rolled-up blankets and thick warm coats.

Rita was dressed and ready for her fire-watch duties, and Louise was sitting close to the range, saying nothing as she stared into the flames. Their early supper had been eaten almost in silence, just as all the meals had over the past few days, and it was beginning to wear Rita down.

'I'll have to leave in a few minutes, Mamma. Are you sure you have everything you'll need in the shelter?'

'Of course,' Louise muttered. 'I've gone there often enough – on my own.'

Rita didn't respond to her snipe. 'I'll be back as soon as I can,' she said, 'but it sounds as if Gerry's going to give us a noisy night, and I have things to do after my shift, so I probably won't see you until early evening.'

Louise shrugged. 'You must do what you want. I no longer have any say in the matter.'

'Don't be like that, Mamma,' Rita pleaded. 'We both have jobs to do if we're to win this war, and up until now you've been quite happy to go to the shelter on your own.'

'It's obviously something I'm going to have to get used to,' Louise retorted, rising from her chair and slamming the kettle onto the hob. 'My opinion no longer counts. I'm not important now you have made your plans to leave.'

Tamping down on a bitter retort, Rita buttoned her heavy coat and wound the woollen scarf round her neck. 'Please don't talk like that, Mamma,' she said stiffly. 'This is hard enough as it is, and I don't want us to fight when Gerry's threatening to blow us all to kingdom come.'

Louise kept her back to Rita as she spooned the last of the tea leaves into the brown china teapot. 'Perhaps it would be best if Gerry did drop a bomb on me. Then you'll be free to do what you want,' she said softly.

Rita took a deep breath. 'Now you're just being over-dramatic.' She went to Louise and took her arms, forcing her to turn and face her. 'I love you, Mamma,' she said firmly, 'and I have never wished you dead. Why do you keep saying such things when all it does is drive a wedge between us? Can't you be happy for me? Can't you see that I've been given the chance to finish my apprenticeship and do what I've always wanted?'

'You promised Tino and Roberto you would look after me until they returned,' Louise replied obstinately. 'I heard you swear to it, right here in this room on the night they were arrested.'

'None of us realised how long they would be gone. It was a promise made in the heat of the moment – a promise I have fulfilled to the best of my ability, and I'm sure Papa would forgive me for breaking it if he knew—'

'A promise is a promise, regardless of how it is made.' Louise sank into the chair and buried her face in her hands as she burst into noisy sobs. 'You are breaking my heart, Rita – and you will break Tino's when he discovers how little you value your word to him.'

Rita had had enough. She grabbed the small bag which held all her important documents, letters, photographs, jewelled combs, pearl earrings and a change of clothes. With her gas mask box over her shoulder and her tin hat perched on her head, she looked down at the sobbing Louise and resisted the profound need to pacify her, for she suspected the noisy sobbing was merely an act.

'I'm due to go to the airfield tomorrow morning for my initial interview and medical examination. I don't know what time I'll be back.'

Louise raised her head from her hands, her eyes strangely dry and bright for one who'd been sobbing moments earlier. 'Go then. See if I care – and if I die tonight, you'll know you were to blame.'

'That's a cruel thing to say.'

'Now perhaps you'll understand what it's like to be me,' Louise snapped, forgetting she was supposed to be in tears. 'It's you who are cruel, Rita. Cruel, thoughtless and selfish.'

Rita was so upset she could barely speak. 'I'll see you tomorrow,' she muttered. She turned in the doorway to discover Louise was placidly making tea as if none of their harsh words had been spoken. 'If you value promises so much,' said Rita softly, 'then perhaps you'll not forget yours to go into the shelter during a raid.'

Louise didn't turn from the range. 'I keep my word, Rita. Unlike some.'

Rita left the house, dumped the small bag in the pannier, and fired up the Norton. Her emotions were in such turmoil she could barely think straight. Louise was using every weapon against her, and she would have to find some way of breaking through to her if either of them were to come out of this unscathed. Their relationship, once so close and loving, was being torn to shreds – but she couldn't simply cave in to Louise's demands, no matter how much pressure was put on her.

Gladys Albright and John Hicks were waiting on the forecourt as Rita pulled up outside the fire station. 'You're looking a bit down in the dumps,' said Gladys with motherly concern.

Rita took off her goggles and silenced the engine. 'I'm fine,' she replied, plastering on a smile. 'Ate my tea too quick and got a bit of indigestion, that's all,' she added quickly when she saw Gladys hadn't believed her. The last thing she needed tonight was the other woman's well-meaning sympathy and homespun philosophy.

'It's going to be a long night, Rita,' said John. 'Gerry's on the move and we're expecting a lot of noise. I want you to take Gladys up with you. Mike Summers is already in position and he'll be manning the radio tonight.'

Rita eyed Gladys, who was regarding the Norton with some trepidation. She was a big woman, and Rita could only hope the Norton's suspension could take her weight. 'Climb on then, Gladys, and hold tight. It's a bit of a bumpy ride, and I don't want you falling off.'

Gladys clambered clumsily onto the bike, leaving Rita very little room on the seat. 'You will take it easy, won't you, dear?' she said breathlessly. 'The last time I sat on one of these things was when Bert and I were courting – and I didn't like it much.'

Rita took off her old leather flying helmet and settled it over Gladys's freshly permed hair, fastening the buckle beneath her many chins before topping it off with her tin helmet. 'Just close your eyes and hold on,' she said soothingly. 'You'll be fine.'

Gladys gripped her round the waist and tucked herself tightly to Rita's back. They set off for the hills at a sedate pace and finally sped up as they began to climb the steep, uneven track across the windswept grass, the partially shielded headlight making little difference to the darkness. They passed the soldiers manning the Bofors guns and the volunteers manning the searchlights, waving back to them as they headed for the circle of sandbags which had been set on the southernmost tip of the chalk cliffs.

Mike Summers was having a crafty fag, leaning against the sandbags as if he was on holiday. Of average height and build, he was in his late forties and usually worked for the corporation as a dustman. He had very dark curly hair and a raffish moustache, which Rita suspected were dyed, and, like his best friend, Jim Reilly, usually had pockets filled with black-market goods which he tried to sell at every opportunity.

Rita cut the engine and helped a rather unsteady Gladys climb off.

Mike stamped on the cigarette and came towards

them. 'Ladies,' he said, with a beaming smile. 'It's your lucky night. I've got packets of writing paper and envelopes which I can let you have at a very special price.'

'Keep them in your pocket, Mike,' said Gladys, who was still a bit flustered. 'We're not interested in your hooky gear.'

'I'm cut to the quick, Gladys.' He put his hand to his heart dramatically. 'My merchandise is of the highest quality.'

'I'm sure it is, Mike,' said Rita, 'but we're not on a shopping trip, so let's get prepared for the real job in hand.' She led the way into the dubious shelter of the sandbags and dumped her gas mask box on one of the benches. 'Have you checked the radio's working, that there's enough water in the buckets, and the stirrup pump doesn't jam like it did the other night?'

He nodded, his good humour still firmly in place as usual. 'All checked, and as you can see, I've even put the kettle on.'

Rita grinned at him. For all his nefarious ways he had a certain charm and reminded her a bit of Jim Reilly. 'Good,' she said, turning off the primus stove as the tin kettle began to whistle. 'It's freezing up here.'

'I've got the answer to that,' he said proudly, taking a small bottle of brandy from one of his voluminous pockets. 'A drop of this in the tea will perk us up no end.'

They sat huddled round the old oil heater and sipped the doctored tea, glad of the meagre warmth and the companionship as the wind howled across the land and tossed giant waves onto the promenade far below them. It was a bitter night, with bright stars and a three-quarter moon not quite hidden by the scudding clouds, and although Rita could appreciate the grandeur of her surroundings, she found them daunting and was relieved not to be out here alone.

The radio crackled into life some half-hour later. 'Alert. Alert. Enemy approaching across Channel. Large numbers fighters and bombers.'

Mike swiftly responded as Gladys and Rita turned off the heater, adjusted their tin hats and picked up their night-sight binoculars to scan the horizon. The sirens began their mournful, blood-chilling wails which built swiftly to a crescendo, and the searchlight beams grew from pale yellow fingers to blinding blue-white spears that pierced the darkness.

A few minutes later Rita saw the ominous dark cloud sprawling across the horizon – could make out the pinpricks of their wing lights and hear the distant thunder of their intimidating and determined approach. They were still beyond the reach of the guns which were no doubt primed and ready to blow them out of the air, but the Hawker Hurricanes and Spitfires were already racing to meet them – to harry and shoot them down before they could reach their target. She looked up, the pride swelling inside as wave upon wave of British fighters came from every nearby airfield to join in the battle.

They watched in awed and terrified silence as Heinkels, Dorniers and Junkers thundered purposefully on while their escort of Messerschmidts became entangled in deadly dogfights with the Spitfires and Hurricanes. The very air trembled with the noise as the big guns boomed in rapid succession, tracer bullets zipped and pom-poms burst brightly amongst the sweeping searchlight beams. The earth shook and the downdraught had them flattened against the wall of sandbags as they desperately tried to keep watch for incendiary bombs.

They gasped in horror as two fighter planes collided in a fiery explosion over the sea, and another spun out of control and crashed in a blaze of flame further down the coast. One of the enemy bombers had been so disabled it turned tail and headed ponderously for the other side of the Channel, harried on all sides by darting Spitfires. Moments before it disappeared in a bright, blinding flash, it dropped its lethal cargo harmlessly into the water, where it caused a giant fountain which threatened to swamp the fishing boats anchored on the beach.

Rita kept the binoculars firmly to her eyes, scanning the skies and all over the town for sight of Gerry's deadliest weapon: the parachute mine.

These acted as blast bombs, detonating at roof level rather than on impact, maximising the blast instead of the shock waves being cushioned by surrounding buildings. These shock waves could reach a wider area than those of a normal bomb, with the potential to destroy a whole street of houses, and blow in every window within a two-mile radius. She had seen pictures of the devastation they had caused in London and Coventry. So far, Cliffehaven had escaped, but it was vital to stay alert and not be distracted by the activity in the skies above her.

The angry swarm of enemy bombers droned relentlessly on, darkening the seaside town in its shadow. And then she saw them – hundreds of tiny parachutes dropping from the enemy planes at the rear of the swarm to drift, sway and spin almost lazily towards Cliffehaven.

'Parachute mines,' she yelled to Mike. 'There're too many to count, and a lot have gone in the sea, but it looks as if the majority will hit the industrial estate.'

She heard him talk urgently into the radio, but was helpless to do anything more than watch as one after the other the mines exploded – lighting up the town, blasting buildings to smithereens as their toxic flames spread in a flash-fire to consume everything in their path. She couldn't make out much detail, there was too much smoke, but knew Cliffehaven well enough to realise the industrial estate and the railway lines were certainly tonight's targets.

The mines continued to explode, even though the enemy was no longer overhead. And as Cliffehaven burned, they could hear the distant thunder and crump of heavy bombing behind them and knew what it must mean.

She and Gladys turned and saw the hazy red glow spreading into the sky. The airfield was under attack.

Mike had seen it too and was talking urgently into the radio as Gladys and Rita returned to their watching posts. They could now hear the clamour of fire engine and ambulance bells, could see the bright orange lick of flames pierce the shroud of acrid smoke and dust that rose above the town.

Rita's hands were shaking and her heart hammered as she tried to focus in on the station and the houses behind it. But the pall of smoke was too thick, and the binoculars weren't powerful enough to reach that far. 'Please, God,' she whispered, 'don't let anything bad happen to Louise.'

'We're all in God's hands tonight,' said Gladys as she put her arm around her. 'You keep praying, Rita, but I'm sure Louise will be quite safe in the shelter. You'll see.'

'I just feel so helpless stuck up here.'

'You're doing a worthwhile job, lass, and those down there know what they're about. They'll be putting out the fires and tending to the injured, relying on us to warn them of any more attacks. Best to just sit tight and get this night over with.'

Rita knew she was right, but there were people down there in the burning town that she loved. Had Barrow Lane escaped the incendiaries? Was Beach View still standing? Had Louise kept her promise and gone to the shelter? As Gladys had said, they were in God's hands, and she had to keep faith in Him and trust no harm had come to those she treasured.

'Grandpa, there really isn't enough room for Harvey in here, and he's stinking the place out. He'll have to be put in the shed.'

Ron gathered Harvey into his lap and held him tightly to his chest. 'You refuse to let us go and help those poor benighted souls out there, and yet you deny this old hero the right to safety in here. What's the matter with you, girl?'

Anne glared at him. 'You're not well enough to be out tonight, and Harvey's been eating pickled onions again. The smell he's making is turning my stomach.'

'He's just a bit on the nervous side, so he is,' muttered Ron, wrapping the dog's rear end in the folds of his large coat. 'And anyway, this place doesn't smell too pretty at the best of times. I don't know what you're complaining about.'

Anne fell silent as the enemy bombers flew in, wave upon wave, above them. They could all hear the fighter planes battling it out, the scream of their engines, the rattle of their guns so sharp against the throaty boom of the big guns. But to Anne those terrifying sounds held a deadly resonance, for Martin was up there somewhere, dicing with death to protect everything they held dear. Her father was out fire-watching on the roof of the cinema as well, doing his bit, becoming more exhausted by the day from lack of sleep as he tried to hold down his normal job and fulfil his duties with the Home Guard.

What a terrible war this is, she thought. It was heartbreaking to think of her mother and little brothers being so far away, and terrifying to be carrying a precious baby who would probably be born in the midst of it all. She folded her cold hands protectively over her bump, feeling the baby move and squirm as if it wanted to be free of her.

'We can only pray they'll all come home,' said Sylvia, taking her hand and tucking it into the folds of her mink coat, which she'd put across their knees. 'I do understand what you must be going through, Anne, but it must be doubly hard to be carrying that baby without your mother close to hand.'

'I know you do,' Anne replied, grateful that at least someone really knew what she went through every time there was a raid. 'But I can't help worrying over Martin. He's so very tired, exhausted really, and it only takes a moment of inattention—'

'I bet you've never had to sit out a raid in a place

like this, Lady Sylvia,' interrupted Ron. 'Damned roof is sweating, there's always a puddle on the floor, and every bang and boom makes it shudder and sing. It's a wonder to me any of us can survive without catching our deaths with pneumonia.'

'Thanks, Grandpa,' said Anne dryly. 'I know I can always rely on you to cheer us up.'

'As a matter of fact, Ron,' said Sylvia above the roar of enemy engines, 'I've spent many a night in places like this. I work as a volunteer at the local cottage hospital, and their shelter is just as grim.'

Ron sniffed and shifted Harvey to a more comfortable position on his lap.

Anne checked on Mrs Finch, who had fallen asleep in her deckchair and would have slipped out of it if they hadn't wedged her in with pillows and blankets. 'There are times,' she said with a sigh, 'that I almost wish I was as deaf as her. At least she gets a good night's sleep.' She reached into the cardboard box and pulled out a packet of biscuits. 'Anyone fancy one of these? They're a bit stale, but they taste all right.'

They sat in the flickering light of the kerosene lamp and munched their rather soggy biscuits, trying not to flinch as a series of distant explosions made the ground tremble beneath them. 'What about a game of I-spy?' suggested Sylvia during a lull.

'Not much to see in here,' muttered Ron.

'Ah, but there is if you let your imagination go

to work and use your mind's eye,' replied Sylvia. 'Think of all the things you like best and go from there. Shall I make a start?'

'Sounds a bit daft to me,' muttered Ron. 'Are you sure you haven't been at the cooking sherry?'

Sylvia laughed. 'Quite sure. I absolutely hate sherry.' She gripped Anne's hand tightly as the scream of a stricken fighter plane ended in an explosive crash somewhere down on the seafront. 'That was a Messerschmidt,' she said calmly. 'I've learned to recognise the sound of their engines.'

'Start the game, Sylvia,' urged Anne. 'It would be good to take our mind off things.'

Sylvia smiled. 'Very well. I spy with my mind's little eye, something beginning with H,' she said determinedly, 'and it has nothing whatsoever to do with Harvey.'

The enemy bombers returned within the half-hour, but it seemed they had spent their deadly cargos and were in a hurry to get back to their bases on the other side of the Channel.

The Spitfires and Hurricanes were not prepared to give up the fight so easily and brought several of their fighters down and crippled quite a few of the bombers. But it had been at a high cost, for Rita and Gladys had counted at least three downed RAF planes, and there had been no sign of the pilots parachuting to safety.

It was almost dawn when the all-clear sounded,

and Rita was wracked with impatience to get home and check on Louise. She fidgeted and paced as they waited to be stood down by the team that would take over from them, and when she saw the truck bouncing over the hills towards them, she told Gladys rather sharply to hurry up and get on the bike.

She was about to ride away when the driver of the truck swerved to cut her off. 'Oy,' he shouted through the window. 'You Rita Smith?'

'Yes,' she managed, the fear for Louise making it hard to speak at all.

'Got a message from John Hicks about your appointment up at the airfield this morning,' he said cheerfully, clearly unaware of the fright he'd given her.

'But it's all been arranged,' she protested.

He climbed down from the truck, slammed the door and spent a moment lighting a fag. 'The airfield's closed,' he said. 'The armoury took a direct hit, the control tower and some of the hangars are so badly damaged they'll have to be rebuilt. The runways are full of craters and they have six funerals to arrange.'

'Dear God,' breathed Rita. 'Do you have news of Barrow Lane, or the public shelter nearby? Do you know if anyone was hurt?'

He shook his head. 'Sorry, luv. The whole town's in uproar, but I do know the factories on the estate took a bashing, and that there were several casualties.'

'I've got to go,' she muttered. 'Thanks,' she shot over her shoulder as she kicked the bike into life, told Gladys to hold on tight, and raced towards Cliffehaven.

She could feel Gladys clinging to her, could hear her anxious pleas for her to slow down, but she closed her mind to everything but the need to see if Louise had come through this hellish night safely.

The devastation was clear to see as they reached the outskirts of the town. Volunteers from every service were helping to put out fires, stem burst water mains, make buildings safe and tend to the wounded. Refreshment tents had been set up by the WVS and the Red Cross, men and dogs were searching for people who might be buried in the rubble, and the air was filled with cloying, greasy smoke and the stench of burning rubber and old paint. Ambulance and fire engine crews were working at full stretch, houses were shattered, and people were wandering in dazed bewilderment through the rubble clutching the few precious things they'd managed to grab from the ruins of their homes.

Rita's mouth was dry and her pulse pounded as she quickly dropped a quaking Gladys outside the deserted fire station, retrieved her leather helmet and sped off towards Barrow Lane.

She was almost afraid to reach her destination, for she had no idea what she might find. If the damage in the town was anything to go by, then they would have been incredibly lucky to escape, being so close to the railway line.

She reached the arterial road that linked the narrow terraced lanes and slowed the bike, letting the engine growl beneath her as she weaved through the piles of smouldering bricks, shattered door-frames and windows and toppled chimneys. The corner shop had gone, and so had the barbershop and the remains of the Italian butcher's. Shanklin Lane and the one behind it had been flattened as if by a giant bulldozer, the windows in every other surrounding street blasted in.

Her heart pounded and she found it difficult to breathe as she realised how deserted it was. Where were the residents of these streets that smouldered beneath the pall of smoke? How come there were no wardens or policemen about? Where were the clean-up crews, the rescuers? The all-clear had sounded at least twenty minutes ago.

She reached the end of Barrow Lane and switched off the engine, chilled to the bone by what was before her.

Barrow Lane lay in absolute, abandoned silence. The gasometer no longer cast its shadow, for it had been blown to smithereens. The terraced houses had been ripped apart, shattered into a million pieces, the rubble strewn in heaps across the road. Water gushed like a geyser from a broken main and rattled against the debris of broken guttering, down-pipes and shattered glass. A net curtain had become entangled in the barbed wire that hung above the remains of the goods-yard wall, and it flapped listlessly in the dawn breeze like a white flag of surrender.

Rita was in a daze as she clambered over the wreckage, her breath sounding impossibly loud in the awful silence. She stood where her home had once been, staring at the charred remains of furniture, the blasted, buckled frame of May's beloved BSA and the solitary shoe that lay half-hidden under what was left of the garage doors. It was one of her father's. Picking it up, she held it to her heart, staring in stunned bewilderment at the wreckage, unable to take in what had happened.

'Get out of there! Can't you smell the gas? This whole place will go up in a minute and take us both along with it.'

She stared at the ARP warden – at his wild, red-rimmed eyes, his soot-smeared face beneath the tin helmet and his bedraggled uniform. Her mind was frozen and his words made no sense.

He grabbed her by the arm and almost dragged her down the lane. 'Go to the Town Hall,' he said firmly. 'They'll look after you there.'

'Louise,' she muttered, her thoughts suddenly clearing. 'What's happened to Louise and all the others from this street?'

His expression became grim. 'She probably went down the public shelter in Brook Street,' he replied, not meeting her frantic gaze.

A terrible suspicion lay black in her heart. 'What happened to the shelter?'

'It got damaged,' he said, his tone less brusque. 'There were some casualties, but they're pulling everyone out as soon as they can.'

Rita was trembling as she stood before him clutching her father's shoe. 'Casualties?' she rasped through a tight throat.

'A few. We won't know until we've got everyone out.' He placed a kindly hand on her arm. 'I wouldn't go there, luv,' he said. 'Best you head straight for the Town Hall.'

Rita backed away, shaking her head. 'I have to find Louise. Have to make sure she's all right.' Still clutching her father's shoe, she ignored his shouts, climbed onto the Norton and almost fell off as she attempted to steer with one hand and took a corner too swiftly. With the shoe tucked inside her jacket, she forced herself to remain calm and focused. It would be very stupid indeed to kill herself now after the night she'd just been through.

She reached Brook Street to find it in chaos. The blast had toppled the old tenement building into a heap of smoking rubble, and the rescue workers were desperately trying to get to the people trapped in the shelter beneath it. Those lucky enough to have already been rescued stood in bewildered, tearful huddles as babies cried, wardens tried to restore order and a shrouded stretcher was carried over the wreckage to be placed almost reverently beside two others.

Rita's fear for Louise was all-encompassing as she looked at those stretchers, but as she warily approached them, she was stopped by a warden. 'There's nothing you can do for them, dear,' he said, his eyes red-rimmed with weariness.

'I'm looking for my mother,' she managed through her tears.

'She's not here,' he replied softly. 'Two little kids and an old man lie under those sheets, God help them.'

Rita took a deep, shuddering breath, sad for the lives lost, but thankful it wasn't Louise. She turned back to the milling crowd that waited by the entrance the rescue workers had dug into the rubble. They seemed determined to stay there, heedless of the wardens' furious shouts to leave. 'Louise,' she yelled. 'Louise, where are you?'

There was no answer, and she pushed her way through the confused, stunned onlookers. 'Have you seen Louise Minelli?' she asked everyone she passed. But they shook their heads, their muttered replies barely intelligible – they were too shocked and afraid to be able to comprehend her urgency.

'Louise, where are you?' she called, close to tears. 'Louise. *Louise!*'

'I'm here.'

Rita spun round and gathered her into her arms.

'Oh, Mamma, I thought I'd lost you,' she sobbed. 'The house is gone, there's nothing left of Barrow Lane, and I thought – I feared . . .'

'It's all right, *cara mia*. We are both alive, and that's all that matters.'

Rita heard the aching weariness in Louise's voice, the hitch of sharp-edged fear, and drew back. Louise regarded her with eyes dull with shock. She was barely recognisable beneath the coating of dust and grime. Her greying hair was straggling from its pins, her skin was as pale as putty beneath the sooty smears, and her hands shook so badly she almost dropped the precious bag of treasured letters and photographs.

Rita put her arm round her. 'Come, Mamma, we'll go to the Town Hall and get a cup of tea.'

Louise remained stock-still as if planted to the shattered pavement. The tears rolled down her face, leaving tracks in the soot that had settled there. 'But how will Tino and Roberto find us now we have no home?' she whispered in Italian. 'They will not know – they will think we have forgotten them.'

'No, Mamma, the authorities will make sure we get their letters. They'll know how to find us.'

'You promise?'

Rita nodded and gently steered her towards the abandoned Norton. Taking the bag from her, she quickly placed it in the second pannier with their gas mask boxes.

'It's a long walk into town, and you're exhausted,'

she said softly. 'Will you agree to me driving you there?'

Louise, who had always refused to have anything to do with the motorbike, wordlessly perched side-saddle as they did in Italy, and clasped her arms round Rita's waist. 'Don't go too fast,' she said, resting her head wearily on Rita's shoulder. 'The road isn't safe and I don't want you getting hurt.'

'No, Mamma,' she replied. 'Whatever you say.'

Chapter Twelve

Beach View and the surrounding houses had escaped the worst of the bombing, but nearly every window had been smashed by the blasts, the gas, water and electricity were off, and all the telephone lines were down. Camden Road had come through unscathed, but one of the smaller hotels on the seafront had taken a direct hit and the debris had made the buildings on either side unsafe.

Wally, the ARP warden, had gleefully told them about the enemy plane crashing into the pier, which was now a twisted, charred iron skeleton sticking out of the sea. He seemed almost to delight in being the bearer of bad news as he described the damage in the town, and on the factory estate; the loss of life at the Brook Street shelter and the devastation caused to the airfield. But, frustratingly, he didn't know any of the details about what had happened to the men and women at the RAF base and had left Anne even more frantic for news of Martin and Cissy.

'I wish to heavens I could go out to the base,' she muttered, 'but as a civilian I'm forbidden to go near it – and I wouldn't be of much use anyway.' She paced the kitchen, unable to settle to anything. 'If only he could telephone.'

'I've always found that it's best to keep busy at times like these,' said Mrs Finch. 'Your mother would be calling on the neighbours to make sure they're all right, and then turning her hand to cleaning this place as if her life depended upon it.'

Anne nodded, unable to speak for fear it would unblock the dam she'd desperately erected to stem the great tide of fear that threatened to overwhelm her.

Mrs Finch looked up at Anne and smiled tremulously as she handed her the broom. 'I've sent Ron to check on the neighbours, and Lady Sylvia has gone to the hospital to see if she can lend a hand there. Let's make a start on clearing away all the broken glass before someone cuts themselves.'

Anne fumbled for the broom, but her mind was numb, her hands shaking too badly to keep it from clattering to the floor. She stared at it in dumb despair, unable to retrieve it.

'Come on, Anne, dear. Sit down and have a cup of tea. You'll feel better with something inside you.' Mrs Finch gently led her to the chair by the range and pressed her into it before pouring the last of the tea from the flask. They'd all forgotten to fill the kettle before they'd rushed for the Anderson shelter.

Anne felt sick and disorientated, the sleepless night and the worry over Martin and Cissy exacerbating the effects of that terrifying raid. Yet she sipped the over-sweet, stewed tea obediently in the hope it might calm her, and tried to garner warmth from the meagre fire in the range. She was cold to the core and couldn't seem to stop shivering.

'Your father should be back soon and then perhaps we'll know more,' soothed Mrs Finch as she retrieved the abandoned broom. 'He's bound to have spoken to one of his pals who were manning the searchlights by the airfield.'

'I want my mum,' murmured Anne, the tears sliding down her face. 'I miss her so much.'

'There, there, dear. Don't cry.' Mrs Finch perched awkwardly on the arm of the chair and held her close. 'Your mother will be home very soon.'

'It's so hard without her here,' Anne managed, 'and I'm terrified something will happen to her – to Martin and to Cissy – and that I'll never see any of them again.'

'I know it's hard,' soothed Mrs Finch. 'But we must keep faith that they'll come home safe and well.'

Faith was such a small word, but it held a universe of meaning Anne found impossible to comprehend while the dark fears haunted her. She placed her trembling hands protectively round her distended belly, feeling the baby move beneath her fingers as she prayed fervently for her family to be spared.

'I don't see why we can't go to Beach View,' said Louise as they came to a halt outside the grey, forbidding building that had once been the local asylum.

'Peggy has always said we'd be welcome should we need somewhere, and this place makes my skin crawl.'

'I've already explained several times, Mamma,' Rita said wearily. 'They don't have any room.' Rita climbed off the motorbike, took the box of emergency rations they'd been given at the Town Hall from Louise, and helped her off the bike.

'I don't mind sleeping on the floor, or in the dining room on the couch,' Louise continued. 'Anything's better than staying here.'

Rita didn't voice her deep concern over Martin and Cissy, but she kept seeing that red glow which had lit up the sky to the north of Cliffehaven, marking the almost complete destruction of the airfield where six people had been killed. Beach View could well be a house of mourning, and this was not the time to go begging for shelter.

'They're using the dining room to feed everyone,' she said firmly, 'and Cissy will be sleeping on the couch when she's on leave. At least, here, we'll have beds.'

Louise looked as if she was about to argue, then gave a sigh of defeated weariness and distress. 'Tino and me worked so hard to make a success of the café,' she sobbed. 'We've lived there all our married life, raising our children and making plans for the future. How is it that everything can be wiped out so swiftly, Rita? What have I done to deserve losing my home and my family?'

Rita had no answer, for she was still mourning the loss of her own home and the garage where she and her father had shared so many happy hours. The memories would remain with her for always, but the pain of losing everything still ran deep and she longed for her father's quiet consolation and reassuring embrace.

'You've done nothing wrong,' she replied a little unsteadily, 'and neither did anyone else who lost their homes and their livelihoods last night.' She took Louise's hand, feeling its tremble and its chill. 'But we have each other, Mamma. We aren't alone.'

Louise snatched away her hand as she turned her tear-streaked face to Rita. 'But you'll be leaving after Christmas,' she said bitterly, 'and then I shall be left with no one and no place to call home. It would have been better to die in the shelter than endure such an existence.'

Rita knew she'd been beaten – that it would now be impossible to pursue her dreams and leave Louise behind – had realised it when she'd found Louise standing helplessly beside the rubble of the collapsed shelter. 'I'll go to the recruitment office tomorrow and see if it's possible to do my training here and fulfil my duties locally. If not, I'll withdraw my application,' she said, her voice trembling with emotion.

Louise's tears dried almost instantly. 'You're a good girl, Rita.' She squeezed Rita's hand, her smile a little unsteady. 'I knew you wouldn't desert me.'

Rita battled with her mixed emotions as they stood hand in hand among the choking weeds of the gravel drive and stared up at the gloomy building that was to be their billet until they could find something less daunting.

Shielded by a high wall and surrounding trees, the Victorian asylum stood in large, unkempt grounds that isolated it from the westernmost heights of Cliffehaven. There were no houses nearby, and the little-used cart track leading up to it from the seafront meandered steeply through clumps of gorse, brambles, wild apple trees and stinging nettles.

It was quite a climb, and even the Norton had had trouble carrying them to the top, but Rita suspected the view would have been quite spectacular if the town hadn't been shrouded in the remains of smoke and ash which still rose from the ruined buildings.

She regarded the asylum warily, remembering the stories she'd heard as a child about this place being haunted. She no longer believed in ghosts, and the poor insane souls who'd once been incarcerated here had all been evacuated at the outbreak of war. But despite the weak sunlight streaking through the clouds, she could feel the dark, disturbing aura of their madness which seemed still to linger in the grey ivy-clad walls, turrets and barred windows.

Rita shuddered at the thought of actually having to sleep within those walls, but they had no other choice and Louise was feeling fragile enough without her voicing her childish fears. 'Come, Mamma. We have to make the best of things, and I'm sure it's much nicer inside.'

They carried their bags of precious belongings up the steps to the sturdy, iron-studded front door. The woman at the Town Hall had told them there would be no one to meet them and to just let themselves in.

The door creaked ominously as Rita pushed it open and they stepped into an echoing, marble-floored entrance hall. A once-grand staircase swept off to one side, the red carpet worn through, the brass stair-rods tarnished with age and neglect. There were faded patches on the walls where large pictures had been taken down, and the chandelier that must have hung from the ornate plaster rose in the high ceiling had been replaced by a single unshaded light bulb. There was no furniture, and it looked as if it had been many months since the place had been dusted and polished.

Rita and Louise moved further into the hall, their footsteps echoing in the silence as they explored their new home. Several rooms led off the square hall, each of them numbered, and, behind the stair-case, a passageway led to a vast kitchen with an ancient range, scrubbed wooden tables and mismatched chairs. Unlike the hall, this room was as neat as a new pin, and still held the aroma of last night's supper. There were pots and pans hanging above the range, plain white china sat on deep shelves or in the wooden drainers above the sink, and a huge stack of logs had been placed in a corner to feed the fire. Several wooden clothes driers were strung from pulleys across the huge ceiling, bearing a collection of underwear, sheets, towels and nappies.

'The woman at the billeting office did say we weren't the only ones here, but I was beginning to have my doubts,' muttered Rita. 'The place feels deserted.'

'What you doing 'ere?'

Rita whirled round in horror to face Aggie Rawlings. 'We were bombed out last night,' she stammered.

'This place ain't fer the likes of 'er,' Aggie snarled, eyes flashing with anger as she glared at Louise. 'There's camps for bleedin' Eyeties.' Her venomous glare settled on Rita. 'And for the likes of you an' all,' she added, folding her arms beneath her pendulous bosom. 'You don't fool me, Rita Smith. You've got more than a drop of Eyetie blood in you, I'll be bound.'

Rita could feel Louise cowering beside her. 'You're entitled to your opinion, Aggie,' she said, 'but I warn you – if you say or do anything to hurt Louise, you'll have me to answer to. And I fight dirty, Aggie. Especially when my family's threatened.'

'You wait till my old man finds out you're here,' Aggie retorted. 'You won't be so big for yer boots then.'

'Drop it, Aggie. There's enough trouble without you making things worse. None of us want to be here, but we have to make the best of it.'

Aggie sniffed and stomped off into the hall, her heavy footfalls ringing out until they heard the slam of a door.

'Who *was* that horrible woman?' Louise shivered and pulled her coat collar to her chin.

'No one important. Just ignore her and don't let her get to you. She's mostly hot air, and not everyone thinks the way she does.' Rita gave Louise a smile of encouragement. 'Come on, Mamma, let's find our room and settle in.'

They checked the numbers on the doors and began the long climb up the stairs to discover their room was at the very top of the house in one of the round turrets. Louise was exhausted by the climb, and Rita was sweating in the heavy fire service overcoat that she'd worn over her old leather flying jacket since the night before. But when she slotted the heavy key in the lock and opened the door they were both drawn instantly to the broad bay windows and the amazing view.

Setting aside their bags and the box of rations, they looked through the sturdy iron bars which had been cemented into the frames. Far below them the smoke had cleared enough for them to see the leafy green hedges and red roofs of Havelock Gardens. The little white kiosk on the seafront that had once served afternoon teas and ice creams to the holidaymakers had survived the raid, as had the roofs and chimneys of the big hotels at the western end of the promenade. They could see very little of the rest of the town from here, but the pier was in ruins, the tail of the enemy plane sticking grotesquely out of the charred skeleton of what had once been the ballroom.

'The room's bigger than I expected,' said Rita with determined cheerfulness, 'and certainly not the padded cell I thought we'd get. This must have been one of those private asylums where the rich hid away their embarrassing relatives.'

She took off the coat and leather jacket as she eyed the two narrow iron bedsteads, the thin mattresses and the stack of clean linen, pillows and blankets which had been left on top of the old-fashioned dresser. The only other furniture was a heavy old wardrobe, a badly upholstered chair and a rather dilapidated oil-fired heater which had definitely seen better days.

Rita regarded it dubiously. 'It's probably best not to light it,' she warned Louise. 'Put a match to that and it's likely to blow up – and I don't know about you, but I've had enough explosions for one day.'

'But it'll get very cold up here at night,' Louise protested.

'If it does, then we'll push the beds together and sleep in our coats. I'm not risking that thing.'

Louise sank onto the worn, thin mattress, her face lined with fatigue. 'How did you know that awful woman, Rita? Who is she?'

'She's just a very unpleasant old battleaxe who works at the factory,' Rita replied airily. 'I've learned to ignore her, and so should you.'

'You never told me you were having trouble at work,' said Louise accusingly.

'You had enough to worry about. I'm a big girl now, Mamma. I know how to look after myself.'

'You used to tell me everything,' muttered Louise.

Rita was too tired and distraught to get into yet another argument. She looked at her watch. It was too late to go to the recruitment office or to see what had happened to the factory, but too early to start cooking their evening meal. 'You stay here and rest while I find the bathroom and somewhere to store the motorbike safely. I'll also see where the shelter is – we might need it before the night's out.'

'Will it be safe here, Rita? What if that woman causes trouble?'

'We'll be as safe here as anywhere, and as long as we don't rise to the bait, Aggie will soon find she has nothing to fight against.' Rita kissed Louise's cheek. 'The door's sturdy enough and we have a key to keep out people like Aggie. Rest, Mamma, and leave everything to me.'

The hours had dragged interminably, and Anne's fears multiplied as lunchtime came and went with still no sign of her father or news from the airfield.

The three nurses were still at the hospital, no doubt dealing with the many casualties, and Lady

Sylvia hadn't been seen since she'd left in the Rolls-Royce this morning. Ron had refused to stay indoors and rest and, after makeshift repairs to some of the front windows, had taken himself off to the Anchor to check on Rosie. After that he planned to see if he could glean any news from his pals in the Home Guard, and track down his son. The telephone was still dead, and it was unlike Jim not to come home as soon as his fire-watch shift ended.

'He'll turn up, dear, don't fret,' said Mrs Finch as she wrung out the dishcloth. The water and electricity were back on, and she and Anne had spent the last three hours cleaning away the dust and debris that had floated in through the shattered windows. 'I expect he's got involved in helping to board up everyone's windows.'

'Then I wish he'd see to ours,' muttered Anne. 'It's freezing in here, and once night falls it'll get even worse.'

She carefully carried the bucket of dirty water down the cellar steps and tipped it into Ron's water butt which he used to water his vegetable plot. Standing in the gathering gloom she pulled her cardigan more firmly round her as she looked up at the sky and took a trembling breath. It was still and silent, the calm after the storm, but inside her heart it was still raging, and she knew she wouldn't be able to rest until her loved ones had returned home.

'Anne, dear,' called Mrs Finch rather sharply from

the kitchen window. 'Can you come inside? Quickly now. I need you.'

Anne's heart skipped a beat and an awful dread settled in the pit of her stomach as she hurried through the back door and up the steps into the kitchen. There had been an urgent edge to Mrs Finch's voice which could only bode trouble.

He was standing by the range, his broad shoulders slumped, his face grey and lined with weariness and pain beneath the bruises and the bandage wrapped round his head.

'Martin,' she gasped, and burst into tears.

He gathered her to him awkwardly, hampered by the sling on his plastered arm. 'It's all right,' he soothed. 'Looks much worse than it really is – I promise, my love.'

She clung to him, the anguish turned to joyous relief that was still tinged with fear. 'Thank God you're all right,' she breathed, 'but where's Cissy?'

'I'm here, Anne.' Cissy appeared in the kitchen doorway, looking very much the worse for wear. Her uniform was filthy, her face was bruised and covered in grime, and she too had one arm in a sling. 'We're a couple of old crocs,' she said with a rueful grin, 'but we'll survive.'

Anne held out her arm for her younger sister and the three of them stood in that tight embrace as their tears of thankfulness spilled and mingled. There were no words to express the joy of being home – of being safe and warm and loved.

Mrs Finch dabbed her eyes with a lace-edged handkerchief and hurriedly put the kettle on the range as Lady Sylvia followed Cissy into the room and sank into a chair.

'It's been quite a day,' Sylvia sighed. 'The hospital was in chaos and, for once, I felt a modicum of respect for Matron. That woman is superb in a crisis. She'd have made an excellent army officer.' She took off her hat and shrugged out of her mink coat. 'I came across these two looking rather sorry for themselves in casualty, and once I realised who they were, I was able to drive them home.'

Anne kept tight hold of Martin, never wanting to let him go, needing his warmth and sturdiness to bolster her. 'Has anyone seen or heard from Dad?'

'He was at the hospital earlier,' said Lady Sylvia. 'I saw him working with the ambulance crew.' She gave Anne a reassuring smile. 'He's unscathed, Anne, and told me to tell you he'll be home for his tea.'

Martin gently prised Anne's arms from his waist and sank into a kitchen chair. 'That cup of tea wouldn't go amiss,' he said wanly to Mrs Finch. 'I suddenly feel rather shaky.'

Anne touched his face, noting the bruises and the black eye, the heavy bandaging round his head, and the lines of weariness. 'We heard about the attack on the airfield,' she murmured, 'and were all so worried. Was it very bad?'

'Cissy could tell you more about that,' he replied,

nodding his thanks to Mrs Finch as she set the large mug of sweet tea before him. 'I was a bit preoccupied at the time with two Messerschmidts on my tail.' He took a sip of his tea and closed his eyes with a sigh of pleasure.

Tears welled as Anne regarded him. He looked exhausted. 'But you obviously got back to base safely,' she managed.

'In a roundabout sort of way,' he said almost nonchalantly. 'The Spitfire had more holes in her than a strainer. The engine had cut out and I'd lost the landing gear, so I had to put her down wherever I could. I could see the damage at the airfield, the runways were destroyed, and the only place I could find was a field.'

He grinned and smoothed his moustache. 'Unfortunately the farmer had just ploughed it, so it was a bit of a bumpy ride and the poor old Spitfire took a thrashing. I hit my head on the instrument panel and was out cold for some time according to the land girls who managed to pull me out.'

'He turned up at the base on the back of the farmer's tractor,' said Cissy with a wan smile. 'The place was in chaos, communications were down and everyone was busy putting out the fires and trying to rescue as much as they could from the burnt-out hangars.'

'We were told there were casualties,' murmured Anne.

Martin nodded, his face ashen. 'We lost several

planes, four pilots and two civilian engineers. All good men, who will be very much missed.'

'What about you, Cissy? It must have been terrifying to be in the thick of it.'

Cissy struggled to light a cigarette with one hand. She blew smoke, her gaze distant as she became lost in the memories of that raid. 'We'd all gone to the shelters the minute the sirens went, but we could hear the bombs going off and the planes overhead. Me and Amy and the other girls were absolutely fine until one of the blasts knocked the shelter wall in. We were buried for a bit, and I honestly thought I'd never see daylight again, but they dug us all out quickly, and no one was seriously hurt. I ended up with a broken arm, and one or two of the others had nasty cuts and sprains, but Amy only had a few scratches and a badly bruised leg, so I guess we were very lucky.'

'Certainly luckier than those poor souls who lost their lives in the Brook Street shelter,' said Jim, who'd arrived in the kitchen doorway without any of them noticing.

'Brook Street?' breathed a wide-eyed Cissy. 'But isn't that the nearest shelter for Rita and Louise?'

'Rita was on fire-watch up top, but Louise made it out in one piece only to find their street had been flattened,' he replied, stroking her tangled hair with infinite tenderness before kissing her cheek. 'But what about you, Cissy me darling? What's happened to your arm?'

Cissy told him about the cave-in at the base shelter.

'I'll be fine in a matter of weeks, Dad,' she assured him, 'but I want to hear what's happened to Rita.'

'There's nothing left of Barrow Lane or any of the streets behind the railway. The gasometer took a direct hit and the place was flattened. We had to get the maintenance crew in quickly to stem any gas leaks, and keep the residents away.'

'Poor little Rita,' sighed Anne. 'We'll have to find a space for them here – though I have no idea where to put them.'

'They could share with me, I suppose,' said Sylvia, 'though it would certainly be a tight squeeze.'

'No need for that, Lady Sylvia,' said Ron as he emerged from the cellar with Harvey at his heels. 'They've been billeted up at the old asylum and will be as comfortable there as anywhere.' He pumped Martin's hand and kissed Cissy's cheek. ''Tis a world of thanks I'm giving to see you two again,' he said.

'It's good to be home, Grandpa,' said Cissy, 'and as we're both on leave until our injuries heal, it means we'll be home for Christmas.'

'This calls for a celebratory drink, so it does. Mrs Finch, break out the glasses while I get the whisky.'

Mrs Finch eyed Ron suspiciously. 'I have no doubt you're feeling frisky,' she said frostily, 'but I really don't see why you have to tell *me*.'

Their laughter was soft and tinged with weariness and relief as Ron hunted out the glasses and poured the whisky. Then he raised his glass. 'Here's to Beach View and all who call it home.'

Anne felt the heat of the whisky at the back of her throat as she regarded them all with deep affection. This family would survive Hitler and come through united and stronger than ever.

Rita and Louise had battled with the ancient plumbing and taken it in turns to share the few inches of water in the bath. They'd used the rather murky water afterwards to wash Louise's clothes and brush down her filthy overcoat, and Rita had strung everything up in the kitchen to dry, thankful they'd both had the foresight to pack a change of clothing and spare nightdresses in what they called their 'air-raid bags'.

Having made the beds, Louise had curled up and was asleep within minutes. Rita had covered her with the heavy fire service overcoat and watched her careworn face slowly relax into peaceful repose. She would sleep for at least a couple of hours, and Rita had decided to take the opportunity to go back into Cliffehaven and try to discover what had happened to Cissy and Martin – and if Beach View Boarding House was still standing.

She had been passing the hospital in Camden Road on her way to Beach View when she'd seen Lady Sylvia walking towards her. It didn't take very long to learn that both Martin and Cissy had come home to recuperate, and that all was well at Beach View. She spent a few minutes relaying her own news and, with a promise to pass on her love and best wishes to Cissy, Lady Sylvia had hurried into the hospital to see her son.

With a much lighter heart, Rita had then headed for the fire station to ask John Hicks if she could have the night off. He'd readily agreed, and she'd set off for Goldman's clothing factory to inform them that Louise would not be working her shift tonight, but would come in the next morning. Mr Simmons, the supervisor, wasn't best pleased, but Goldman had overheard their conversation and quickly intervened. Louise did not have to go into work until the following afternoon.

Feeling much better about things, Rita headed for the allotments. But as she rode past the quiet, empty streets of ruined homes, her heart ached for how it had once been, and she deliberately avoided going anywhere near Barrow Lane.

The vegetable plots had been planted on an empty tract of land the council had once planned to use for new housing. The nearby houses seemed to be hardly damaged, but for the windows which had been boarded up, and the allotment had come through the raid unscathed. But Rita suspected that such bounty wouldn't survive the thieves, and she'd dug up as many potatoes, carrots and onions as she could, putting them into the sacks Tino kept in his little shed. The cabbages and Brussels sprouts wouldn't keep for long, so she'd take them with her, the rest could stay locked in the shed.

She didn't stay longer than necessary, for the

allotment reminded her too sharply of Tino, and she'd suffered enough loss for one day. With everyone she loved so far away and her home in ruins, it didn't help to linger on thoughts of what might have been. She stowed the tools away and padlocked the shed, then quickly tied the neck of the sack she was taking with her and carried it through the allotment to the bike.

With the sack wedged between her and the handles, she'd had to ride the bike slowly and carefully back to the asylum. It wasn't an easy journey, and it had taken much longer than she'd planned. She could only hope that Louise hadn't woken and become distressed to find she was alone in such strange surroundings.

Having tucked the Norton safely inside one of the many outhouses, Rita lugged the sack over her shoulder and let herself in through the front door just as Vi came down the stairs and Aggie peered round her door.

'Hello, Rita,' said Vi cheerfully. 'You've been busy. What you got in there?'

She closed the front door behind her, ignored Aggie's inquisitive eyes, and joined Vi Charlton on her way to the kitchen. 'Vegetables,' she replied. 'Thought I'd make a big pot of soup to eke out the emergency rations.'

'Yeah, they don't give us much, do they? And I had a tin of biscuits in my cupboard at home that I was saving for Christmas an' all. The damn thing's probably burnt crumbs now – just like me lovely clothes and shoes.' Vi looked down at the dowdy skirt and worn cardigan she'd been given from the piles of used clothing stored at the Town Hall.

'Still, we've got a roof over our heads, – though it comes to something when we're sent to an asylum,' Rita said wryly. 'What's your room like?'

Vi put her box of rations on the scrubbed kitchen table. 'Not too bad; I'm sharing with two other girls from Shanklin Street. We're down on the ground floor, so we can get in and out without alerting the nosy parkers.' She shot a glance at the two older women who were gossiping as they stirred pots of something on the range.

'Aggie's here,' muttered Rita, 'and she seems to be lurking about the hall every time I come downstairs.'

'No one takes notice of Aggie,' said Vi. 'She's managed to upset so many people over the years she has very few friends here.' She paused as she reached into the box for the brown paper bag which held her weekly ration of tea. 'Has Louise heard anything of her husband and son?' she asked quietly so the others couldn't hear.

Rita shook her head. 'But we hope the authorities will let them write to us for Christmas. It would help no end to know they're all right.'

'They've got to be better off than us,' Vi replied, carefully spooning some of the precious leaves into a pot. 'Have you seen what's happened to the factory?'

'Is it very bad?'

'Not enough damage to shut it down completely, but Major Patricia has had a team of men working through the day to make it safe. It'll be business as usual tomorrow morning, I bet.' She took the kettle off the range and poured the boiling water into the pot. 'Want to share this with me?'

'That would be lovely,' sighed Rita. 'I'll just go and check on Louise. Keep an eye on that, will you? I'll be back in a minute.'

Vi regarded the sack thoughtfully. 'If I make a start on preparing the veg, do you think I could share some of your soup?'

'Of course, Vi. But don't do too many potatoes and onions, they'll keep in the sack for ages yet.'

Rita hurried out of the kitchen, caught Aggie's malevolent glare through the chink in her door and raced up the stairs. It would be a relief to get back to work and some kind of normality – but she still needed urgently to speak to that woman at the recruitment office. Although her head was telling her she'd probably lost her chance of fulfilling her dreams, her heart still yearned for it not to be so.

Chapter Thirteen

Rita had fallen asleep almost the minute her head had hit the rather lumpy pillow. When she woke, she experienced a moment of disorientation before she remembered they were in the asylum, and that earthy smell was coming from the sack of vegetables in the corner and the onions she'd strung together from the hook on the door.

Lying there in the relative warmth of the thin blankets and the profound darkness of the blackout curtains, she listened to Louise's soft breathing and knew she still slept. But she would wake soon enough to the trials and tribulations of adjusting to their new home and the people who shared it, and Rita could only hope that her time at the clothing factory had given her enough self-esteem to be able to cope and make friends.

She stared into the darkness, loath to begin the day, for although she had few qualms about their living arrangements and was quite happy to muck in with everyone else, she dreaded the visit to the recruiting office.

Unable to go back to sleep, and with her troubled thoughts churning, she climbed out of bed, hauled on her fleece-lined leather jacket over her nightdress, and tiptoed across the room to peek through the blackout curtains. The condensation had turned to ice on the inside of the windows and she had to scrape it away to see anything. It was hardly worth the effort, for the dawn was depressingly grey, with low clouds veiling the sea and the buildings at the bottom of the hill. Rain spattered against the glass, gulls cried mournfully as they hovered and swooped, and she could see the path of a brisk wind in the surrounding trees.

She sighed and let the curtains drop back into place. The only good thing about such a murky day was that Gerry would probably stay at home and leave them in peace to clear up the mess the Luftwaffe had left behind yesterday.

Not wanting to wake Louise, Rita quickly got dressed, used the bathroom and hurried downstairs to make a pot of tea. The kitchen was warm and welcoming, and, despite the early hour, was already quite busy. She greeted the other women who were sleepily preparing breakfast, feeding babies and helping one another to adjust to a different way of living.

Most of them were neighbours from the streets surrounding Barrow Lane, and had known each other for years, and it seemed that past enmities and niggling irritations had been set aside for now. Regardless of age, they were all in this together, with one goal: to get through this war, see their men home, and start again.

Rita spent some time chatting with them as she waited for the kettle to boil and the toast to brown, and was gratified and relieved to discover that Louise was no longer considered an outcast. In fact, she learned, Louise was regarded quite kindly now she'd proved she could hold down a proper job and go it alone – which Rita found most amusing in the circumstances, although she kept that to herself.

Louise was still curled up in bed when Rita brought the tray of tea and toast into the bedroom, but she was awake and threading the rosary beads through her fingers as she murmured her morning prayers and gazed at her photographs of Tino and Roberto.

'I'd stay in bed for as long as you can until you have to go to work this afternoon,' Rita said cheerfully. 'It's horrid out there.'

Louise slipped the rosary beads round her neck and sat up. 'Do you have to leave just yet?'

Rita nodded as she poured the tea. 'I'm due to start my shift at ten, so it'll give me time to go to the recruiting office first.' She fell silent, her appetite for tea and toast dwindling at the thought of what she had to do.

'You'll be far safer staying in Cliffehaven,' said Louise, tucking into the toast, oblivious to the irony of her words considering their situation. 'And the job in the factory pays very well. I can't understand whatever possessed you to enlist with the WAAFs in the first place.'

Rita stirred the few grains of sugar she'd put in her tea, unable to reply. Louise would never understand – could never accept that there were opportunities and challenges for a girl like her outside the confines of Cliffehaven.

'You'll be much happier here amongst the people you know,' Louise continued. 'And when the men come home you'll realise how much you really love Roberto, and settle down to a happy and contented life. A woman's place is in the home with her husband and babies – not fooling about with engines and dashing around on motorbikes.'

Rita remained silent. She might only be eighteen, but she'd learned enough to know that happiness and security didn't have to depend on marriage – that sometimes it had the opposite effect. She'd seen enough of the trials Vi had gone through with her brute of a husband, had heard the stories of drunkenness and bullying from the women who'd once gossiped on the doorsteps of Barrow Lane, and seen the black eyes and bruises – and the hopelessness that seemed to weigh them down. Not everyone was lucky enough to have a marriage like Tino and Louise's.

'I'd better be going,' she said, pulling on her jacket and reaching for her gas mask box and overnight bag. 'I don't think there'll be any raids today, the weather's too bad, but it might be an idea to keep your bag packed just in case.'

Louise nodded. 'Could you get my washing from the kitchen before you go? It must be dry by now.'

'It's best if you fetch it, Mamma. You'll have to mix with the others sooner or later, and as you know most of them it shouldn't be too hard.'

'I don't want to bump into that Aggie person,' she muttered.

'She's on early shift today,' said Rita firmly. 'Please, Mamma, you have to try and muck in with everyone here, or they'll think you're stand-offish.' She shot her a warm smile. 'They're not your enemies, you know. In fact they all asked after you, genuinely concerned about how you are.'

Louise pushed the tray to one side of the bed and slid beneath the blankets. 'I'll go down later,' she replied. 'What time will you be back?'

'At about six. The rest of last night's soup is in the pot over there for your lunch, and I'll make sure there's something hot for you when you get in at eight.' Rita bent to kiss Louise's cheek.

'Will you go to the post office and see if there are any letters?'

'I'll do my best, but I might not make it during opening hours. Take care going down that hill and wrap up warm. It's raining harder now and the wind's getting up.'

Louise pulled the blanket over her head, her reply inaudible.

There were very few people about in the town, apart from the few hardy souls waiting mournfully outside the bakery for their day's ration, and the men who were still labouring to shore up one of the large buildings which was leaning dangerously against its neighbour.

There were huge gaps all along the upper end of the High Street, and at the top of the hill the station looked forlorn now it had no roof and only the remnants of one wall. Rubble had been piled high into the bomb craters, and the shops closest to the station had had their windows blown in during the blitz of parachute mines that had all but obliterated the railway lines, bus depot, and the houses behind it.

In the gloom of the misty rain and the cold wind coming off the sea, Cliffehaven didn't look at all festive, and it seemed in keeping with the sadness that lay heavy in Rita's heart as she parked the Norton outside the recruiting office.

The door was locked, but as she peered through the misted windows, she could see there was a light on inside and someone was moving about. She rapped on the glass, impatient to get this over with.

The figure loomed towards her and an angry face peered through the glass. 'We're closed until ten.'

'I have to be at work by ten,' shouted Rita. 'I need to speak to you now. It's urgent.'

The recruitment officer glared at her, then turned the key and opened the door just far enough to talk through. 'This is most irregular. What do you want, Miss Smith?'

'I need to talk about my application.' Rita tucked her chin into her collar as the rain dripped from her leather helmet and down her neck. 'Please can I come in?'

The woman gave a great sigh and, with little grace, let her in. 'Stand on the mat,' she ordered. 'I've just cleaned this floor.' She slammed the door shut. 'So what is it, Miss Smith?'

Rita pulled off the sodden leather helmet and shook out her hair. 'I need help and advice,' she replied. 'You see, I was bombed out, and of course I couldn't go for the initial interview and medical because of the raid on the airbase.'

'I am fully aware of the consequences of that raid, Miss Smith, but I cannot see how your lack of accommodation is any of my concern. As for your medical, you will be given another date as soon as possible.'

'That's just the point,' said Rita. 'I don't know if I should take it in the circumstances.'

The older woman's eyebrows shot up. 'Why ever not?'

Rita quickly explained. 'I don't need much training, and I was hoping I could stay in Cliffehaven to carry out my duties,' she finished breathlessly.

There was a long, tense silence in which Rita could hear the thud of her heartbeat.

The other woman's steely gaze never faltered. 'One cannot pick and choose, Miss Smith. The WAAFs command obedience and total commitment. The training is compulsory, and carried out several miles away. You will then be posted wherever you are needed most.'

Rita's eyes swam with hot tears. 'Then I have no choice but to withdraw my application,' she said shakily.

'But you were so keen,' said the woman, her expression softening. 'I remember when you first came in here at the beginning of the war begging to be allowed to work as a mechanic on the airbase. Now you have the chance to finish your apprentice-ship and do just that. Surely you don't really want to throw this opportunity away?'

'It's the last thing I want to do,' Rita admitted as she battled the tears, 'but I can't abandon Louise now she's homeless.' She looked up at the woman, saw the understanding in her eyes and could battle no longer. 'Please,' she sobbed, 'isn't there some way I could work at the local base during the day and stay with Louise at night?'

'Oh, my dear.' The woman put her arm round Rita's shoulder and held her as she cried. 'I'm sorry, but that just isn't possible. You'd be part of the team, don't you see, and expected to live at whichever base you're assigned to so that you're on call day or night. Joining one of the services is not like working in a factory or a shop. There aren't set hours, and leave is erratic at the best of times.'

Rita was aware that her tears were dampening the stiff serge of the other woman's uniform jacket – and it was a bit disconcerting to be mothered by someone she'd always found daunting. She eased from her embrace and hastily blew her nose. 'Is there a form I have to sign?'

The woman wordlessly walked to her desk, found a sheaf of forms and a pen and hesitated before she handed them over. 'There're always forms to fill in,' she said with a sad smile. 'Are you really sure about this, Miss Smith? Isn't there anyone else to look after Mrs Minelli?'

Rita thought longingly of Beach View Boarding House. If only Peggy wasn't away. If only the house wasn't already so crowded there might have been a chance. 'No,' she replied, her voice catching.

'Then, I'm sorry, my dear.' The woman pushed the forms towards her.

Rita could barely see through her tears as she swiftly signed them. 'Thanks anyway,' she muttered. She gave a wan smile and headed for the door.

'If things change, then come back,' the woman called after her. 'The WAAFs could do with more girls like you, and I will guarantee that your re-application will be rushed through.'

'You're very kind,' said Rita. 'Thank you.'

She was sobbing as she ran into the rain and

climbed on the Norton. She could hardly see through her tears as she kicked the bike into life and headed for the factory. Her dreams were shattered. Although she was chilled to the bone and soaking wet, at least the rain acted as a perfect camouflage for her tears.

Ron knew he wasn't fully recovered, for he'd attempted to smoke his pipe this morning and had ended up coughing his lungs out. His chest still ached where he'd pulled the muscles, and the shrapnel was moving about again in his lower back. All in all he was feeling a bit sorry for himself, and the only way he knew of countering that was to go and see Rosie.

It was almost opening time when he slipped out of the back door with Harvey and hurried down the passageway that ran between the terraces to the end of the street. Jamming his cap firmly over his head, he pulled up his coat collar and buried his chin. It was only a short walk down Camden Road to the Anchor, but it was raining and the strong gusts of wind threatened to knock him over.

Harvey trotted along beside him, tongue lolling, fur plastered to his head and back making him look more like his greyhound sire than ever. He didn't seem to mind the weather at all; in fact, he appeared to be relishing it.

Ron tugged on the leash as Harvey tried to water every lamp post and sniff every scent. 'Not the weather for that, ye auld rascal,' he muttered. 'Let's get in the warm.'

He shoved his way through the ancient oak door and went down the single step into the stone-flagged bar that held the aroma of decades of beer and tobacco. A fire was blazing in the inglenook, sending dancing shadows over the heavy dark beams, and glints of light on the diamond-paned windows and collection of copper pots. Every table and chair had been polished to a gleam, the cushions on the old pews beneath the windows were plumped and inviting, and Rosie had strung tinselled branches of holly and mistletoe everywhere. It was like coming home.

Harvey headed straight for the fire and stretched out on the flagstones with a deep sigh of pleasure, his nose on his paws, his eyes watching Ron's every move.

Rosie was behind the bar looking gorgeous as usual and she shot him a warm smile of welcome. 'Hello, Ron. I didn't expect to see you this early in the day.'

'I worked up a thirst sitting about in that hospital.' He took his coat off and dumped it on a stool. 'Did you want a hand bringing up the crates or changing the barrels?'

'It's all been taken care of,' she said, her gaze avoiding him as she reached for the beer pump. 'Do you want your usual, or a drop of whisky to keep out the cold?'

'To be sure, a drop of the heather would see me right.' He frowned with concern as she kept her gaze averted, reached for the bottle under the bar and poured him a generous measure. 'You seem a bit distracted,' he said as he took the glass.

'I've a lot on my mind.'

Ron was still frowning as he gulped down at least half of the whisky, but he decided to bide his time and say nothing until she was ready to confide in him.

Harvey got to his feet and ambled across the room to rest his front paws on the bar, tail wagging as he grinned at her. He was thirsty too, and liked a drop of beer now and again.

'Here you go,' said Rosie with a smile as she came round the bar and placed the shallow bowl on the floor. She patted his head distractedly as he enthusiastically lapped up every drop and pushed the bowl round the floor in search of more. Rosie retrieved it, smoothed her skirt over her slender hips and returned to her place behind the bar.

Ron's concern deepened. Rosie was in a dither about something, and it was most unlike her not to straighten the seams on her stockings and freshen her lipstick before she came into the bar. 'Are you all right, Rosie?'

'Of course,' she said rather too brightly.

He looked at her from beneath his bushy brows. 'You can't fool me, Rosie Braithwaite. What's the matter, girl?'

'Nothing,' she said firmly, her gaze darting to the opening door behind the bar.

Tommy Findlay emerged carrying a crate of bottles which he dumped on the bar. He then stood beside Rosie as if he owned the place. His hair was slicked back with Brylcreem, his moustache was twirled, and his weaselly eyes gleamed with proprietorial victory as he gave Ron one of his greasiest smiles. 'Morning, Ron. Glad to see you're on your feet again so soon.'

Ron felt a chill of loathing run down his spine. 'I didn't realise you were still here,' he muttered.

'That's not very welcoming, Ron,' Tommy replied with all the bonhomie of a rattlesnake. 'I thought you'd be pleased to know that someone's looking after Rosie while you were laid up.'

'That depends on who's doing it, Findlay.'

'Now boys, please play nicely,' said Rosie with determined cheerfulness. 'I've got a pub to run, and my customers prefer a happy atmosphere. Another whisky, Ron?'

He looked into her eyes and saw the plea in them to hold his peace. 'Aye. I will that, Rosie, but I'll take it over there by the fire, if you don't mind. The company's better.'

Tommy's laugh held nothing but derision. 'My, my, Rosie,' he said, giving her waist a squeeze. 'I do believe the old fool's jealous.'

She jerked away from him. 'Keep your hands and your opinions to yourself, Thomas Findlay. This is my pub and Ron's my friend. If you can't behave, then sling your hook.'

'Do like the lady says,' growled Ron, his fists curling, itching to swipe that supercilious grin off his face.

Harvey leaped to his feet at the sound of his master's voice, ears pricked, lips drawn back in a snarl. He was big enough and fast enough to take the bar in one leap and have Tommy's throat in his jaw within seconds. All it would take was Ron's command.

Tommy eyed the dog warily, his cocky smile faltering. Then he shrugged and stepped back, easing the lapels of his flashy jacket and straightening his gaudy tie. 'I was only having a bit of a laugh,' he said. 'Didn't realise you'd lost your sense of humour, Ron.'

'You weren't being funny,' snapped Rosie with an unusual show of temper.

Tommy was about to reply when the front door crashed open, bringing a gust of wind and flying debris into the bar along with a group of Canadian soldiers. 'Hey, Rosie,' one of them called cheerfully. 'Set 'em up, honey. We got a mighty thirst today.'

Ron and Tommy regarded each other with mutual loathing as Rosie hurried to serve the Canadians. 'I have a fair idea of what you're up to, Findlay,' muttered Ron, 'and you'll have me to answer to if Rosie's hurt in any way.'

Findlay made a disdainful noise in his throat. 'Yeah? You and who else's army?'

Ron took a swig of his whisky. 'You'd be surprised,' he muttered, slamming the empty glass on the bar. He glowered at the other man, unfazed by the age difference. He'd learned a great many skills in the special operations unit during the last war – skills that were as honed today as they had been then. 'I've got my eye on you, Findlay,' he said with quiet menace.

Something flickered in Findlay's eyes and Ron knew he'd got the message. He grabbed his coat and turned for the door, the faithful Harvey at his heels.

Rosie was busy pouring pints, but he could see she was flustered and, as he passed, she shot him a look that held a world of meaning. He nodded that he understood, shrugged on his coat, rammed on his cap, and went out into the rain. He would go back this afternoon after she'd shut the pub and seen Findlay off the premises. And then perhaps he'd learn why Findlay was hanging about, and what hold he had over Rosie.

Major Patricia had been very understanding when Rita had asked if she could stay on at the factory. She'd listened as Rita had explained her predicament, sympathised with her and swiftly welcomed her back.

Rita was in the canteen eating a lunch of mince,

boiled potatoes and cabbage when one of the Major's secretaries came to find her. 'You've got a telephone call,' she said breathlessly. 'Major Patricia says you can take it in her office.'

Rita pushed back the chair in alarm. She'd never had a telephone call before, and it could only bode trouble. 'Who is it?'

The girl grinned. 'It's your dad.'

Rita rushed out of the canteen and into the Major's deserted office, slamming the door behind her. The receiver was lying on a pile of papers and she tentatively picked it up. 'Hello?' she shouted. 'Dad?'

His voice sounded distant and unfamiliar through the static. 'Rita? Rita, is everything all right with you and Louise? I heard about the raid the other night.'

'We're both fine,' she hurried to assure him. 'But the house is gone, Dad. The gasometer finally did for the whole of Barrow Lane and most of the other streets surrounding it.'

'Dear God,' he breathed. There was a long pause as he tried to take this in. 'Is there nothing left?' he asked finally.

'I found one of your shoes, but I haven't had the chance to go back and look through the rubble. They closed the whole area off because the gas was still leaking.'

'Thank heavens you and Louise weren't there,' he said. 'I can't bear to think how close you must have come to being killed.'

She decided not to tell him about the collapse of the Brook Street shelter, or the risks she'd taken during her nights of fire-watching. 'We're both fine, Dad, really.'

'But where are you living now? Have you gone to Beach View? Is Peggy looking after you?'

Rita told him about the situation at Peggy's and hurried on to explain about the asylum, keeping her tone light and cheerful so as not to worry him further. 'It's not too bad,' she said breezily, 'and most of the others are from round our way, so we've got plenty of good company. Louise and I are back at work today, so life will soon get back to normal.'

'I want you and Louise to get out of Cliffehaven,' he said flatly. 'You're right in the thick of it down there and it's not safe. Major Patricia can arrange travel warrants for both of you, and I'll find you a billet up here.'

Rita blinked away her tears. It would be lovely to see him again, and just the sound of his voice gave her such comfort. But leaving Cliffehaven was fraught with difficulty. 'We both have jobs here, Dad, and Louise still hasn't heard from Tino. She won't leave – and I can't desert her now she's lost everything.'

'Don't be ridiculous,' he stormed. 'Tell Louise I'm ordering her out of there. I have to know you're both safe, and the only way to do that is to get you up here where I can keep an eye on you.'

'I'll try,' she sighed. 'But you know how stubborn she can be.'

'Stubborn or not, she should be thinking of your safety – not dithering about waiting to hear from Tino,' he said crossly. He gave a great sigh. 'It's frustrating being so far away, but all leave is cancelled until further notice, and getting to you would take too long. You have to talk some sense into her, Rita.'

'I'll try,' she said, 'but getting Louise to agree to leaving Cliffehaven is only the start of it. The train lines have been blown to smithereens, and the bus depot took a direct hit. Unless you want us to steal a car or walk, there isn't any other way of getting out.'

'The railway is an important lifeline. It will be fixed soon enough,' he said obstinately. 'Look, Rita, I don't have long to talk, the Sergeant Major is already pacing outside the door and looking at his watch. Work on Louise and make her see sense, and I'll ring you again as soon as I can. Once you've persuaded her, ask Major Patricia to make the travel arrangements. She's already said she'll help any way she can.'

A great wave of longing swept over Rita. 'I miss you, Dad,' she said with a catch in her voice.

'I miss you too, darling,' he replied, his soft voice almost lost in the hiss of static. 'And I wish I could be there with you. Christmas was always our special time, and it's going to be horrible without you.'

Tears rolled down Rita's face and she smeared them away. 'We'll be at Beach View on Christmas Day,' she managed. 'Perhaps you could telephone me there?'

'I'll do my very best, my darling, and send my letters straight there from now on. Now I've got to go. Stay safe, talk to Louise and get up here as soon as you can. Goodbye, Rita. Goodbye.'

She stared at the receiver and slowly set it back into its cradle. Her future plans had turned to dust, she had no real home and no one to turn to but Louise, who was so wrapped up in her own misery she couldn't see anything beyond it. But the thought of going to live near her father, of beginning again somewhere new filled her with hope, and she left the office with a broad smile. Her father had been so positive about everything it had given her heart, and a new goal. Louise would see reason once she realised Jack Smith would not take no for an answer. She was sure of it.

Ron had decided he couldn't just sit about waiting for two o'clock, so he took Harvey back home, dried him off and left him asleep by the range in the kitchen. It wasn't visiting hours, but as Christopher was in the private wing it didn't matter – and if Matron Billings crossed his path, then she'd better watch out. He was just in the right mood to tell her a few home truths.

Ron had visited Christopher several times before.

The lad certainly looked a much better colour today as he slept peacefully against the soft pillows. Ron tiptoed in and smiled at Lady Sylvia, who'd been reading a book at his bedside. 'He looks well, so he does,' he murmured, dumping his sodden coat over the iron bars of the radiator. 'What does the doctor say?'

She smiled warmly and tucked the book in her bag. 'Mr Carling has said he can begin his physiotherapy once the plaster cast is off – which should be in about six weeks. And that if he continues to improve he can come to Beach View for Christmas Day.'

'That's good news. I'm glad he's on the mend.' He fidgeted with his pipe, decided against smoking it and shoved it back in his pocket. Leaning back in his chair he surveyed the room for a moment and then shifted about, trying to get comfortable.

Lady Sylvia folded her hands in her lap and regarded him evenly. 'You seem restless,' she said quietly. 'Is it too hot in here, or is something bothering you?'

Ron eyed the steam rising from his coat and rescued it before the lining got singed. 'These places are always too hot. Perhaps, as the boy's asleep I'll leave you to it and come back tonight.'

'Sit down, Ron, and tell me what's got you in a lather,' she said firmly.

'You don't want to be listening to my troubles,' he muttered.

She reached out and took his arm. 'I regard you as a friend,' she said softly, 'and friends should be able to talk their troubles through.'

He was almost persuaded, for he did want advice on how to get Rosie to talk to him. 'A trouble shared is a trouble halved,' he said with a wry smile. 'It's a bit of a cliché, Lady Sylvia.'

'That it might be,' she replied, 'but it does hold true.' She looked up at him. 'My time is yours, should you want to discuss anything, and I promise that whatever is said in this room will go no further.'

Ron sat down and spent some time filling his briar pipe with sweet-smelling tobacco. He didn't plan to smoke it, but it gave him something to do as he thought about what he should say.

He didn't really know where to begin. He was worried that she might find his story distasteful, and it took him a while to decide how to convey his deep affection for Rosie and his very real fear that Tommy Findlay would bring trouble to her door, but, having started, he was surprised at how easy it was to confide in her, and found himself telling her everything.

As the time ticked away and she quietly began to question and counsel him, he realised there was a great deal more to this charming young woman than mink coats and diamond rings. She was a woman with experience far beyond those high walls of her stately home – a woman who, he suspected, had had to learn many a harsh lesson before she'd become Lady Anstruther-Norton.

The rain had eased, but the sky was still leaden, the wind even stronger as Ron made his way out of the overheated hospital room and into the street. He could hear the roar of the sea as it crashed against the cliffs, clawed its way over the shingle and boomed against the concrete shipping-traps that had been placed across the wide mouth of the bay. Gulls called fretfully as they wheeled and swooped and clattered over the loose tiles on the roof of the Daisy Tea Rooms and tried to find shelter and purchase beside the chimney.

He pulled up his coat collar, tucked in his chin and headed down the narrow side alley for the back door of the Anchor. Stepping inside he closed it behind him and listened. He could hear light footfalls upstairs, but no voices. Was Rosie alone, or had Tommy refused to leave? Either way, he was going up there to find out.

'Rosie?' he called from the bottom of the stairs.

'Come up, Ron. I've just put the kettle on.'

She sounded cheerful enough, and that gave him heart, so he checked that his boots hadn't brought half the street in with him and hurried up the stairs to the large room above the bar that was Rosie's sanctuary.

It was a feminine room, with chintz upholstery and curtains, lace antimacassars on the backs of the couch and armchair, and china ornaments on every flat surface. A large, ornate mirror had pride of place over the fireplace, and a bowl of dusty dried flowers sat in the hearth. The whole place was a bit overblown for his taste, and there were too many cushions on the chairs, but Ron had come to appreciate its comfort over the past months, and enjoyed sharing the quiet lull with Rosie between opening hours.

'Sit down and relax,' she called from the small kitchen. 'I won't be a jiffy.'

Remembering Lady Sylvia's advice, he made no mention of Findlay and kept things simple. 'A cup of tea certainly wouldn't go amiss,' he said, taking off his coat and cap. 'It's filthy out there.'

She emerged from the kitchen carrying a tray laden with china. She'd kicked off her high heels and put a thick cardigan over her frilly blouse and tight black skirt. 'I've managed to get some scones as a special treat. They'll be lovely with the blackberry jam Peggy gave me.' She set the tray down on a low table and fussed with the china. 'How is Peg?'

He made no comment on her red-rimmed eyes, although it hurt to keep silent, and plumped down in the overstuffed chair, wriggling his way round the cushions until he could get comfortable. 'She phones when she can,' he said gruffly. 'They've had no raids so far, and it sounds as if she's having the life of Reilly down there with the boys.'

'Well, she would, wouldn't she?' She gave him a weary smile. 'She is a Reilly after all.'

He grinned back at her. 'She is that, to be sure, and it's the very divil keeping our latest adventures from her. The questions that woman asks are a minefield – so I leave most of the talking to Jim. He's better at circumnavigating than I'll ever be.'

'So she knows nothing of your heroics, or your stay in the hospital, your escape on the back of a motorcycle – or that you have an illustrious lodger?'

'Lady Sylvia answered the telephone one day when we were out – but all Peggy knows is that she's staying while her son recovers.' He grinned. 'Lady Sylvia is a rare woman, so she is. Knows when to keep her mouth shut.'

She raised a finely plucked eyebrow. 'Goodness, Ron. That's high praise from you.' Her gentle smile was teasing. 'The lovely Sylvia has certainly got you where she wants you, hasn't she? Do I smell romance in the offing?'

Ron didn't want her to think she had a rival for his heart. 'She's a nice woman and happily married,' he muttered, 'and I'm me own man. We're friends, that's all.'

'Mmmm.' She was still smiling as she poured the tea and handed him a scone liberally spread with butter and jam. 'There's no cream, unfortunately, but I could spoon the top of the milk over it if you'd like.'

He shook his head. 'This is just fine,' he murmured.

For all her bright talk and teasing smiles, he'd caught the fleeting shadows in her eyes, and the way she kept chewing at her lip. She was trying very hard not to let him see how on edge she was, and his need to comfort and console her was a gnawing pain deep in his heart. But Lady Sylvia had made him see that he must be patient, give her time – let her be the one to broach the subject of Tommy Findlay.

'Sit yourself down, Rosie, girl, and stop mithering. You've already had a busy lunchtime, and tonight will probably be even busier.'

'Yes,' she sighed, as she sank into the corner of the couch opposite him. 'I could do with a bit of a sit-down. My feet are killing me.'

Ron ate his scone in silence. He was sure it was delicious but he couldn't taste a thing, for it was agony not to blurt out his concerns. He watched her sip her tea and nibble at the scone. The silence was stretching now, becoming awkward.

'I know you don't like Tommy Findlay,' she said finally, 'and I have to admit that I'm finding his frequent visits a bit of a trial. But it can't be helped.'

Ron's pulse jolted. 'He's not staying here, is he?'

She gave him a soft, genuine smile. 'Of course not. Give me some credit, Ron.'

He ate the last of the scone and set the plate aside, his thoughts churning. 'Are you doing business with him then? 'Cos if you are, you need to watch out, Rosie. Findlay's a spiv, and if you're caught dealing with him the police will nab you as well, and you'll lose your licence.'

'We've done business in the past,' she murmured, her gaze on the loose thread she was slowly drawing from the upholstery. 'But not this time, Ron. I've had my fingers burnt before.'

'Then why do you even give him the time of day when you clearly can't stand the sight of him?'

She reached for the packet of Park Drive, pulled out a cigarette and lit it with a match. 'We go back a long way,' she replied, blowing a stream of smoke, 'and a friendship that enduring deserves a certain loyalty.'

'Loyalty?' spluttered Ron. 'That weasel wouldn't know loyalty if it bit him.' He cocked his head and eyed her closely. 'What's he got over you, Rosie? How come you put up with him when you've proved in the past that you don't suffer fools or people on the make?'

She regarded him with a look that told him he'd probed too far. She tapped the ash from her cigarette into the ashtray and changed the subject. 'I was wondering if Anne needed any help preparing the Christmas food now she's got so many to feed? She's very welcome to my ration of extra dried fruit and sugar if she wants to make a cake.'

Ron knew then that Rosie would say no more about Tommy Findlay, and that if he persisted in questioning her it would ruin their friendship. All he could do now was bide his time and hope she'd come to trust him enough to confide in him very soon. He just prayed that it wouldn't be because Findlay had hurt her.

'I don't care what your father said. I'm not leaving Cliffehaven.'

The argument had been going on for at least half an hour. Rita's impatience was rising and she was finding it almost impossible not to grab Louise and shake some sense into her. 'We can get the post office to forward any mail,' she said through gritted teeth, 'and leave our new address at the police station so the authorities can get in touch. Tino will find us, Mamma, wherever we are.'

'You can't be sure of that, and I'm not prepared to risk it.'

'But Cliffehaven's already seen some terrible raids, and you can be certain more will follow. Please, Mamma, think about it. Dad just wants us to be safe.'

'I'm not going – and that's an end to it.'

Rita finally snapped. 'Then I'll go without you,' she retorted. 'I'll pack my bag and leave you here with Aggie.'

Louise slapped her with such force Rita staggered in shock.

'You don't speak to me like that,' she shouted in rapid-fire Italian. 'You are a wicked, selfish girl and I'm ashamed of you.'

The stinging slap had obliterated Rita's jag of

temper, but Louise's accusation pierced her to the heart. She cupped her cheek and fought back blinding tears. 'Don't you *dare* call me selfish,' she stuttered. 'I've done everything you've asked of me and more, and yet you keep on demanding – keep on pulling those apron strings tighter and tighter until I can hardly breathe.'

'You're a black-hearted girl to say such things after all I've done for you,' shouted Louise.

'And what about all the things I've done for you?' Rita dashed away the tears, determined to stay in control of her emotions. 'I gave up my dream for you, Mamma.'

Louise's lip curled. 'I didn't ask you to,' she snapped.

'Not in so many words,' Rita replied, 'but with all those long silences and emotional outbursts you made it impossible for me to see it through.'

'I was simply trying to make you see how foolish you were being,' she retorted. 'Girls like you need to know your place. And it is with me – your mamma. Not on some airfield.'

Rita's frustration was burning again. 'What about my need to be with my father? Isn't that important? Or can't you see anything beyond your own needs?'

'It's different for me,' Louise stormed. 'Your father is safe and well. I don't even know if my Tino and Roberto are still alive.' She burst into noisy tears, collapsing on the bed in a huddle of misery.

Louise had a point, but it was clear she couldn't

think beyond her own misery – couldn't understand anyone's needs but her own – and wasn't prepared even to try. Rita took a deep, trembling breath, shocked that it had come to this, and mortified by her own lack of self-control. Their harsh words couldn't be taken back, and she feared the consequences to their once loving and close relationship.

Rita perched on the end of the bed, knowing she had to do something to make amends. 'I do love you, Mamma,' she said softly, 'and I'm sorry I've upset you. But talking to Dad made me realise just how much I miss him, and this is a chance to be with him again.'

There was no response from Louise, and Rita took a steadying breath. 'I know it's hard for you without Papa Tino . . .'

'You know nothing of how I feel.' Louise sat up and glared at Rita through the tangle of her greying hair, her eyes swollen and red-rimmed, her face streaked with tears. 'Go to your father!' she shouted. 'Leave me. See if I care.'

Rita closed her eyes. 'You know very well I could never leave you while things are so uncertain,' she murmured as the tears spilled down her face. 'But please, Mamma, think about Dad's offer and don't just dismiss it out of hand.'

Louise collapsed back onto the pillows and reached for the rosary beads and family photographs that rarely left her side. 'I will wait in Cliffehaven until they return,' she sobbed. 'If you really loved me you'd understand and stay with me.'

Rita's head was pounding and she could still feel the heat of Louise's slap on her cheek, but as she regarded the huddled figure on the bed, she ached for her understanding. Yet it was obvious Louise was deaf to everything, and would continue to use emotional blackmail to keep her tied to her. The love and respect she'd always had for Louise had been badly dented, and she wondered if either of them could emerge from this night's terrible confrontation unscathed.

'I need fresh air and time to think,' she said wearily. 'I don't know how long I'll be, but try and sleep, Mamma. We'll talk again in the morning.'

Louise emerged swiftly from the pillows and grabbed Rita's arm. 'Don't go,' she begged, her eyes wild with fear. 'Please don't go, Rita. I'm sorry. I'm so sorry I said so many terrible things. I didn't mean them. Really I didn't.'

Rita gently moved out of her clutches, pulled on her leather jacket and reached for her gas mask box. 'I know you didn't,' she said, drained of emotion and weary to the bone. 'And I'm sorry too. I should never have spoken to you like that – but I've had enough, Mamma. I've really had enough.'

Louise stared at her, shock and distress battling in her eyes. 'What do you mean by that, Rita?'

'Don't worry, Mamma. I'm not leaving you for more than a few hours. But we both could do with some time alone to think about everything – and to try to work out where we go from here.'

Louise scrambled off the bed, fresh tears streaming as she followed Rita to the door. 'But there's nothing to think about,' she rasped through her sobs. 'We love each other, and when Tino and Roberto come home we will be a family again.' She grabbed Rita's jacket sleeve. 'Please, *cara mia*, don't go. Don't leave me.'

Rita hated pulling away from her, loathed herself for leaving the room and closing the door sharply between them. But her spirit and strength had been sapped by all that had happened over these past months and she needed to escape.

She heard the door opening as she ran down the stairs – heard Louise's pleas for her to return ring out in the echoing stairwell, and closed her mind to them.

But her heart heard them, and she knew she would answer those calls before the night got much older. For now, she needed the wind and the rain and the throb of the powerful motorbike engine beneath her – needed the freedom of the tracks lacing the hills and the silence of the night to help her heal.

Chapter Fourteen

It was Christmas Eve and Anne had spent the morning with Mrs Finch and Lady Sylvia in the kitchen. Now the cake was safely cooling in the larder, the birds had been plucked and stuffed, and she needed to sit down and rest. The baby had been particularly restless since last night, her ankles were swollen and her back ached.

'I'll help Mrs Finch tidy up,' said Sylvia kindly. 'Drink this cup of tea and rest, dear. You look all in.'

She sipped gratefully at the very weak tea and closed her eyes. The morning's baking had all been a bit last minute, but Rosie had supplemented their extra rations of dried fruit and sugar with her own, and it had been decided that Christmas wouldn't be the same without a proper cake. Now the heavenly aroma of brandy-soaked fruit and rich cake drifted through the house, making it at last feel festive.

The clock ticked loudly on the mantelpiece and Anne settled deeper into the comfortable chair. Martin and Cissy had wrapped up like Eskimos to go for a tramp across the hills to forage for mistletoe and holly with Grandpa Ron and Harvey, the nurses were not expected home until teatime and her father had fed the chickens and was now outside chopping wood for the fire. It was lovely to be at home; to have Martin with her every night and not have to worry about him – and he looked so very much better already after only a few days' rest.

But she missed her mother dreadfully, and although it was selfish, she wished she hadn't gone all the way to Somerset to be with Bob and Charlie. Peggy had been away for only two weeks, but it felt like months, and Christmas just wouldn't be the same without her.

The sharp rap on the front door startled her and she snapped from her rambling thoughts and struggled to get out of the chair.

'I'll go,' said Sylvia, not bothering to take off the rubber gloves as she pressed Anne back into the chair and hurried into the hall.

Anne could hear her talking to someone on the doorstep, and then her quick footsteps returning across the hall.

'It's arrived at last,' Sylvia said triumphantly. 'I knew they wouldn't let me down.' She dumped the enormous wicker basket on the kitchen table, her eyes shining in delight as she peeled off the rubber gloves.

'Good heavens,' muttered Mrs Finch, eyeing the basket with suspicion as she fiddled with her buzzing hearing aid. 'Are we taking in laundry now?'

'It's the hamper from Fortnum and Mason's,' said Anne.

'Camping fork basins? That doesn't make sense, Anne.'

Anne struggled from the chair and spoke directly into Mrs Finch's ear. 'It's the hamper from Fortnum and Mason's,' she said loudly.

'Well, why didn't you say so? Hurry up, Sylvia, and let's see what's inside.'

Sylvia laughed and unbuckled the sturdy straps, letting the wicker lid fall open. The three of them stood there in stunned silence as they regarded the bounty before them. They hadn't seen food like this for over a year, and it was almost too much to take in.

Anne reverently drew out the oranges, the circular box of crystallised fruits, the little bag of walnuts, the two pouches of tobacco, and the twelve packets of Sobranie cigarettes. They were the exotic kind that were wrapped in pastel coloured papers, with gold foil tips – a rare and special treat never before seen at Beach View.

Mrs Finch cooed over the ornate canisters of tea, coffee, sugar and cocoa, and lovingly caressed the tins of shortbread and mince pies. 'I'd better put my very best teeth in for these,' she muttered.

They all gasped at the sight of two precious bars of foil-wrapped chocolate, and the beribboned box of tiny pink and white sugared mice. Digging deeper into the fragrant pale yellow straw, Sylvia found a Christmas pudding, a joint of ham, a box of cheese and a packet of plain crackers. She delved still deeper and examined the labels on the bottles of wine, champagne and brandy and pronounced them to be just as she'd ordered.

They stood and grinned at each other in delight, but as Anne regarded the treasure trove that now stood on the battered old kitchen table, she realised they must keep it secret. 'We'll have to hide it from the men,' she murmured. 'If they even get an inkling of this in the house, they'll plunder it.'

'A wise decision,' said Sylvia. 'We'll put it all back but the ham, which I'll cook now, and keep the hamper in my room. We can have the champagne and the wine with lunch, but the rest will stay out of sight until tomorrow afternoon. We don't want anyone spoiling their appetite for Christmas lunch – not after all the trouble we've taken.'

They quickly packed everything away and Sylvia hauled it upstairs, leaving the kitchen only moments before Jim tramped in from the garden, his arms laden with firewood. 'Did I hear someone banging on the front door?'

'You must have been mistaken,' said Anne, quickly covering the ham with a tea towel and shooting the giggling Mrs Finch a warning look. 'I expect you'd like a cup of tea after chopping all that wood?'

'Aye, I would that,' he said as he stacked the logs neatly in the corner by the range. Straightening, he looked from Mrs Finch to Anne and frowned. 'What's going on? The pair of you look like guilty children.'

'Nothing,' said Mrs Finch, who was desperately trying to keep a straight face.

'Here's your tea, Dad,' said Anne hastily, biting her lip.

'Is there not a biscuit to go with it?'

Anne and Mrs Finch burst into giggles and he eyed them suspiciously. 'To be sure,' he muttered, 'I'll never understand women.'

'Better that we hold a bit of mystery, Jim,' said Sylvia as she came back into the kitchen. 'We need something to keep you men on your toes.' She avoided looking at Anne and Mrs Finch, but the corners of her mouth twitched as she pulled the rubber gloves back on and began to vigorously scrub the pots and pans.

'Something's going on here,' he muttered good-naturedly, 'but I suppose I shouldn't be too surprised – not with a house full of women and Christmas only hours away.' He sniffed the air appreciatively. 'Something smells delicious,' he said. 'Are we having cake for tea?'

'It's not to be touched until tomorrow,' said Anne sharply. 'I'll find you something else to be going on with.' She reached into the larder and pulled out the biscuit tin. There were only a few broken digestives in the bottom, but they would have to do.

'Is that it?' He eyed them in disgust. 'I thought you bought some the other day? Have you hidden them?'

'You ate them, remember?'

The loud rap of the door-knocker saved Anne from a prolonged inquisition and she hurried into the hall to open the door.

The daunting figure of her Aunt Doris stood on the top step, resplendent in her best mink coat, pearls and natty hat. Her furious expression did not bode well.

'You should have told me,' she said without preamble as she brushed past Anne and stepped into the hall. 'I would have come sooner if I'd known. It was most lax of you not to give me some warning.'

Anne heard her father's hasty retreat back into the garden as she closed the door. Her mother's sister was difficult at the best of times, and Jim couldn't stand her when she was on her high horse. By the look of her, she was saddled up and ready to go into battle.

'I don't know what you're talking about, Aunt Doris,' she said, despite the fact she understood all too well. 'But it's nice to see you,' she added with a wry smile. 'You look in robust health.'

Doris waved away her compliment with a gloved hand. She wasn't about to waste time on social niceties. 'I see the Rolls-Royce is parked outside,' she said briskly. 'Is Lady Anstruther-Norton receiving visitors?'

'Oh,' said Anne, trying to keep a straight face. 'And here's me thinking you'd come to wish us a happy Christmas.'

Doris bristled. 'Well?' she asked impatiently.

'She's in the kitchen doing the washing-up,' said Anne, the giggles bubbling very close to the surface now.

Doris's eyes widened and she paled beneath the careful make-up. 'You don't ask a *Lady* to do the washing-up,' she hissed. 'Even *I* have a girl to do that.' She quickly checked her appearance in the hall mirror, straightened her hat a fraction over her stiffly set brown hair, and walked purposefully into the kitchen.

Anne followed her and quietly sat by the fire to watch the fun.

Doris swept past a startled Mrs Finch as if she was invisible and held out her gloved hand. 'Lady Anstruther-Norton,' she said in her most refined and strangulated accent. 'May profound apologies for not presenting mayself sooner.'

Sylvia paused a fraction of a second before she turned from the sink, her hands swathed in bright yellow rubber gloves that dripped soapsuds. 'How do you do?' she said coolly.

'This is my Aunt Doris,' Anne hurriedly explained as Doris eyed the rubber gloves, thought better of shaking Sylvia's hand and ruining her own, and awkwardly clutched her handbag.

'We haven't been introduced, Lady Anstruther-Norton,' Doris simpered, 'but Aye do believe we have a mutual acquaintance.' She paused for effect. 'My dear friend Lady Charlmondley sends her regards.'

'Good grief,' said Sylvia. 'Is that old battleaxe still going?'

Doris looked distinctly put out. She cleared her throat and forgot momentarily to keep up the strangled accent. 'Lady Charlmondley is very much alive,' she said. 'In fact she and I are on the board of many of our local charities.'

'Aurelia always did enjoy bossing everyone about,' muttered Sylvia as she pulled off the gloves and placed them on the wooden drainer. She looked at Doris and smiled, 'but a doughty lady nevertheless. I'm sure you're both a great asset to Cliffehaven's charitable institutions, Mrs . . .'

'Mrs Williams, but please, call me Doris,' she replied hastily, deeming it safe now to risk shaking hands. 'May husband Edward and Aye are delighted to welcome you to Cliffehaven, Lady Anstruther-Norton.'

'Thank you,' Sylvia said with a gracious dip of her head, a smile twitching the corner of her mouth.

The introductions over, Doris got into her stride. 'May husband Edward is the area manager for the Home and Colonial Company, you know, and we are *terribly* concerned about your welfare – and that of your son, of course. How is that poor, dear *brave* young man?'

'Christopher is getting stronger by the day,' Sylvia replied, 'but I don't really see why you should be concerned over *my* welfare.'

'Well,' said Doris with a disapproving glance sweeping past Anne and Mrs Finch to the clutter on every flat surface. 'It's hardly what you're used to, is it Lady Anstruther-Norton?'

Sylvia raised an eyebrow. 'It's homely and warm and welcoming, and the people who live here have been kindness itself. Are you implying that my home in Wiltshire is not the same?'

Doris reddened. 'No, of course not,' she blustered. 'I just meant that you must be finding it all a bit . . . a bit . . .' She leaned forward like a conspirator. 'Working class,' she hissed disdainfully. 'James and Ronan can be so *terribly* uncouth at times, and their humour is questionable, to say the least.'

'Really?' Sylvia eyed her coldly. 'I find both of them delightful company. And if it hadn't been for dearest Ron, I would have lost my son. As far as my husband and I are concerned, he's a hero.'

Clearly disconcerted that every approach had been skilfully turned against her, Doris fidgeted with her coat collar and patted the triple strings of pearls at her throat. But she was not a woman to be thwarted. She was here on a mission and nothing would stop her. 'May husband and Aye would be honoured if you'd stay with us in Havelock Gardens,' she said determinedly. 'We have a naice detached house in the *better* part of Cliffehaven.'

'You're very kind,' Sylvia said smoothly, 'but I'm quite content here.'

Doris frowned. 'Are you sure, Lady Anstruther-Norton? Only Aye've had may gel prepare a room for you – with your own bathroom, of course. May son is away on important, *secret* business with the MOD, so there is plenty of room.' She hurried on before Sylvia could interject. 'You'll be very comfortable, Aye assure you, and of course Lady Charlmondley is a frequent visitor, and Aye just know—'

Sylvia cut in. 'I'm grateful to your girl for going to so much trouble, but I will not be leaving Beach View.' She smiled and held out her hand, forcing Doris to shake it. 'It was kind of you to come,' she said pleasantly as she slowly drew Doris towards the door. 'But as you can see, we are rather busy this morning, and Anne needs to rest. Please pass on my regards to Aurelia when you see her.'

Anne watched in admiration as a flustered Doris was expertly steered into the hall.

'Perhaps you would do me the honour of attending may little tea party next week?' Doris asked in a final desperate bid. 'It's a trifling thing really, arranged more for charity than may own pleasure, but one has to do what one can in such troubling times, doesn't one?'

'One certainly does,' murmured Sylvia as she opened the front door.

'Ay'm sure your august presence would lend cachet to the occasion and help raise the much-needed funds for all those poor souls who've been made homeless,' Doris gabbled. 'When one is as fortunate as you and Aye, it is our duty to do what we can, don't you think?'

Anne watched in amusement from the kitchen doorway as Sylvia moved in such a way that Doris had no choice but to step outside.

'It is indeed,' said Sylvia. 'But I'm here to care for my son, not to join in the social whirl of Cliffehaven.'

Doris dithered on the top step, the light of rising panic gleaming in her eyes. 'Lady Aurelia was especially looking forward to seeing you and will be most disappointed,' she muttered, nervously tugging at the strap of her handbag.

Sylvia dug in her skirt pocket and pulled out a large pink crumpled pound note. 'Please accept this small token towards your charity. I'm sure the recipients are truly grateful for all your sterling work.'

Doris discovered that she was now on the second step down, the pound note crushed in her gloved hand. 'Thank you, Lady Anstruther-Norton,' she managed. 'It is most kind . . .'

'Not at all,' said Sylvia with some asperity. 'Now, I really do have to go and help in the kitchen. Goodbye, Doris.'

'Goodbye, Lady Ans . . .'

Sylvia closed the door quietly but firmly, and leaned against it with a deep sigh of relief.

'Well done,' breathed Anne as she came into the hall. 'Aunt Doris was worse than usual today. It must be your august presence and fetching rubber gloves that brought it on,' she added with a chuckle.

Sylvia grinned. 'I don't wish to be rude,' she said, 'but please tell me your mother is nothing like her sister.'

Anne laughed. 'Mum's the exact opposite and she'd have applauded that performance. Aunt Doris is always turning her nose up at our home and making snide comments about Dad and Grandpa. She winds Mum up like a cuckoo clock.'

'I know how Peggy feels,' Sylvia admitted. 'In fact, Anne, I think my cuckoo expired about ten minutes ago due to an overdose of pomposity and strangled vowels.'

They burst out laughing, and linked arms as they made their happy way back to the peaceful sanctuary of the untidy kitchen.

Three days had passed since that awful confrontation and Rita knew that neither of them would ever forget it. The harsh words had remained between them like an unseen third presence, the thorny topics of leaving Cliffehaven and Rita's broken dreams firmly avoided.

But as they stepped out of the church after the beautiful midnight mass, and heard the joyous ringing of the bells, Rita felt Louise reach for her hand, and knew that the sense of peace that had come with the lovely service had touched her heart too.

'Happy Christmas, Mamma,' she said softly.

'Happy Christmas, Rita,' she replied, tucking her hand into Rita's arm as they stood in the churchyard which glistened with frost and listened to the bells.

They made a joyful sound compared to the awful, spine-chilling wail of the sirens and the drone of enemy planes, and Rita's pulse quickened with hope that this war would soon be over and the bells could ring every night.

'Come, Rita, let's get going before we freeze to death.'

They waved goodbye to their friends and set off from the church for the long walk home. Rita had decided it was far too dangerous to ride the bike down the hill in such weather, and anyway, there was only just enough petrol in the Norton to get them to Peggy's in the morning. As Rita would be on fire-watch duty tomorrow night, she would refuel at the fire station on the way.

They were bundled up in their thickest coats, scarves wrapped round their heads and necks to stave off the bitter cold, gloved hands dug deep into their pockets. The wind coming off the sea nipped at their noses and made their eyes water, and in its breath was a promise of snow.

'Perhaps we'll have a white Christmas,' said Rita,

as they carefully walked along the slippery pavement towards the small park on the edge of Havelock Gardens.

'I've lived here all my life and never seen snow fall on Christmas Day,' Louise replied.

'We're probably too far south,' muttered Rita as she concentrated on where she placed her feet. She paused and looked round. 'But it's beautiful, isn't it? Look how the frost is all lacy in the trees, and the way the spiders' webs are glittering with it.'

Louise tugged at her arm. 'It's too cold to be admiring the view,' she said, huddling into her coat collar, 'and we've got that hill to climb yet.'

It was only a short walk through Havelock Park to the far western end of the promenade, but the pavement was treacherous and they kept hold of one another until they reached the gravel path that ran through the heart of the small park. The elegant iron benches and ornate railings and gates had been taken to be melted down and made into fighter planes and tanks, and the carefully ordered flower beds and arbours had been demolished to provide vegetable plots and air-raid trenches.

They silently passed the pond and the deserted swings and slides and headed towards the high hedges and grand houses that lined the broad streets of Havelock Gardens. They could still hear the bells, but now they were accompanied by the mournful moan of the foghorn and, as they began the long climb to the asylum, they could see the fog coming in from the sea in swirling clouds.

Disregarding all the blackout rules, Rita switched on the powerful torch she'd borrowed from the fire station. They were now shrouded in fog and couldn't see a thing. 'Not much chance of Gerry being out on a night like this,' she reassured Louise as they slowly went arm in arm up the winding track and negotiated the frozen ruts and icy puddles.

Neither of them regarded the asylum as home, but on this bitter night its promise of sanctuary and warmth drew them ever onwards, safe in the knowledge that no matter how tough things became, they would always have each other.

It was Christmas Day, but the routine of life on a busy farm went on as usual and, once again, Peggy was woken by the low of cows, the rattling of buckets, the crow of roosters, and the fussy clucking of hens. The days began before first light here, for the cows had to be brought in for milking and there always seemed to be something to do.

She lay in the comfortable bed, enjoying these few moments of tranquillity before she went down to help Violet in the vast flagstoned kitchen. It felt odd without Jim lying next to her, for they'd never spent a night apart since their wedding, but it was rather nice to be able to stretch luxuriously across it, wrapped in all the blankets and burrowed in a stack of pillows.

Her room was beneath the heavily beamed eaves of the isolated farmhouse. Warmed by the chimney breast that ran up one side of it, it was a pretty haven with sprigged curtains and bedspread, dark sturdy furniture, faded Turkish rugs, and a tiny latched window that looked out over the farmyard to the fields and the distant lake.

She appreciated the beauty of the rolling Somerset landscape but still couldn't get used to the emptiness of it all. A town girl at heart, she preferred to have shops nearby and a firm pavement beneath her feet. It was all very well for the boys, they didn't mind getting muddy and wet, and had no objection to the wide open spaces where they could roam at will from dawn to dusk.

She smiled as she thought of Sally Hicks' little crippled brother, Ernie. Violet was his aunt, and she had given all three boys sanctuary for the duration. Ernie had blossomed, his once wan face glowing with health, his shambling gait in the restricting caliper much improved as he followed her boys about. It did Peggy's heart good to see how much he'd come on – for she remembered all too well how desperately needy both he and his sister had been when they'd arrived at Cliffehaven as evacuees at the start of the war. Now Sally was married to the fire chief, John Hicks, and Ernie was thriving in this good country air.

But despite Violet Cardew's warmth and generous hospitality, Peggy knew she didn't belong here. She was missing Beach View and the sound of the seagulls and clattering trolleybus, and wished she could gather up her boys and take them home.

Peggy closed her eyes and tried not to mind that Bob and Charlie seemed so content to be here – that, like Ernie, they had so swiftly taken to the warm, motherly Violet, and regarded this rambling farmhouse as their new home.

They'd been thrilled to see her, of course, but after the initial excitement of showing her around the place, they'd happily gone off to help the land girls in the fields, and she hadn't seen them again until supper. Over the past two weeks she'd barely had more than a snatched hour or two with them as they went about their daily chores, and got embroiled in making camps in the woods or fishing in the nearby river that fed the large pond at the bottom of the field.

She'd tried to join in, but realised fairly quickly that she wasn't cut out for such rough and tumble, and that they were quite happy to be left to their own devices – in fact, they seemed to prefer it. Feeling rather sorry for herself, she'd turned to the understanding and ever-patient Violet, who'd gentled her out of her misery and made her see that her boys were just behaving quite naturally and that she shouldn't take it personally.

The evenings were the best times, for after their bath and tea, they'd sit with her by the blazing fire in the inglenook, wrapped in dressing gowns, drinking hot cocoa and telling her about their day's adventures. Bob was still the quiet, more thoughtful of the three and, at thirteen, seemed to be taking his responsibility for Ernie and his young brother very seriously indeed. Charlie was his usual exuberant self, chattering away nineteen to the dozen, his little face glowing with health and happiness.

She didn't resent Violet, in fact she was profoundly grateful that her boys were being so well looked after, but she could already see an indefinable change in them, which would become more apparent the longer they stayed. And yet she had no choice but to leave them here where it was safe. She'd heard about the awful raids along the south coast, and Jim had told her about the damage in Cliffehaven. She couldn't expose her sons to that, no matter how much she wished them by her side.

Impatient with her dissatisfied thoughts, she clambered out of bed and prepared for the day. The presents were all under the huge tree in the sitting room, and she could smell the turkey roasting. There would be no turkey at Beach View this year, but Jim had assured her there would be plenty of pheasant and duck, courtesy of Ron and Harvey, and that Rosie had donated her extra rations so they could have a proper cake. It sounded as if half of Cliffehaven would be round the table today, for apart from the family and the lodgers, Rosie, Rita and Louise had been invited.

She drew her thick cardigan round her and stared

out of the window, not really seeing the view as her thoughts settled on home. She'd had to make some tough decisions recently, and was still torn between the need to be with her boys and the draw of home and the rest of her family. 'Damned war,' she muttered crossly. 'Why did it have to spoil everything?'

She gave a sigh as she put on her sturdy shoes and tied the laces. There was little doubt she would continue to be tormented by her family's enforced separation, and yet, frustratingly, everyone seemed to be managing very well without her. Her boys were thriving, Martin and Cissy had survived the raid on the airfield, and Beach View was still standing despite the shattered windows. But she had an unsettling feeling that when she'd telephoned, they'd been keeping something from her.

She paused as she reached for the wooden latch on the door. Jim had a glib tongue and could sell sand to the Arabs, but she knew him too well, and suspected he wasn't telling her the half of it. Anne had been equally evasive, and although her story about the titled lady seemed plausible enough, it somehow didn't sit right with her.

Lady Sylvia had sounded charming on the telephone, and very posh, but what on earth was she doing at Beach View when she could have stayed in any one of the far grander hotels that remained open? Not all of them had been taken over by the forces, and their accommodation was much more suitable than that draughty bedroom at the front of the house.

She bit her lip, determined not to give in to the awful niggle of doubt, and to enjoy this precious Christmas Day with her sons, for her visit would soon be over, and she had no idea when she might see them again.

Chapter Fifteen

Rita and Louise had exchanged their small gifts of handkerchiefs and cheap scent before they left their billet and set off for Beach View in a happy mood. The snow promised the night before had not materialised and the fog had cleared, so they had an easy run on the Norton.

Beach View dining room was now alive with the chatter of many voices, the delicious aroma of the roast dinner and plum pudding they'd just finished lingering throughout the house. Wrapping paper and bits of string and ribbon littered the floor, and Cissy's camp bed had been exiled to the cupboard under the stairs.

There had been fewer presents this year, for no one had much money and the shops offered a very poor selection. Rita had managed to find pretty brooches on a market stall for Cissy, Anne and Mrs Finch, and socks for Ron and Jim. She and Louise were delighted with their colourful woolly scarves, gloves and berets.

Rita was happy to sit back and sip wine as she listened to them talking and laughing. Peggy and Jack had both managed to telephone that morning, but their absence was keenly felt, reinforced by the programme on the wireless earlier that day which had arranged for parents and children separated by war to talk to one another.

Listening to those tearful voices, it was as hard for Rita and Louise as it was for Peggy's family – but she refused to let thoughts of her father, Papa, Roberto and May cloud her happiness, for it was wonderful to be in a real home again, and warming to see how loving and big-hearted the Reilly family was. She gazed about the room, content to soak up the atmosphere.

The big bay windows in the dining room had been boarded up after the last raid, but with the curtains pulled, the room was cosy with the flickering fire in the hearth and the many candles. Holly and ivy had been draped artistically over the mantelpiece and round the big mirror above it. There was a decorated, sweet-smelling pine tree in the corner that had been carried down from the hills by Ron and Jim, and someone had taken the trouble to hang a vast number of paper chains across the ceiling. These acted as a reminder of Bob, Charlie and Ernie, who'd made them the previous year and, according to Jim, they would remain there now until they came home to make new ones.

Rita glanced at Louise, saw that she was talking earnestly to Fran – the nurse with the Irish accent and fiery hair – and returned to her quiet observance.

There were fourteen sitting round the tables that

had been put end to end and covered in crisp white linen cloths, and although the china, cutlery and glasses were mismatched, and the chairs had come from just about every room in the house, it didn't matter a jot. It was the people who counted, and the opportunity to share this special day in a happy atmosphere.

As Rita looked round the table and listened to the laughter, she was made shockingly aware of how dreary her life had become since Tino and Roberto had been taken away. Her horizon had become constricted and she'd fallen into the habit of mirroring Louise's moods – of not seeing beyond the high walls of their relationship, and burying herself in work and duty.

She glanced at Louise, wondering if she too was aware of the different atmosphere, of the lightness and warmth that could still be maintained despite the dark consequences and fears of the war. But Louise was dabbing at her eyes as she talked to a very patient Fran about Tino and Roberto, and the tragedy of being bombed out. It seemed she would never emerge from that all-encompassing grief.

Rita turned her attention to the others again, unwilling to be drawn into Louise's unhappiness today. Cissy looked very pretty in a soft pink woollen dress, her damaged arm in a very fetching pink and white scarf which she'd made into a sling. Martin still had some nasty bumps and bruises on his face and around one eye which had turned a jaundiced yellow and angry blue, and his arm was also swathed in a sling – albeit the white one provided by the hospital. The bandage round his head remained, and Rita thought he looked rather like a dashing pirate with his twirled moustache and winning smile.

The three nurses were off duty for once and so they'd dressed in their best clothes for the occasion, and Jim and Ron looked very smart in the suits, shirts and ties that Anne had insisted they wore today. Sylvia was elegant in a moss green skirt and creamy silk blouse, and hadn't seemed to notice the suspicious glances Rosie shot her every time she laughed and chatted to Ron.

Rita thought it odd that Rosie should feel threatened by Sylvia, for not only was dear old Ron clearly head over heels in love with her, but she looked quite magnificent in the beautifully tailored navy dress that showed off her curvaceous figure admirably.

Anne looked radiant in a sprigged smock and matching cardigan, and she sat next to Martin and held his hand like a new bride. Dear little Mrs Finch was festive in her best grey dress, string of pearls and the paper hat she'd made from an old newspaper.

Christopher had struggled into a shirt and tweed jacket to make up for the pyjama trousers and slippers, the heavy plaster cast on his leg and the cumbersome wheelchair, which had been drawn up at the top of the table where he could sit with a tray across the handles to eat his dinner.

Harvey had been groomed and bathed, and now sat on the floor beneath the tray, waiting patiently for tidbits. Everyone had been warned not to give him vegetables or anything too rich, unless they wanted him to disgrace himself and send them all scurrying for fresh air.

Rita knew she didn't look half as smart as the others, but the jewelled comb in her hair and the pearl earrings suited her very well, and she was glad her best cardigan, blouse and skirt had been packed in her emergency bag, and not blown sky-high with everything else.

But she did mourn the loss of her one pair of decent shoes, and the make-up Cissy had given her. The rather worn low-heeled pumps she'd found among the donated clothing at the Town Hall had definitely seen better days, and were half a size too small, which meant her toes were being pinched. She'd kicked them off under the table, and just hoped she could get them back on again when it was time to leave.

Ron had brought the wireless into the dining room so they could listen to the King's speech at three o'clock, and as the time approached, he twiddled with the knobs and they all fell silent. His speech wasn't very long, but it was clear that he was still struggling with his terrible stutter. But they all agreed it was a vast improvement on the speech he'd given at the outbreak of war.

They were discussing the speech, and the five

thousand jerkins that had been parachuted by the RAF into occupied Corfu for the children who were facing enemy action in a bitter winter, when Sylvia came bustling into the room. She was armed with clean glasses and several bottles which she placed in front of Jim.

'These should be cold enough now,' she said. 'I put them in the shed overnight.'

There was an audible gasp as everyone eyed the expensive bottles, and Sylvia smiled at a goggle-eyed Jim. 'Would you open them, please? I never did get the hang of popping champagne corks.'

'To be sure, Lady Sylvia, you've a great sense of occasion, so you have,' said Ron.

She smiled at him and winked at her son. 'We Anstruther-Nortons know how to celebrate, don't we, Christopher?'

He winked back, his soft blond hair falling over his forehead. 'I should say so, Mother, and if Pa was here, he'd agree wholeheartedly. But just a snifter for me, please, I shouldn't really be having any alcohol.'

Jim carefully poured the straw-coloured foaming champagne, and Ron passed the glasses round the table. They all looked at Sylvia expectantly.

She stood and raised her glass, the diamonds flashing on her finger and in her ears. 'The King,' she said.

They all stood and toasted the King.

But Sylvia wasn't finished. 'I now propose we

drink to those who cannot be with us today.' She looked round the table. 'A toast to Peggy, my husband James, and our two sons Bertie and Matthew – and to Antonino, Roberto and Jack Smith. May they return to the bosom of their families very soon.'

They drank the toast in thoughtful silence, and Rita felt the onrush of emotion as she thought of her father being so far away. There were so many families praying for their men to come home safely, but how much worse it must be for those whose loved ones would never return. She sniffed back the tears and counted herself lucky. Jack Smith and the Minelli men were safe. They would come home eventually.

'Right,' said Martin, breaking the solemn mood. 'Now it's my turn. Here's to all the courageous boys fighting this war – and the women who so bravely wait for them.'

The mood lightened immediately and there was a rousing cheer.

Within moments of putting down his glass, Ron had called for a toast to all the rescue dogs. Then Jim proposed a toast to Lord Cliffe, who had unwittingly provided the birds for the table that day, and Fran offered a toast to 'Matron and all who sail in her'.

They collapsed into laughter and quickly opened the last three bottles. When they were empty, Rosie produced a large bottle of gin out of her capacious handbag, and it all got a bit messy.

Someone put a record on the gramophone, the rug was rolled back into a corner, and the noise level rocketed. Rosie dragged a protesting Ron from the table for a dance, June grabbed an unsteady, but very willing Jim, and Martin held Anne with his uninjured arm and, with the mound of their unborn baby between them, managed a passable stab at a two-step.

'I think it's time we were leaving,' muttered Louise.

'But the party's just getting started,' replied Rita, who was flushed from too much champagne and desperate to join in the dancing.

'Precisely.' Louise was tight-lipped as she watched Rosie trying to teach Ron how to jitterbug. 'And some don't seem to care that they're making a show of themselves.' She gave a derisive sniff. 'I'm surprised Anne allows that floozie in the door, let alone to sit at her table.'

Sylvia must have overheard, for she leaned across a highly embarrassed Rita, her voice low so that it wouldn't carry to the others. 'Rosie has a heart of gold,' she said flatly, 'and makes Ron feel eighteen again. Don't condemn out of hand, Louise. You can't always tell a book by its cover, you know.'

'It's not proper to be prancing about at her age – and in that dress. It's almost indecent,' muttered Louise as her sullen gaze followed the bouncing bosom and wriggling hips.

'I admire her energy,' said Sylvia, 'and it looks like fun. Come on, Rita, let's give it a go.'

'Rita is on duty tonight,' protested Louise.

'Then she should have some fun before she has to leave,' replied Sylvia.

Rita happily followed Sylvia into the centre of the makeshift dance floor. 'She doesn't mean to be rude,' she said quickly, 'but she's had a very sheltered life and is often more Italian than the Italians in her way of thinking.'

Sylvia nodded as they tried to copy the steps Fran and Suzy seemed to have conquered with ease. 'It's often the way in mixed marriages,' she said lightly. 'But never mind. I'm sure she'll see how much fun we're having and will soon join in.'

Rita doubted it very much, but she didn't have time to think about Louise, for the music was enticing and she and Sylvia were beginning to get the hang of the dance.

It was now late afternoon. Rita was taking a bit of a breather from all the dancing and enjoying a welcome cup of tea with a slice of the delicious Christmas cake when there was a knock at the door, and June and Suzy raced out of the room.

Fran turned to Jim, who was trying unsuccessfully to flirt with Sylvia. 'I hope you don't mind, Mr Reilly, but we asked a couple of friends to join us.'

Jim raised an eyebrow as he heard the voices in the hall. ''Tis my guess these friends are not nurses from the hospital,' he slurred, his eyes twinkling with alcohol-fuelled good humour.

'Um, no. They're Yanks from the airbase – and as they're so far from home and it is Christmas, we thought it would be nice to show them how we celebrate it here.'

'You'd better get them in then instead of keeping them in my hallway,' he said expansively.

'Thanks, Jim, to be sure you're a darlin' man.' She kissed his cheek and hugged his neck before rushing off.

Jim looked bashful as he caught Mrs Finch's disapproving glare. 'To be sure, she thinks of me as a father,' he blustered.

'As long as you remember that and don't get ideas, Jim Reilly,' she retorted.

'Ach, woman,' he snorted. ''Twas nothing.'

He turned from Mrs Finch and eyed the young Americans who hovered uncertainly in the doorway. Clean-shaven and wholesome, they looked smart in their uniform greatcoats, their hair short and slicked back with Brylcreem beneath the jaunty caps which they hurriedly removed.

Jim staggered to his feet, swayed alarmingly and had to sit down again. 'Come in, come in, me boys, and introduce yourselves.'

Rita went scarlet and almost swallowed her tea the wrong way. The last man to enter was Chuck – the boy she'd met outside the recruitment office all those weeks ago – and as his gaze found her and he smiled, she felt a little thrill of pleasure. He remembered her too.

Their spokesman snapped off a smart salute and stood ramrod straight as if he was on a parade ground. 'Squadron Leader Rory Banks, at your service, sir.' He indicated the men beside him. 'Flying Officer Lewis Carmichael, Flight Lieutenant Harry Jablonski, and Pilot Officer Chuck Howard.' All three saluted and stood to attention as Jim introduced everyone.

Mrs Finch giggled and went pink. 'Ooh, what fun. You haven't got any chickens hidden away in those big coats, have you?'

'Chickens, ma'am?' Rory Banks looked puzzled.

'To be sure, we had some Aussie boys come over once,' said Jim. 'They brought chickens and eggs and cooked us all steak. It was a rare treat.'

Rory Banks grinned. 'You can always trust the Aussies to make a grand gesture.' He cleared his throat, his expression becoming serious again. 'Mr Reilly, we're real grateful for your hospitality on this Christmas Day,' he said, 'and although we don't have any chickens or eggs, we hope you'll accept these small gifts.'

Jim's eyes widened as several cartons of American cigarettes were placed on the table alongside a tin of ham, a dozen slim boxes of stockings and two bottles of whisky.

He gave a long, low whistle. 'Well, to be sure, 'tis a pleasure to be welcoming you. Sit down, boys, and let's open that bottle so we can drink a toast to cementing our friendship.'

As the men opened the whisky and settled down to drink and chat, the women fell on the stockings and hastily tucked them away as if afraid they might be taken back.

Even Mrs Finch was quick off the mark and stuffed a pair into her ever-present handbag. 'Make sure you keep the last few pairs for Peggy,' she ordered Anne. 'They'll be a lovely welcome home present.'

Rita carefully put the precious stockings into the pocket of her overcoat which hung on the back of her chair, and shyly smiled her thanks at Chuck, who was still watching her.

'I don't think we should accept such intimate things,' muttered Louise, who wore thick lisle stockings regardless of the time of year. 'We don't know these men and it's not proper.'

'Well, if you don't want them, I'll have them,' said Rosie cheerfully. 'It's murder on nylons behind that bar, and it's been ages since I had a decent pair.'

Louise gave her the sort of look that would have stunned a more sensitive soul – but Rosie seemed unperturbed as she continued to look hopefully at the stockings on the table.

Louise picked up the flat box and neatly slipped it into her handbag. 'It's time we went, Rita,' she said firmly. 'Tino would not approve.'

'But it's still early,' Rita protested.

'We are going,' Louise replied flatly.

'Hi there.'

Rita looked up and found Chuck standing beside her. 'Hello,' she said, all too aware that Louise was glaring at them both. 'Nice to see you again, Chuck. How are you?'

He grinned bashfully as he twisted his cap in his hands. 'I'm okay, I guess, but it's sure hard to still be on the sidelines of this war. We weren't sure if we'd be welcome today.'

'Of course you're welcome,' she said awkwardly. 'The Reillys rarely turn anyone away,' she blushed again as she added, 'especially when they come with such lovely presents.'

Louise jabbed her with her elbow. 'You know this person?'

Rita nodded, her gaze fixed on Chuck as she introduced them. 'Chuck's brother has a Norton just like mine,' she said.

'That's correct, ma'am,' he said pleasantly. He disregarded Louise's disapproving glare and sat down. 'My brother and I have always had motorbikes, and when I saw Rita's Norton, I just had to talk to her. You must be very proud of her, Mrs Minelli. Not many girls can build a bike from scratch.'

Louise regarded him stonily for a long moment and then reached for her cardigan. 'Rita and I have to go,' she said.

'Not yet, Mamma,' Rita said firmly. 'I'm not on duty at the fire station until ten, and it's only six.'

'But you have to drive me home first and get changed. I really think . . .' The rest of her protest was drowned out by the lively sound of the Glenn Miller orchestra pouring from the gramophone.

Chuck and Rita looked at one another and took advantage of the moment, jumping to their feet and joining the others on the makeshift dance floor.

'So, you're not married,' he said.

She shook her head, suddenly shy to be in his arms.

'Is your mother always so protective?'

She nodded and blushed and couldn't meet his eye, let alone go into a long explanation of her relationship with Louise.

'Can't say I blame her at all,' he shouted above the music. 'A pretty gal who owns a Norton is a rare find.'

She didn't really know what to say to this and suddenly wished she was as adept as Cissy when it came to flirting.

They danced in silence for a while and when the record came to an end he leaned close and murmured in her ear, 'You have to be at the fire station at ten?' At her shy nod, he smiled. 'Would it be okay if I came along to keep you company?'

'I don't know,' she said hesitantly. 'The station manager doesn't allow visitors, and he could be sending me anywhere tonight.'

'There won't be any raids, you know. There's what you Limeys call a pea-souper out there, and Gerry can't fly in the fog.' He grinned and took her hand as the music began again. 'Come on, let's dance while we can. After all, it *is* Christmas.'

Sylvia watched Rita and the young American and was glad for the girl. She'd heard her story from Anne and Cissy, and had witnessed the way Louise clung to her. It was such a shame that one so young should be tied down with responsibilities. With the war on, and survival being so precarious, it was important to live every minute as if it were their last.

'You're looking thoughtful, Mother,' said Christopher as he stroked Harvey's silky ears.

She smiled at him lovingly and resisted the urge to brush the hair back from his forehead. 'I was just wondering if there was anything I could do to help little Rita,' she murmured, aware that Louise was nearby and could probably hear.

He grinned as he watched Rita and the American enjoying one another's company. 'I think young Rita's perfectly capable of helping herself,' he said wryly. 'She might be small and skinny, but you shouldn't let that fool you, Mother. There's a toughness there, believe me.'

Sylvia patted his hand, the swell of love reminding her how lucky she was that he'd been spared from paying the ultimate sacrifice. 'You know me,' she murmured. 'I never could resist a child in need.'

'She's hardly a child, Mother,' he retorted. 'Leave well alone, I say. She'll be all right.' He ruffled

Harvey's rough fur and sneaked him a morsel of cake that still clung to his plate.

Sylvia decided to say no more. Christopher knew nothing of Rita and Louise's story or circumstances, and certainly had no inkling of her own humble beginnings. He probably wouldn't understand much of it if he had been told – and she had often wondered how he would react. Her coming to live at Beach View, and the easy way she'd settled into the routine of this household, had shocked him enough – how much worse it would be if he and his brothers discovered that their mother had once been an orphan waif begging for food in the London slums.

She took a deep breath and became lost in her thoughts. James had gently tried to reason with her, but she had refused to be talked out of staying here, seeing it not only as a way of showing her appreciation to the man who'd saved her son's life, but as an opportunity for Christopher to experience life outside his cocoon of wealth and privilege.

This class divide had been a knotty problem right from the start of her marriage for, much to her disappointment and chagrin, James had been adamant that none of his sons should be exposed to the rougher elements of society, those whose lives were one long struggle for survival. He chaired several charity boards and donated generously. In his opinion, that was enough.

She had done her best to widen her sons' horizons

so they might have a better understanding of the world outside their privileged existence, for she firmly believed it would make them better men. But they were too like their father, and regarded charity donations as the only way to carry out their duty to those less fortunate. She could only hope that their time in the services would make them see things differently.

She let the noise and bustle go on around her as she allowed her thoughts to roam. She was a socialist at heart, and held strong, some might say radical, opinions on the welfare of the poor – though she'd never quite dared reveal them to James or the rest of his staunchly Conservative family. But the last war had seen many changes on the estate, and this one would carry on that process.

The women were earning good money now and taking a pride in themselves and their achievements, no longer prepared to slave for a pittance below stairs or take orders from bullying husbands. The big country houses no longer had manservants and an army of gardeners and estate workers to keep them going, so half the rooms had been put in mothballs for the duration – or taken over by the military as hospitals.

The harvests were being brought in by old men and land girls, the formal gardens turned into vegetable patches, the imposing iron gates sent away to be turned into tanks and aeroplanes. It would be a very different world that those fighting men would return to, and as fortunes were made and lost, those once grand estates would be taken on by the new money, and the class divide would blur again as it had in the nineteen twenties.

She smiled as she thought how horrified James would be if he could read her thoughts this minute. But the inevitability of it all could not be denied, and she rather looked forward to that day.

Selecting a lavender-coloured Sobranie cigarette from the dainty box, she lit it with her gold Dunhill lighter and gathered her wayward thoughts. She needed to concentrate on the problem of Rita and Louise.

Sylvia could imagine what heartache Louise must be going through, and the frustrations and divided loyalties Rita had to be contending with. It was clear Louise could only really function when she had someone to rely upon and, without her husband, she was like a lost soul, clinging to Rita for every need.

As the music and dancing continued, and Christopher and Martin fell into a serious discussion with two of the Americans about the lack of planes and fully qualified pilots, and the setback caused by the recent attack on the airfield, Sylvia watched the different expression flit across Louise's face.

Rita had told Sylvia that Louise was 'more Italian than the Italians'. It couldn't be easy to be Italian at the moment for despite the pact they'd signed with Germany and Japan, the Italians weren't faring well in this war. Their fleet had been crippled at Taranto back in early November. Later that month, the Greeks had defeated the invading Italian army – and now the British and Australians had begun a desert offensive against them in Northern Africa.

Louise was fortunate in a way that her menfolk were safe in some internees' camp, far from any strategic areas that might be bombed. Yet not to know where they were, or how they were faring, must be agony.

'Is there a smudge on my face? Is that why you're staring at me?'

Sylvia snapped out of her thoughts. 'I'm so sorry, Louise,' she said quickly. 'I wasn't really looking at you – I was just very deep in thought.'

Louise lifted her chin and patted the stray wisps of hair back into the knot at her nape. 'It's the occasion to turn our thoughts to more serious things than loud music and dancing. Without our loved ones, it all seems rather pointless.'

Sylvia shook her head. 'Sad, maybe, but not pointless, Louise. We must all make the best of things, and it does everyone good to let their hair down occasionally – especially the young.' She saw Louise wasn't convinced and shifted her chair a little closer. 'Have you heard from the authorities yet?'

'There's still no word,' Louise replied dolefully as she blinked away the ready tears. 'It's been five months now, and I'm beginning to believe I'll never see them again.' When there was no response from Sylvia, Louise blew her nose and heaved a deep sigh as if the cares of the world were on her shoulders.

Sylvia remained silent as she watched this performance. Louise was as dramatic and emotional as any Italian, but then she'd been living amongst them all her married life, so it was hardly surprising. But she suspected Louise had used tears and emotional blackmail to get her way far too often, and although she felt deeply sorry for the woman, she wanted her to stop being so selfish and think about Rita for a change.

Louise glanced at her and took a sip of tea. 'Without my husband, it's very hard to keep Rita safe, especially now we're homeless,' she said, her voice unsteady. 'She's a good girl, and has decided to give up her silly idea of working as a mechanic at the airfield because she knows her place is with me. But I'm afraid for her with so many foreigners about.'

Sylvia shot a glance at the happily dancing Rita and felt a stab of fury. The poor girl had probably never stood a chance to realise her ambitions, not with Louise's constant neediness. Now it seemed Louise was taking advantage of the girl's devotion, determined to keep her hidden away and rob her of any kind of life.

'Rita seems to have a good, sensible head on her shoulders,' Sylvia replied tightly. 'Let her make mistakes, stretch her wings and get a taste of life, Louise. They're all a part of growing up – and she needs to be prepared to face what could be an uncertain future.'

'Her future is not uncertain,' Louise replied smugly. 'She will marry Roberto and come to live with me and Tino. It's my duty to protect her honour until Roberto comes home. My own parents were very careful with me, and it did me no harm.'

Sylvia was of the opinion that it had done a great deal of harm, and that now Louise was passing it on to poor little Rita. The news that Louise planned to marry her off to her son simply made things worse, and Sylvia was deeply concerned for the girl. If something wasn't done soon, Rita would find herself forever trapped in Louise's soft, smothering web of need.

Deciding she would give it some careful thought over the next few days, she willed herself back into a happier frame of mind, slid back her chair and stood to face Ron.

'Now, Ron,' she said gaily, 'it's your turn to lead me onto the dance floor, I think.'

He glanced at Rosie and made a great show of reluctance. 'To be sure, Rosie's had me prancing about all afternoon and me feet are already killing me.'

'Your aching feet are simply a reminder that you're still alive,' she retorted, 'and I'm sure Rosie won't mind me borrowing you for just one dance.'

Rosie's expression was unreadable, but the folded arms, the gleam in her eye and the tilt of her chin warned Sylvia not to overstep the mark.

It had been a wonderful day, and although Rita wished it could have gone on until late into the night, she still felt the glow and the buzz of wine and music and the warmth of Chuck's smile as they'd danced.

She'd been aware of Louise's disapproval, and she and Chuck had spent their time together on the other side of the room. When she and Louise had returned from Beach View, Rita had virtually flown up the stairs to their room to get changed, emboldened by the day and the happy atmosphere at Beach View.

She closed her mind to all of Louise's dire warnings and threats as she dragged on the thick trousers and boots and buttoned the heavy overcoat. But as she caught a glimpse of her reflection in the dressing-table mirror, she realised why Louise had been berating her, for her eyes were shining, her cheeks were flushed and she seemed to be veiled in a soft glow that made her look almost pretty. It was obvious she was in the thrall of something very new and exciting.

'I'll be back at the end of my shift,' she said, cutting into a long monologue of woeful and terrible things that had happened to young girls who'd had their heads turned by men in uniform. She bent to kiss Louise's cheek. 'Sleep well, Mamma.'

Louise shot off the bed. 'How can I sleep when I know you've arranged to meet that boy?' she snapped. 'And don't deny that's what you've planned, Rita Smith, because it's written all over your face.'

'I haven't denied anything,' she replied calmly.

'There's nothing wrong with spending time with someone whose company I happen to enjoy.'

'You shouldn't want other men's company when you are promised to Roberto,' Louise stormed.

Rita stared at her in horror. 'I'm not promised to anyone,' she gasped. 'And I'll see who I like.'

'Roberto is expecting you to wait for him – to keep yourself pure for him like I was for his Papa on our wedding day. I will *not* allow you to bring shame to this family.'

Rita felt something cold crawl up her spine. 'Roberto and I have no such understanding. We are not engaged, or even courting – and never likely to be, either. Why do you refuse to believe me?'

Louise waved away her protest with a grimace. 'You're too young to take such decisions. It's up to me and Tino to make sure you—'

'It's not up to *either* of you to rule my life,' Rita stormed. 'I don't want to marry Roberto. I don't love him – not in that way, and I need to have some experience of life and everything it has to offer before I even begin to *think* about marriage.'

Louise shook her head mournfully. 'You will learn soon enough that life does not always give the things it seems to promise. You will see that I'm right.'

Rita took a deep breath. 'I need to find that out for myself, not just take your word for it,' she replied with as much calm as she could muster. 'The world won't end because Chuck and I are planning to sit together and pass the time while I'm on duty.'

'I forbid it,' Louise retorted. 'Fraternising while on duty is against the rules. John Hicks will not allow it either.'

Rita had had the same thought, but she snatched up her gas mask box and ugly tin hat and opened the door, determined to cross that bridge when she came to it. 'Well, I'm going to see Chuck anyway,' she said firmly. 'He's meeting me on the corner by the fire station.' With that, she shut the door and was halfway down the stairs before she heard Louise yelling after her.

Rita had never defied Louise before, and it was with a mixed sense of dread and excitement that she rode the Norton down the hill and headed for the fire station. There would be hell to pay when she got back to the billet, and it would be simply awful if Chuck wasn't waiting for her.

But he was standing on the pavement, his coat collar turned up against the cold, his hands cupping the flame as he lit a cigarette. 'Hi there,' he said softly.

She ripped off the goggles and helmet and shook out her hair, hoping she didn't look too much of a fright. 'Are you sure you don't mind sitting about for hours?' she asked hesitantly, 'only it can get pretty boring.'

He grinned back at her. 'I'm sure we'll find something to talk about.'

Rita let him wheel the Norton along the pavement as she walked beside him. He was tall and broad-shouldered and very handsome, and she still couldn't quite believe he wanted to spend this cold, foggy Christmas night with her.

All was quiet at the fire station and John Hicks was busy doing an inventory of the supplies when they walked through the door. He smiled at Rita, shot a questioning glance at Chuck and set the clipboard aside as Rita launched into a garbled explanation of why the American was with her, and why he should be allowed to stay.

Rita finally ran out of breath and looked at him hopefully.

'You know visitors aren't permitted, Rita,' he said quietly.

Hope plummeted.

John picked up the clipboard and flicked through the sheets of paper, his chin down so she couldn't see his expression. 'The fog's closed right in and Gerry's staying home, so you'd better make the most of a night off,' he said.

Hope was alive again. 'A night off? Really?'

He looked at them both and grinned. 'That's what I said. Now, go on, get out of here before I change my mind.'

Rita grinned up at him, grabbed Chuck's arm and almost dragged him out of the fire station.

'By the way, Rita,' called John, 'if the siren goes I want you back here pronto – and without the Yank.'

'Will do,' she called back, hastily putting on her leather helmet and goggles. 'He wasn't being personal,

Chuck,' she explained as she kicked the bike into life. 'But there are rules.'

The Norton dipped as Chuck settled on the seat behind her. 'That's okay,' he said lightly. 'So, Rita, where are you taking me?'

Rita had to think quickly. 'The pubs will probably be shut tonight, but I'm sure we could find a nice warm hotel bar to sit in – as long as you don't mind being seen with me in this get-up.'

He shifted on the seat until he was leaning against her back, his arms sliding round her waist. 'Lead on, Rita. I'm all yours.'

Chapter Sixteen

It was three days after Christmas and Peggy was fighting back the tears as Charlie clung to her waist and buried his head in the folds of her coat. She'd been dreading this moment, for she'd known their parting would be far more painful the second time round.

'Will you be coming back soon?' asked Charlie, his voice muffled.

'I can't say,' she murmured, ruffling his hair through her fingers and sinking her lips into it. 'But I'll try, Charlie. Really I will.'

'Why can't we come home with you, Mum?'

Peggy looked at Bob, who was a solemn bystander fighting his own battle to appear stoic. He put his hand on his young brother's shoulder, his voice breaking a little. 'Mum's already explained,' he said. 'Don't keep badgering her, Charlie. Can't you see you're making her upset?'

'But I . . . I . . .'

Bob put his arm round them both, the tremble in his young arms the only sign of how much this was affecting him too. 'It's all right, Charlie, really it is,' he murmured. 'We'll go home when the war's over, you'll see, but for now we have to stay here.'

He drew away and eased Charlie's grip from their mother's coat, making him turn to look at him. 'But it's nice here, isn't it? We have lots of fun with Ernie, and Bess is about to have her puppies. You don't want to miss that, do you?'

Peggy was overwhelmed by her son's under-standing of the situation, and the love he so clearly had for his little brother. She blew her nose and tried to pull herself together. 'Puppies,' she breathed. 'How lovely, Charlie. You certainly don't want to miss out on them, do you?'

He looked up at her, his little face blotched with tears. 'Puppies are all right,' he said, trying desper-ately not to show how much he was being torn. 'But I miss Dad and Grandpa and Harvey.' He gave a hearty sniff and dashed his tears away with his sleeve. Being brave and grown-up like his big brother was terribly hard.

'We all miss you too – both of you.' It took all of Peggy's determination to stem her own tears.

He slipped his grubby little hand into hers and looked at her trustingly. 'Don't be sad, Mum,' he said. 'Me and Bob will be all right until you come back. Just don't leave it too long, that's all.'

Peggy pulled them both to her and held them tightly. 'I'll come as soon as I can, and remember we all love you both very much,' she said, her voice gruff with unshed tears.

Violet let go of a tearful Ernie's hand, her round, sweet face soft with concern. 'It's time to go, Peggy,' she said softly. 'The girl's waiting in the truck outside, and you don't want to miss the train.'

Peggy wanted very much to miss the train – to stay here, to be a part of her sons' lives again. She hugged them fiercely, knowing she had to deny herself – knowing it was best for all concerned if she left now before she made a complete fool of herself.

She kissed Ernie again, stepped back and picked up her case as Violet opened the front door. 'Goodbye, my darlings, look after one another, won't you?'

Bob slung his arms round Charlie and Ernie's shoulders and mussed their hair. 'Don't worry about us,' he said. 'I'll make sure these two don't get into too much mischief.'

She swiftly kissed them all again and stepped outside into the gloomy day. The rain was a mist that veiled the surrounding hills and soaked through her best coat and hat as she carried her case out to the farm truck. She didn't look back, for if she did, she would never leave.

She climbed into the truck and slammed the door, blinded by her tears, her heart heavy.

'Ready?' asked the young land girl as she crunched the gears.

'Not really, but I suppose I have no other option.'

'Must be horrid for you,' the girl said sympathetically. 'Glad I don't have any children to worry about.' She released the handbrake and the truck began to roll forward.

Peggy wiped away the condensation on the side

window and looked out. Violet and the boys were standing on the doorstep in the pool of light coming from the porch. She blew a kiss, holding her fingers to the glass as if she could touch them through it.

They waved and blew kisses back, but the truck was already moving away from them, gathering speed as it splashed and jounced through the farm-yard puddles and scattered the ducks and hens.

As the farmhouse was lost in the mist behind them and they reached the narrow, winding country lane that would take them to the station halt some miles away, Peggy felt a great surge of the grief that had been building since yesterday. It overwhelmed her like the breaking of a dam, and she buried her face in her hands, yielding to it in a storm of bitter tears.

It seemed Hitler was giving them some respite, for there had been no bombing raids since before the holiday. The nasty weather had closed in with misty rain blotting out the hills and thick, freezing fog rolling in from the sea, but Cliffehaven was preparing for the New Year celebrations. The talk at the factory was an excited babble as the women discussed their plans, what they would wear, and who they would be dancing with. It took all of Major Patricia's leader-ship skills to keep them focused on their work.

Rita was looking forward to the celebrations, too, for she and Chuck had met every day since Christmas, and he'd already bought tickets to the biggest and best dance being held at the Galaxy Ballroom, which was in the Grand Hotel on the seafront. To celebrate, she'd splashed out on a lovely pair of dancing shoes she'd found in the market, and had begun to worry about what to wear with them.

Ever the romantic, Cissy had insisted she have one of her many party dresses, and Rita had asked John Hicks' wife, Sally, to take it in and shorten it. It was a lovely dress of turquoise blue, and both Sally and Cissy had assured her that it brought out the darkness of her hair and eyes and made her very pretty indeed. Rita had never been one for party frocks before, or bothered much about her looks, but things had changed since meeting Chuck, and even she had to admit she looked rather nice.

She had known it wouldn't be long before her friendship with the young American became common knowledge, but she refused to be drawn into the factory gossip and denied there was anything serious in their being seen together. She hugged the memory of her shy, first sweet kiss to herself.

The end of her early shift had come at last, and although it was only three in the afternoon it was already quite dark outside. She quickly pulled on the thick fire service overcoat over her dungarees and old sweater, wrapped a scarf round her neck and pulled the beret Anne had given her for Christmas over her curls. Picking up the canvas bag containing the remnants of her lunch, and the gas mask box, she slung their straps over her shoulder, dug her gloved hands deep in her pockets and hurried away from the factory.

The Norton was safely locked away in one of the outbuildings at the asylum, and it was a long walk back, but she had an appointment with John Hicks first and didn't want to be late. His message had come through to Major Patricia's office telephone. She had no idea why he wanted to see her, but suspected he was going to cut down on some of her fire-watch shifts now things were quieter.

The station was a hive of activity as the fire engines were hosed down and polished to a gleam, the yard was scrubbed and the whole place made shipshape in readiness for the next raid. There was a chorus of greetings which Rita returned before climbing the wooden stairs up to John's office.

'Come in and sit down, Rita,' he said cheerfully as she opened the door and walked in. 'Want a cup of tea?'

'That would be lovely.' She held her hands over the paraffin heater to warm them. 'It's bitter out there.'

'Before I forget,' he said, 'your dress will be ready Tuesday morning. I'll bring it in so you can pick it up here. If there are any problems, Sally will be at home all day, so she can sort them out.'

Rita experienced a little thrill of excitement. 'I'm sure it will be perfect,' she breathed, imagining herself dancing the night away in Chuck's arms like a fairytale princess.

'Yeah, my Sally's clever with the needle. Her home

dressmaking business is going from strength to strength.' He poured the tea and set the cup and saucer on the table with a couple of digestive biscuits. 'She tells me I'm getting fat,' he said comfortably, patting his midriff, 'so don't let on I've sneaked these into work.'

Rita smiled and blew on the hot tea, her hands cradling the cup. 'It's our secret as long as you keep sharing them out,' she murmured. She watched as he settled into the chair by his desk, his injured leg stuck out before him. Rita knew it still caused him a degree of pain, and although he limped quite badly when he was tired, she'd never heard him complain about it.

'Your father telephoned about ten minutes ago. He said he was sorry he missed you, but couldn't hang on because the Staff Sergeant had only given him five minutes.'

Rita felt her spirits ebb. 'It would have been lovely to speak to him,' she said softly. 'Will he call again, do you think?'

'I don't know, Rita, but I'm sure he'll try.'

'Is he well? Nothing's wrong, is there?'

'He's absolutely fine.' He regarded her in silence for a moment. 'He rang because he got your letter. He's not happy about you staying here now the house is gone, and asked me to make you see sense and get you on the next train out of Cliffehaven.'

'I can't leave without Louise, and she's refusing to budge. I explained all that in my letter.'

'I also understand you've withdrawn your

application to join the WAAFs for the same reason,' he said, his gaze steady.

'How on earth did you know that? Dad couldn't have told you, because I never let on to him I'd even applied.'

He didn't smile, simply looked rather sad. 'Cliffehaven's a hotbed of gossip and rumour. You should know that, Rita.' He fell silent for a moment and then gave a deep sigh. 'So it's true then,' he said. 'What a shame.'

'I really had no choice once we'd been bombed out.' She had a sudden, rather alarming thought. 'I hope you didn't say anything to Dad about it.'

He shook his head. 'He never mentioned it, so I didn't either.'

The relief was immense. Her father would blow a gasket if he'd known and would probably have gone AWOL to come down and read her the riot act. She hated keeping things from him, but what he didn't know couldn't hurt him, and she'd worded her letter very carefully.

She sipped the hot tea, and then remembered he'd asked her to come here long before her father had telephoned. 'What did you want to see me about, Mr Hicks?'

He shifted in his chair and fiddled with some of the papers strewn across his desk. 'As you seem so determined to stay in Cliffehaven, I was wondering if you'd consider taking on a full-time job here. I'd pay the going rate.'

Rita put down her cup, afraid she'd spill the tea. 'As a fireman?'

'As a driver and fill-in mechanic.'

A little thrill sparked inside her as her thoughts raced. 'Mechanics earn more than drivers,' she pointed out, more in hope than expectation.

He laughed. 'There're no flies on you, are there, Rita?'

'It's too jolly cold for flies,' she returned with a smile, 'and I need the money.'

'Tell you what. I'll pay the rate for a driver when you drive, and the rate for an apprentice mechanic when you fix my engines. How about that?'

Rita grinned. 'That sounds fair to me. You've got a deal.' She drank the last of her tea and stood. 'When do you want me to start?'

'On your next shift, and then full-time once you've worked your notice at the factory,' he said. 'Mr Wickens will be on hand to help. He might be old and a bit doddery, but he knows more about engines than you ever will.'

Rita liked Mr Wickens, even when he was grumpy. He reminded her of Ron Reilly, for no matter how much he grumbled, there was always a twinkle in his eye.

John looked back at her, a grin tugging at his lips. 'I don't think I've ever seen you smile so broadly,' he said, 'or look so happy. Still seeing that young American?'

'It's nothing to do with him,' she said quickly, not

wanting him to think she was a dreamy girl with cotton wool for brains. 'I'm just thrilled you're giving me this chance, and I can't wait to get my hands on a decent set of tools again. Dad's were lost when the house blew up.'

'You're always welcome to come in and tinker during your hours off at the factory,' he said. 'I'll pay for any work you do on our engines.'

'Thanks, Mr Hicks.' She shifted from one foot to the other, the excitement battling with sudden doubt. 'I might need a bit of practice before I take one of the engines out on the road,' she said nervously. 'I know the mechanics, but the practical side of actually driving anything is a bit hazy.'

He laughed. 'Come in tomorrow and I'll give you a lesson. It shouldn't take long. You're a bright girl.'

Rita knew she was grinning from ear to ear in delight. 'Is it all right if I go now? Only Louise is waiting for me to walk her back from the factory, and I want to tell her the good news.'

He frowned. 'Why aren't you using the Norton?'

'Not enough petrol to keep running all over the place, and she's developed a strange knocking sound which I need to investigate.'

'Bring it down here and work on it in the garage during your spare time,' he said as the telephone began to ring. 'You'll need it to get about now you're stuck up at that asylum. It's not safe walking up there in the dark.' He picked up the receiver and his expression softened. 'Hello, Sally. I thought it might be you . . .'

Rita closed the door on his private conversation with his new wife, but was still grinning fit to burst as she raced down the stairs and declared her marvellous news to all and sundry.

Warmed by their congratulations and encouragement, she felt as if she had wings on her boot heels as she all but danced along the pavement and headed for Goldman's clothing factory. Chuck was meeting her outside the Odeon cinema at seven, she was about to start doing what she loved most, and would even learn how to drive a fire engine. Her world couldn't be more perfect.

Rita was amazed at how simple it had been to look at life differently, and see that it didn't have to be conducted in a haze of gloom and hopelessness. That Christmas Day at Beach View had opened her eyes to how low Louise had brought her, and although she would never leave Louise to cope alone, she'd slowly begun to loosen the apron strings.

She and Louise didn't argue over her seeing Chuck any more. They'd said everything they had to say, and Rita was no longer so easily swayed by Louise's tears and long, meaningful silences. Louise clearly wasn't happy at the change in Rita, but they'd reached an uneasy truce, relying on their love for one another to carry them through this sea-change in their relationship.

The news of her new posting at the fire station

was greeted with a warm, knowing smile by Louise, who couldn't resist commenting that she'd always known Rita would be much happier staying in Cliffehaven, and that she hoped this would be the end of all that silly talk about joining the WAAFs.

Rita had just smiled, kissed her goodbye and left their billet with a light heart to ride the Norton down to the fire station on the way to meeting Chuck at the cinema. She was still concerned about the strange noises it was making, and if it hadn't been for her date tonight, she'd have stripped the engine down and given it a good going over.

It was a filthy night and the fire station was all but deserted. After greeting the volunteer who was manning the telephone and reading his newspaper, she wheeled the Norton to the most distant corner of the vast garage and pulled her 'air raid bag' out of the pannier.

Locking herself in the small canteen, she changed into her best clothes. Once dressed, she brushed her hair and fixed May's sparkling comb firmly amid the curls and then made sure Tino's earrings were safely pinned in her earlobes. May had been right, they didn't hurt at all now.

There wasn't a mirror, but she could just make out her reflection in the shining steel dome that sat over the empty cheese platter. Her reflection was distorted in the curved metal, but as far as she could tell, she didn't look too bad, even though she was wearing no make-up and hadn't had the time or the spare money to get her hair done.

She donned the heavy fire service overcoat, which must look very odd with high-heeled shoes, but was the only protection she had against the appalling weather, gathered up her motorcycle gear and carefully folded it and the hold-all away in the panniers. Giving the Norton a pat, she called a cheerful TTFN to the volunteer. The night was hers, and she meant to make the most of it.

She crossed the echoing space, past the three red Dennis fire engines, her heels tapping on the concrete. Opening the door, she grimaced at the rain that was teeming down and gurgling in a rush along the gutters. She'd forgotten to buy a new umbrella, and her hair would end up a horrible frizzy mess.

As she dithered in the doorway a noisy jeep swerved across the road and pulled up with a squeal of brakes, the big tyres sending a slew of dirty water across the pavement.

She leaped back with an angry gasp and only just escaped getting her shoes and stockings ruined. 'For goodness sake,' she muttered crossly as she checked for damage.

'I'm so sorry, Rita. I was on my way to pick you up from your billet and only just saw you. I didn't know there was a puddle there. Are you okay?'

She looked up at Chuck and her anger fled. 'Only just,' she teased. 'You really should look where you're going.'

He grinned and took her hand. 'I can't help it if you guys drive on the wrong side of the road, and then confuse us poor ol' country boys by turning out all the lights.'

'We do it especially, just to wind you up. So, where did that come from?'

'One of my buddies back at base lent it to me for the evening. I didn't want you getting wet, and it's a long walk to your billet.'

Rita smiled back at him, her pulse missing a beat. 'What a treat,' she said. 'I've never been in a jeep before.'

'No time like the present. Come on, or we'll miss the show.'

Rita felt the warmth of his hand as they ran into the rain, felt the strength of him as he virtually lifted her into the cab of the jeep and slammed the door on the wind and rain. She was a lucky girl and no mistake.

As he climbed in beside her she eyed the jeep's interior. It was very basic – just a shell of metal really, with only a couple of dials fixed behind the large steering wheel, two bucket-shaped leather seats and a canvas roof which let in a terrific draught. The engine was noisy so it was impossible to carry on a conversation, and the suspension left a great deal to be desired. But it was fun, so much fun, and she blessed him silently for being so thoughtful.

Chuck parked the jeep with typical gung-ho American verve. He helped her down and they ran up the steps past the colourful posters advertising *'Broadway Melody of 1940*, starring Fred Astaire and Eleanor Powell,' and into the warmth of the dimly lit foyer.

Rita knew how quickly tickets sold out for a Hollywood musical, so had advised Chuck to buy theirs in good time. They quickly found their way to the stalls, where an elderly usherette clipped their tickets, switched on her torch, and showed them through the baize doors to their seats.

The large cinema's three blocks of seats were already packed, cigarette smoke drifting in clouds to the high, domed ceiling as people chattered, waved to friends or tapped along in time with the music from the ancient but ornate Hammond organ that had been raised to stage height from the orchestra pit. The organist was a familiar character to the residents of Cliffehaven, for he always wore full evening dress and a top hat when he played – even for the matinees.

Rita waved to Cissy and Anne, who were sitting in the far block. She recognised several of the women from the factory, and even saw Vi Charlton tucked up in the back row with her American. She blushed and smiled back at Vi's knowing wink and quickly followed Chuck, apologising as they had to edge past knees and feet to get to their seats. They were only just in time, for the organ was slowly and majestically being lowered back into place and the lights were dimming.

The faded and much mended velvet curtains rattled open and silence fell, the anticipation for the Saturday night's entertainment almost tangible as the beams of light from the projection window at the back battled through the cigarette smoke. The music coming from the speakers on either side of the stage was familiar and quite loud as the screen sent its reflective glow over the audience and the crowing and rather imperious Pathé News cockerel appeared.

Rita felt Chuck reach for her hand and they entwined their fingers as they watched the newsreel flicker on the screen, and listened to the plummy voice of the reporter.

The British offensive against the invading Italians in Northern Africa was going well, and it was expected to be a great success. An enemy raider had been driven off by British naval ships escorting a convoy in the Atlantic, and closer to home the belea-guered Londoners were going about their daily lives and celebrating Christmas in defiance of the devas-tation wreaked upon their city by Hitler's blitz. The expert view from the Home Office was that the lull in the air raids over Christmas had been more to do with bad weather in Northern Europe than any altruistic gesture by Hitler – and that the citizens of Great Britain must remain alert.

As the newsreels came to an end Rita and Chuck settled further into their seats, comfortable and easy with one another as they held hands and waited for the first of the two films they would see tonight. It might be raining outside, but they were warm and snug and very happy to be together.

They came out of the cinema humming 'Begin the Beguine' along with everyone else. It had stopped raining, but there was a chill wind, and Rita shivered.

'Let's warm up in a pub,' suggested Chuck.

'That sounds like a jolly good idea, but I can't stay too late,' she said regretfully. 'I'm on early shift tomorrow, and I'll have to walk to work. The Norton's been playing up and I daren't risk it any longer on that steep hill.'

He helped her climb into the jeep. 'Want me to have a look at it?'

She shook her head, jealous of anyone touching her motorbike, even Chuck. 'I'll sort it out after work tomorrow. You can lend a hand if you want,' she added quickly.

'I can't tomorrow night,' he shouted over the engine noise. 'I'm on duty. Maybe the next day?' He glanced swiftly across at her and, at her nod, shot her a beaming smile. 'It's a date,' he yelled.

He drove down the High Street and along Camden Road, stopping outside the Anchor. 'I thought we might try it for a change,' he explained once he'd killed the engine. 'Ron and Jim gave it high praise.'

'It's not the pub Ron's in love with,' said Rita and chuckled. 'It's the lovely Rosie Braithwaite.'

Chuck helped her down and they strolled arm in arm towards the Anchor and the raucous singing that drifted out into the street. 'Can't say as I blame the guy,' he drawled. 'Rosie's quite a gal.'

Rita tugged at his arm playfully. 'I didn't realise you liked the more mature woman,' she teased.

'Only when they look like Betty Grable's mother,' he replied with a twinkle in his eyes.

'Betty who?'

He laughed. 'I see I'm going to have to fill those yawning gaps in your education, Rita. But for now, let's get inside out of this cold.'

The singing was so loud it was almost impossible to talk, but the songs were well known and they'd joined in, adding to the noise. Rita was aware of the time flying past and of how early she would have to leave the asylum in the morning to get to work – but she didn't care. She didn't need sleep – not while she was having such fun.

It was almost closing time when the door opened and Jim stepped in and surveyed the still crowded bar. Rita waved to him and he elbowed his way through the melee to the bar, bought a drink and battled his way to the corner settle they'd found next to the back window.

'Cissy told me you'd be in here,' he shouted above the noise. 'She saw the jeep outside when she and Anne were coming home.'

'I'm sorry we didn't give her a lift, but there's only room for two,' explained Chuck.

'No matter. They took it slow and got home safely.'

Jim lifted his glass and swallowed half his pint in one steady go. Wiping the froth from his lips, he then dug into his coat pocket. 'I came to find you because there's a letter arrived this afternoon that looks important.' He regarded Rita, his expression solemn. 'I'd've taken it to Louise at the factory, but I'm thinking it's best you read it first in case it's bad news.'

Rita's hand was shaking as she reached for it. A chill swept through her as she read the stamped words, 'Home Office', in the left-hand corner. It could only mean news of Tino and Roberto.

She quickly tore it open. There was no address at the top, and the signature was indecipherable, but there was little doubt that it was official.

Dear Mrs Minelli,

   This is to inform you that Antonino and Roberto Minelli are at present being held in custody at a secret location somewhere in Britain. It is reported that both men are in good health, and have been given permission to correspond with you in the very near future. I regret I have no further information at this time.

   Yours sincerely,

Rita stared at the scrawled signature, but it meant nothing to her. She looked up at Jim and Chuck. 'It's quite good news,' she said, and showed them the letter.

'At least Louise will get some comfort at last,' muttered Jim.

Rita reached for her coat and gas mask box. 'Thanks for bringing it, Mr Reilly.' She turned to Chuck. 'I'm sorry to cut our evening short, but Louise needs to see this. Could you please take me home now?'

Chuck parked the jeep at the end of the gravel drive and switched off the engine. Rita happily leaned into his embrace. 'Thanks for a lovely evening, and I'm sorry it ended so abruptly.'

'A kiss might make up for that,' he replied, nuzzling her cheek with his lips.

Rita became aware of the gap between the seats and the awkwardness of trying to embrace someone with a huge steering wheel in the way. But his kiss was soft and sweet, and the sensations he was arousing made her forget everything for a blissful moment.

She pulled away reluctantly, and he got out, opened the door and helped her down. 'I'll see you at the fire station the day after tomorrow,' he said, holding her for just one moment more before he had to let her go.

Rita blew him a kiss and ran up the drive. She opened the big front door as the jeep roared away, saw Aggie watching her from the kitchen doorway and raced up the stairs. She could only hope that Louise hadn't gone to sleep already. It was quite late, almost ten-thirty.

Louise was awake, sitting in bed, flicking through a rather tattered magazine someone had left in the kitchen.

'There's been a letter, Mamma,' Rita said as she dug it from her coat pocket and quickly explained the contents before handing it over.

Louise's lips moved as she struggled to read it word by painful word, and then she burst into tears and held the letter to her heart. 'I must go to them,' she sobbed. 'Rita, you must *make* them tell us where they have been taken.'

Rita had suspected there would be tears and demands and had prepared for them. 'They won't tell me anything more,' she said evenly, 'and I certainly can't force them to break an official secret.'

'But I'm his wife,' Louise retorted. 'I have a right to know.'

Rita took off her coat, sat on the bed and held Louise close. 'Papa will write soon,' she said calmly against the storm of Louise's tears, 'the letter says so. We have to be patient for just a little while longer, Mamma, and then Papa will tell us what has been happening to him and Roberto.'

'It's so unfair,' stormed Louise. 'Why do I have to suffer like this?'

'You're not alone, Mamma. There are lots of other families going through the same thing. Just be glad that they're alive and well, and look forward to Tino's letter, which I'm sure will come very soon.'

Louise nodded, the letter still clutched to her

heart. 'It's very hard for me, Rita,' she breathed through her tears. 'I miss them so much.'

'I know,' soothed Rita, glad the storm was over. 'But you'll feel so much better once you hear from them. Then we can write back, and perhaps send them a parcel of treats.'

Louise dried her tears, carefully put the precious letter back in the envelope and picked up the stub of a pencil, which she handed to Rita. 'We will make a list of all their favourite things,' she said purposefully. 'And once we know where they are, we will take everything to them.'

'I don't know if we'll be allowed to visit them,' warned Rita.

'Of course we will,' Louise retorted. 'Even murderers get visits in prison, and my Tino is not a criminal.' She handed a clean sheet of writing paper to Rita, her expression alive with hope. 'They will need warm clothes and fresh underwear,' she began.

Chapter Seventeen

The fog had finally lifted around lunchtime to reveal a watery sun and a steely sea. It being Sunday, Cliffehaven was quiet, the shops closed, the pubs not yet open for the evening session, but several people were strolling along the promenade, taking advantage of this minor break in the weather.

The day had gone swiftly for Rita, despite the fact she was still feeling tired after the late night and very early start. She had returned to their billet at the end of her shift, snatched a couple of hours' sleep, and was now walking back down the hill with Louise, who was struggling to carry her 'air raid bag' as well as her gas mask box and handbag. It was only four o'clock, but the night was already closing in.

'What on earth have you got in here?' Rita asked, her arm almost wrenched from its socket as she took it from her.

'My best clothes and shoes, the Madonna statue and family photographs, four potatoes, the rest of the onions and two tins of bully beef. There's also a small tin of Spam, and one of condensed milk as well as the last of the sugar and tea.'

'Good grief,' muttered Rita, changing it from hand to hand. 'No wonder it weighs a ton. What on earth possessed you to bring our entire larder into town?'

'I don't trust that Aggie not to steal it. Nothing's safe in that kitchen with her around.'

'They would have been quite secure locked in our room,' Rita said evenly.

'I feel easier having them with me.' Louise continued walking, her expression set.

Rita sometimes wondered what on earth went on in Louise's head, but she made no further comment. They reached the western end of the promenade, walked past the big houses in Havelock Gardens and through the small park to the High Street, where they would go their separate ways.

Rita put the heavy bag down and flexed her aching fingers. Louise was going to the early show at the Odeon before she started her night shift. 'Why don't I drop this off at the factory while you go to the flicks? It'll be quite safe in your locker.'

Louise lifted the bag and hugged it protectively. 'I'll keep it with me,' she said stubbornly. 'Those lockers can be broken into very easily.'

Rita gave in. 'Well, I'm off for my first driving lesson. I'll see you back at the billet tomorrow morning.' She gave Louise a warm hug and watched her trudge up the High Street towards the Odeon, the heavy bag dragging on her arm. 'Bless her,' she muttered, before turning off into Camden Road.

The fire station was next to Goldman's factory,

which now sprawled the length and depth of an entire block. John Hicks was waiting for her beside the bright red Dennis fire engine that stood on the forecourt. 'Right,' he said without preamble. 'In you get, and I'll run you through the basics before you terrify the life out of the locals by driving on our roads.'

Peggy was exhausted, not only by the anguish of leaving her boys behind, but by the interminably long and frustrating journey. It seemed there were still lines up everywhere, despite the fact there hadn't been a raid of any significance for at least ten days.

Her passage home to Beach View had been interrupted constantly, stopping and starting all through the previous day. She'd had to change trains, wait on lonely platforms in the middle of nowhere, with nothing to show where she was, or how far she still had to go. She'd climbed on and off ramshackle buses that lumbered through the ever-darkening countryside at a snail's pace, and had finally managed to snatch some sleep in the crowded second-class compartment as the train chugged and puffed towards morning.

Now she sat wearily in the refreshment room of a large crowded station, drinking stewed, weak tea. There was nothing to eat, so she made do with a cigarette. She'd managed to wash her face and hands and brush her hair in the ladies' convenience, but her reflection in the age-spotted mirror had not been flattering. There were dark circles beneath her eyes, her skin was the colour of whey, and there were soot smears on her coat and dress. Even the jaunty feather in her hat was drooping as if it too had had enough of this seemingly endless journey.

She looked at her watch, stubbed out her cigarette and picked up her case. Her train was pulling into the station, and if she didn't hurry, she wouldn't get a seat. Her feet were killing her in these silly shoes, and she certainly didn't have the stamina to stand all the way.

The porter was very kind, finding her a nice seat by the window and stowing her case in the rack above. She settled down, pulling up her coat collar to ward off the draught, and was asleep even before the train pulled out of the station.

There had been some activity this afternoon from the nearby airbase, with Spitfires and Hurricanes sweeping over the town, but as the sirens weren't sounded and there were no reports of enemy sightings, the firemen and volunteers went on with their duties unperturbed.

'You did well today, Rita,' said John Hicks. 'If we have any call-outs tonight – which I suspect we might, now the weather's cleared – you're more than ready to drive one of my engines. I'll see to it you get some first-aid training as well. It could come in handy.'

Rita grinned with delight as she finished tightening the last nut with a spanner. 'It was fun,' she said, cleaning the grease off her hands with a dirty rag. 'Thanks, John.'

'How's the Norton? Fixed the problem?'

She nodded. 'As I suspected, it was just a faulty connection, nothing serious.' She'd been going to let Chuck give her a hand fixing the bike, but when it came down to it, she hadn't been able to resist doing it herself. She put the spanner back with the other tools, eager to put the Norton through its paces before her shift started. It was almost six o'clock. Louise had most of their food in her bag, so there was no point in going back to the billet, and Rita was starving. 'I'll just go and see if the chip shop's open. Does anyone else . . .?'

The telephone rang with that peculiar sense of urgency that always heralded bad news, and everyone stopped what they were doing and looked towards the office.

'Enemy sighted,' shouted the volunteer from the top of the stairs moments later. 'Heavy presence coming in fast. Full alert. Stand by, stand by.'

The volunteer fire-watchers quickly moved towards John to be given their orders and then raced away on an assortment of bicycles, old vans and motorbikes to man their observation posts. The firemen donned their helmets and boots and made final checks to their reels and hoses before the lights were switched off, plunging the vast garage into darkness.

Rita and the other two drivers pulled on their heavy coats and rubber boots, clamped on their helmets and climbed into the cabs. She wasn't supposed to be on duty for another two hours, but she knew all too well that every pair of hands mattered when Gerry was on the prowl.

The huge folding doors at the front of the station were drawn back just as the sirens began to wail, and above the rooftops of the houses opposite, Rita could see the searchlights flicker into life and slowly build in strength. She no longer felt hungry or tired, for the air was charged with expectation and she was more than ready to do her bit.

Every head was turned towards the distant but growing resonance of many powerful engines approaching their shores. No one spoke or moved as the sirens shrieked, the searchlights split the sky and the rumble of menacing thunder grew.

Rita could feel the air tremble and the sturdy fire engine vibrate around her as the big guns on the seafront began to boom. But the first wave of enemy bombers were above them now, stacked seven or eight deep, hiding the moon and erasing the stars as they headed inexorably inland.

Red tracers stitched through the sky. Pom-poms from the guns up on the hills exploded like giant chrysanthemums as the ack-ack guns rattled and stuttered and the Spitfires and Hurricanes harried and darted, their guns blazing.

But still the Luftwaffe came in wave after terrible

wave – as black as scavenging ravens, as menacing and as numerous as all the demons from hell, their thunder filling the air and echoing deep within the very souls of those who watched in awed silence.

Rita's mouth was dry and her hands were slick on the steering wheel as she stared up at that terrible sight. She had witnessed nothing like this before, and was suddenly made terrifyingly aware of the enormous strength of Hitler's air force, and his absolute determination to bring England to her knees.

Peggy was woken by the guard shouting and the train coming to a screeching, slithering halt. She couldn't see where they were because the shutters had been drawn down over the windows, but the illuminated dial on her watch told her it was two in the morning, and in the distance she could hear a deep rumble that was all too familiar.

'Everyone off the train,' yelled the guard, blowing his whistle. 'Air raid. Air raid.'

She grabbed her suitcase from the rack, hitched her gas mask box and handbag straps over her shoulder and slowly shuffled with the rest of the passengers into the corridor, where they were filtered towards the doors and down the step to the grassy embankment. She could just make out a platform and a huddle of buildings ahead and felt a little relieved. At least they weren't in the middle of nowhere, without cover or shelter.

There was no sign to tell her where they were – they'd been removed long ago – but she suspected they were in one of London's western suburbs. Yet it was strange how light it was considering the late hour. Small and slight, she was hemmed in on all sides, unable to see where she was going as she was carried along by the tide of people. The distant thunder of enemy planes and the answering booms of the guns continued, but the lack of true darkness worried her. It felt wrong, it looked wrong, and was eerie enough to make her skin crawl.

It seemed she wasn't the only one to feel it, for the crowd began to slow, and she could hear people muttering.

And then a woman close to her cried out. 'Oh, my God. Look at that.'

Peggy clambered onto a nearby bench to see – and froze. Everyone was still now and no one spoke as all eyes turned to the horrifying source of that strange and frightening light.

The sky was glowing on the horizon, reflecting the furnace heat of the flames which rampaged beneath it. Smoke billowed and boiled in grey clouds tinged with orange and pink and yellow as the colossal hunting pack of enemy planes circled like carrion crows and unleashed their lethal cargos. The distant boom of the guns, the probing fingers of searchlights waving back and forth in a desperate bid to pinpoint the enemy, were accompanied by the zip of tracers and the bright yellow bursts of the pom-poms.

It seemed that hundreds of incendiaries exploded even as she watched, and new tongues of flame shot into the broiling mass of smoke as they feasted and spread and added to the turbulence.

To Peggy it was the apocalypse of the book of Revelation – for the great and ancient city of London was being consumed in hellfire – and her sister Doreen was right in the middle of it.

There was hardly any lull between the enemy's arrival and departure. The numberless swarm had still been coming from across the Channel when the first wave returned from their attack. But it seemed they had little interest in Cliffehaven, and swept over the seaside town without dropping a single bomb.

It was now five in the morning and still the demonic noise continued. There had been a couple of distant booms and several bombs had exploded harmlessly into the sea – but there were no fires reported from the watchers up in the hills.

'They must be reloading on the other side of the Channel and coming in for a second and third go at poor old London,' muttered John. 'The Luftwaffe doesn't have that many bombers – or at least I hope to God they don't.'

Rita's ears rang with the continuous roar overhead, and her nerves were shredded. She was thankful

Cliffehaven seemed to have escaped this particular raid, but the tension over the past eleven hours had been almost unbearable.

There was a deep boom to the west, swiftly followed by another. That sounded close, too close, and Rita shivered.

'Fires reported. Fires reported.' They all listened as the man on watch gave precise coordinates over the two-way radio.

'It's the old asylum,' shouted John, scrabbling for the appropriate clipboard which held the list of residents. 'You'll need this,' he said, passing it to Rita. 'One and two engine, go, go, go.'

Rita's mouth was dry and her heart hammered as the three firemen leaped aboard. She started the engine of number two and swiftly followed her colleagues in number one. The enemy planes were still overhead, but she couldn't hear them as the fireman beside her yanked enthusiastically on the bell. Louise would be in the shelter beneath the clothing factory, but there were over thirty women billeted at the asylum, some of them with babies and toddlers. She just had to hope they were all right.

The fire engines raced through Havelock Gardens and began to climb the steep, winding road up the hill. Rita could already see a red glow in the sky and yellow tongues of flame licking at the roof and the turrets, reaching for the trees that crowded in behind the old building.

She brought the engine to a screeching halt and jumped down, ready to help in any way she could. But the firemen were well trained and they moved in unison to release the hoses and aim the jets of water from their big emergency tanks onto the flames. The heat was tremendous, their faces aglow with it, their shadows distorted by the flickering light as black smoke billowed from the inferno.

Rita felt helpless as one of the men raced to the water main, swiftly unlatched it and plugged in the largest hose. It took three of them to hold it steady as the pressure forced them to counter it with their own weight.

She looked towards the deep trench that had been dug on the far side of the grounds. It was the only air-raid shelter for the evacuees in the asylum, and was protected, not with a sturdy roof, but with high surrounding walls of sandbags. Had everyone got out of the building? Did anyone know if all the residents had been accounted for?

Rita was about to run over and check when there was a piercing scream. She looked up, her pulse racing wildly. A woman was leaning out of the bay window in the turret – Rita's room – the fire glowing behind her as flames licked across the roof.

Rita froze in horror.

'Bring the engine closer so we can use the ladder,' yelled one of the men on the giant hose.

Galvanised into action, Rita ran to the fire engine and swiftly drove it as close as she could to the inferno.

Pressing the correct button, she heard the hydraulics whining as the fifty-foot ladder slowly rose from the back and locked into place.

When the fireman shouted it was correctly placed, she switched off the engine and clambered out. The heat scorched her face, then the freezing jets of water played over the wall and the roof surrounding the window, soaking her to the skin.

Her eyes were stinging from the acrid smoke as she watched the fireman race up the rungs towards the window. It was a long way up and the ladder rocked alarmingly. She could feel the heat searing her exposed face and hands as the flames defied the jets of water, but her whole attention was on the woman above her. Had Louise left the factory early? Was that her up there, trapped and in terrible danger?

Rita could hear the woman's terrified screaming through the hungry crackle and roar of the fire – could see amid the swirling clouds of smoke that her arms were outstretched towards the fireman. But in the shifting shadows she still couldn't tell who it was.

She craned her neck, watching as the fireman clambered through the window, grabbed the hysterical woman unceremoniously and slung her over his shoulder. As he swung his leg over the window-sill and grasped the ladder with his free hand, the turret roof collapsed in a shower of ash and sparks and made him lose his balance.

Rita held her breath as he hung from one hand, the woman over his shoulder, his feet scrabbling for purchase. 'Right foot to your right,' she yelled above the roar of the inferno. 'Down, down. Right a fraction more.'

He found the rung, steadied himself and began the slow, steady descent back down to the ground. 'Thanks, love,' he rasped. 'Now get the engine away from here before it blows up.' With the woman still slumped over his shoulder like a rag doll, he raced away from the building.

Rita's eyes stung so badly she could hardly see, and the metal was hot as she opened the door and climbed into the cab. Not bothering to bring the ladder down first, she reversed the engine out of harm's way.

With the ladder back in place, she ran to the woman who was now sitting on the grass wrapped in a blanket. 'Louise?' she cried fearfully.

Aggie Rawlings shifted the blanket a little nearer her face, her gaze sliding away. 'I wasn't stealing nothing,' she muttered. 'It just happened to be the only room not on fire.'

Rita eyed her coldly and turned away. Aggie's room was on the ground floor, and she had no business being upstairs, or even in the house while everyone else was in the air-raid trench. Rita had a very clear idea of what she'd been up to.

The firemen had almost extinguished the flames now, and she needed to make sure that everyone had been accounted for. She told one of the men what she was going to do and he nodded, still busy with dampening down. Grabbing the clipboard from the cab, she ran across the large expanse of neglected garden, startled to realise that there were still bombers overhead. In all the excitement, she hadn't even heard them.

They were huddled in the deepest part of the trench, wearily clutching their small children, their few possessions, and each other. 'Is anyone hurt?' Rita shouted above the din of a low-flying Spitfire.

'We're all fine,' said one of the younger women, 'but Aggie's missing.'

'We found Aggie. She's all right,' Rita said shortly. 'Anyone else?'

'We don't think so.' She reeled off the names of the women who were at work, or known to be somewhere in the town, and Rita ticked them off her list. 'I did check all the rooms before I left the house last night,' the woman assured her. 'There's no one in there.'

'How bad is it, Rita?' asked one of the other women, clutching her baby close.

Rita gave a deep sigh. 'We won't be going back there,' she said. 'Sorry, girls, but it looks as if we're all homeless again.'

There was a groan of weary acceptance as Rita trudged back out of the trench. The air was thick with smoke and the smell of burning wood. Flakes of ash drifted and swirled in the wind coming off the sea, and there was a soft slither of something falling with a sigh inside the almost gutted house.

It was just after six, and she looked up at the sky which was now lightening over the eastern hills, the last few stars fading and dying in the emptiness. The silence was almost absolute. The raiders were gone.

Peggy had stood for over an hour watching the fires destroy London, wondering if Doreen had escaped, fretting that she might have been caught in one of the collapsing buildings, or be lying injured somewhere. Surely no one could survive such a firestorm?

Heartsick and dispirited, she'd eventually turned her back on it and found a space on the floor of the ladies' waiting room. Sitting with her back propped against the wall, her handbag tucked safely under her arm and her suitcase and gas mask box on her lap, she'd doubted she'd be able to rest at all until she knew her younger sister's fate. But exhaustion meant she'd fallen asleep within minutes, oblivious to everything around her.

It was the distant screaming all-clear sirens that woke her. She checked the time. It was six-fifteen in the morning, which meant she'd been on the move for almost forty-eight hours. She picked up her belongings and trudged wearily out onto the platform.

People were sprawled everywhere, making do with every inch of space, but they were rising now, bleary-eyed, their first thoughts – as Peggy's had been – for London.

She stood on the platform and looked across the fields and the distant huddle of houses. The horizon still glowed – a false dawn against the soft velvet of the night sky that was clouded by smoke.

Peggy turned away, unable to comprehend the enormity of what she'd witnessed. She wanted to go home – needed Jim's arms about her and to see her daughters' smiles. She yearned for Beach View and the familiarity and warmth of those she loved. But her most pressing need was to get to Doreen.

She saw the station master emerge from his office and hurried across. 'Will our train still be going into London?' she asked breathlessly.

He shook his head. 'All the lines are up and access has been forbidden anyway,' he said wearily. 'I've been talking on the radio to my opposite number at Paddington. London's off limits until they can restore some order.'

'But my sister lives there. I need to find her and—'

'Sorry, madam. There's nothing I can do to help.' He looked down at her, his expression kindly. 'Were you supposed to be going to London, or just passing through?'

'I'm on my way to Cliffehaven,' she murmured, 'and was going to visit Doreen for a couple of hours before I caught my connection home.'

He gave a deep sigh. 'You've got a long journey ahead of you, I'm afraid. The trains will have to skirt the city, and it'll mean you going on very small branch lines to get to the coast. Even then, we have little idea of the damage that's been done further down the country, so you'll have to be prepared to take buses as well.'

'I see,' she said quietly. 'I don't suppose I could use your telephone to let my family know? Only they'll be worried by now.'

'All telephone lines are down, and our radio is for rail personnel only.' He squeezed her arm in sympathy. 'I'm sorry I can't be of any help.'

Peggy nodded her thanks and lugged her suitcase back into the station building. She found an empty stall in the ladies' lavatory, locked the door and leaned against it. 'Damn you, Hitler,' she hissed as tears of fury ran down her face. 'Damn you to hell.'

Anne put down the telephone receiver with a clatter. 'The local lines are all right,' she told Martin, 'but everything beyond Cliffehaven is down. I can't reach Mum, or Auntie Doreen.'

Martin put his arm round her shoulder and steered her gently into the kitchen where Mrs Finch was sleepily making the first cup of tea for the day. 'Both of them will telephone when they can,' he consoled Anne. 'They'll know we'll be worried.'

'Mum was due home today,' she said. 'I hope to goodness she wasn't caught up in it all.' She plumped down into a chair, her expression a mixture of fury and exasperation. 'Why do things have to be so complicated?' she snapped. 'Why hasn't someone invented a telephone system that doesn't break down the minute something like this happens?'

Martin kissed the top of her head. 'I'm going up to the base today. I'll see if I can get any sense out of the boys at Croydon airfield. They might be able to shed some light on what's happening with the railways.'

Anne felt a jolt of panic. 'Why do you need to go up there today? You're not fit for duty yet.'

He ran his hand softly over her shining hair. 'I might not be able to fly, but I've still got responsibilities, Anne, and I'm perfectly fit enough to sit behind a desk.'

'You never said,' she muttered. 'I thought . . .'

'I know,' he soothed, 'but I can't be on holiday while my men are putting their lives on the line. They need me there, Anne – and I need to be with them.'

Anne bit back the tears, knowing they wouldn't sway him, knowing they would just make things worse for him. 'Then we must give you a good breakfast,' she said, dredging up a false bright smile. 'Will you be coming back tonight, or staying at the barracks?'

'I'll be back here for New Year's Eve – unless Hitler has other ideas.' He grinned in an attempt to lift her spirits. 'Just be sure to wear your prettiest dress. I've booked tickets for the dance at the Galaxy and intend to whirl you very sedately round the floor.'

Anne rose from the chair and softly kissed him before she went outside to see if there were any fresh eggs for his breakfast. But the hens had been upset by the enemy planes and there were no lovely brown eggs hidden in the straw.

Tears pricked and she determinedly blinked them away. The world of certainty she'd once taken for granted had been twisted out of shape – her family scattered and her nerves stretched to the very limit. But her mother would keep smiling through, and so would she, regardless of how much effort it took.

Rita had been hosing down the garage floor when Louise came to find her. She'd spent the night in the shelter beneath Goldman's, and had burst into hysterical tears as she was forced to digest the fact they were homeless again. Rita had swiftly bundled her up the stairs to John's office, where she parked her by the heater with a cup of tea and the gentle but firm order to calm down and not get in the way.

The day had dawned cold and grey, but Rita was feeling surprisingly chirpy as she helped clean the fire engines and tidy away the equipment. She stank of smoke and her face and hands were black with soot, but her most precious belongings were safely tucked in the Norton's panniers, she and Louise had come through without a scratch, and if the worst came to the worst, they could always camp out in Tino's shed until the authorities could find them another billet.

Chapter Eighteen

Louise had refused to camp out in Tino's shed, so she and Rita had had no option but to move into the emergency shelter provided by the many rooms in the Town Hall. They had now been there for two days. It was noisy and chaotic, every moment spent against the background noise of screaming babies, shouting toddlers and arguing women. The close proximity of so many crammed into one place did not make for easy living, and tempers, already sorely tried, were quickly frayed.

The large assembly room downstairs had long been the clothing and utilities centre for the WVS, while two of the side offices had been turned over to the almoners and housing people, who had the unenviable task of trying to find billets for the dispossessed. The Mayor's parlour hadn't been invaded, but the rest of the offices and meeting rooms had been turned over to row upon row of camp beds. A vast kitchen had been set up to provide food, and this was run by a small army of volunteers.

This morning they'd seen the headlines in the newspapers. The raid was being called the 'second fire of London'. There had been surprisingly few casualties, although the Guild Hall and six city churches had been burnt to the ground, which made everyone very angry. The damage was such that it could take a long time to restore order to the city, and the pictures that accompanied the articles were graphic, showing the full horror of what the Londoners had gone through.

But the photograph that had everyone gasping with awe, showed St Paul's dome rising above the smoke and the flames to stand proudly in defiance of everything the Luftwaffe had thrown at it. It was a symbol of the spirit of London and the people who lived there – proof, if it was needed, that Britain would not cower under Hitler's jackboot.

'It makes you feel proud to be British,' said Rita as she passed the newspaper to Louise. 'If the Londoners can survive that, then we can survive anything.'

'Do you know if there's any news of Peggy's sister?'

Rita shook her head as she made the beds. 'I saw Anne yesterday, and she said there was no news of Doreen, but she thought Peggy was probably stuck somewhere south of London, still trying to get home.' Rita paused. 'Poor Anne. She looked exhausted by all the worry. I wish there was something I could do to help.'

'It would have been nice if she'd offered us a bed at Beach View,' said Louise sourly.

Rita began to repack their bags. Aggie and one or two others she didn't trust were billeted in the same building, and as she and Louise would be out at work all day it seemed wiser to keep their precious things with them. 'That's unfair,' she said flatly. 'There's no room, and Anne has enough to worry about.'

'What about that Mr Hicks at the fire station? I hear he's living in a big house.'

Rita was close to losing her patience. 'He lives with Sally and his mother, and there are only two bedrooms. He offered us the floor in the lounge for a couple of nights, but we're better off here where we don't make extra trouble for anyone.'

'It comes to something when we have to rely on charity,' Louise muttered.

'Better that than sleeping in Tino's allotment shed.' Rita pulled on her moth-eaten flying jacket and picked up her bag. 'I'll be back at about five after I've picked up my dress from the fire station,' she said. 'What are your plans for the night?'

'I'm going to the pictures with two of the other women at the factory. We're of the age when dancing the night away with strange men holds little appeal,' Louise said stiffly.

Rita kissed her cheek and left. It seemed Louise was never happier than when she could have a good moan.

Ron was as concerned as the others over Doreen and Peggy, for he adored his daughter-in-law and admired Doreen. Peggy's younger sister had a verve and dash about her which probably came from escaping Cliffehaven to live and work in London. Her visits had been few and far between, but he'd come to like her very much indeed, for there were no flies on Doreen, and she stood up to toffee-nosed Doris and gave as good as she got.

He finished polishing his shoes over a piece of newspaper on the kitchen table, then went down to his basement room to get dressed in his best suit and tie. Every night at the Anchor was lively, but he suspected it would reach new heights tonight, and had promised Rosie he'd help behind the bar.

There had been no sign of Findlay since Christmas Eve, and Ron hoped he'd finally realised he wasn't wanted and had slung his hook. Rosie certainly seemed much happier and more relaxed with him out of the picture, and Ron hoped it would remain that way. But he was still intrigued by Rosie's relationship with Findlay, and knew that sooner or later he would have to persuade her to explain.

He put down his hairbrushes, eyed his freshly shaven chin and winked at his reflection. 'Not bad for an auld fella,' he muttered. 'You've still got it, Ronan Reilly.'

'Talking to yourself again, Da?' Jim appeared in the doorway and gave a low whistle. 'My word, you're looking sharp tonight. Rosie won't stand a chance.'

Ron ignored him, trying not to look too pleased

at the praise as he settled the soft felt hat carefully over his brushed hair. 'Some of us have got it, son – and know how to use it.' He turned to Jim, noting that he too looked very smart. 'I thought you were working tonight?'

'That I am, auld man, but I mean to have me a little drink or three after to welcome in the New Year. Most of the pubs have got an extended licence for the night, and I'll be thirsty after sitting in that projection room.' Jim's smile faltered and he became thoughtful. 'Besides, this house will be empty of everyone but Mrs Finch, and I need to take me mind off Peggy.'

'Aye, this place doesn't feel right without her,' agreed Ron, 'but knowing Peg, she's doing her best to get home.'

He went up the stone steps into the kitchen just as Anne and Martin were preparing to leave. Anne looked lovely in her long, flowing dress of buttercup yellow, and Martin was handsome in his freshly pressed uniform. 'Where's everyone else?' Ron asked. 'We might as well walk together as we're going the same way.'

'Cissy and the other girls have already left and Sylvia is staying at the hospital to see in the New Year with Christopher,' said Anne as she pulled on long gloves and reached for her warm cape. 'Mrs Finch has gone next door to play gin rummy with Mr Ferguson and two other old cronies. I think she's planning to make a bit of a night of it, as she said she'll be staying over at number forty-two with Ena West and her sister.'

'Let's be going then,' said Jim. He looked at Anne and grinned. 'To be sure, you're looking well, me darlin' girl.' He held out his arm. 'Will you be letting your Da escort you to the end of the street?'

Anne laughed and took his arm as Ron whistled for Harvey. The four of them left the house, determined to put their worries behind them. But as they ambled down Beach View Terrace, the spectre of Peggy's unknown fate shadowed them.

Louise had already left the Town Hall when Rita had rushed back from the factory and picked up her lovely frock. There was very little privacy at the Town Hall, and she'd had to wait an age to use the washroom. There were no bathing facilities, but the queue at the public baths down the road was endless, so she'd made do with a thorough scrub with a flannel. Now she was finally dressed, and Cissy was doing her make-up and hair.

'It's sweet of you to come and do this,' she said as she perched on the edge of the truckle bed and tried to keep still.

'I couldn't let you go out on such an important date without make-up,' said Cissy, who was finding it a bit awkward to work left-handed. 'Besides, you've more than earned a treat after what you've been through. I only wish there was a bed for you at Beach View. It would have been quite like old times sharing a room again. Still,' she went on breathlessly, 'anything has to be better than the asylum, and you're much nearer to everything now. We can see each other every day until I'm well enough to go back on duty.'

'You've still not heard from your mum or Aunt Doreen?'

Cissy shook her head, her platinum hair gleaming in the light from the very grand chandelier that still hung from the ceiling. 'No news is good news, as they say,' she said with determined cheerfulness. 'But I did hear something you might be interested in.'

Rita laughed. 'Go on, spit it out.'

'I heard that May has almost completed her training and has taken her first solo flight.' Cissy carefully painted Rita's lips scarlet. 'She'll be on operations within the week, and is bound to fly down here at some point.'

'Goodness,' breathed Rita. 'Well done, May. Who would have thought it?'

'She's braver than I'll ever be,' muttered Cissy as she concentrated on tweaking Rita's hair and covering it liberally with hairspray. 'There you go,' she said. 'All done. You look a treat, Rita, and no mistake. Chuck won't be able to keep his eyes – or his hands – off you.'

They giggled and hugged, careful not to crease their dresses or smudge their make-up. 'What's your date like?' asked Rita.

Cissy grinned. 'His name's David and he's an RAF fighter pilot. He's very handsome and dances like a dream.'

'What about your Australian?' asked Rita warily.

'He's in the thick of it in North Africa somewhere.' Cissy's smile faltered as she plucked at the sling over her arm. 'I haven't heard from him in a while, even though I did as you suggested and wrote him lots of chatty letters.'

'You know the post is unreliable. I'm sure you'll hear from him soon,' Rita murmured. She gave Cissy a warm smile. 'So, are you ready for a night on the town?'

'Absolutely,' she replied, twirling the frothy skirts of her silvery dress as her happy mood revived. 'The boys should be waiting outside by now. Let's show them how well we scrub up – even if one of us has to wear a blasted sling.'

They reached for the warm woollen wraps Cissy had provided for the evening and were still giggling as they carefully made their way down the grand staircase in their high heels to the ground floor. As they reached the main doors they looked at one another, took a deep breath and sailed out into the frosty night.

Chuck and the young English pilot stared in

delighted amazement, and then quickly helped the girls into the borrowed car. Within moments they were heading for the seafront and the Galaxy ballroom.

Peggy was almost on the point of collapse. She'd been travelling for four days, and these last few miles seemed to be the longest as the bus trundled through the night past darkened villages and down winding country lanes. Her family must be worried sick by now, but she hadn't been able to contact anyone during that horrendous journey, and could only hope that someone would be at home to welcome her.

As the bus pulled in by the station, she wearily dragged herself out of the seat, hauled her case from the rack and slowly followed the other passengers down the steps to the street. There was no one there to greet them, but then they hadn't known when they would arrive. She looked at her watch. It was almost ten o'clock.

It was pitch-black, but Peggy could still make out the wreckage of the station buildings, the gaps and yawning skeletons of the houses and shops that had once stood close by, and the absence of the bus terminus and the wall that had once shielded the ugly shunting yards.

She dreaded to think what other damage there was in Cliffehaven, but she didn't have time to dwell on that, for the trolleybus was just pulling up on the other side of the street. She quickly clambered on and discovered she had to stand, for every seat was full. She clung to the strap as the trolleybus clanked and rumbled down the High Street, steadying herself every time it came to a halt to let people off.

Most of them were gone by the time the trolleybus turned the corner, and she sank into a vacated seat as they began the long journey down the seafront. She'd lost track of the date, and was surprised to realise it must be New Year's Eve. Despite the war, it looked as if Cliffehaven was celebrating, and she smiled wearily as she saw the knots of young people outside the pubs, hotels and dance halls. There had even been a long queue outside the Odeon, and she wondered if Jim was working tonight, or out drinking with Ron at the Anchor.

It seemed everyone was determined to have fun, to pack away their cares and keep smiling in the hope that 1941 would be a better, more peaceful year. But she was too tired to think straight, let alone celebrate. What she needed now was her family around her, the kitchen fire, a soft chair and a cup of tea.

The trolleybus came to a screeching halt at the end of the promenade and Peggy stepped off. It was a cold night, the wind carrying the salty breath of the sea which splashed and dragged reassuringly against the pebbles. It was a sound she'd missed – a sound that meant she was home.

She looked up the steep hill, thinking of her family who she hoped would be waiting there, and found the energy to pick up her case again and begin the climb.

Everywhere was in darkness, but she could hear raucous singing coming from the Anchor as she passed Camden Road, and the music from several wirelesses as she turned into Beach View Terrace. She eyed the old house lovingly. It was still standing despite the barricaded windows, the chipped paint-work and the smashed lamps at the bottom of the steps. It was as much a symbol to her as that photograph of St Paul's was to the Londoners. As long as they both remained standing, they would come through this.

She slotted her key in the door and stepped into the hall. The house was silent and there was no sight or sound of Harvey as she closed the door behind her. It seemed everyone was out, and it was far too late to disturb Mrs Finch.

But as she stood there feeling rather sorry for herself, she noticed there was a glimmer of light coming from beneath her bedroom door, and her heart did a little jig. Jim was home.

Her weariness fled as she put her things down and quietly slipped off her coat, hat and gloves, imagining his surprise at her just walking in. Oh, what a reunion they would have with the house all to themselves. She tiptoed across the hall and reached for the door handle.

The throaty, unmistakable chuckle of a woman came from the other side of the door.

Peggy froze. Her heart was racing now, not with pleasurable anticipation, but with dread. She leaned nearer the door, listening, the blood drumming in her ears, her thoughts in turmoil. She could hear the woman's voice, muffled and distant, and the answering deeper male tones, then the sounds of more giggling and scuffling.

Peggy had heard enough. She crashed the door open. 'Jim Reilly, I'm going to kill you,' she stormed.

June shot up, the sheet pulled to her naked chest, her face reddening, eyes and mouth wide with shock. 'It's not . . .'

Peggy stared at her, then gathered her wits. 'Get out, you little tart,' she snapped, her whole focus now on the mound beneath the bedclothes. 'At least have the courage to show your face, Jim Reilly,' she barked. 'Then you can get out as well.'

'But—'

'Shut up, June, and get your knickers on.'

The mound moved and a stranger emerged shamefacedly from beneath the covers. 'There's no need to blow a bleedin' gasket,' he said crossly as he shook the hair out of his eyes. 'We was only . . .'

The relief was immense but it did nothing to quell the rage that was like a red mist in Peggy's head. 'I'll blow more than a bloody gasket if you don't get out of my bed and out of my house.' She snatched the big clothes brush from the top of the dressing table and waved it threateningly.

He grabbed his trousers and Peggy turned to face June, who was rapidly trying to get dressed. 'You've got fifteen minutes to pack your bags,' she snapped.

'But I—'

'I don't want to hear your excuses,' Peggy interrupted. 'How *dare* you sneak a man in here – and into *my* bed?'

'You were away and everyone was out,' said June sullenly. 'I was going to change the sheets.'

Peggy took one look at that almost defiant expression and slapped June hard, the sound ringing through the silent house. 'Get your things, you *slut*,' she said, giving her a push that sent her stumbling into the hall.

'You've no right to hit me,' June shouted furiously.

'I've every right, and at this moment if you want to make something of it, I'm more than ready to prove it.'

June must have seen Peggy's very real intention to hit her again, for the fight went out of her and she burst into tears and raced up the stairs.

Peggy saw the young Cockney soldier still lurking in the bedroom. '*Out!*' she yelled. He scuttled for the front door and she slammed it behind him and leaned on it, breathing heavily. Where the hell she'd found the energy to explode like that, she'd no idea, but she suspected that her fear had played a major part. How could she ever have suspected Jim of doing such a thing – and in their bed?

June came downstairs and Peggy silently handed her back her food ration book and took her keys. She opened the door, her expression brooking no argument or plea.

As June went down the steps, Peggy slammed the door and strode into the kitchen. Putting the kettle on the hob, she returned to her bedroom, flung open the windows to get rid of the smell of June's cheap perfume, and furiously stripped the bed.

The anger was still with her and her tears were hot as they rolled down her face. 'How *dare* she after all this family has done for her? *Tart*. Filthy, dirty little *tart*.' Yet her anger was also aimed at herself for ever doubting Jim, and she knew it would rankle long after this evening.

Gathering everything up, she carried it down to the washtub in the basement, poured hot water and a dash of bleach over it and left it to soak. She would have a cup of tea and a cigarette and then see what there was in the larder. The welcome home had been far from the one she'd expected, but by golly it had given her one heck of an appetite.

She'd made the bed with fresh linen and closed the window, liberally spraying the room with her most expensive perfume to make it her own again. Having eaten a vast Spam sandwich and three biscuits washed down with a gallon of tea, she laundered the bedlinen then sat and waited for her family to come home.

Anne and Martin arrived first and she hugged and kissed them, made a fuss over Anne and told them about the awful journey she'd endured to get home. She said nothing about her to-do with June. Ron and Jim came in together, both of them unsteady on their feet, and she said nothing about it to them either.

Once their joy at her homecoming was overcome by weariness, Anne and Martin went to bed and Ron staggered down to the basement, leaving Jim alone with Peggy in the kitchen.

'Will you be coming to bed, Peg?' said Jim. 'You're looking exhausted, darlin'.'

'I'll be with you soon,' she replied, giving him a kiss, wanting very much to climb into bed with him. 'But I won't rest easily until the other girls get in.'

'Cissy's staying with Amy tonight,' said Jim, 'and the others could be hours yet. Come on, Peg. I've missed you something terrible, and you look as if you're about to drop.'

She wavered and was about to give in when she heard Fran and Suzy coming into the hallway with a burst of giggles and a lot of shushing. 'I need to have a quiet word with those two,' she said. 'It won't take long.'

There must have been something in her expression,

for Jim frowned. 'What's the matter, Peggy? Has something happened?'

'I'll tell you later,' she promised. 'Best you leave this to me.'

He eyed her thoughtfully and then left, saying goodnight to the girls on his way and telling them Peggy was home.

They flew into the kitchen and Fran threw her arms round Peggy and gave her a kiss. 'It's so lovely to have you home again,' she said. 'We've missed you something terrible.'

'Yes, Peggy, we're so glad you're back,' said quiet little Suzy. 'We were all so afraid you'd been caught up in that terrible raid on London.'

'I saw it from the distance,' she said as they poured the last of the tea from the pot and raided the biscuit tin. 'Fran, Suzy, there's something I have to tell you.' Her tone of voice stilled them and they looked at her warily. 'I've had to tell June to leave,' she said flatly.

Fran sighed. 'Oh, God, what's she gone and done now?'

Peggy told them without mincing her words. 'I know she's your friend, so I'll fully understand if you decide to find another billet,' she finished.

Fran tossed back her fiery hair, her eyes flashing with disdain. 'She's no friend of ours if that's how she carries on,' she said. 'Oh, Peggy. I'm so sorry. What must you think of us?'

'It wasn't you I caught in my bed,' said Peggy.

She gave them both a hug. 'I'm glad you've decided to stay. I just hope it doesn't have repercussions with June between you all.'

'She always was a bit wild when it came to men,' said Suzy quietly. 'You don't have to worry, Peggy. Me and Fran aren't like her at all, and we'd never do such a thing to you – not after you've given us a lovely home and mothered us and everything.' She burst into tears.

Peggy found her a handkerchief and gave her a cuddle until she'd calmed down. 'I know, Suzy, really I do, and you can be sure that I've said nothing to the rest of the family. Jim will have to be told, of course, but the others will be led to think she's decided to move into the nurses' home.'

'I doubt she'll get a room there,' said Suzy. 'It's full to the rafters.'

'That's June's lookout,' said Fran with a sniff. 'Come on, Suzy. It's bedtime. Peggy's clearly exhausted, and we have to be on duty tomorrow afternoon.' They said goodnight and ran upstairs.

Peggy dumped the dirty china in the sink, turned off the lights and went in to Jim, who was sitting up in bed waiting for her. She was weary to the bone, almost sleepwalking as she swiftly stripped and pulled on her winceyette nightdress.

'Come on, me darling,' he murmured. 'Climb in and hold onto me. It looks as if you've been ship-wrecked.' His smile was warm and loving. 'Problems sorted?'

'I'll tell you in the morning.' Peggy eyed the bed, realising she could never have climbed into it without him there – not after what she'd witnessed earlier. Pushing that memory firmly to the back of her mind, she slid in beside him and into his waiting arms.

'I've missed you, me darling,' he murmured, holding her close, his lips buried in her dark curls.

She rested her cheek against his chest, hearing his heartbeat and knowing she was finally home. She closed her eyes. 'You're my anchor, Jim Reilly,' she murmured, warm and soft with love, 'and don't ever let me doubt it.'

Rita and Chuck had happily agreed to walk back to the Town Hall while David drove Cissy and Amy and her young man back to Amy's. He'd promised to come back for Chuck within the hour and drive him back to the American airbase, which wasn't so far from his own.

Like many other couples, they were strolling along the seafront arm in arm, reliving the evening, and making plans for their next date. The moon was like an apostrophe, playing hide and seek with the scudding clouds, and the waves broke against the shingle, sending diamonds of water into the air. It was cold, but Rita didn't feel it, for Chuck's arm was about her waist and she was snuggled into his side. Her very first grown-up New Year's Eve had fulfilled her highest expectations.

They reached the High Street and slowed their steps as they approached the Town Hall. It was almost two in the morning, but like the other couples drifting by, neither of them wanted the night to end. Chuck pulled her gently into the shadows of a shop doorway and gathered her into his arms for a kiss.

Rita dreamily closed her eyes, forgot about people passing by, and gave into the melting sensations that made her feel weak and pliant. But then she became aware of his hand sliding down from her waist, his fingers gripping her bottom, pressing her tightly against him. She could feel he was aroused, knew that if she didn't stop this now, things would go too far.

'I've got to go,' she said breathily, pushing away from him.

He resisted and held her closer. 'Just a few minutes more,' he pleaded, his hand urgently hitching at her skirt, his fingers finding the tops of her stockings, the soft flesh of her thighs and the hem of her camiknickers.

'No.' Rita pushed him harder and stumbled away from him. 'I'm not that sort of girl, Chuck.' She straightened her dress, aware of the amused and curious glances of the people passing by, and furious that he should have taken such liberties.

'Aw, gee, honey, don't be like that.' He smiled at her as he reached for her again. 'You can't kiss a guy like that and not expect him to think . . .'

She evaded his outstretched hands. 'I have a very clear idea of what you were thinking,' she said, tugging her wrap more firmly about her shoulders. 'And I'm sorry if I gave you the wrong impression, but if you want more, then you should find another girl.'

'I'm sorry too,' he said shamefacedly. 'I should have known you were different.' He took her hand, keeping his distance, the very model of remorse. 'I really like you, Rita,' he said softly. 'I just got carried away in the moment. Please say you'll forgive me?'

She eyed him thoughtfully. He certainly looked repentant, but did he really understand that she wouldn't allow any further liberties? 'If you promise not to try it on again, then I'll see you on Thursday outside the Anchor,' she said.

'I'll be there, and I promise to behave, Rita.'

She smiled at him, glad he was being so reasonable. 'Thanks for a really lovely evening, Chuck.'

'It was my pleasure,' he replied, not attempting to kiss her again.

Rita walked away from him, her emotions in turmoil. It had been a wonderful evening, but that little scene had spoilt it somehow – had brought her up short and reminded her of all Louise's dire warnings. If they had not been in such a public place, could she have handled the situation quite so easily?

She turned and waved to him as she reached the Town Hall steps.

He didn't see, for he was standing on the street corner, hands in pockets, looking totally unruffled and rather too sure of himself as he chatted to another American.

Rita pushed through the heavy double doors and walked into the hall. She still liked him, found him funny and bright and excellent company, but perhaps, if she was to go on seeing him, it would be best to keep away from dark shop doorways and isolated places from now on. For she wasn't so naïve as to think tonight's performance wouldn't be repeated.

Chapter Nineteen

They had made love sweetly and languorously, renewing and confirming their commitment to one another, falling asleep softly bound within each other's arms. But when Peggy woke, it was to find the other side of the bed empty. She looked blearily at the bedside clock as she prepared to snuggle back under the blankets, and then shot out of bed, appalled to see that it was almost midday.

The house was quiet, but she could see Ron attending to the chickens while Harvey ignored his sharp admonishments and investigated the compost heap. She smiled as she gathered her things together and headed for the bathroom. Life was going on despite everything, and perhaps today she'd be able to get hold of Doreen.

Washed, dressed and ready for what was left of the day, Peggy tried to telephone London without any luck, then went into the kitchen. Mrs Finch was looking rather tired as she dried the dishes and stacked them on the table, and Peggy gently took the cloth from her and gave her a hug.

'Oh, my dear,' Mrs Finch sighed. 'I'm so very glad

you're back. The house just hasn't been the same, and you wouldn't believe the shenanigans.'

Peggy smiled. Beach View was so often the scene for some drama or other she wasn't surprised, but at least the old lady had been spared June's carrying-on. 'Let's leave the drying up for a bit,' she said. 'I want to hear what my family has been up to.'

Mrs Finch looked suddenly uncertain. 'It's not my way to tell tales,' she murmured, 'and no real harm was done.'

Peggy eyed her sharply. 'I think this calls for a cup of tea and a cigarette,' she said. 'Sit down, Mrs Finch. You look a little peaky.'

'I'm not being sneaky at all,' the old lady protested.

'I never said you were,' shouted Peggy. 'You look tired.'

'Oh. Well, I spent the evening playing cards and then stayed with Ena and her sister Mabel.' She reddened. 'I'm afraid I drank rather too much sherry,' she confessed, 'and don't feel terribly chipper.'

Peggy found her two aspirins to wash down with her tea and then sat by the range. 'So,' she prompted. 'You were going to tell me what's been happening since I left.'

Mrs Finch giggled. 'It was quite funny really,' she began. 'You hadn't been gone more than a few hours before the fun started.'

Peggy listened with growing alarm as Mrs Finch relayed the story of Ron, the pilot, Lady Sylvia, the parachute, and the hidden cache of whisky and cigarettes that had had to be quickly moved else-where. She might have known she couldn't leave Beach View without someone doing something daft. But Ron had proved his bravery and stamina, Cissy and Martin had come through the attack on the airbase, and it seemed Christmas had gone extremely well, with the added bonus of nylon stockings, Sobranie cigarettes and Fortnum's goodies.

The news that Doris had come round to ingratiate herself with Lady Sylvia came as no surprise, and she laughed as Mrs Finch did a brilliant impression of how the conversation between the two women had gone.

'Ron was thrilled that Rosie agreed to come on Christmas Day,' Mrs Finch continued. 'I think he was getting rather worried that she had another suitor.' She twiddled with her hearing aid, making it whine quite alarmingly. 'Some horrid chap called Findlay, I think. Nasty piece of work according to dear Ron.'

Peggy felt a chill. She knew Findlay of old and had thought him long gone. What on earth was he doing back in Cliffehaven? Realising it was pointless to ask Mrs Finch, Peggy helped her adjust the hearing aid and changed the subject. 'June's decided to move out,' she said. 'She left last night.'

'I'm not surprised,' Mrs Finch sniffed. 'A bit too fond of the men, that one.' She looked at Peggy over her teacup. 'I suppose it's all right to tell you now she's gone, but I caught her only last week trying to sneak some man into the house.'

'Oh, Mrs Finch,' Peggy experienced a deep sense of shame that this sweet little old lady should be involved in such tawdry business. 'How awful for you. I'm so sorry.'

Mrs Finch giggled. 'Nothing for you to be sorry about,' she said airily. 'I quite enjoyed sending him off with a flea in his ear and giving that hussy a piece of my mind. Just because I'm old, doesn't mean I'm daft, you know.'

Peggy patted her hand and smiled. 'No one would ever make the mistake of thinking you weren't as sharp as a box of knives.'

Mrs Finch sipped her tea. 'If June's gone,' she said thoughtfully, 'then we can move people about and give poor little Rita and that Louise woman somewhere to stay.' Her little face puckered with concern. 'It's heartbreaking to think of her being bombed out twice. And now that most of the houses around Barrow Lane have been flattened, as well as the asylum, the Town Hall isn't the nicest place to be with so many crammed in there.'

'Rita's been bombed out again?' Peggy listened as Mrs Finch told her about the asylum taking a direct hit and burning almost to the ground. Looking at the clock, Peggy finished her tea and reached for her coat. 'Where're Jim and the others?'

'Jim's doing the matinee. He said to let you sleep as long as you wanted because you were clearly exhausted by that awful journey. Anne's at the hospital for her regular check-up, Cissy is still at

Amy's and Martin is back at the airbase. Fran and Suzy just left for work, and I think Ron's in the garden.' She looked thoughtful for a moment. 'Oh, and Lady Sylvia is at the hospital discussing the possibility of Christopher going home for his recuperation and physiotherapy.' She smiled. 'With so many people in the house I can't keep up with all the comings and goings.'

'I'm looking forward to meeting Lady Sylvia,' Peggy said as she pulled on her coat. 'She sounds just the sort of woman I'd like.'

'She's very similar to you in many ways,' said Mrs Finch, 'and doesn't put on airs and graces like your Doris. She's fitted in here very well.'

'No doubt we'll meet eventually.' Peggy reached for her handbag, gloves and gas mask box. 'I'm off to find Rita and Louise. Do we have enough food in the larder, or should I try and find something in the shops to eke it out?'

Mrs Finch nodded. 'Jim came home with several tins of bully beef the other night.' Her eyes twinkled with fun. 'I didn't bother asking where he'd got them – he'd only have given me some old blarney. There's plenty of Oxo, potatoes and onions, so I can do a nice hash and mash, with stewed apples to follow.'

'Would you mind terribly making a start on tea? Only it may take a bit of time to find them both and then get back here and move the rooms round.'

'Not at all,' Mrs Finch replied. Her lips twisted.

'I don't know how well that Louise will fit in here, though.'

Peggy frowned as she did up her coat and reached for a headscarf. 'It's not like you to take a dislike to anyone without reason. What is it about Louise that's ruffled your feathers?'

'She's far too hysterical and dramatic for my liking, and turns her nose up at the first sign of Rita having any fun. I suspect that poor little girl has had to put up with a great deal from that woman – even to the point of having to withdraw her application for the WAAFs.'

Peggy absorbed this new piece of information with a heavy heart. 'Don't worry, Mrs Finch,' she said evenly, 'once Rita's under my roof, I'll see she gets all the love and support she needs, don't you fret.'

The Town Hall was in chaos as usual, with harassed volunteers manning tables piled with donated clothes, household utensils and toys, and racks crammed with coats and jackets, and boxes full of shoes. It was a complete bun-fight as women rummaged, babies wailed and toddlers got under everyone's feet.

There was no sign of Doris, who was supposed to be in charge, but then that was hardly surprising. The 'great unwashed', as she referred to the dispossessed, were merely to be administrated from afar – getting involved in the actual day-to-day running of this WVS centre was not her cup of tea at all. She left that sort of thing to women like Peggy, who happily did several shifts a week.

Peggy smiled, waved back at the many greetings, and hurriedly did a search of the downstairs rooms before climbing the grand staircase to the assembly rooms, where she spotted Rita almost immediately. Standing unseen in the doorway, Peggy watched her for a moment.

Rita was a small, still island in the midst of the bustle, her head bent as she busily repaired what looked like a tear in her overalls. Her hair was shining, her skin was glowing and there seemed to be an air of contentment about her as she ignored the noise and concentrated on her needlework. There was no sign of Louise.

Peggy moved towards her and Rita looked up. Peggy opened her arms, and with a gasp of delight, the girl abandoned her sewing and raced to her, holding her in a hug that had them both stumbling.

'I'm so glad you're all right,' Rita breathed, looking lovingly into her face. 'When did you get back?'

Peggy smoothed back her riot of dark curls, warmed by the girl's welcome and the sight of her lively, pretty face. 'Late last night,' she replied, 'and now I've come to take you and Louise home with me. It'll be a bit of a squash, but I've got a spare room now, so you don't have to stay in this bedlam any more.'

'Oh, Aunty Peg, you really don't know how much that means to me.' Rita gave her a watery smile. 'It's been a bit of a roller coaster these past few weeks, and it'll be lovely to have somewhere to call home again.'

'Beach View will always be your home for as long as you need it,' said Peggy softly. 'I'm just so sorry I've been away, otherwise I'd have found you both a corner somewhere.'

'Anne's had enough to worry about, what with Ron and Lady Sylvia,' replied Rita. 'We were fine, really, Aunt Peg.'

'You certainly seem to be glowing with health despite all you've been through. The resilience of youth is a wonderful thing.' Peggy eyed the two truckle beds that were squashed in a corner. 'Where's Louise?'

'She's at Goldman's, but her shift won't be over for another four hours.'

Peggy eyed the dungarees and flying jacket which were lying on the bed next to a lovely blue dress she could have sworn once belonged to Cissy. 'Is that all you managed to rescue?' she asked in astonishment.

'You can't risk keeping stuff here,' Rita said, glancing at Aggie who was glowering on the other side of the room, 'too many light-fingered chancers. My very best and most precious things are safely locked in the pannier of the Norton, which is at the fire station.' She gave Peggy a beaming smile. 'Mr

Hicks has taken me on as a driver-mechanic,' she said breathlessly. 'I have a week left at the factory first, but it's ever so exciting, and you'll never guess, my first outing was to the asylum.'

'You've certainly had a bit of a time, haven't you? But it seems you're happy enough.'

'Oh, Aunt Peg, I am happy, and I've got so much to tell you.'

'Let's get your things together and tell Louise where you'll be first.' She picked up the moth-eaten flying jacket that had somehow survived since the last war and handed it to Rita. 'We'll go to Beach View on the motorbike, I think.'

Rita looked at her in amazement, and then laughed. 'I don't think you'd find it very comfortable, Aunt Peg – especially not in a dress.'

'It's long enough to cover the essentials,' she said airily, 'and if Ron can sit on the back of that thing, then so can I.' She giggled at Rita's shocked expression. 'I've always wanted to see what it was like, and there's no time like the present.'

Rita gathered up her few things and tucked her hand in the crook of Peggy's arm. 'It's lovely to have you home again,' she said. 'I've missed not being able to talk to you.'

'Well, I'm here now,' Peggy said with a soft smile, 'and once we've sorted out a room for you, we'll sit down and you can tell me all the things you've wanted to say while I've been gone.'

Goldman's factory was twice the size now his

brother-in-law, Solomon, had relocated from London, and the building sprawled across an entire block. Peggy marched in and told the po-faced supervisor, Simmons, why they were there. She waved to Sally Hicks, then hurried to find Louise.

Louise's face lit up as Peggy told her her plan, and although it was obvious to Peggy that she was longing to quiz Rita about something, she kept silent and quickly handed over the big bag that was stowed beneath her sewing machine table.

Rita put it in the second pannier and then helped Peggy to keep her dignity as she perched on the seat of the Norton, tucking her skirt beneath her and wrapping her coat over her exposed knees.

Peggy was a little nervous as Rita revved the engine, and she clutched her waist as they set off down Camden Road. She grinned at the astonished expressions of the people they passed, and would have waved if she hadn't been holding Rita's jacket so tightly. She was fine while they were going in a straight line, but didn't like it at all when Rita leaned the bike at an angle to take a sharp left then right at the junction.

As they pulled up behind the gleaming Rolls-Royce that was parked outside Beach View, Peggy experienced a rush of regret as well as relief. That had been scary, but fun – perhaps she'd get up the nerve to do it again.

Rita swung off the Norton and grinned. 'Did you

enjoy it, Aunt Peg? I went very carefully so as not to frighten you.'

'It was a bit hair-raising,' she admitted. 'The next time, I think I'll wear trousers.'

'Next time?' Rita chortled. 'Goodness, you *are* full of surprises today.'

'I might need a little help getting off, dear,' muttered Peggy. 'Don't want half the street getting a view of my knickers.'

They were both giggling as Rita helped Peggy dismount with as much decorum as possible, and she was straightening her skirt and adjusting her coat when the front door opened and a very elegant, beautiful woman emerged.

'That's Lady Sylvia,' muttered Rita as she took off her helmet and goggles and shook out her hair.

Peggy was all of a dither as she eyed the immaculate vision standing on her doorstep. What must she be thinking? 'Hello, there,' she said breathlessly. 'I'm Peggy Reilly.'

Sylvia grinned. 'I thought you might be,' she said, coming down the steps and shaking her hand. 'Delighted to meet you at last. I admire your pluck, Mrs Reilly. I don't know that I'd be brave enough to ride that.'

Peggy relaxed immediately. 'Please call me Peggy,' she said, 'and I wasn't very brave at all if the truth be known. I was hanging onto Rita for dear life.'

They smiled at one another, sharing the intimacy

of two women of the same age who had found a like-minded friend.

Rita began pulling the bags from the pannier and dumped them on the pavement. 'I don't have to be at work until tomorrow,' she said with an impish grin, 'so if you'd like a ride on the Norton, Lady Sylvia, you only have to ask.'

Sylvia laughed. 'I may take you up on that – give me time to think about it.' She eyed the bags. 'Are you moving in with us, Rita?' At her happy nod, Sylvia smiled. 'How lovely,' she said enthusiastically, grabbing one of the bags and carrying it up the steps into the hall.

Peggy was warmed by her natural smile and the easy way she seemed to want to muck in – and yet she was intrigued by Sylvia and wondered what her story was. Everyone had a story, and Peggy suspected that Lady Sylvia Anstruther-Norton's would be very interesting indeed.

Hugging this thought to herself, she followed Rita up the steps and closed the door behind them. 'It'll be a bit of a squeeze, but there's just about room enough for two beds in June's old room,' she said to Rita.

Sylvia made no comment on June's whereabouts, merely raised a fine eyebrow. 'I'll move in there,' she said. 'My room is big enough for two beds, and I really don't need all that space just to sleep in.'

'I can't expect you to do that,' gasped Peggy, who'd been told about her paying the rent on top of the government grant. 'Rita and Louise will be fine up there.'

'I insist,' said Sylvia, and without another word, went upstairs to her room and began to pack her cases.

Peggy and Rita looked at one another. 'She's ever so nice, isn't she?' said Rita.

Peggy nodded as Mrs Finch came into the hall and welcomed Rita into the fold. Then she became businesslike, took off her coat and gloves and went in search of fresh linen. 'I'll help Lady Sylvia do the bed upstairs, and leave you to do yours and Louise's. Ron should be about somewhere, he can put the iron bedstead together that he's stored in the shed, and bring it upstairs for you. Then I think we should have a spot of lunch. It's almost two o'clock.'

Rita chatted with Mrs Finch for a few moments before she found Ron and asked about the bed and mattress. Then she carried the bags upstairs and dumped them on the landing as Lady Sylvia emerged from the big front room with a cheerful smile.

'It's all quite clean,' she assured Rita. 'I gave it a good once-over just this morning.' She didn't wait for a reply, and hurried up the stairs to the single room under the eaves.

Rita walked into the room and stood for a moment absorbing the tranquillity and familiar scents and sounds of this old, much loved house. Beach View had been a part of her life since childhood, and now it would be her home. She would be safe here, warm and loved and given the encouragement her father would have provided if only he could be here too. Perhaps now Louise would feel more secure, and at last begin to learn to let go.

She took her father's battered and scarred shoe from her bag and placed it almost reverently on the small mantelshelf. It might look incongruous there, but it was all she had left of him and Barrow Lane, and it made the room feel homelier than ever.

Humming one of the tunes from last night's dance, she put away her few clothes in the drawers and the wardrobe, and waited for Ron to assemble the other bed. John Hicks' wife Sally and her little brother Ernie had lived in this room when they'd been evacuated from London at the beginning of the war, and Sally had told Rita how she'd come to love it as well as the warm-hearted people who'd taken them in. Now Rita could finally be more at ease, the burden of responsibility for Louise lifted and shared: 1941 was going to be a good year.

Peggy and Sylvia got to know one another a little more as they swiftly stripped the bed and remade it with fresh linen. June had left a mess, which wasn't surprising after her rapid departure, and as Peggy swept and dusted, and Sylvia unpacked her things into the drawers, Peggy learned all about Sylvia's two sons who were on battleships protecting the Atlantic convoys, and her hopes to take Christopher home very soon.

'I'm very lucky in that I have good transport,' she said. 'He can rest easily in the back of the Rolls with his leg propped up. But the doctor said I should leave it another two weeks just to further the healing process.'

Sylvia paused in the act of folding a caramel-coloured cashmere sweater into a drawer. 'It's been lovely staying here,' she said on a sigh, 'and everyone has been so very kind, but I miss my home.'

'Home is certainly where the heart is,' agreed Peggy, 'but my two youngest are so far away, and I'm constantly torn.' She surreptitiously watched Sylvia as she continued unpacking. 'What about your husband? He's in London, isn't he?'

Sylvia nodded. 'I haven't seen much of him since this war started,' she said softly. 'He's very involved with the Foreign Office as well as in the House of Lords.' She sank onto the dressing table stool. 'I have no idea how he fared in that terrible raid,' she said on a tremulous sigh. 'The blessed telephone lines are still down.'

'My sister Doreen was in the middle of it all, as well,' said Peggy. 'I've decided to accept that no news is good news until I can get hold of her.'

Sylvia smiled at her. 'This war doesn't make things easy, does it? But at least James was in a position to stir some life into the authorities over Louise's menfolk.'

Peggy knew nothing of this, so Sylvia went on to tell her. 'It seems Antonino and Roberto sort of slipped through the gaps in the system,' she concluded, 'but now James has alerted the authorities, I'm sure Louise will soon know where they are.'

'That was very kind of you both,' said Peggy. 'Louise is lost without Tino and . . .' She decided she'd said enough.

'Knowing where they are will give Rita some respite,' finished Sylvia. She smiled. 'She was the reason I got James to see what he could do. That poor child is so loyal to Louise, I don't think she realises how expertly she's being manipulated.'

Peggy's estimation of Sylvia rose higher. 'Thank you for caring enough,' she murmured. 'Most people wouldn't have even noticed.'

Sylvia laughed and moved away from the dressing table. 'I have an eye for such things,' she said enigmatically. 'Now, I don't know about you, but I could do with a cup of tea. I'll go down and put the kettle on.'

Peggy finished the dusting, eyed the room with satisfaction and closed the door. Sylvia might belong to a social class way above the humble Reillys, but she had a heart of gold, and Peggy regarded herself as fortunate to have the chance to get to know her.

Rita and Louise had been at Beach View Boarding House for two weeks. They'd settled in quickly, and despite Louise complaining that Rita was always going out with Cissy and her friends, she seemed much more willing to give Rita her freedom. Perhaps

Peggy had had a few words with her after their long chat on her first evening – or perhaps Louise just felt she didn't need her quite so much now she had other people to lean on. Either way, Rita was delighted to be young and carefree again.

Rita had met Chuck outside the cinema as planned, but as they'd sat in the back row, he'd tried to put his hand up her skirt again, and she'd told him straight that she was having none of it. She'd been so angry that she'd slapped his face and left her seat to a chorus of titters before the film ended, pushing past the other people before storming outside.

She hadn't waited to see if he was following her, and had run down the High Street and round the corner into Camden Road, the tears blinding her, the shame of her very public exit from the cinema warming her face. Half of Cliffehaven must have seen.

Cissy and her friends had been coming out of the Anchor and, after one glance at Rita's expression, she had linked arms with her, said goodbye to her friends and steered her back into the pub. Rosie also seemed to realise something was wrong and gave them drinks before shooing them upstairs into her parlour so they could have a private heart-to-heart.

Cissy had listened as Rita's tale poured out, offered quiet advice and related some of her own horror stories, which had made Rita feel a lot better. They'd come to the conclusion that it would be best to stick to English officers in the future and to always be one of a crowd.

Rita always left the Norton at the fire station now she'd finished working at the factory. Being so close to Beach View meant she didn't really need it, and it was safer there than in Ron's shed. She loved her work at the fire station and was learning a great deal from George Wickens as they serviced the engines and did repairs and replacements of parts to the collection of vans, motorbikes and bicycles that were used by the volunteers.

There had been some activity from the local airbase over the past two weeks, but although they'd heard distant booms, and enemy bombers had raced towards the Thames, no bombs or incendiaries had fallen on Cliffehaven.

However, the RAF had been very busy. They had attacked Turin and Calais, and repeatedly bombed Bremen in reply to the heavy raids on Cardiff, Bristol, Portsmouth and Plymouth. The North Africa campaign was progressing very well, with Bardia falling to the ANZACS and the British forces, which were now sweeping towards Tobruk and almost certain victory. Shipping losses were at their lowest for eight months, and an important convoy got through to Greece after a skirmish in the Mediterranean.

The only piece of news that really touched Rita was the disappearance of Amy Johnson, whose plane had probably come down over the Thames.

It made her think of May and all the other brave young women who were playing their part in ferrying vital machinery and men from one end of the British Isles to the other, thereby releasing the RAF pilots to concentrate on defending Britain and doing as much damage as they could to the Nazis on their home territory.

It had been bitterly cold all day, and as Rita stepped outside into the darkness, she was met by swirling snow. It was very pretty, dancing and floating, lying in soft drifts on the road and dusting the rooftops, deadening the sound of her footfalls as she pulled up her coat collar and headed for home. The temperature seemed to have risen now the snow had started to fall, and by the look of the sky, there was still plenty more to come.

She slipped and skidded down the pavement, past Goldman's factory and the bomb site where a block of flats had once stood next to the school, which had closed for the duration. The Anchor looked dark from the outside, but she knew that if she pushed open the door she'd be blinded by light and deafened by noise as the tightly packed crowd tried to make themselves heard above the singing and the thumping of the piano keys. She carried on walking, for she and Cissy were planning a night out tomorrow and she needed to catch up on her sleep.

The short parade of shops was in darkness, the taped windows shuttered to protect them from bomb blasts. As she reached the end of the road and crossed over into Beach View Terrace, she saw someone open their front door, careless of the light streaming out onto the pavement.

'Turn that light out. I won't tell you again, missus.'

Rita's heart did a jump and she recoiled in shock. The warden's yell had come from the shadows beside her and she'd had no warning. 'You could give someone a heart attack, yelling like that,' she said crossly.

'That damned woman has been opening that door every five minutes,' he snapped. 'If she's anything to do with you, tell her that I'll arrest her if she don't stop it. She's breaking all the blackout rules.'

She quickly assured him it wouldn't happen again and ran up the steps. 'Get inside,' she hissed, giving Louise a nudge and shutting the door firmly behind them. 'The warden's on the warpath.'

'I was waiting for you to come home.' Louise dismissed the warden with a wave of her hand and grabbed Rita's arm. 'I've had a letter from Roberto,' she breathed. 'I need you to read it to me.'

Rita took the letter Louise was thrusting into her face. She could hear the lively chatter in the crowded dining room and smell something delicious that made her stomach clench with hunger. But a letter from Roberto was far more important, and she could understand Louise's impatience to read it. 'I'll just tell Peggy I'm home and then I'll read it to you upstairs where it's quiet.'

'You don't have to do that,' snapped Louise. 'She already knows the letter has come and I can't have her knowing that I need you to read it to me.'

Rita followed an impatient Louise up the stairs to their bedroom.

'Read, read,' implored Louise, wringing her hands.

Rita struggled out of her damp coat, unwound her scarf and kicked off her boots. Lighting the gas fire, she warmed her hands so she could feel them again, and carefully slit the envelope.

The letter was in English and several pages long, the writing small and filling every square inch. Rita sat on the bed and began to read it out.

'"Dearest Mamma and Rita, Papa and I are well, and we have been given warm clothes and plenty of food, so we are not cold or hungry. Papa is sitting beside me now and asks me to send you many kisses, Mamma and Rita, and wants to know if Mamma remembered to give you the earrings for your birthday."'

Louise flicked a dismissive hand. 'Go on, go on,' she urged. 'How are they, where have they been?'

Rita continued as if she hadn't been interrupted. '"After our arrest we were kept in the cells overnight and then, with Gino, his brothers and their sons were taken to Wormwood Scrubs prison. For Gino it was much worse, as their women and children had been taken away and sent to an unknown place. At least we knew that you and Mamma were safely at home."'

'But our home is gone,' Louise wailed. 'Poor Tino, he'll be heartbroken.'

Rita continued calmly. '"Papa and I were allowed to stay together and we shared a very small cell in one of the wings that hadn't been used since the days of the Suffragettes, so Papa and I had a bit of a task to clean away all the pigeon droppings and make it habitable. But it was good to be doing something useful, it kept our minds off what might be happening to you."'

'He cannot know the half of it,' Louise muttered.

'"There are aspects of prison which I will not go into here, but it can be very degrading, and I learned to hate the lumpy lukewarm porridge which was given to us every morning without fail. The bedtime bread and cocoa was welcome, but only because when cooled, the cocoa formed a layer of butter which we used to make candles so we could see after lights out, which was on the dot of six every night.

'"After six long weeks we were all ordered to gather our few possessions and were taken from the Scrubs under military escort to a train. None of us knew where we were being sent, and I think Gino and his brothers hoped that they would be reunited with their women and children.

'"But it was a false, cruel hope, for our destination was Ascot, and after we were marched to the outskirts of that town, we arrived at a place surrounded by pine trees. It was the winter quarters of Bertram Mill's Circus, and we were all expected to make the best accommodation we could in the various animal houses. Papa and I helped Gino and his brothers clear out the elephant house, but the smell of the beasts remained the whole time we were there.

'"It was the height of summer and very hot, but there was plenty of water, so none of us went thirsty. But we were all very hungry, and soon discovered that although there were plentiful supplies of food, no provision had been made to feed us. When we were made to strip and line up in rows for a roll-call in the blazing heat, some of the older men fainted."'

'*Mamma mia*,' gasped Louise. 'My poor Tino, my poor Roberto! Such shame for them to be naked among strangers.'

Rita silently agreed, but said nothing. The letter was a long one, and with all of Louise's interruptions, it could take half the night to get through.

'"Being Italians, most of us could run a kitchen, so we set to and scrubbed and scrubbed until everything was clean and shining. Then we made a hearty vegetable soup and everyone was fed.

'"Conditions improved over the next few weeks, and we made many friends, entertaining ourselves with readings from books, little shows where everyone had to sing a song, juggle, or tell a joke – we even had cookery lessons. But none of us knew what would happen next, or if we'd be sent somewhere else, and this made us uneasy. Rumour was rife, and we all dreaded the thought we might be shipped off to Australia or Canada.

'"We had been at Ascot for five weeks when we were again taken by military escort on a very long train journey. Papa and I came to the conclusion that the circus people wanted their winter quarters back now it was November, and we hoped they appreciated the lovely clean kitchen we'd left behind.

'"Papa and I and the other men from Cliffehaven had hoped we might be taken south, but the train went north and we ended up at an internment camp on York racecourse. The main grandstand and administration buildings had been converted to house us, though it was very cramped beneath the grandstand, and it felt much more like a prison than the last place, for it was surrounded by barbed wire and patrolled by the military.

'"We had no chance to cook for ourselves at York, and every meal was dominated by badly cooked rice – this plain, tasteless fare made a little less dull by the lovely smell of chocolate that drifted into the camp from the nearby Terry's factory.

'"We remained in York for only two weeks, each day marked off in the hope that our liberation would come soon. But then we were separated from Gino and the others and taken to Huyton, a half-finished council housing estate on the outskirts of Liverpool. It was surrounded by anti-aircraft guns which made it almost impossible to sleep at night when there was a raid on the city.

'"The conditions were bad, and we had to make our own beds by stuffing grass into sacks left behind by the builders. The unfinished houses were mostly rat infested and full of rubble, so we lived in tents. It was only a few weeks before Christmas and the weather was very bad. We supplemented the awful diet with the dandelion leaves that grew everywhere, but it was the boredom and the cold that defeated us more than anything. We had nothing to do and Papa got a bad cold which settled on his chest. I was afraid for him, but he has since made a very good recovery and is well now."'

Louise groaned and rocked back and forth. 'I should have been with him,' she sobbed. 'I should have been told he was so ill.'

'Listen to this, Mamma,' said Rita excitedly as her gaze skimmed the last of the letter.

'"It was like a miracle, for one day an officer came and questioned me for a long time and then ordered that Papa and I were to be removed from Huyton immediately and sent south to a farm near the Brecon Beacons in Wales.

'"We packed our few things and were on a train under escort of a soldier until we arrived at our destination to be met by the farmer and his wife. Papa got well again very quickly, and although we couldn't understand much of what the farmer or his wife said – their accent was almost impossible to decipher – we both realised this, at last, was our chance to play our part in the war effort.

'"The farmer, Mr Hugh Jones, and his wife, Nerys, already have several other Italians working for them and we are all housed in a big, comfortable barn. There are no guards and we can come and go as we please as long as we are in the barn by ten o'clock at night. It is very quiet and isolated so there's nowhere to go, but some of the other men have their English wives and children billeted in the tiny nearby village, so they sneak out at night to be with them."'

Rita looked up to find that Louise's eyes were shining with hope. She quickly returned to the letter.

'"I think the farmer knows this but turns a blind eye, and Mrs Jones is very keen to learn our recipes for Italian food and does her best to find all the ingredients. On Christmas Day she made us a beautiful dinner and invited the women and children as well. We missed you so, Mamma, Rita, and think of you all the time, but it was especially hard to see the other families celebrate together and not to be with you on that special day."'

'For me too,' sighed Louise as she shot Rita a reproachful look. 'Some of us did not forget you on that day.'

Rita ignored the barb and finished the letter.

'"As you see from the address at the top, you can write to us now, and if it is at all possible, you could come to visit. There are some nice people in the village and it may be possible for you to find a billet with the other wives. This little Welsh valley seems to have taken us to its heart, and I know you will find a welcome here.

'"It would be wonderful to see you again, but we both understand how difficult it would be for you to make such a journey. We've heard about the bombing in Cliffehaven and the terrible attack on London, and we pray with all our hearts that you remain safe and well, and that Peggy and the Reilly family have come to no harm either."'

'So like my Roberto,' murmured Louise, 'always thinking of others when he is in trouble himself.'

'It sounds as if they've both fallen on their feet,' said Rita with a wry smile. 'Let me finish the letter, it's almost done.

'"Papa is strong again and I am feeling much more useful now I have work around the farm. I'm learning to milk cows, drive the tractor and plough the fields, and Papa is making butter and cheese the Italian way, and has begun to make ice cream too. Mrs Jones sells it all at the big market and gives him a share of the profit.

'"We send kisses and hugs to you both, darling Mamma, dearest Rita. And hope we will hear from you very soon. Your loving Roberto and Tino."'

'We must make arrangements immediately,' said Louise, snatching the letter and holding it close. 'Peggy will sort out travel warrants, and we can be on our way to this Wales place by the end of the week.'

Rita had been afraid of this. 'I can't go to Wales,

Mamma,' she said calmly. 'I have a job here and responsibilities.'

'Aaach. That job means *nothing* – not when Tino and Roberto are waiting for us – *longing* for us to be with them again.'

'My job means a great deal,' said Rita, 'and I doubt John Hicks will let me take time off to go all the way to Wales.'

'But I can't go alone!' Louise's voice rose several octaves. 'You must give in your notice – tonight. He can always find someone else to drive his engines.'

'I don't want anyone else driving my engine,' said Rita, her pulse beginning to thud. 'And I absolutely refuse to give in my notice. If John—'

'You selfish girl,' yelled Louise as she lifted her hand to strike.

Rita grabbed her arm. 'Don't you dare,' she snapped. 'Hit me again and you're on your own, Mamma.'

'But I've waited so long to hear from them,' Louise wailed. 'How can you be so *cruel*, Rita? Why do you wish to hurt me this way?'

'Mamma, be still and listen for a minute.' Rita's tone was commanding enough to snap Louise from her hysteria and get her attention. 'I was going to say that if John agrees to me going off for two weeks, then I will travel with you.'

'But you'll stay with me in Wales? You and I can share a billet?'

'No, Mamma. I'll be coming back here.'

'Why?' Louise's voice was rising again. 'First you don't want to be in Cliffehaven – you want to be on the airfield. Now you want to be in Cliffehaven, but not with me and Tino and Roberto. I don't understand you, Rita. I really don't.'

Peggy marched into the room unannounced. 'What on earth is happening here? We can hear you all the way downstairs.'

Louise let out a torrent of passionate Italian accompanied by hysterical tears, and Peggy looked at Rita hopelessly. 'You'd better tell me what all this is about,' she said grimly.

Rita told her the gist of Roberto's letter and Louise's insistence that she travel with her to Wales. 'I can't just leave Mr Hicks in the lurch,' she said finally. 'He's been very good to me, and I really don't want to lose my job.'

Louise interrupted with another harangue of rapid-fire Italian, which was now accompanied by sharp little slaps on Rita's arm.

'Stop that at once, Louise,' snapped Peggy. 'You have no right to hit Rita, and I will not have behaviour like this in my home.'

Louise sniffed and sobbed and kept a wary eye on Peggy, but at least the hysterics had been firmly quelled.

'Right,' said Peggy. 'Rita, you come down for your tea. You must be starving by now. Louise, go and wash your face. When you've pulled yourself together and can conduct a sensible and controlled conversation, I will see you in the kitchen.'

Rita felt her heart swell with love for Peggy as she followed her down the stairs. At last she had someone on her side who understood just how difficult it was to get Louise to see reason.

But as she tucked into the delicious plate of corned beef hash, she knew Louise would never be able to make such a journey alone, and began to fret once more over her own future. She would have to go with her, but how on earth could she persuade Mr Hicks to let her have so much time off when she'd only been in the job a week?

Chapter Twenty

Peggy had been feeling much more cheerful as she had at last got hold of Doreen on the telephone and been reassured that her sister was unharmed, but the argument between Rita and Louise had soured the evening. Now she was determined to restore order to her home and give Louise a piece of her mind.

As Fran and Suzy helped to clear the table before they went into town, Peggy left Rita to finish her meal in Cissy's company and went into the kitchen. The girls had stacked the dirty dishes on the wooden drainer and Sylvia was already pulling on rubber gloves.

'You don't have to do that,' said Peggy.

'I actually quite enjoy it,' Sylvia replied. 'There's something very satisfactory about having lovely clean china and a tidy kitchen.'

Peggy fetched a drying cloth and they happily worked together, their silence companionable as Mrs Finch snored peacefully by the range. Ron had left for his Home Guard duties, Jim had gone to the pub to see a man about something, and Anne had gone to bed straight after the meal. Martin was at the airbase most of the time now, so she and Cissy were sharing the room again, and she liked to be asleep before her younger sister came to bed.

With everything tidied away, Peggy made them a cup of tea. There was still no sign of Louise, and Peggy was hoping she hadn't simply gone to bed in a huff. The woman needed talking to, and that was a fact. 'I'm just going to make a telephone call,' she said to Sylvia. 'I won't be long.'

She hurried into the hall and dialled a number she knew by heart. 'Hello, Sally,' she said warmly. They spoke for a few minutes, catching up on things, and then Peggy said, 'I was wondering if you could help me with something.'

Peggy returned to the kitchen some minutes later, feeling much more confident that things could be sorted out for Rita. Sally Hicks had been her first evacuee – a sweet, lost and rather lonely girl, who'd been in sole charge of her little crippled brother, Ernie. She'd become one of the family, and Peggy knew she could rely on her to work on John Hicks and persuade him to help Rita through this latest drama.

'It's so lovely having the telephone working again, isn't it?' said Sylvia. 'Which reminds me, I need to pay for my long call to James.' She dug in her handbag and pulled out some notes which she placed on the kitchen table.

'That's far too much,' said Peggy, her eyes widening.

'If it is, then spend the rest on something special

for yourself – but make sure it's frivolous and fun and makes you smile. You deserve a treat.'

'That's very generous of you,' Peggy murmured, tucking the notes into her handbag, her thoughts on the little dress shop in the High Street.

Sylvia lit a cigarette with her gold Dunhill lighter. 'Actually, Peggy, while we've got a quiet moment, there's something I have to tell you.'

Peggy looked at her, guessed what she was about to say, and was surprised at how sad she felt. 'You're planning to leave, aren't you?'

Sylvia nodded. 'The doctor has given Christopher the all-clear to travel at the end of the week, depending on the weather, of course. James has organised our travel passes to get through all the checkpoints I'll have to drive through, and Jim managed to get me six cans of petrol, which are stored in the boot of the Rolls.' She gave an impish grin. 'I'll probably get arrested for hoarding, but Jim reckons I can easily talk my way out of any trouble. He seems to think I have his gift of the blarney, though I've never set foot in Ireland.'

'Jim got you the petrol?' Peggy chuckled. 'Trust him.'

'Yes, I do, actually.' She paused. 'And if you don't mind me saying so, you should too.' She smiled. 'I've seen the way you are together, and although he's a silver-tongued rogue with an eye for a pretty woman, his heart is very firmly in your hands, Peggy.'

Peggy was about to deny her ever doubting Jim's faithfulness and then realised Sylvia was far too astute. 'I've always believed in keeping him on his toes,' she replied instead. 'He knows how far to go before I reel him back in.'

They giggled and Sylvia reached for Peggy's hand. 'We've only known each other a fortnight, but it seems as if we've been friends for ever,' she said fondly. 'I'm going to miss you and everyone at Beach View.'

'We'll miss you too,' murmured Peggy.

Sylvia was about to say something else when Louise walked into the room. 'I'll leave you to it,' she said quietly.

Louise had a sour expression that didn't bode well. Peggy quelled her rising impatience with the woman and forced a smile. 'I expect you'd like a cup of tea,' she said pleasantly. 'Sit by the fire and get warm.'

Having made the tea, Peggy perched on a nearby kitchen chair. She wouldn't mention her telephone call to Sally, for nothing was settled. 'Rita is a sweet girl,' she began, 'and has done her very best to help you through what must have been a very tough time for you both.' She rushed on before Louise could interrupt. 'But she is not your guardian or your mother – that is your job – or it was until you both moved in here, and I will not have you bullying her.'

'A little slap now and then does her no harm,' said Louise sullenly. 'She knows how long I've been waiting to hear from Tino and Roberto, and now she's refusing to come with me to be with them.'

'You won't be able to travel for a few days yet,'

said Peggy firmly. 'There's thick snow on the ground and the trains won't be running.'

'Then we'll go on the bus,' Louise said stubbornly.

'Have you any idea of how far it is to Wales?' Peggy rummaged in the dresser and yanked out one of Charlie's old school atlases. Stabbing her finger on Wales, she dragged it across the map to Cliffehaven. 'It could take days.'

Louise shrugged. 'I don't care how far it is. I need to be with my husband and son.'

Peggy closed the atlas. She was beginning to realise what a complicated maze Rita had had to negotiate these past months. 'As the weather is the deciding factor at the moment, I suggest you write to them, perhaps send them a little parcel. Then, once the trains are running again, you can travel to Wales – but on your own.'

'Rita must come with me,' Louise said flatly. 'I've never travelled outside Cliffehaven, and the thought of getting lost on such a long journey terrifies me.'

Peggy finally lost patience. 'Rita has already sacrificed her place with the WAAFs for you. Do you expect her to give up this job too? Are you *really* that selfish, Louise?'

'It's her duty to look after me,' Louise retorted. 'She promised Tino.'

'I don't care *what* she promised. It's time you acted your age and took responsibility for yourself. Good heavens, woman, you're almost sixty, and yet you behave as if you're a half-witted five-year-old.'

Louise stood, her face ashen, her expression grim. 'You have no right to speak to me like that. Rita and I will be leaving first thing in the morning.'

Peggy stood to face her, sorely tempted to slap that obdurate expression off her face. She folded her arms tightly about her waist instead. 'Leave if you want, but Rita stays here. This is her home now, and her father is happy she's settled at last.' Peggy could see the battle being waged in Louise's mind and wanted to tell her to sling her hook and good riddance. But she waited, arms still folded, determined to say no more until Louise came to a decision.

'We will stay until the weather improves,' said Louise finally. 'Rita will make up her own mind as to where her loyalties lie – and you'll find it's with me, not you, Peggy Reilly.' She turned her back on Peggy and marched out of the room.

Peggy lit a cigarette, furiously blew smoke and plumped down in the chair. She had a fair idea of the emotional blackmail Louise would use to get her own way. 'But you've got me to contend with now, Louise Minelli,' she muttered crossly, 'and I can tell you straight, you won't know what hit you if you force Rita into anything again.'

The snow was still coming down thick and fast as Rita trudged through it the next morning to get to the fire station. Her argument with Louise still rankled, even though Peggy had assured her she was free to make up her own mind about whether she'd go to Wales or not. She had spent the night on the couch in the dining room, unwilling to return to her own bed and have Louise constantly nagging at her.

One of the fire engines was already out on a call to sort out a burst pipe, but the other two were being washed and polished. She looked up at the office and saw John Hicks talking on the telephone. She'd wait a while before she went to tell him she needed time off. It was an interview she dreaded, for she didn't want to let him down after he'd been so kind, nor did she want to get the sack.

Tugging off her gloves and scarf, she greeted George Wickens who had his head buried amid the innards of an ancient truck. She was about to join him when John Hicks called down to her. 'Rita, can you come up for a minute?'

Her heart began to pound, and she reluctantly trudged up the wooden stairs. She could put it off no longer.

'Sit down, love,' he said kindly. He twisted back and forth in his office chair, his hands folded at his waist. 'I understand you need some time off to go to Wales,' he said without preamble.

Rita knew then that Peggy had forestalled her, so she quickly told him the reason. 'She can't possibly go on her own, and I'm the only one who's free to take her,' she finished.

'But you're not free, are you, Rita? You have a job here and a responsibility to me and the rest of the fire crew.'

Rita couldn't meet his steady gaze. 'I was rather hoping you'd let me take two weeks off,' she murmured.

'Two weeks is a long time, and I can't afford to lose one of my team at such short notice.'

'I won't be able to go until the snow stops, anyway,' she said, 'and that could be some time yet.' Rita's heart was thudding so hard she was certain he could hear it as the silence fell between them. 'Perhaps I could do the trip in a week, or ten days,' she said hopefully. 'I'll work really hard when I get back, I promise, and I won't take any other time off at all to make up for it.'

John took a deep breath and let it out in a long sigh. 'I've had Sally and Peggy at me since last night,' he said wearily. 'They both think I should let you go.'

Rita looked at him, silently begging him to agree.

'But if I do that,' he said, 'I can't guarantee you'll have a job when you return.'

Rita's pulse was racing. This was what she'd dreaded.

His dark blue eyes regarded her steadily. 'If we have a series of bad raids while you're away then I'll have to take on another driver. And it wouldn't be fair to have to dismiss them on your return.'

'I understand. But if there weren't any raids, do you think I might still have a job here?' Rita looked up at him, blinking back the tears in a desperate bid to stay calm and not fall on her knees and beg him to reconsider.

He regarded her steadily for a long moment of silence. 'You have a good chance of George getting you through your final mechanic's exams,' he said eventually, 'and I think you've proved you can be a good member of my team.'

Hope rose and Rita held her breath.

'I don't want to lose you, Rita, but my hands are tied. Head Office will be down on me like a ton of bricks if I don't fill my quota of personnel, and this is a big town, we're a busy station.'

Rita's hopes dwindled and her anxiety grew as John paused once more.

'If you go, then it will be your annual leave and I'll find a temporary replacement,' he said, a smile tugging at his lips.

'Thank you, oh, thank you.' She leaped from the chair and threw her arms round him. 'You won't regret it, I promise, I promise, I promise.'

He gently disentangled himself and cleared his throat. 'Don't let me down, Rita. I'm relying on you to get back here within two weeks. Any longer and I'll have to dismiss you.'

Rita was close to tears. 'Thank you, Mr Hicks,' she said, giving him a watery smile. 'I'll make sure I don't lose this job.'

'Good,' he said, becoming businesslike and turning to the stack of papers on his desk. 'Now get out of here and find something sensible to do.'

Rita ran down the steps, her heart light with happiness at the thought that she could visit Papa and Roberto, appease Louise and still come back to the job she'd come to love. All was right with her world, and nothing and nobody could spoil it now.

Cliffehaven looked like a picture postcard in the snow. It smothered roofs and chimneys, lay in sparkling white drifts in the hollows on the hills and over the gardens. Glittering in the trees, it hid the rubble of the bombed-out buildings and muffled every sound.

But it was a damned nuisance, for it had brought almost everything to a grinding halt. The trains and buses weren't moving, and the day-to-day business of getting about had become dangerous as the slush froze and turned pavements and roads into ice rinks. Shops began to run out of supplies because nothing was coming into Cliffehaven; coal, anthracite and paraffin were at an all-time low just as they were most needed; and there were constant calls to the fire station to deal with burst pipes, chimney fires, and damage to roofs already weakened by bomb blasts.

It was almost another week before the snow began to melt, but then the residents of Cliffehaven had to cope with enemy planes flying overhead, constant air-raid warnings, and the inconvenience of having to sit huddled in a freezing Anderson shelter for hours on end. To add to the misery, the government had decided to ration gas and electricity, and there were constant blackouts, sometimes lasting for half a day, which meant it was almost impossible to cook, clean or even bathe properly.

Peggy had had enough. She'd been down to the Town Hall to do her two-hour stint for the WVS and had bumped into Doris, who seemed determined to tell her every last detail of her current charity fundraising, and her burgeoning relationship with Lady Charlmondley. Doris had thrown broad hints about coming back with Peggy to see Sylvia, and Peggy had told her straight that Sylvia was due to leave today and didn't have time to put up with her fawning all over her. Doris had taken umbrage and Peggy had happily left her to stew.

She carefully made her way along a pavement slick with dirty snow and slush, her mind working over everything she had to do before she could sit down with a cigarette and a cup of tea. With Sylvia and Louise leaving there would be spare beds again, and she supposed she should tell the Welfare people. The Town Hall was still packed with the homeless and, although Peggy felt terribly sorry for them, she actually just wanted a bit of peace for a while amongst people she knew and loved. It was an effort to make strangers welcome and attend to the problems they seemed to bring with them.

Perhaps it was her age slowing her down – after all, she would be forty-four in three weeks' time, and most women her age were beginning to take things easy. Not much chance of that, she thought crossly, not with a houseful and Louise getting worse by the day as the snow kept her in Cliffehaven. She'd be glad to see the back of her.

At least Rita seemed happy enough to go with Louise now she knew her job was safe. Of course Louise still wouldn't accept that Rita would be returning to Cliffehaven, but Rita was proving to be much tougher than she'd thought, and now she knew she had Peggy's support, she would deal with Louise – Peggy was sure of it.

She tramped up the front steps, knocked the snow from her boots and went inside, to be greeted by the sound of laughter in her kitchen. She unwound her scarf, took off her gloves and boots and hung her coat on the newel post. It seemed that everyone was home, and the kitchen was so crammed she could barely find somewhere to sit. Sylvia was holding court, pouring champagne, chattering away nineteen to the dozen to Fran and Suzy.

'Rosie managed to find a few bottles at the back of her cellar,' muttered Ron. 'Sylvia wanted to throw a bit of a party before she left.'

Peggy took a glass and lit a cigarette. She realised that nothing much would get done for a while, so she relaxed and watched the others. The five girls were chattering and giggling, Ron was looking stoic and Jim was flirting with a delighted Mrs Finch, who clearly couldn't hear a word he was saying but was enjoying the attention anyway.

Louise was looking sullen as usual, refusing the champagne and sipping a glass of water instead.

She still hadn't forgiven Sylvia for refusing to give her and Rita a lift to Salisbury where they could have caught a train into Wales. She simply couldn't – or wouldn't – understand that with Christopher taking up the entire back seat, there wasn't room for passengers.

Beneath the hubbub of noise, Peggy turned to Ron. 'I understand Tommy Findlay's been sniffing around again,' she murmured.

'He was,' he said round the stem of his pipe, 'but there's been no sign of him since Christmas.' He eyed her through the pipe-smoke. 'Do you have any idea why Rosie puts up with him?'

'She has her reasons,' Peggy replied. 'It's not up to me to tell you what they are.'

'He's not some old flame, is he? Or the missing husband? Braithwaite's her maiden name, you know.'

She patted his arm as she nodded. 'Don't worry, Ron, she's still your girl.'

He narrowed his eyes. 'I wish I could be certain of that,' he said gruffly.

'Then do something about it,' she said. 'Tell her how you feel and put things on a firmer basis. You'll find she'll be quite open to the suggestion.' She grinned at him. 'Trust me, Ron. I know about these things.'

He grinned back. 'Aye. I suppose you do.'

'Can I have everyone's attention?' called Sylvia. She smiled as the babble died and all eyes turned to her. 'I would just like to say thank you for giving me such a loving and happy home for my short stay here. Ron, I owe you my son's life and my eternal gratitude. Jim, you've been a constant source of entertainment, good food and black-market petrol.'

Everyone laughed, and she turned to Mrs Finch. 'Thank you, Cordelia, for being such a lovely companion, and to all you girls for providing much-needed laughter and fun.' Her smile faltered as she looked at Peggy. 'Peggy, we haven't known each other long, but I think of you as a good friend. Please stay in touch, and perhaps after this war is over, we can pick up where we've left off.'

Peggy nodded, saw that Sylvia was close to tears and knew that there would be no protracted good-byes. She hated them too and understood.

Sylvia raised her glass. 'To Beach View Boarding House and all who are lucky enough to live here.'

Peggy met Sylvia's gaze as she raised her own glass. She would miss her, certainly, but they would stay in touch and meet again.

Sylvia finished her glass of champagne and with a smile to everyone, made her way through the crush and into the hall. Her cases were already stowed on the passenger seat, the petrol cans and food for the journey safe in the boot of the Rolls-Royce. All that was left for her to do now was leave.

She slowly drew on the mink coat and gloves, the chatter from the kitchen drifting out to her. Peggy had seen her slip away – had understood that she hated long goodbyes and wanted to go quietly and without fuss. Dear Peggy, what a good friend she'd been.

Smoothing back her fair hair and adjusting her hat, she caught her reflection in the mirror and gave a wry smile. Her life might have been very different if she'd grown up in a warm and loving family like this, with a mother like Peggy. It had been her dream as a child, and now, through the vagaries of fate, she'd had the chance to experience it for a while. The memories of Beach View and the Reilly family would remain with her for the rest of her life.

She quietly opened the front door and slowly went down the freshly salted steps to the Rolls-Royce. Christopher was waiting for her at the hospital, James had promised to come home for a few days next week and her other two sons were due for leave within the next month. Her own precious family needed her now, and the enrichment of her few weeks in Cliffehaven would carry her through whatever lay ahead in her strange and rather wonderful life.

Sylvia took a deep, enlivening breath of the cold sea air. The sun was brilliant on what remained of the snow, a good omen for the long journey – a bright, shining hope for the future.

The next day dawned just as brightly, and Rita was as eager as Louise to begin their long journey to

Wales. It would be lovely to see Tino and Roberto and get Louise finally settled – but the best part would be coming home again to Cliffehaven and Peggy.

It was strange how her priorities had changed over the past weeks – the dream of being in the WAAFs fading as the new and exciting job at the fire station offered all she'd needed. Perhaps Louise had been right all along, she thought wryly, for she had found everything she'd yearned for, right here in Beach View.

Rita had spent the previous evening with Cissy, who left early that morning for the airbase, her arm finally out of plaster. She'd said goodbye to Fran and Suzy as they rushed off for their early shift at the hospital, and tried not to lose her patience with Louise as she fussed and dithered and raced about like a headless chicken.

Now it was time to leave, and although she knew she'd be coming back soon, she still felt rather tearful as Jim and Ron hugged her and Mrs Finch gave her a kiss. 'Take care, Anne,' she said, giving her a gentle hug, 'and give my best to Martin.'

'You take care too, Rita,' Anne replied, 'and we'll see you soon.'

'She's staying with me,' said Louise, glancing yet again at the clock. 'Come on, Rita, or we'll miss the trolley.'

Rita turned to Peggy. 'I'll be back,' she murmured as they hugged. 'Keep a space for me.'

'You'll have June's old room,' Peggy replied, 'and I'll make sure it's all ready and waiting for you, don't you fret.'

'Waste your time all you want,' said Louise. She eyed Peggy with barely disguised triumph. 'Rita won't be back.' She didn't bother to say goodbye as she marched into the hall and picked up the heavy bag that was straining with all the things she'd bought for Roberto and Tino as well as her own precious belongings.

Rita kissed Peggy and followed Louise into the hall. Her own bag was very light, for she didn't need much for such a short time away. As Louise opened the door and hurried down the steps, Rita shot Peggy a smile that held a world of love, and the promise to return as soon as she could.

The journey seemed endless as they had to change trains, catch buses and wait for hours on lonely platforms for their connections. Louise never stopped complaining. She muttered her ill-will over Lady Sylvia's selfishness, moaned about the delays, the draughts in the carriages, the terrible food at the stations, the lack of decent facilities, the crush, the noise and the inconveniences she had to bear.

Rita hadn't listened to half of it, preferring to read the magazines Cissy had given her, or to look out of the window or watch the other people in their carriage. She let her mind drift to how she would feel on seeing Roberto after all this time. Would the experiences he'd had have changed him? Her own experiences had changed her, that was a fact, and she hoped with all her heart that he didn't expect anything more from her than sisterly kinship.

They finally arrived at the tiny station in Wales and clambered down onto the platform. It was a neat, pretty place, with a small cottage next to the signal box, a vegetable garden beside the embankment and fresh paint on the doors and window frames.

Louise dumped her bag and peered through the clouds of smoke as the train chuffed away. 'They should be here,' she said fretfully. 'Where are they? They knew what time we were to arrive.'

'Mamma! Rita!'

'Roberto! Tino!'

The four of them clung to one another, exchanging kisses and hugs, drinking in the sight of their beloved faces, rejoicing in their reunion.

'It's wonderful to see you again, Rita,' said Roberto as Louise and Tino continued to embrace. 'You look very well, considering what you've been through.'

Rita grinned up at him in delight. 'So do you – but what's with that moustache?'

He thumbed it bashfully. 'Thought I'd give it a go,' he muttered.

'It makes you look very distinguished,' she replied, trying her best not to laugh. It actually looked like a caterpillar crawling over his top lip, but she would never say so. She glanced at Tino, who was lovingly kissing away Louise's tears. 'Papa's lost weight,' she said quietly. 'Are you sure he's fully recovered?'

'Fitter than ever now he has so much physical work to do around the farm,' said Roberto, reaching for her bag. 'Come on, we've arranged for you to stay in the village. They're a nice old couple and have plenty of room, and you'll find there are other wives and their families close by, so you won't get lonely.'

Rita caught his arm. 'I can't stay long, Roberto,' she warned.

He looked crestfallen. 'But I thought you and Mamma were coming to live here?'

She shook her head. 'I'm sorry, but as I explained in my letter, I have a home with Peggy Reilly and a good job at the fire station. I'll be going back on the next train the day after tomorrow.'

'I've had no such letter, Rita.' He glanced across at his weeping mother. 'Mamma will take a bit of time to settle in – you know how she dislikes change – and we can only visit on our time off and in the evenings.' He turned back to her, his dark eyes concerned. 'How does she feel about you going back?'

'She's not happy about it,' Rita said truthfully, 'but she'll be fine once she settles in, and with you and Papa, and the other families nearby, she won't miss me at all.'

He grinned at her and linked arms. 'So, tell me

all about this job,' he said. 'I thought you wanted to go into the WAAFs?'

The elderly couple was as delightful as their little thatched cottage which stood within a flourishing vegetable garden on the edge of the small village. Their bedrooms were neat and pretty with chintz curtains and bedspreads, the sitting room and kitchen warm from the blazing fire in the inglenook and the large range.

Rita unpacked her toothbrush, flannel and night-dress, leaving everything else in the bag. She ambled into the other room as Louise chattered away happily to Tino, who was sitting on the bed. Louise hung up her clothes in the wardrobe and put the Madonna and child statuette in pride of place on the chest of drawers under the window. 'There,' she said softly. 'Now it is truly home.'

Rita looked round the room as Louise continued to settle in. There was a large double bed in here, and the view from the window looked over miles of fields to the distant craggy mountains. It might be isolated, but it was warm and cosy, and Rita could see that Louise was already feeling quite at home now she had Tino and Roberto close by.

Within the hour they had met the families of the other Italian men who'd been sent down to this remote part of the country for the duration. There were five wives, who had numerous small children, as well as several older girls who were out working for the land army on the many surrounding farms.

A large welcoming tea had been arranged in the church hall, and as Louise clung lovingly to Tino while he introduced everyone, Rita could see she was beginning to be her old self again. She would be happy here, for these women could speak Italian, and understood what she'd been going through.

As night fell, the tea was cleared away and steaming bowls of home-made pasta and freshly baked bread replaced the sandwiches and cakes. The locals drifted in along with the Italian husbands and sons from their farm labours. It was quite a large community, but the locals seemed to enjoy this influx and happily joined in, bringing their own Welsh additions to the table.

The noise rose as the numbers increased, the familiar and musical sound of Italian blending with the equally tuneful Welsh, and filling the hall. Someone began to play an accordion, and this was soon joined by a couple of violins, a guitar and the out-of-tune piano that stood in the corner of the hall. Chairs were pushed back and people began to dance.

Tino managed to escape Louise's clutches for a few minutes while she became involved in helping to clear the tables. He took Rita in his warm embrace and kissed the top of her head. 'Thank you for looking after Mamma so well, Rita,' he murmured. 'I know it can't have been easy.'

'She was lost without you and Roberto,' she replied simply.

'My Louise needs much care,' he murmured. 'She is not strong.' He smiled down at her. 'Roberto tells me you will not be staying.'

She shook her head and explained everything.

'It is good you have plans,' he said, his eyes brimming. 'Of course we shall miss you, but to learn about life, one must live it – and my poor Louise never really understood that.' He hugged her again. 'I wish you all the luck in the world, my little Rita, and when you get the time, please write to us. We don't want to lose you completely.'

'You'll always be my Papa Tino,' she murmured.

Louise was hurrying towards them. 'Just remember we love you,' he said, 'and don't worry, I will help Louise understand your reasons for leaving.' Louise claimed his attention, and with a wink and a smile to Rita, Tino allowed her to steer him into the dance.

Rita had danced with Roberto and was now happily sitting this one out so she could watch Tino and Louise move round the floor. Louise had shed her cares, the years dropping away, making her seem young again as she gazed into Tino's adoring eyes. Louise had to be the most demanding and difficult person Rita had ever dealt with, but with Tino she was very different. Theirs was a wonderful love story, and Rita could only hope that one day she would find a husband who would look at her that way as they grew old together.

Her attention was snatched from the dancers as several young women made a dramatic entrance into the hall. They'd clearly prepared for the party, dressed in lovely frocks, with their hair all shining and their make-up freshly applied. Farm work and a plentiful supply of meat, eggs and milk obviously agreed with them, for they were glowing with health and energy as they greeted their families and joined in the fun.

Rita was about to make a comment to Roberto when he moved from her side and hurried across the room. The girl whose hand he claimed was the prettiest of them all, with dark, feline eyes, olive skin and long hair as black as jet.

As Rita watched, the girl gave Roberto a radiant smile and moved into his arms with the ease of familiarity. Roberto was clearly entranced as they moved to the music, his gaze capturing her, his expression rapt. Rita gave a sigh of deep pleasure. Roberto was in love – which probably explained the ridiculous moustache and smart new haircut. How lovely.

The time had flown by and now it was early morning on her last day. Rita stretched and yawned, blissfully happy not to have to share a bedroom with Louise and eagerly looking forward to going home to Cliffehaven. She had said goodbye to Tino the night before, and he'd again given her his blessing and told her not to worry – Louise now fully understood why she had to leave, and was quite happy about it.

Rita rolled onto her side and thought over this short time in Wales. The Italian community had been warm and welcoming, and Rita had soon learned that they congregated every night to share their evening meal and to dance. It was their way of returning to the old traditions, a way of confirming who they were and what they stood for.

Rita had met Nuncia when she and Louise had gone to the farm to meet Mr and Mrs Jones. Nuncia worked there as a land girl, and Rita had liked her very much, for it was clear she was as in love with Roberto as he was with her. Louise, unfortunately, didn't share Rita's joy for them, and made it clear at every possible moment that she didn't approve.

Rita was relieved that she wouldn't be around to witness Louise's next foray into emotional blackmail. She climbed out of bed and pulled back the curtains. It was a clear, crisp, sunny day, and she could smell the delicious aroma of bacon frying downstairs. Hurrying to wash and dress, she stuffed everything back in her bag, stripped the bed and went down for breakfast.

Mrs Hughes was in a hurry this morning – she had a sick neighbour to visit – so Rita said goodbye to her and thanked her for looking after them so well.

Breakfast was delicious, with lashings of butter on the toast and two fried eggs to go with the bacon. Rita finally pushed back the plate and patted her stomach. 'That has certainly set me up for the day,' she sighed.

'What time's your train?' Louise looked at her over her teacup as they sat at the scrubbed kitchen table.

'Ten thirty.' Rita looked at her watch. 'Roberto's picking me up at nine as it's such a long way to the station.'

'I need to go to the church hall to prepare for tonight's supper,' said Louise. 'If you're packed, then I could do with a hand.'

She was being very reasonable, and Rita felt tremendous gratitude that Tino had at last made her understand and accept her leaving. 'Of course, Mamma,' she said and smiled. 'I'll bring my bag down and leave it by the front door with a note to tell Roberto where I am.'

'That won't be necessary. I've already asked Mrs Hughes to keep an eye out for him. She'll be back in plenty of time.'

Rita wrote a note to Roberto anyway, and tucked it beneath the handle of her bag as she deposited it on the doorstep. Linking arms with Louise, she accompanied her down the steep cobbled street to the village hall.

Louise unlocked the door and began moving tables and chairs in a businesslike fashion as Rita opened the curtains, found freshly laundered table-cloths and replenished the candles which would be lit if there was a power blackout. Plates and cutlery had been washed and stacked on the drainer in the tiny kitchen, and she carefully laid the tables which had been pushed together to form two long ones.

Half an hour had passed when she stepped back and admired their handiwork, almost sorry that she couldn't be a part of the noisy, lively gathering tonight. 'We'd better go back to the cottage,' she said. 'Roberto will be here in a few minutes.'

'Go in the kitchen and find the broom first,' ordered Louise. 'There are crumbs on the floor and they'll encourage vermin.'

Rita went into the kitchen at the back of the hall and was reaching into the cupboard for the broom when she heard the key turn in the lock. Frowning, she tried the handle and pushed at the door. Her heart began to thud. 'I can't open the door,' she called.

'It's staying locked until you promise you won't leave.'

Rita knew now that it had all been an act. 'I'm not promising you anything, Mamma. Not until you unlock this door.'

'Then you'll stay there.'

'Don't be silly, Mamma,' she said, trying her best to keep the panic and anger out of her voice. 'You know you can't force me to do anything.'

'I'm the one with the key.'

Rita checked her watch. Roberto would have left

the farm by now and be on his way to collect her. 'But I'll miss my train and there isn't another until next week.'

'It will give you time to think about your loyalties, Rita. My Roberto has had his head turned by that girl – but now you're back, he'll soon realise you are the only one for him. I'll make sure of it.'

'He doesn't love me and I don't love him,' Rita shouted. 'Papa has given me his blessing to go back to Cliffehaven and he'll be very angry if he finds out what you've done.' She banged her fist on the door. 'Unlock it, Mamma.'

'Papa will see things my way,' said Louise implacably. 'Your place is with us.'

Horrified, Rita heard her footsteps cross the hall floor and the squeak of heavy hinges on the front door. 'Louise, if you leave me in here I'll never speak to you again. Do you hear me?'

The slam of the front door was her only reply.

Rita hit the kitchen door with her fist, rattled the handle and gave it a furious kick. Gathering all her strength and anger, she ran at it, hitting it with her shoulder and bouncing off it with a yelp of pain. All she'd gained was a shooting pain in her arm and hip. The door was sturdy, the handle firmly screwed into place, the lock bolted.

She looked wildly around her. There were no windows, no other way out. Then she remembered there was a larder. It had a small mesh-covered square above the stone shelves which let in cold air from outside.

She looked at her watch again. Time was flying. She had to get out of here – or at least let someone know where she was. She hurried into the big larder and looked up at the mesh. It seemed very sturdy, and had been nailed firmly over the opening.

Returning to the kitchen, she turned on all the lights and began a hurried scrabble through the drawers and cupboards for something to prise out the nails. All she could find were some knives. 'They'll have to do,' she muttered.

The nails were embedded in the wooden surround, some of them at a twisted angle, the heads battered and difficult to get beneath. She broke the shaft of the first two knives as she desperately tried to get leverage and her hands became slick with sweat. She cut her finger twice, but she hardly noticed, for all her focus was on her task.

She was sweating profusely now, her hands sticky with blood, her shirt and sweater clinging unpleasantly to her back. But she gritted her teeth and carried on. Roberto would be at the cottage now. He would see the bag and her message. He would come to find her.

But Louise had left some time ago. Had she returned to the cottage, found her note and hidden it and the bag away? Was she, at this minute, telling Roberto she'd decided to stay? But how could she explain where Rita was? Would Roberto believe her?

The thoughts and arguments raged in her head as inch by painful inch the nails slowly came out. Cutting her hands on the sharp wire mesh, she wrestled with it, peeling it back like the lid on a sardine can.

She stopped to catch her breath and look at her watch. If she wasn't discovered soon she would miss the train. But the square opening was too narrow for her to climb through – not even big enough to be able to stick her head out.

Rita stood on tiptoe and craned her neck, discovering that the opening overlooked the side garden of the hall. Beyond that was a big field without a house in sight. She yanked off her sweater and waved it. 'Help me,' she yelled. 'Help! Is anyone there? I'm locked in the village hall.'

She listened as the seconds ticked away. The only sound she could hear was the lowing of cows and the drum of her heart. 'Help,' she screamed, waving the jumper frantically through the hole. 'Help! Help!'

It was now after nine o'clock and it was almost an hour's drive to the station. The train would be on its way, getting ever nearer – and she would not be there to catch it.

She had a sudden thought that Louise might be outside the hall, waiting for her to give in. 'Louise,' she yelled furiously. 'If you can hear me, then open this door. I promise to do whatever you say, just let me out of here so we can talk.' She had absolutely no intention of discussing anything with Louise, but if it meant being freed she didn't care what promises she made.

'It's all right, Rita. I'm coming to get you.'

'Roberto?' She pressed her face against the opening. 'Roberto?' she called again, wondering if in her panic and distress she'd been hearing things.

The key turned in the door behind her and she whirled round.

Roberto caught her as she fell off the stone shelf, and she clung to him. 'I thought you'd never find me,' she rasped, her throat sore from shouting.

'Papa came with me and made Mamma tell him where you were. We both knew you didn't want to stay.' He gently steadied her. 'She told me she wanted us to marry, to all live together.' He looked at her warily, a question in his eyes.

'Neither of us wants that,' she said firmly. 'You have Nuncia, and I'm sorry, but I don't love you – not in that way.'

'We're to be married in the summer,' said Roberto, 'and I would ask you to the wedding if the journey here wasn't so difficult.' He kissed her on her hot forehead. 'Come, Rita, your bag is in the Land Rover, and we should make the station in time if we hurry.'

They left the hall door swinging as they ran down the short path and piled into the truck. 'Where's Louise?' she asked as Roberto turned the key.

'Papa has taken her for a long walk to calm her down. He sends his love.' He shot her a glance. 'She'll be fine. You know how Mamma is.'

Rita did indeed, but she kept that dark thought to herself.

The train was just pulling in as they clambered out of the truck and raced for the platform. Rita threw her arms around him. 'I'll write regularly,' she promised, 'and good luck on your wedding day. Nuncia's lovely, and I'm sure you'll be very happy.'

He was still standing on the platform as she found a seat by the window and the train began to chuff slowly away from the little station halt.

She waved to him until he was lost in the clouds of smoke and steam and then sank back into her seat. She was free to follow her dreams, free to be young and carefree again, but her smile was wry as the train clattered along the rails.

The greatest irony of all was that for all her dreams of adventure, she now simply wanted to go home. Home where the heart lay. For Roberto, it was here in this Welsh valley with Nuncia and his parents. For Rita, it was in Cliffehaven with Peggy and the family who lived at Beach View Boarding House.

ALSO AVAILABLE IN ARROW

There'll be Blue Skies

Ellie Dean

**It's 1939 and the first evacuees are arriving at Beach
View Boarding House . . .**

When sixteen-year-old Sally is evacuated to the English south
coast, she is terrified by what lies ahead of her. All she knows is the
sights and sounds of London's East End – but Sally swallows her
tears as they leave the familiar landmarks behind, knowing that she
has to be a Grown-Up Girl and play mother to her six-year-old
brother Ernie. Playing mother is nothing new for Sally – their real
mother Florrie, a good-time girl, hasn't even come to the station to
wave them off and Ernie, crippled at an early age by polio, is used
to depending on his older sister.

When they arrive in Cliffehaven, they're taken to live at the Beach
View Boarding House where they're welcomed by the open-hearted
Reilly family headed up by warm, loving Peggy, and life begins
to improve. Sally gets a job in a uniforms factory to help pay her
way – and to pay for Ernie's expensive medicines – but then Florrie
arrives in Cliffehaven, bringing disaster with her. And Sally is forced
to work out where her true loyalties lie . . .

arrow books

Far From Home

Ellie Dean

Would she ever see her loved ones again?

It is 1940 and Staff Nurse Polly Brown has been granted a posting at Cliffehaven Memorial Hospital on the south coast to be near her badly injured husband, Adam. But her decision has meant that she has had to part with their beloved five-year-old daughter, Alice, who is travelling to safety in Canada.

Polly's heart is torn in two as she says goodbye to Alice and heads to the Beach View Boarding House in Cliffehaven, where she throws herself into her work.

But as she confronts the fact that Adam may not survive his injuries, a telegram arrives at Beach View. The boat Alice was on has been torpedoed by a German U-boat . . .

arrow books